08-18-05

Flame War

Flame War

a cyberthriller

JOSHUA QUITTNER and MICHELLE SLATALLA

WILLIAM MORROW AND COMPANY, INC.

NEW YORK

It is the policy of William Morrow and Company, Inc., and its imprints and affiliates, recognizing the importance of preserving what has been written, to print the books we publish on acid-free paper, and we exert our best efforts to that end.

Library of Congress Cataloging-in-Publication Data

Quittner, Joshua.
    Flame war : a cyberthriller / by Joshua Quittner and Michelle Slatalla.
        p. cm.
    ISBN 0-688-14366-0
    I. Slatalla, Michelle. II. Title.
PS3567.U57F58   1997
813'.54—dc21   97-737
                                                                CIP

Printed in the United States of America

First Edition

1 2 3 4 5 6 7 8 9 10

BOOK DESIGN BY JO ANNE METSCH

FOR ZOE AND ELLA

Flame War

chapter one

B rown butcher's paper, crisp edges folded with a sol-
dier's precision, an address in block letters. Blue ink.
Someone pressed down hard. The parcel was no bigger than
a comic book.

I know now this is how it all started.

Tossed into a bulky pile of a hundred, no a thousand, a
million other packages just like it, the parcel resignedly
thumped its way up a humming, moving belt.

Barely touched by human hands, the parcel anonymously
navigated the busiest mail-sorting center in the United States.
No one knew its secrets, or remembered the next day that it
had been nudged off the edge of the conveyor, where it had
dangled dangerously like a boulder about to roll down a cliff,
then dropped to the linoleum. A postal worker retrieved it
and tossed it into a mail bin. Eventually, the bin emptied into
the bed of a long semitrailer, where the package lay, patient,
with its hand-stamped FRAGILE peeking out from beneath the
edge of a much larger, heavier box. It was boarded on a truck

that drove onto the interstate, headed toward darkness and a thunderstorm rolling down like a curtain on the horizon.

In that way, the package came to my town in northern New York State.

The next morning, I was late for work. I pedaled down the windy, muddy road that dead-ends at The Vines, cranking my legs and slowly stressing out. Not that being late mattered to me much. I was far less concerned about the boss's reaction to my tardiness than I was about the persistent rub on the rear brake pads on my mountain bike. I'd adjusted that once. I hate to do things twice.

It was the start of the Last Summer for me, ten weeks of complaining about the weather and the blackflies up here in the Adirondacks. In the fall, I'd be gone. For good, maybe. I had memories to escape. But that didn't keep me from admiring the smoke rising from the water as I took the wide curve on the state road.

Timber Lake, usually so calm, was kicking up a chop. I must have taken that same ride a thousand times in my life, but somehow the snapshot of that day stays fresh in my mind: me in cutoffs, clocking around the final bend to the finish line, heading to the gravel parking lot. Beyond, the Kodak moment: fir trees, the shingled main lodge, and the endless expanse of lawn that rolls lazily to the lake's deep-blue edge.

There's no way to make a decent living here in the middle of the mountains. My dad tried. I wasn't going to repeat his mistakes. My choices would have been limited anyway. Open one of those greasy pit stops where all the waitresses feel insulted by any remark spoken in a tourist's Manhattan accent? Or maybe run a charter service, do my little bit to slick the lakes with gasoline and oil runoff? No thanks.

After all these years, though, I'd miss some things. The geology of the place still blew me away. I pedaled past the craggy hills that had been carved by glaciers so long ago, a daily reminder that it's possible to move slowly and still change the face of the world. And don't forget the pine trees. Some perch right on top of boulders, four feet in the air, no dirt in sight, huge trunks held aloft by roots like tentacles encircling rock. Those trees don't know what precarious is.

Neither did I. I had just graduated from law school, and had to fly a holding pattern until the bland but venerable firm of Hart, Monroe & Weinmiller could find a permanent spot for me in its Syracuse offices in September. I'd worked there the previous two summers. They liked me. I liked the prospect of paying back my student loans. A nephew of one of the partners was leaving at the end of the summer. Ergo, a comfortable fit. At least on the surface.

Secretly, I dreaded my career choice the way some young men fear marriage. But an undergraduate degree in English lit hadn't exactly prepared me for the Fortune 500. At the time I had entered law school in Boston, I believed that I was doing it solely to shut up the four million people—everyone from my mother to my thesis adviser to my roommate—who were warning me that my innate ambivalence would lead to ruin. I'd stopped waffling long enough to get into law school, where I then waffled away for three years.

Of course, here I was now, sixty-five thousand dollars in debt and with essentially the same Top 10 list of skills I'd always had. Number one, I could read. Number two, I knew how to fish. Number three, I knew how to deal with unbelievably arcane jargon. I'll think of the other seven later.

I didn't learn how to fish at school. My mother taught me that to snare a smallmouth bass you lurk in the shallow, rocky waters near the shore, and then flick your wrist just right to sink your hook after you feel the first tug. My mother doesn't like to let anything get away. Panfish, bluebellies, trout, and salmon. We used to take out a canoe in the mornings, because she swore the big fish could hear our motorboat coming.

I worked the early shift for Peterson. Which meant I was supposed to get to the resort at seven. Ha. I stashed my bike against the shingled lodge, then pulled a couple of chairs out onto the lawn, as if I'd been doing it all morning. I noticed that the old aluminum canoe, left out for the guests, was banging against the dock, so I went down to pull it up. Hauling on the rope, I practically knocked over a fat kid who appeared behind me. He was maybe eleven. He wore a white sailor's hat. I remembered that age. It didn't lead to pleasant memories.

"Were you going out in that thing?" I asked. His family had checked in the day before, Cottage 6 with the sleeping loft. They were from Brooklyn. This morning they were wandering around, addled by the fresh air. He'd been hanging out at the dock ever since, eyeing the narrow boat, handling the paddles, perhaps gauging his parents' reaction to his plans. He could afford to take his time acclimating them to the idea of their son out alone on the lake, because his was one of those families who came to The Vines for such an extended visit that we jokingly said they were "taking the cure."

"Nope," the kid said in a guilty "who me?" voice.

"The canoe's for the guests. You don't have to pay extra or anything." But he skittered off.

I wished I could get out in the long canoe myself because the wind was stiff and I'd get a fight if I tried to steer into it. I weight the front end with enough heavy rocks to hold a course, and then point it into the foam and listen to the buoyant sound of bow slapping water. The boat wasn't heavy enough to navigate in a real storm, and I wouldn't recommend it for amateurs.

I swept a few pine needles from the porch, looking appropriately busy when John Peterson poked his head out through the office door.

"Finish painting the south dock yet?" He was working a toothpick between his two front teeth. He looked like Telly Savalas—Who Loves Ya, Baby—only thinner and tanner than the guy I knew from cable reruns.

"I was going to do it after I get the outboard back together."

Peterson gave no indication that he even heard the empty excuse, and instead fiddled with a grommet on his cotton fishing cap. "Let me know when you run out of paint."

He marched off to inspect the clay tennis courts. After last night's rain, I figured he'd have me roll the courts and relime them too. I kind of liked pushing the heavy roller in the hot sun, as much as I liked anything. I could be alone, stripped down to the waist in case it turned out that the woman in No. 5 had a fetish for guys who looked like Dobie Gillis. The last time I'd seen her was up at the lodge eating breakfast yesterday, red hair bent over a plastic bowl of corn flakes and blueberries. She was around my age, only with a polish that speaks of prep school and summers in Fra-ahnce. Her willingness to lounge on a chaise at the we-trucked-in-the-sand beach was the only fringe benefit to my job. I had never spoken to her and knew little about her beyond the fact that she favored bikinis. Did I really need to know more?

The mail truck clattered round the bend. I went to meet it—I'd ordered a featherweight tire pump—but got distracted by the sight of the canoe out on the water. The city kid had taken my advice. He was a few hundred yards out and twirling like a weather vane.

The kid couldn't get control, and fought the water with his rude paddle instead of just giving up and letting the wind push the boat shoreward. This created a crazy whirlpool, with the front of the boat in the air and water cascading in the back.

A gust swept across the lake and tipped the canoe.

The kid was gone. The water was deep enough to drown in, nearly twenty feet out past Swimmers' Shoal, and he didn't have a life jacket. Behind me, a few people gathered and someone yelled, "Help him!" Being a lifeguard was not part of my job description, but what else could I do? Waffle? The motorboat wasn't at the dock, so I jumped into a dinghy and started rowing, hard. I saw the kid's head bob in the water. But whenever he tried to right the canoe and heave himself over its side, it tipped over again. He was wearing heavy street clothes, jeans and a long-sleeved shirt, and I could tell his swimming skills were about what you'd expect from a kid from Brooklyn.

Then he disappeared again.

I put my legs into the oars, pushing from the knees, paddling in reverse, careful to keep my attention fixed on the exact spot where I last saw the hat. I triangulated my destination, using a tall tree on the far shore as a reference point, and rowed like Popeye after he'd sucked down a can of spinach.

When I got to the spot where I last saw him, there was nothing. Just the shiny canoe. I stood, and practically passed out from hyperventilating. I squinted and searched for him, for the floating sailor hat, for anything. The glare of the sun bounced off the water, sharp white loops of neon, tricking my eyes.

Then I saw him, just below the surface, ten feet to the west. I threw the small lead anchor overboard and dived, with hardly enough time to take a gulp of air. My lungs felt it too, and my sneakers weren't making things any easier. I flashed on the thought of a double burial, my mom left all alone and the image of a fatuous intern I'd worked with last summer getting my job after all. I peeled off my Nikes and felt eighty dollars' worth of shoes sink away while I rocketed back to the surface. I sucked air, then dropped underwater again, sleek as a pencil, fanned out my arms and dived, headfirst into the deep. With a frog kick I glided down, my vision cleared, and I saw him, his arm dangling, limp like kelp, head lolling. I grabbed hold of my quarry, hugged the dead weight of his torso, kicked as hard as I could, and we surfaced.

Exhausted, I sidestroked like an old man toward the boat, wondering how the hell I was going to get him into the dinghy. Then I heard the roar of Peterson's outboard motor. Who Loves Ya, Baby, was at the wheel, his expression too neutral for me to see if he was mentally calculating the cost of his liability and negligence. Jed, the caretaker, was along for the assist, scrambling toward me with a boat hook. Life preservers rained down.

Jed administered CPR. I watched while hanging limply off the side of the boat, panting like a hot hyena. The kid had been out for less than a minute. Lucky for him.

On the ride back to the dock, Peterson clapped me on the shoulders. "Must be in your genes, Harry old boy," he said.

"Thanks," I said, not meaning it.

I hate when people invoke the ghost of my father.

Enough excitement for one day, right? But after I begged a doughnut from the kitchen and received congratulations all around, I saw the mail, stacked on the counter in the lobby. Somebody had to deliver it. Might as well be a hero. I scooped up the pile, which included a tightly wrapped parcel that was headed to Cottage No. 5. Persnickety handwriting, addressed to Dr. Frederick Ames, c/o The Vines. Beyond that, the parcel provided few clues to the mysterious occupants of Cottage No. 5. No return address. I first noticed Ames and the woman on the day they checked in. They paid in cash, in advance, which was kind of weird. When I sneaked a look at their registration card, their address was simply New York City. The card gave no clue to their relationship. I had wondered whether she could really be dating an old guy like that. I mean, he was in good shape, tall and lean as me, and he had a rocket tennis serve. Still, he must have been pushing sixty. The only times I saw them were on the tennis court, where they played fiercely, and in the dining room, where they ate in silence. Maybe they were married. But it seemed like a companionable silence.

I knocked and heard her voice coming from the other side of the screen.

"Door's open."

I cradled the parcel like a running back, and the screen door whipped open a little too hard. It smacked into the wall, causing the room's two occupants to look up in alarm. Enter the gladiator. The cabin had a toothpaste-and-soap, early-morning smell. Ames wore white shorts and a Lacoste shirt, and was drying his Einstein hair with a towel. The woman sat at an old desk, probably something that Peterson salvaged from a schoolhouse, and her long, too-skinny legs were cramped under it. She looked like a redheaded crane. She was intent on the object that dominated the desktop: a remarkable computer screen.

A computer, of course, is not exactly unusual. We even used one here in the sticks for itemized bills and an annual winter newsletter, which updated guests on renovations and nudged them for next year's deposits. What was unusual was seeing a computer, especially such an expensive-looking one, in a guest cottage. The monitor was one of those flat panels I'd read about, as wide as the twenty-inch TV screen in the lounge but no thicker than a ream of paper. It was attached to a sleek laptop. The whole setup couldn't have weighed more than five pounds, and had to have set its owner back five grand. That's a thousand dollars a pound.

"Package for you, Doctor Ames." I couldn't bring myself to call anyone sir, not even someone with such an air of total confidence in himself, and his place in the world. To him, the package was a small annoyance, simply by virtue of being unexpected. "Thanks, Harry," he said. I guess he couldn't bring himself to call me knave, either.

"What is it, Dad?"

Dad. Yesss.

I must have smiled, because Dr. Ames's daughter volleyed one back. She had these way-cute, tortoiseshell glasses perched on her head and her gray eyes blared with a happy intelligence. I love smart-looking girls. That's not my most important criterion for choosing female companionship, but it's a nice bonus. You can keep Ginger; I'll take Mary Ann every time.

I moved in to get a better look at the monitor.

"Cool," I said, neutrally. What I was thinking was, Hey, we got us a Girl Geek sighting here. I didn't want to startle the specimen, so I leaned down to peer over her shoulder. Like I was interested. There was a creamy image of a scrap of parchment on the screen and the picture was clear enough for me to see some kind of ancient-looking black script inscribed on it. "Are you running a CD-ROM?" I asked.

Score.

"No, it's a browser," she said, pleased that someone else in the world apparently shared her desire to spend a perfectly sunny day in a dank cabin copping a computer tan.

My experience with computers at law school had been limited to cruising my free Lexis-Nexis account to keep up on the latest baseball scores. I'd used the mighty bank of available personal computers to write papers, play solitaire, and send E-mail to old high school buddies at other universities. I knew from watching my friend Blaney back in the Dark Ages of computer lab that you could cruise the Internet and hook up to electronic destinations as wildly diverse as the University of Miami and Kankakee Library. My own interest, though, hadn't extended much beyond the utilitarian.

It didn't seem to matter, now. While I was looking at the screen, I surreptitiously took a sniff of her hair. Johnson's baby shampoo. Dream date.

Ames was yanking on the twine that held the parcel, and it twanged, unyielding as a banjo string. "Annie," he said. "Did you bring scissors?"

"Look in my backpack. Outside compartment, I think."

Ames left the room.

"These are pictures of the Dead Sea Scrolls. I'm getting them off a Web site in Jerusalem," Annie said as she put her palm over a computer mouse and nudged it forward. The pointer on her screen moved to the first line of ancient script. She clicked on a word highlighted in blue, and suddenly the image on the screen changed. Now there was a picture of a cave near the Red Sea and a locator map with one of those blinking you-are-here arrows. She clicked again. This time we were looking at the floor plan for a pyramid in the Yucatán.

"Each one of these is a different Web site, a different multimedia document stored on a computer somewhere that's programmed to let the public in," she said. "Don't you have a home page?"

"Do I need one?"

But Annie was already clicking away again. Hot yellow and black horizontal stripes shuttered the screen, and then the words WELCOME TO ANNIE'S PLACE! danced across the top.

I'd seen enough home pages—starting with my college roommate's—to expect banality. The ones I'd browsed had seemed like highly personalized, multimedia family albums. And about as interesting to people outside the family as the predigital versions of "Our Summer Vacation in Europe." Maybe people get carried away by the novelty of being able to publish their autobiographies without a book deal. Hang a home page on a server, and you've just broadcast your inner self directly to twenty million Web denizens.

It must be a wildly liberating feeling, this electronic narcissism. That's the only possible explanation for the lack of inhibitions evident on most home pages: wedding photos, lists of personal hobbies, wedding-night photos, lists of favorite books, lists of favorite beers. My old roommate's enthusiasm for the home page genre led him to scan in his own photographic image of a dorm-sized refrigerator. If you clicked on the door, it opened to reveal a graphically realistic hunk of moldy cheese and a green Jell-O mold.

I squinted at Annie's page, ready to utter a meaningless banality about how interesting it wa—

That was the first time she surprised me.

Instead of looking at the multimedia yearbook entry I had expected, I saw an amazing map of an ancient city. It was depicted as a black-and-white line drawing. The only color, along the faint roadways, was little sepia-colored piles of brick and stone, the ruins.

"That's pretty cool," I said, in spite of myself.

"Click on anything, and you get a closer look."

"Where are we?" I asked.

"Palenque. What's left of an ancient Mayan city."

With my finger, I touched the screen where half-realized images of rising mist obscured a signpost. I read, "This way to the Temple of Inscriptions."

She clicked on it, and immediately we zoomed in, like a camera. We were standing at the entrance to a dark, yawning space, with toppled columns on either side, and a tendril of vine curling up, over the stone pathway.

"It's my own interpretation, of course," she said. "It's more about what I felt when I was there than what I actually saw."

She clicked again, and the page filled with an article titled "Field Observations of Annie Ames." A small photo of her, in dusty overalls, appeared in the corner.

"You worked on this a long time," I said.

"Yeah, I'm an anthro geek."

"That's not what I meant."

"Click on my picture," she said. The computer whirred as if it were trying to wake from a nap, and then a small diagram appeared on the screen. It looked like a drawing of a CD player, with buttons that said PLAY, REWIND, FAST FORWARD. A voice piped through the computer's built-in speakers: "Hi! I'm Annie. Welcome to my home page."

"That's me saying the same thing in Mayan," said Annie as I heard more sounds. "It was hard to come up with a decent translation of 'home page.'"

She dug into the pocket of her shorts and pulled out a smooth, triangular shard of clay, about the size of a penknife. "I got to go to Belize in the spring, on a dig of some Mayan ruins. I found this." She handed it to me. A string of small ideographs ran across it.

"Filching priceless artifacts from a dig," I said. "Classy."

She didn't get the joke.

"The director said I could borrow it for a while, to research what these glyphs represent," she said. "We think it's part of a huge mural. Several of us got to take pieces home to analyze. We keep in touch by E-mail."

"Is this your job?"

"I'm working for my dad. For now. I just got my degree," she said. "Anthropology. There aren't a lot of jobs."

I turned the potsherd in my hand. Then I reached over her shoulder and clicked on a button at the bottom of the page that read "Other Hobbies."

Type appeared: "Annie Says Anything's An Anagram! Try it."

Annie blushed. "That's a little program I wrote. You type in a word and it spits back a list of the words you can make by combining letters of the word into other words."

I clicked on another button that said "Links to Annie's Favorite Pages." The list that appeared on screen was eclectic: The Netly News, The Digital Diva, a page that archived Rickie Lee Jones lyrics, a digital camera that piped back the view from the seventy-seventh floor of the Empire State Building, a digital camera called Shoe Cam, which sent images, over the Net, of people's sneakers.

"You're a foot fetishist?" I asked. "Not that that's bad."

She tried to grab the mouse away, but I clicked, instead, on "My Pet."

A digitized photo of a tortoiseshell cat filled the screen. It wore a studded collar that said Bootsie.

"Attack cat?"

"You don't like cats?" she asked.

"He's very attractive," I lied.

"She."

"That's what I said," I said. "I could tell from the necklace."

"Do you have any pets?"

"I had a dog once."

"I'm sure she was very loyal," she said.

"He," I said.

F
L
A
M
E
W
A
R

She clicked on a tiny box in the corner of her screen. The home page disappeared. On screen a question popped up, accompanied by a beep: ARE YOU SURE YOU WANT TO LOG OFF?

She punched Y, and the computer responded: GOOD-BYE, ALA5.

"Ala5?" I asked.

"Anna Louise Ames," Annie said. "There must be at least four users on my computer system with those initials, since I'm ala5."

"Why didn't you tell them you wanted to be number one?" I said.

"First come, first served," she said. Then, maybe I imagined that hint of a judgmental tone creeping into her voice: "Aren't you on the Net at all?"

"I used it at law school."

Mis-take.

"Law school?" I had forgotten that people actually wrinkled their noses in this day and age.

"Law review," I lied. I don't know why, just that her look of faint disapproval egged me on. I might as well have said "I'm an ax murderer."

"I always hear people talk about law review, like it's some kind of religion," she said. "And I wonder, what's the point, anyway?"

"The point, young lady," I said, "is to make the world a better place."

She laughed. But didn't want to.

It was probably just as well that her father interrupted our awkward tête-à-tête (sorry, I don't know the Mayan synonym) at that point, ripping open the parcel as he entered the room. "At last," he said, extracting a floppy disk and tossing its wrapper into the trash.

"Do you want to use this machine, Dad?"

Ames considered the question. "No," he said. "I'll run it on the other laptop. Is it in your room?"

"I'll get it for you." She stood up.

Joshua Quittner

"Don't bother," he said. He couldn't wait.

As he disappeared, I realized that I should too. Time to paint those docks.

"Well, thanks for the lesson," I said, wondering why I had a desire to continue standing there, smelling her hair. She definitely wasn't my type.

"Ah, here we go," I heard Ames say from the other room. I heard a few computer beeps. A half dozen of them, like a garbage truck backing up. "That's odd," Ames said. "Annie—"

And then the room flashed red, and a roar that must have come from the center of the earth reached up to engulf me as an explosion tore apart the cottage.

F

L

A

M

E

W

A

R

chapter two

F ire ants were excavating my skull. It felt like they were swinging pickaxes in there. I opened my eyes and saw a hand lying on whiteness, brown and weathered against cotton sheet. My hand. I turned my head to locate my other arm, but that was a bad idea. Less than twenty degrees of motion and I thought the pain would split me.

"Harry."

Harry. I'm Harry.

"Are you awake?" the voice said. "Harry, it's Mom."

Then I was gone again.

The next time, the insects had left my brain, and it didn't hurt as much to open my eyes. I was in a white room, bags of clear fluid hanging from wire frames around my bed. Hospital.

People were watching me. My mother looked the same as always, wearing khaki pants, Top-Siders, and a buttoned-down shirt. She had that ageless L. L. Bean look. She could have been forty or she could have been fifty. With her nearly shaved graying hair—I thought of it as the chemotherapy look—and her year-round tan, she looked like a junior high phys. ed.

teacher. Hang a whistle on a string around her neck, and the nurse taking my pulse would unquestionably drop and give her twenty. For the first time in about ten years, I wasn't annoyed to see her. Funny how a near-death experience can do that for a relationship.

Next to her sat a stranger.

The nurse put a hand on my forehead. I felt the coldness of her wedding ring.

When I opened my eyes again, two new strangers appeared in orange molded chairs. This time there was no familiar face in the room.

"Who are you?" My voice.

"Hello," one of them said, smiling weakly. "How you doing, kid?"

They asked me if I knew my full name.

Harry Davidson Garnet.

They asked me if I knew who the president was.

Teddy Roosevelt.

This elicited bare smiles.

They were from the FBI. Drove up from Utica, eighty-six miles. They looked almost identical with their blue suits and black shoes and shaved necks. The only difference between them that I could see was their choice of necktie. One wore red. One wore stripes. They wanted to know about the bombing. I considered the question, and thought: What bombing?

Then it came back: the roar, the shock, the smell, fire, splinters, heat, and moaning. I tasted grass and cordite. I saw an auburn head bent over a computer screen. "What about the others?"

"The girl's okay. Her dad . . ." Striped Tie shrugged and looked at his companion for support.

"He didn't make it, Harry," said the other one. "But you lucked out."

Didn't make it. Why skirt the issue? He died. A healthy man with tennis on his mind had been blown to bits. Didn't make it. That empty phrase had no relation to the bits of blood and hair and bone that used to be Fred Ames, all the mess that had been inside a body splashed across the walls.

"Fred Ames died?" My voice was harsh. Death is harsh.

"Instantaneously."

Did they think that made it sound any better? At least no one said he didn't suffer. Because he did. He suffered like hell.

I thought of myself, of Annie, of her father, three people whose hearts were pumping, whose brains were firing, whose lungs were sucking in oxygen. And the next second, one of them didn't exist. It made me crave Annie. I wanted to confirm her existence. I wanted to confirm mine. Then suddenly I felt so tired.

Striped Tie stood and moved closer to my bed, looking at my left forearm. It was bandaged, down to the hand. In fact, the whole left side of my body was covered in some kind of protective wrap. It throbbed.

"What happened?" I asked.

"That's what we're here to ask you."

They wrote down everything I remembered, prompting me here about what time the mail truck arrived (I wasn't wearing a watch), and there about whether I noticed any strange people hanging around with Dr. Ames (just his daughter). They lost interest at about the time they realized that I knew nothing special.

During the interrogation, my mother came in, wearing her green uniform and leather holster, and greeted the FBI agents like old friends. She was a cop first, a mother second. That had always been the problem.

"Chief Garnet," I said. "Maybe you could tell me what the hell happened?"

"You fell off your bike, Harry," she said. "How many times do I have to tell you to wear a helmet?"

The FBI agents looked a little surprised at the tenor of this tender mother-son interchange. But there's a comfort to the familiar, and so I welcomed the wisecrack. It meant I wasn't about to die on her watch.

She told the agents, "I think he can handle it."

Red Tie said, "When the package bomb went off, you were standing near enough to the door to actually get blown out of it. You landed on your upper back about three feet away, in the gravel walkway that connects Cottage Five to the main path." The concussion of the blast, plus slamming my head on the way down, explained why I felt as if I had spent the evening single-handedly drinking my way to the bottom of a keg.

Of the three people in the cottage, I had been the farthest away from the explosion. That had been on Monday.

"What day is today?"

Thursday.

"What happened to Annie?"

"She was lucky too. Minor burns. She's almost ready to be released," my mother said. "She got air-vac'd down to Albany."

There was not a hell of a lot they could tell me beyond that, which I took to mean there was not a hell of a lot they wanted to tell me. "Until we have something more concrete, we don't want to speculate," the agent said. "Our forensics people were in there and sucked up every bit of evidence. If there's anything left behind, we'll find it."

"What was Doctor Ames mixed up in?" I asked. "Why'd anyone want to kill him?"

Blank stares.

Stripes shut his notebook and slipped it into his blazer pocket. "Harry," he said. "We don't have the lab reports back, as we've said. However, despite my partner's fear of speculation, I think I can say it's likely that this bombing is the latest in a chain of incidents that goes back three years."

"Incidents?"

"Other mail bombs. This is the fourth."

"I thought you guys caught the Unabomber."

"We caught one," Stripes said.

Red Tie cut in: "We don't want to mislead you. This string of bombings is very different, in a lot of ways, from the Unabomber's trademark style. We ruled him out as a suspect even before there was an arrest."

"But this guy's a copycat?" Could there be two?

"Like, do you think this one also lives in some remote cabin in the wilderness and survives the winters by eating rabbits he shot?"

"We'll ask him when we get the chance," Red Tie said.

"How do you even know these four bombings are related to each other?"

"The same way we knew that the Unabomber was behind all the bombs that he built. Bombings are distinctive events, in their own way as unique as fingerprints. At each juncture, the bomb maker has to make certain decisions about the materials used, the way the explosive is packaged, whether to carve tiny initials like 'FC' into it. Patterns emerge," Red Tie said.

"It helps when all the bombs come packaged in the same way," said Stripes.

"As a floppy disk," I said, suddenly remembering.

"A floppy disk filled with plastique," said Red Tie. "A micro detonator inside sets it off when it engages in the disk drive. A computer makes a surprisingly deadly weapon when it's blown apart from the inside. All those little frags of hard plastic and wire. A claymore wouldn't be more thorough."

"Is he another anarchist?" I asked.

"Right now we know more about the victims than the perpetrator. You were a bystander. But what we need to figure out is what Ames or his daughter had in common with the previous victims: a woman, a teenager, two other adult males. All got floppies in the mail."

"Who is Ames? I mean, what's he do for a living?" I said.

"He was a mathematician in New York City," said Red Tie.

"He did a lot of his work on computers, exchanged data with people all over the world. Probably got a floppy in the mail a few times a week. That's what mathematicians do these days. Obviously, we're still checking him out."

"So what's the connection?" I asked.

"If we knew that . . ." said Red Tie.

"Any more questions?" asked Stripes.

"Yeah. Do you guys have names?"

A few days later I got released. I was still bandaged, but the burns were healing, and I hadn't sustained any permanent brain damage. I had a loose T-shirt and some tight running shorts to wear, and while I was in the bathroom trying to remember how to put on my clothes, a nurse knocked on the door.

"I brought your personal effects."

Like I was a corpse.

I opened the door, and saw a small cardboard box sitting in the middle of the unmade hospital bed. It wasn't much bigger than the mail bomb package had been, but the contents were more benign. The key to my bike lock. A charred little piece of paper, which I managed to identify as a receipt for the cherry Coke slush I bought at Swanee's the day before the explosion. My wallet, miraculously unscathed, and still holding safe within its Velcro flaps a driver's license and sixty-seven cents. There was one more object, which I noticed by accident, after I tossed the box toward the trash and heard something rattle. I limped to the garbage and found a tiny dark shard of clay.

It was Annie's treasure.

I wasn't strong enough to go back to my place, so I moved in with my mom for a few days. It was about as bad as you'd expect. People who don't know her would think of her as a charming eccentric. She lived in a small frame house that looked like a cabin, set back down a dirt road near a bend in the Big Moose River, the same house that she was born in. The Big Moose River flowed into Timber Lake, so I could take a canoe to work every morning, if I felt like paddling for seven miles. I figured I wouldn't be in shape for the rapids for a few more weeks, though. Technically, the house had indoor plumbing, if you didn't mind pouring a bucketful of water into the tank every time you wanted to flush the toilet.

Other people in town lived in a collection of idiosyncratic buildings that appeared to have been recklessly plopped, here and there, onto the side of a mountain or in a little valley near water. We had no indigenous style or regional architecture to call our own, unless you counted the few former Great Camps that sat moldering beneath their National Register plaques. My neighbors inhabited cheap A-frames built in the seventies during the ski craze, or little, squarish cinder-block boxes designed to defend themselves against the onslaught of winters, or prefab split levels that opportunistic contractors had cobbled together in the past decade. Any sense of history that this region commanded came not from the rickety structures that man had imposed, but rather from the permanence of the land itself—with its broadleaf cottonwoods that grew ninety feet high or more, shagbark hickories that bloomed in May, mighty stands of northern red oaks that had withstood a century's storms. The central Adirondacks forest, stretching northward to the High Peaks, had always been fertile land. It had lured sportsmen to its clear streams and hunters to the deer-infested underbrush ever since the titans of the Industrial Revolution built their summer camps and ensconced their servants for the season. In those days, a man who wanted to mount a moosehead above his fireplace might journey the 144 miles from New York City to Albany via railroad, then change trains to Riverside, then catch a stage for the six-mile jaunt to Pottersville, then board a steamer to Schroon Lake. The trip would take the better part of two days, if a man were lucky and the steamer *Effingham* was running. The fare, point to point, would cost $9.75. The trees and the rocks and the lichen had seen all the arrivals, had witnessed history. One foggy night, Theodore Roosevelt traveled recklessly by carriage down the side of a mountain to meet the early train in North Creek, stooped to one knee to read a telegram in that station, and learned by the light of a lantern that he had become president, courtesy of an assassin. He missed most of the hunting season that year.

I hadn't lived with my mother since I went away to college seven years ago. Even in my current underemployed state, I was managing to pay the rent on a seasonal cabin whose owner only showed up to kill deer in the fall. It was rustic but it had given me the illusion of leading a private life.

"This place looks like a shrine," I said, limping into my old bedroom, still wallpapered in bumper stickers and posters of Jerry Garcia and Ernest Hemingway. My teenage yin and yang.

"The maid called in sick," my mother said, placing my box of personal effects in the middle of the bed. She smoothed the worn blue coverlet. "If you think I'm a lousy housekeeper, wait until you taste dinner."

That last threat was empty, thank God. She expertly grilled some hamburgers, rare, with some onions. And corn. I wolfed down about six helpings.

"Peterson called," she said, spanking the bottom of the ketchup bottle.

"Wants to know why I haven't finished painting the dock yet, I suppose," I said.

"No. In fact, he's sending you two weeks pay."

"Why?"

"I guess your heroics on the beach softened him," she said. "Why didn't you tell me?"

"I was going to, but I got blown up."

She laughed, then clamped a hand down on her head and scowled, just like Peterson when he grabs his hat and smashes it over his shiny pate. Which he does about ten times an hour. She caught the essence of the man in that one motion. She's a brilliant mimic when she's in the mood.

"Do Jed," I begged. She could capture his lackadaisical attitude perfectly every time she drawled, "Well, I was going to fi-i-i-x it, Mr. Peterson, but I couldn't find the right to-o-o-l."

"Can't. Mouth's full." She bit deep into a bun.

I was ten years old when my mother went back to work, rejoined the local force. Actually, I should say that she became the force, because for all intents and purposes, the police chief of Timber Lake was the sole extent of the local law in our part of the county. She wrote the speeding tickets (tourists mainly). She drove out to the bridge at the gorge to talk down Bill Marcus whenever he got drunk and climbed the suspension cables. Now, she was the local liaison to the FBI.

"What did Annie Ames tell the feds?" I asked her, thinking about the talisman I carried in my pocket.

"About the same as you. Zilch."

I wondered if Annie had responded to the FBI agents in Mayan. I kept flashing on that last second of contact with her, with my body language saying, "I don't get involved with women who call their cats Bootsie," and her stance answering, "I was intrigued at first, but you're clearly not boyfriend material." Then suddenly a bomb went *ka-pow*, as they used to say on Batman. Holy Life-Altering Occurrence, Boy Wonder.

If there had been no explosion, Annie Ames and I probably would have run into each other a couple of times more during her stay at The Vines. Maybe it would have been a little awkward, with her arriving at the courts in her tennis whites while the hired help was still rolling out the clay. I probably would have made another run at her then, just because I hated to see my seasonal average suffer, but she instinctively would have shied away. She wasn't gullible. She had the look of someone searching for something I didn't want to offer—a man to replace "My Pet" on her list of Other Hobbies. She might want him to wear one of those collars with little bells, so she'd know where he was all the time.

But that scenario had disappeared. Hell, the whole world had almost just evaporated. I'm not saying I missed her. How can you miss somebody you don't know? I'm just saying that I wouldn't have minded talking to someone else who just experienced the odd sensation of being tossed like a handful of wedding rice out onto a gravel path.

"I have something of hers," I told my mother.

"You should have told the FBI." Exit Rich Little.

"It's just a little souvenir rock she found on her last vacation. She was showing it to me when the bomb went off."

"Well, she's down at the medical center in Albany." She stood to clear the plates. "You could call her there."

I got the hospital's number from directory assistance, but the switchboard cut me off twice and then mistakenly transferred me to billing records a third time before a clerk admitted, "That patient has been discharged."

Dis-charged. Dis-aster. But wait. The generic FBI agents had said her dad was a math guy in New York. Back to directory assistance.

"What borough, please?"

"New York City."

"There are five boroughs, here, sir," the operator said. "Checking Manhattan . . . There is a Frederick Ames, but he has an unlisted home number. I'm not showing an office number."

I remembered that she said she had gone to Columbia University, so I called the alumni office. I sat through an after-hours recording that informed me that alumni searches would be conducted by mail or fax only and to please allow ten working days.

I'm not a guy who gets carried away by much (except my bike), so it was a strange feeling, all that adrenaline coursing through my body, focused on one thing: find her. I hate it when people tell me no. But there was more to it. I might have a lot to say to her if we ever connected. So if I had to, I would call every Ames in Manhattan. One of them must be a cousin or something, someone who would know Annie Ames. I called back directory assistance.

"What borough, please?"

"Manhattan."

"Yes?"

"I need the phone numbers for every person named Ames," I said.

There was a pause.

"Sir, there are dozens of people with that last name," the operator said. "I can't give you the whole list. Do you have a street address or a first name?"

"No. I have to find Annie Ames!"

"Checking," she said. "No one named Anne or Annie Ames listed."

I went to bed wondering if the Timber Lake library had a Manhattan phone book. This wouldn't have been a problem if I were already working for Hart, Monroe & Weinmiller. There, I could just order one of my slaves, er, assistants to run one down. But for now, stuck in a little house on a dirt road an hour from anywhere, I might as well have been seeking a double iced decaf cappuccino, hold the cinnamon. The library housed its modest collection in a mildewed trailer near the dump, where tourists went most nights to watch the bears feed. The library's hours were less regular than the bears'. And what if the Frederick Ames listed in Manhattan was different from the one I was looking for? I got into one of those loops, where my mind knotted, and every plan was another tangled rope. I slept the sleep of the sore and the thwarted that night.

I felt better after the sun came up. Funny how that happens. I woke late, heard sparrows at the bird feeder outside the window, thought of Annie, walked into the kitchen, got distracted by a list of phone messages my mother had left before she went to work: "Blaney called at 9:30—left no number." "Call Dr. McCubben's office to schedule a follow-up." "Peterson wants to know if you can drive." I would have walked down to The Vines to retrieve my bike, except for one thing. Moving hurt like hell. The fire ants were back. On my right leg this

Joshua

Quittner

time. Being alone in this house reminded me of being a kid, wondering if my mother would come back for supper. Usually she didn't, but sometimes she remembered around seven o'clock to call Mrs. Etterson and ask her to come over to heat up a bowl of soup. Mrs. Etterson kept horses. Some days, after school, she let me go over and pitch hay.

Alone on the itchy brown couch in the living room, I jabbed the remote control.

Cable was cool, but there wasn't enough wacko stuff on for my taste. I wanted more channels, bring on the weirdness.

There was a game we used to play a lot back in law school, mostly right after exams, and mostly in off-campus barrooms. It was called Dream Cable. You'd think up some outlandish idea and then poll the table: Who here would pay for this kind of programming? The game stayed the same even if the faces around the table changed. I remembered a guy named Sinclair. I didn't even know him well enough to know if that was his first or last name, but it suited him, either way. He had the kind of forever boyish look that women love, with unruly hair falling in his eyes and a complexion that looked just slapped. He also had enough charm to cadge the occasional free pitcher of beer from the waitresses. I never had any classes with him, but I believed Sinclair would make a fine courtroom lawyer one day because he loved to take outrageous stands and then argue their merits convincingly. You need that kind of audacity to face a jury.

One night Sinclair had put forth his own modest proposal, The Execution Channel. I hadn't bought into the idea back then, even though I agreed the X-Channel would cream anything else in the Nielsens. Its programming would revolve exclusively around capital punishment, Sinclair had said, ticking off on his fingers all the possibilities: documentaries on guys who were fighting the death penalty; live reports on their executions, with footage from Death Row; the Last Supper, the Last Mile, the Last Words. "Let's do it."

I remembered that he clambered up on a scarred wooden

table for the big finish: "What if teenagers started committing murders just so they could get onto Death Row and sell their movie rights?" I think we pelted him with popcorn soon after.

But now that I was lying in pain on the couch, I didn't think it was totally a joke anymore. I wondered where old Sinclair was, and if he had thought about pitching the X-Channel to any networks. I wouldn't even mind co-producing. I could recommend the first person to star in a pilot episode: the bomber who almost offed me. Every time I thought of the guy, who I pictured as some squirmy and pale hunchback wielding tweezers and wires at a basement workbench, I wanted to see him fry. The original thing about The Execution Channel would be that you, the viewer, could vote on the method of death. Take the case of the mail bomber. He might make a plea for lethal injection over electrocution (wouldn't you?). The audience could consider his request, then viewers could call a 900 number and vote. Proceeds from the calls would go to a victims' restitution fund.

I clicked off the TV and forced myself up. I remembered the copy of *The Armies of the Night* I'd bought for seventy-five cents a while back, and limped down to the basement, to the fake pine-paneled rec room where the bookshelves were.

The room had that sweet-rot smell that screamed out for a dehumidifier. The overhead fluorescents did strange things to my skin color. The dartboard and the macramé wall hanging were vestiges of a hope for normalcy that my family had long since abandoned. Desk: a weathered door straddling a couple of sawhorses. That door had come from the front of the house, relegated to the cellar a few years back, after the dog had chewed off the edge of it. I sat in the desk chair, ran my hand over the fang marks, and swiveled.

That's how I came face-to-face with my fate.

It was my old computer, which I got for my twenty-first birthday. The idea was that I'd use it for term papers. Wrong. As an undergraduate I had mainly used it to play to-the-death matches of Tetris, Flight Simulator, and Zork.

I'd never even taken the thing to law school, though, since the university had a bunch of laptops lying around on just about every horizontal surface. There were so many, you could practically pick one up in the men's room. They were perfect for taking lecture notes. In the three years that had passed since I last flipped the switch, this computer had become hopelessly outdated, lame, a paperweight. Looking at it was like catching a glimpse of a Ford Pinto parked on the street. Your eye would be drawn to it, because there would be something a little off about the design of the body. It was the same way with my old computer: the case was too blocky, the keyboard was too filthy, and the screen was too convex, like a contact lens designed for the severely myopic. Its vestiges of "high-tech style" had long since lost their charm. No mouse feel.

I needed new wheels, metaphorically speaking. I needed the equivalent of new-car smell. Maybe one of those speedy new laptops. A flat panel, like Annie had.

All this before I even flipped the switch.

I heard a once-familiar whirrrrr, the motor lumbering into the clearing one more time after all these years. The monitor frizzed electrically, and the screen lit. Then there was a beep: I am awaking from my slumber, master. How may I serve you?

I looked at the cursor blinking in the upper left-hand corner of the screen, and then I typed: CONNECT ME TO ANNIE.

What I really needed was a modem, of course. Hard to imagine, but back when this baby was new, a modem was still considered an add-on, a newfangled, red-blinking alien. People were just starting to care about making a connection between their personal computers and the rest of the world. Back in those Dinosaur Days of the early 1990s, the general public was first forming the syllables of that word *In-ter-net*. Now I needed one of those new modems, the ones that pumped data through the phone line at a rate of 56 kilobits per second. That's a lot of *0*s and *1*s, but then, I had a lot to say.

I knew where to find the modem. But I dreaded the thought.

Blaney.

How does one introduce Richard Blaney? How to cushion the blow? Let me describe the scene I came upon the following day, after I had played on my mother's guilt ("If Mrs. Etterson hadn't shown up to tell you were running late, Ma, I would have gone crazy with worry"), and she had offered me the keys to the Sentra as penance. Despite my persistent pains and soreness, I climbed into the car to drop her at work, then drove for two hours down to Albany. I whizzed along the Northway, and exited the highway half a mile from the target, a strip mall. Snapshot of the end of the century: the parking space to customer ratio is about one to five hundred and the competition is fierce among the Americans in their too-big four-wheel-drive vehicles. They all woke up this morning convinced of the need for a bucket of chicken, closeout ceramic tile, and a manicure. Using a mother and child crossing the asphalt as a diversion, I outmaneuvered a Ford Expedition with a Labrador panting in the backseat and slid into a spot right in front of Computer Nation, the biggest computer electronics store in a hundred-mile radius.

I knew I would find Blaney here. He was the kind of geek who you couldn't just *call* on the phone, because as a rule he wouldn't answer the phone, and if he did, just once by accident, and you were able to make an appointment to meet him somewhere, well, chances were he wouldn't show up. Blaney was unable to *connect*, because even if his intentions were good, he had no ability to follow through. He lived below the line of human nicety. He was pure id, distracted easily by the physical twinges of his always worrisome body: too sleepy, too sick, too hungry, too anxious about being late to be anything but late. If I wanted to see Blaney, then I had to confront him—

physically show up at the premises he currently occupied, present myself to him and then start talking.

Why bother with Blaney at all? Well, a lot of people didn't. In college he had relied on a modern version of the farmer's old-time barter system to get by. Instead of trading livestock for services, delivering a fresh-killed chicken to the doctor's door to pay for medicine dispensed yesterday, Blaney traded information. He dispensed bits and pieces of his knowledge about computers—how to copy a file, where to download the best software games for free, how to fix the printer—in return for the services he needed. Beer and free rides, mostly. It was a user's way of life, mainly, but not by choice, I was sure. If Blaney had possessed a larger portion of the things the rest of us trade for services—good looks, charm, the ability to tell a joke—he wouldn't have been forced to rely, so blatantly, on his hoard of hacker tricks. Did Blaney have a good heart? I had no idea. But I have a taste for strong personalities, and something about his eccentricities satisfied that craving.

Computer Nation might have been invented with Blaney in mind. If Blaney hadn't gotten hired as a salesman, he would've volunteered to mop the floors just to be near the new-gadget, shrink-wrapped odor that emanated from the shelves.

Inside, they had what they touted as EQUIPMENT! Thousands and thousands of square feet of HARDWARE! and SOFTWARE!, CD-ROMS!, and PERIPHERALS! like spongy computer mouse pads and wrist rests and joysticks. The shoppers pushed their carts up aisles as wide as a supermarket's, loading up on printer paper and extra megs of RAM! and the latest multimedia upgrade.

In the back of the store, in front of a beat-up old computer that tracked inventory, my quarry hunched. That deflated-doughnut silhouette was unmistakable. I could see from a distance that my Blaney wore a silly red apron emblazoned with a stylized image of a computer being struck by lightning: Computer Nation's logo. Hard to believe somebody got paid to think that up.

Catching sight of Blaney triggered a repressed memory. I would say "unpleasant," but the word would be redundant in any statement concerning him. I had met him years ago, as an undergraduate. I had an eight-page paper due in an hour. I dashed into the lab to print it out, sat down, logged on, and tried to call up the file that contained "Dickens and Chancery: A Bleak Relationship." Brilliant thesis. Anyway, I couldn't retrieve my paper. The computer said FILE NOT FOUND. I started flipping through different directories, getting more and more desperate as time passed, and then, all of a sudden, this ominous message flashed across the screen:

Application Error
WIN.COM has caused a General Protection Fault in module_LIB.DLL at 0009:046F

Then the system froze. I hit RETURN. Nothing. I tried to reboot. Nothing. I flipped off the computer, then hit the switch again. Same message. I tried to hit the ESC key, the CTRL ALT-DEL keys in tandem, the XYZ-PDQ HELP ME NOW key, but the damn thing wouldn't budge. Just kept blinking that message. I pounded my fists on the keyboard.

That was when I heard a maddeningly nasal voice from behind my left shoulder say, "Are you trying to kill that computer or just rape it, Frat Boy?"

I turned to confront a lumpy individual in a short-sleeved buttoned-down shirt. No lie. He sat attached to a nearby computer like mold on a petri dish. Empty bags of Cheetos, dented Coke cans and piles of computer magazines with names like *Unix Review* all littered his desk.

Before I could leap for his throat, he sidled over to where I sat.

"You've just experienced a GPF," he said, and reached for the mouse next to my keyboard. He deftly clicked on the CLOSE button at the top of the screen, and the hateful error message disappeared. Then he closed down a succession of other applications I had unwittingly opened. Finally, DO YOU WANT TO QUIT WINDOWS? flashed across the screen.

Y, he typed.

"You had too much going on at once, so you fried the thing," he said, blinking vacantly in my direction. "Two programs were competing for the same space in your memory. It's a General Protection Fault."

As he spoke, he restarted the software program, and suddenly my file appeared on the screen. PRINT, he directed, and I heard the whine of the laser printer as it struggled to meet the challenge. I felt only hot relief.

"Thanks," I said and flashed him one of those smiles of earnest, clean-cut gratitude that seemed to work so well with the professors.

But Blaney had been immune to my charms. "You know what your problem is?"

"I didn't know I had one."

"I've been watching you. You rush in here every few days, expect the computers to behave like your servants, run back out. You don't take the time to learn anything," he said.

I would have been angrier if I hadn't sensed that he was truly saddened by what he perceived as my callous treatment of his friends, the machines.

"Your problem is that you're a natural," he said. "You usually don't have to work hard to get what you want, do you? So you go nuts if something doesn't go your way."

Nobody had ever talked to me like that before. To hear such words emitted from the mouth of a lumpish stranger was wild. It was kind of interesting, to tell you the truth. Most people like me from the start. Blaney didn't.

"So why'd you help?" I asked.

"Out of respect."

"Thanks."

"Not for you, idiot. For the computers."

Months would go by and I wouldn't see him. But then I'd

decide I wanted a dose of something sour. Maybe I wanted a wakeup call from time to time. Seeing Blaney felt like having the coach come out to the pitcher's mound to tell you to knock it off with the fancy curve balls. I wasn't fooling him.

Why he socialized with me, I don't know. He didn't have a lot of human friends. He inhabited the computer lab as ubiquitously as the stale air, and he was always there to witness—and correct—any amateur's computing mistakes. He never extracted payment in money. But two thirds of the sophomore class owed him.

He probably wouldn't have described our relationship as a friendship. That was too intimate for him. When we got together, he liked to say it was because he was collecting debts. He called in favors sporadically. Usually he needed a ride to the mall. Or cash for a large order of cheese fries. I could overlook his obnoxious behavior, his circus-refugee wardrobe, and his propensity to put on vaguely superior airs. When somebody provides an invaluable service, it's best to put up with their little quirks.

I knew little about his personal life, and his past remained shadowy. He lived somewhere off campus, and was a classic paranoic. He believed that people were following him. Blaney graduated a couple of years after me. He was one of those dudes who wanted to take their college nice and slow, maybe make a career out of it, the type who ends up running a business on the edge of campus, selling U. of Whatever T-shirts and emblazoned jockey shorts.

Now, as I approached him, Blaney blinked. As usual.

"Hey, Blaney, thanks for calling my mom." She said he'd phoned to see if I was okay.

He recoiled in embarrassment. I loved that.

"Gar-net, bombing victim, ex-classmate, boob vivant. I called to see if you still had your typing fingers, that's all," he said. "Did you come in for a Tetris tutorial? Let me see if I have Tetris for Dummies in stock."

He was the first person I'd talked to in days who didn't ask me what had happened, whether I was feeling better, if I needed any help. He wasn't programmed for small talk. That made it easier for me to get to the point.

I told him I needed to send E-mail.

"You joined the human race! What kind of machine are you using?"

"It's an NEC," I said. "A 486."

"Big fins and a beavertail hanging from the antenna?" he said. "Wouldn't a Morse code clicker be easier?"

I told him I wanted to buy a modem.

At that point, a customer who had been perusing the Compaq display nearby interrupted. "Excuse me, I couldn't help but overhearing. I'm looking for a modem too." He looked like an insurance salesman. He looked like an easy mark.

Instantly Eddie Haskell emerged.

"Certainly, sir, perhaps I can help you find a superior model," said Blaney. I had no idea he could feign such unctuousness.

"Well, I'm not sure what I need." The customer took out a piece of paper from his pocket. "I wrote down the model of my computer." Handed it to Blaney.

Who cleared his throat.

"Sir, I think your computer already has a modem. An internal modem built into it." I heard the regret. His heart breaking, Blaney led the customer down the aisle to a display of personal computers. I trailed. "Let me show you."

He flipped around the big toaster component, which he identified as the CPU, and pointed to a spot on the back of it where you could plug in a phone line.

"It's already in there, sir. All you need, sir, is to sign up with an online service, plug in the phone cord, and off you go. You'll be online in a jiffy." A jiffy?

The man thanked him, wandered off.

"Do I have one like his?" I asked.

"No," Blaney said, pulling a box off a shelf, still transition-

F
L
A
M
E
W
A
R

34

ing out of that helpful Haskell mode. "You need an external modem. Easier to install."

"How much?" I asked.

"Just charge it, Garnet. You're a big-shot lawyer now, right?"

He had a point.

"Want to get a beer later?" he asked.

"Sure," I said.

"You get a six-pack and I'll configure the modem for you."

Configuring modems. How hard could it be?

"Nah, but I do need you to help me figure out how to send someone E-mail."

"What's to figure out? You just send it."

"I don't know her address."

"Her?" I swear he giggled.

"I know part of it. She calls herself ala5."

"Ala5 is not an address. It's a user name. You've sent enough E-mail to know that, Garnet," he said reprovingly. "You don't know her Internet provider?"

"She has an account from Columbia University."

"That's probably where she checks for mail, then. Even if she has another account, she'd get her mail forwarded. Do I need to spell it out for you?" He wrote on a sales slip: ala5@columbia.edu.

"Try that."

I gathered up my modem and my sales slip, and I headed for the cash register. I left him standing there in his too-tight apron, hands on hips, inventory scrolling across his screen. But he called me back. "Hey, you owe me," he said.

"I'll see you later at Joe's-Bar-dot-com. I'll buy."

"No—something else," he said. "I need a ride next week. You still driving the shuttle for Peterson?"

"You need to go to New York?" I asked. "Why?"

"Business." He oozed off.

chapter three

If they'd spent their summer vacations anywhere else, the six people in the back of Peterson's Chevy Suburban would be coming home with trophy sunburns. But up in the Adirondacks, you can't even get a wristwatch mark in July. In the rearview, I could see them shift on the queen-size bench seats, these pale folks who'd piled into the shuttle at dawn for the long ride back from the resort. They preferred to take their vacation pains in the form of hiking-boot blisters, shoulder aches from fly casting, and hands callused by canoe paddles—souvenirs they could flaunt back in New York City.

I'd made this drive before and knew that when we crossed the county line into Westchester, where the tributaries of traffic converged at the headwaters of the metropolitan area, all the guests' hard-won relaxation would start to seep out and be replaced by poison. They were headed back to heavy mortgages and Wall Street worries and legions of homeless guys who pestered them for a meal. My fear was simpler: just don't let anyone crowbar my bike off the back of the Suburban at a stoplight. After I jettisoned my passengers at Grand Central

Station, I planned to dump the car in some three-hundred-dollar-a-night garage. Then I could travel light.

"You hit another pothole." My navigator was wedged against the passenger-side door, periodically blinking up from the muffin-sized chronometer on his freckled wrist. "Your speed has dropped to fifty-two miles per hour over the past eight point seven miles. If you keep decelerating at a constant rate, we might never get there, thereby proving Xeno's paradox."

Yeah, the passengers were tightening up, all right, but it could have been from prolonged exposure to Blaney.

I was feeling it myself. I suspected he only wanted to be helpful, in the same way that the computer in *Lost in Space* was trying to be of use every time it waved its arms and shrieked, "Danger, danger, Will Robinson!" Blaney loved computers so much, and spent so much time with them, tinkering, typing, installing video cards, and just breathing in the air that blew off their motors, that he had inhaled their essence. His brain had morphed into a machine. The same thing could probably happen to a newly hatched duckling who set eyes on a Windows PC and believed it was his mother.

Everything Blaney said was accurate, of course. But this version of the Blaney model had a few bugs. Somebody needed to write a few new lines of code to make him less annoying. It would be easy to grab him by his drip-dry shirt collar, rattle the bottle of eardrops in his pocket, and growl, "Knock it off, jerk." But it would just hurt his feelings.

I usually managed to ignore Blaney's delusions. But today he seemed almost panicky. He had begged me to pick him up before the guests, because he didn't want them to see where he lived. He had wanted to know who would be riding in the Suburban—a passenger list, as it were—and he wouldn't say why. He wanted me to drop him off last. It had to be at a precise time at the northwest corner of Forty-eighth Street and Sixth Avenue. "Follow my instructions," he had pleaded. "And while we're driving down to the city, please do not, re-

Joshua Quittner

Michelle Slatalla

37

peat, do not address me by my name in front of those people, okay?"

"Who are you meeting?" I asked.

"Who wants to know?"

So much for conversation. For nearly six hours, his drive-time patter had consisted of criticisms of my speed, punctuated by long lapses of gazing at the rest-stop billboards that lined the New York State Thruway. On this stretch of highway, we passed vehicles bound for vacation, with canoes lashed to their roofs, bikes jammed onto trunk racks, suitcases and extra pillows and folded-up tents filling the back cargo spaces. Volvo station wagons and Jeep Cherokees, their sides busting with the weight of possessions too precious to leave behind, looked like yuppie versions of the Joad family truck.

I knew from previous trips that Blaney liked to eat at the Adirondacks-theme McDonald's, the highway rest stop where the vinyl tables were printed with a fake wood-grain pattern and the twig chairs were really made of molded plastic. But today, he didn't even ask. Now and then he'd smile to himself nervously or tick off some imaginary items on his fingers. I didn't bother to try to draw him out. He may have been the de facto copilot on this shuttle, but I didn't want to be drawn into whatever furtive scheme he was planning. I was, frankly, dreading the fact that I had agreed to crash overnight with him in some eau-de-sweat-sock walk-up in Greenwich Village where his cousin kept company with a pack of Norwegian gray rats. "Come on, it'll be too late to drive back," he had whined.

Whatever. The memorial service would be over too late for me to drive back today, anyway.

Dr. Frederick Ames, who had held the Alistair V. Melton endowed chair of mathematics and the title of distinguished professor in his department, would be eulogized at 3:00 P.M. at Riverview Chapel on Manhattan's Upper West Side. It was a small building, and Dr. Ames used to say that its gothic pretensions amused him whenever he walked past and saw its spire, jammed between two enormous, many-storied apartment buildings. The little chapel had been there first and had refused to give way. That had appealed to Ames.

How did I know all these things? The professor's daughter told me, in E-mail, of course. "My father loved architecture. Maybe he was just trying to order the world, figure out how it all went together, by studying the buildings as if they were a carefully arranged pile of wooden blocks. A benefit of that approach was that he always noticed unusual gargoyles up on a balcony, or the secret door on the side wall, or the little plaque that said the Whyfe family had housed their pigs here in the 1860s."

"Do you study buildings too?" I had written.

"No, people. Remember? (anthro)."

We had exchanged a number of messages. Modem magic. Actually, I no longer thought of her as Annie but as ala5@columbia.edu. It was funny how fast the sum total of a human being's identity could be replaced by one line of text on a computer screen. I got five or six E-mail messages a day from ala5 now. I'd sent a lot of E-mail before but none of my pen pals had been so conscientious. Or, for that matter, considerate. Indeed, during my freshman year of college, a bunch of my high school buddies set up a little mailing list. It was intended to be a way to keep our supposedly eternal friendship alive. And thriving. No matter where we were. But what passed for clumsy jocularity in person turned into disaster online. (Joe told Jeff he saw Fern—Jeff's ex—at a party and boy, did she look hot. Jeff, still smarting from the breakup, told Joe to get bent. Max leapt to Joe's defense. And a full-scale flame war erupted, incinerating an otherwise beautiful friendship.)

This is a serious pitfall of the communications revolution. A few poorly chosen words set off a devastating sequence of events. Party A sends a message to Party B, and something gets lost in the translation (a wink, a shrug, a nudge . . . and please, don't talk to me about smiley faces). Words miscoded on the far side cause awful consequences.

I didn't have that problem with Annie. Maybe we communicated better just because she was a better writer. She managed to avoid any landmines. Our correspondence immediately fell into an almost physical, healthy rhythm. We might as well have been on a tennis court, volleying. Every time I lobbed one over the net, she hit the ball back. With topspin. The first reply she sent had thrilled me. Garnet, you're a genius, I'd thought, when I saw that mail was waiting for me. You figured out how to get to her.

I'd called it up, trembling with as much anticipation as one of Jane Austen's heroines breaching a wax seal on a catty note from a neighbor.

> Henry: How nice of you to write. I am at my mother's, as well, so we have something in common after all. My arms still hurt but no permanent scarring (according to the plastic surgeon). People send flowers, which makes the apartment smell like a funeral home. I kept the yellow roses but gave the vase of glads to the doorman, who put them by the mailboxes in the lobby. I don't really remember much from that day. Do you? // Annie

I wrote back immediately.

> Amy: I remember a lot of things about that day. I remember thinking I would knock off work early to go fishing. I remember that my biggest worry (before my near death experience) was bike maintenance. I remember that the tag on your T-shirt was sticking out, and that it said medium. Oh, also that you have a beautiful neck. Signed, H-A-R-R-Y. Let's review that, class, H-A-R-R-Y

Her next message was profusely apologetic. How difficult things had been lately. How distracted she was planning the memorial service for her father—"my mother, who didn't even like him while he was alive, is more concerned with getting a notice about the date of the service into *The Times* than

F

L

A

M

E

W

A

R

she is about his death"—and how lonely she was, sitting in that big apartment, unable to concentrate on her work, on a book, on anything.

I took pity on her.

> Addie: Here's a trick to limit your emotional liability. Imagine the worst-case scenario unfolding . . . memorial service a nightmare with mother bad-mouthing your dad to his relatives; mother pressures you to move back home permanently; cries if you say no. Bootsie gets a big tick on her neck even though she's an indoor cat; apartment requires fumigation; clothes smell of stink bomb; professor who led your dig gets indicted for stealing artifacts.
>
> You realize—reality will be a cakewalk in comparison.
>
> This is my patented method for stress relief—very 1990s. It works. no? Signed, Henry

I wasn't even sure why I bothered. She was as different from me as Blaney, only in a much cuter way. Her mother was a professional cellist, away on tour six months of every year, whereas mine was a cop, away just about every day convincing drunks not to smash beer bottles over each other's heads outside Buford's Tap Room.

> Harry, if that is truly your name: what does a tick look like? I might have seen one in the lobby by the elevator. //Annie

When I pointed out to the city girl the incongruity in our upbringings, she wrote: "What about your family dynamics? In mine, it was weird because for years I never really knew him (Father). They separated when I was little and I barely saw him until I started to work for him this summer."

I wrote back: "In my family, we don't believe in dynamics. Just fate. Ours was unlucky."

*   *   *

Information arrived in little niblets. Quick thoughts that got sent off before there was time to reconsider or punctuate. Annie's messages were frozen in time: March 16, 1999. Her computer's time stamp was stuck.

She was trying to decide what to do for the rest of the summer. She had been planning to organize all her father's research notes for an article he was writing, "but suddenly no one requires my administrative services. maybe i'll get his notes in shape anyway."

"Why don't you take it easy for a while instead?" I wrote. "Don't push yourself."

"Some people like to push themselves."

"I'd like to come to the memorial service," I wrote, inexplicably. The truth is, there's nothing I hate more than memorial services, with the cloying scent of too many roses and the mourners' somber expressions to remind me of the people I had buried. But I wanted to come to this memorial service; it could just as easily have been in my honor as Ames's. Had I been standing a couple of feet closer to the bomb, or at a different angle from the center of the explosion, the boys up in Syracuse would already be interviewing alternate candidates for the endowed chair of long hours and lowly chores. I wanted to know more about Ames, about what such an apparently mild guy had said or done that could inspire so much hatred. The bomber had dedicated a lot of energy, days or weeks of tedious and meticulous work, to erasing Ames from the face of the earth. I hated the bomber. But I knew nothing, was powerless to do anything about him. If I learned more about Ames, that would be a start.

There was also the small matter of Annie's shard. "I was holding it when the bomb went off, and it was still clenched in my fist in the emergency room," I wrote to her.

"I would like to have it back, so I hope someone managed to pry it loose from your fingers," she responded.

"A nurse did that."

F
L
A
M
E

W
A
R

"If she bruised you, you should sue. It could be your first big pain-and-suffering settlement."

"Why do you have such a bias against lawyers?"

In reply, she sent directions to the chapel.

Annie's directions stank. I had to settle for the last remaining folding chair, just inside the door, the price of arriving late at a crowded, tiny chapel. I had expected some Columbia faculty, a couple of students who weren't away for the summer, family members and friends. I hadn't expected two hundred people who looked like they should be attending a Senate subcommittee hearing. Most of the men were in dark, well-cut suits and sported the severe haircuts of the very ambitious. Only a few women were in the audience, and most seemed as if they had stopped in for a few minutes in between high-pressure client meetings. They carried briefcases, and sneaked peeks at wristwatches. The message this crowd broadcast was that Frederick Ames was someone whose passing commanded notice, even if he hadn't been a particularly close friend. Attendance was their tithe.

Unfortunately, the air conditioner had broken, and it was hotter than midday out on Peterson's dock. Casement windows haphazardly cranked open here and there did nothing to create an actual breeze. Beads of sweat appeared on my forehead. Two standing fans, facing each other across the aisle, aimlessly recirculated hot air.

Annie was in the front row, in a small hat with a veil, the kind Jackie Kennedy wore in the old, black-and-white footage. Once she turned around to look for someone, and I saw a small stickpin, which caught the sun like a searchlight when she moved. It made her sparkle incongruously. Her mother, an older version of Annie—same red hair, pale skin, and muscular frame—sat next to her, now draping an arm in consolation, now withdrawing it. I recognized that scene of confused single parenting.

Annie went up to the podium and cleared her throat. "I want to thank you all, on behalf of my mother and myself, for coming to say good-bye to my father. Like me, he was an only child, so he considered his colleagues and his friends to be his family. It would have pleased him to see so many of you here today."

She looked and sounded steady, as if she were used to speaking to crowds on emotionally wrenching occasions. She gripped both sides of the lectern with her hands, and a pulse in her throat was the only sign she gave of strain, as she said, slowly, "I only recently began to spend time with my father, but it has always been apparent to me that he prized his work. While I was lying in a hospital, thinking about how he died, what bothered me most was the fact that he left this world so abruptly—in the middle of projects, with unfinished papers littering his desk, with his thoughts and his life's work severed before they could reach their natural conclusion. It seemed a particularly cruel fate for a man like my father, who needed to finish every last detail of every single thing he undertook to be satisfied. To die like this, in midstream, that was unfair, I thought. But then, a few days passed, and what I came to realize about my father was this: No matter how long he lived, or how he died, he would have departed in the same way—in midstream. He was involved. His curiosity was like a persistent flame, and the only way to put it out was to snuff it unceremoniously. He was always working on a new project, a new problem, a new way of looking at things. The course of his life shows that he kept growing intellectually—in mid-career, he quit his job at a government agency to accept an academic position. Who knows where he would have gone next? What he cared about was the pursuit of ideas, and even if he had lived to be a hundred and five, he would have left unfinished business. That was one of the most wonderful things about him.

"When I came to that conclusion, I felt peace, for him and, for the first time, for my relationship with him. We may not

F
L
A
M
E
W
A
R

44

have been close, but he left behind, for me to inherit, his curiosity and his love of learning. Those are the two best legacies I could hope for.''

She hesitated then, as if she wanted to say more, but consciously stopped herself. "Some people who knew him longer and more intimately than I did have asked to speak about my father today. I'd like to introduce one of his oldest friends, Edmund Alsace.''

As I watched Annie walk back to her seat, I realized someone was watching me. He was a solidly built man in a light gray suit, bald except for a monk's fringe of close-cropped brown hair, with a square, linebacker's head. A few years older than me, the man wore brass-rimmed aviator-frame glasses and had a ruddy complexion, a survivor of serious teenage acne. He stood against the wall a few rows behind Annie's seat, and made no effort to disguise the fact that he was looking at me. I ignored him, after a bit, and concentrated on the eulogies.

At the podium stood a man with prematurely white hair, unshaven and unkempt in what had to be his only blazer. Perspiration stained his armpits, as he read from the few pages still clinging to a dog-eared yellow legal pad. He acted like someone who always carried a legal pad, needed it for when he wanted to jot down notes and appointments with his mechanical pencil. Without it, he would be lost.

"Freddy was not a quitter, nor did he abide people who gave up easily," the man read. "For him, arriving at a solution was less satisfying than attacking the problem. I remember a time, back when we both worked for the Department of Defense, when Freddy had locked himself out of his office. Now, the obvious answer would have been to call security, get a skeleton key. But Freddy eschewed the obvious—and never mind the fact that he had a report due by lunchtime involving an odd cipher the NSA boys had picked up over Tehran. For more than an hour that morning, Fred toiled away at the door, at the keyhole, using a series of paper clips, a nail file, and a credit card to jimmy that darned lock. I don't need to tell the people in this room that Frederick was perhaps the first person to ever break into an office at the Pentagon." A few nervous chuckles. Ames's colleague consulted his legal pad.

The door pushed open behind me, inches from my chair. Somebody was sliding in even later than I had. There were no more seats, so the man wedged himself between my chair and the wall, whispering, "Excuse me." I looked up, ready to give him a nod, but he was caught up in his grief and didn't seem to care if I minded his intrusion. He was as tall as me and even thinner, and managed to look elegant in a denim shirt and slightly wrinkled chinos. He had long, graying hair, good thick hair, pulled into a perfect ponytail. His blue eyes were sad; just looking into them made me recognize the gravity and sorrow of the moment.

I glanced at Aviator Glasses and saw that he had lost interest in me in favor of the recent arrival.

Ames's friend was winding down, whether because he had run out of things to say or because he was afraid of passing out if he didn't sit down in this heat, I couldn't say. What always strikes me at funerals is how people tend to eulogize someone's life as if it had had an intrinsic structure, a well-plotted beginning, middle, and end, with clear themes running throughout. Sometimes, there was a denouement—a pinnacle reached, like being made CEO; a battle won, against alcoholism or disease—which made for a dramatic story. But the surprise endings, like Frederick Ames's, were always hard to handle. A good eulogizer tried to bring the ending hastily into context.

What story would people be telling if the bomber had gotten me too? Probably the "he had so much promise" routine. Or better, the irony angle: "For such a young man, Harry left surprisingly few loose ends."

Ames's friend reached into a shirt pocket and pulled out a crumpled wad of a handkerchief, which he used to swipe ineffectually at the sheen on his forehead. As he paused to sip from a glass of water, I saw Annie quietly stand and walk over to the windows. Unobtrusively, she cranked open the two nearest the front. Then she shut the rest of them, except for the window in the very back of the chapel, near where I sat. Was she trying to bake us like pork chops?

Then, on her way back to her seat, she stopped in front of one of the standing fans and shifted its angle toward the back of the room. She positioned the second fan to draw air from the open windows, and blow it toward the other fan, which broadcast the air throughout the room.

I felt the breeze immediately. I tried to savor it unobtrusively, but what I really wanted to do was to gulp in greedy breaths of it. I marveled at her ingenuity. I could not have been more impressed by her innate grasp of air currents and angles if she had just sunk the nine ball into the side pocket after banking it off the far end of a pool table.

The eulogizer looked gratefully at Annie as she slid back into her seat, and then he said, simply, "Fred adhered to his own moral code. And the rest of us be damned."

The rest of us be damned. Did that attitude lead to his death? The FBI must be here, staking out the scene in case the murderer showed up to gloat at his handiwork. I covertly surveyed the room. Couldn't tell. I knew from Annie's E-mail that no one had figured out the bomber's motive: "the fbi keeps asking more questions about enemies. But he had none i knew of. did he act odd, or nervous, before he was killed? no. did he talk about anything that was bothering him? no. then they go away for a day or two. but they always come back."

The formal service ended, and it was time for the bonus round: audience participation. People awkwardly navigated the rows of folding chairs to approach Annie and her mother. Like a sweaty reception line at an outdoor summer wedding, people shook their hands or patted their shoulders or offered a stiff hug. Among the uncomfortable stickiness of the other mourners, the man with the ponytail stuck out as crisply as starch on a shirt. He had been in the direct path of the fans, a lucky recipient of Annie's science-fair smarts. As he moved toward the door, a look of pain flashed in his eyes. His gaze hit me like a sucker punch, and I wondered if he was a relative of Fred's, maybe a distant cousin. I thought he was going to say something, but then he slipped out.

I made my way toward the front of the room, where Annie suddenly looked strained and small among the red faces and dark suits that surrounded her. When she saw me, she smiled.

"I'm sorry about your father." I augmented that obligatory condolence with a discreet squeeze of the shoulder.

"Thank you for coming."

It had been much easier to converse with the virtual version of Annie. E-mail had given me the illusion that we had known each other for years. Now I was confronted with the inescapable fact of a living, breathing, complicated person, with an eyelash that needed to be brushed off her cheek, and I realized that what stood in front of me was a stranger.

"He had a lot of friends." I gestured around the room.

"I don't recognize most of them," she said.

Her mother turned to her. "Annie? Are you ready? We should try to get home ahead of the others."

"Mom, this is Harry Garnet. I told you about him. He was in the cottage with Daddy and me."

She looked at me, a little shocked, I guess, like the Messenger of Death—"What the hell are you doing here?" Then she caught herself, and forced a smile, extended a hand. "Hello, Harry," she said. "It's a long drive down to the city, isn't it?" She spoke very softly, tentatively, like a fortune-teller. I had to strain to hear her, a ploy, I quickly realized, that made everything she said seem more important.

"I asked him to come," Annie said.

Her mother looked at me a little more closely. "I hope you're feeling better," she said. And then to Annie: "We should be going."

"Come with us," Annie said.

She took my arm, and we walked out of the chapel into the sunlight.

On the corner, waiting for the light to change, I said, "Where'd you get the First Lady hat?"

She reached up to pull the veil of black net down over her eyes, and said, mysteriously, "It belonged to my grandfather's favorite sister, Thea. She wore it to church during Lent, and to the weddings of nieces who were marrying beneath them."

"How'd you get it?"

"She left it to me in her will, specifically."

"As an omen to protect you from a disastrous marriage?"

"Hardly," Annie said. "She thought I was the most likely candidate, among the great-nieces and -nephews, to carry on her tradition of stern, prune-faced disapproval at family gatherings."

She pursed her lips theatrically. "You are a sour thing," I agreed, and sucked in my own cheeks. We laughed, in danger of spitting all over ourselves. I caught a glimpse, a half block away, of the man with the ponytail. He was standing at a pay phone, receiver to his ear. Before I could ask Annie who he was, the light turned green, and she pulled me impatiently into the street. "We're late," she said, eyes on her wristwatch.

"I'm surprised you actually showed up. I thought you were just being polite when you said you would. You don't seem like the type to make . . . *gestures,*" Annie said fingering the shard I had just returned to her. "Why *did* you come?"

"Because I'm really a very polite guy." I had my nose up to the edge of the window sash in the living room of her mother's apartment, trying to see the Hudson River. If I closed my left eye, and looked through the narrow slit of light between two brick buildings across the street, I could see water. It wasn't exactly blue.

About thirty-five people were crammed into the apartment, which had been designed to accommodate far fewer. A maid was passing a doily-lined tray of finger sandwiches, and some tasteful classical music filled the spaces of the room that the people couldn't reach. The music sounded like geometry. I'd guess Bach.

"Well, thanks." She must have thought I wasn't paying her enough attention, because she elbowed me away from the view, a scene she must have seen a million times in her life, and said, "Give me a turn."

The view was definitely improved now that Annie's face obstructed it. Maybe her still, quiet look was evidence that she was thinking about her father, who, it had been revealed at his memorial service, had lived in an apartment very much like this one when he was growing up. Frederick Ames, the only son of a well-to-do furrier, had been offered many choices that fell outside the realm of retail vs. wholesale. While he had attended college at nearby Columbia University, Ames had lived at home, in an apartment his parents rented on the Upper West Side and which probably offered a similarly inferior view of New Jersey. He worked for his father during summer vacations, carefully labeling the minks and sables that arrived for storage, and probably lingering longer than necessary in the cool vault where they were kept. Ames's early days were comfortable, and predictable, and it was no surprise that he had returned to Columbia after he left civil service. He had worked for the government during a disillusioning age, after all, when a young man would have had to question his service to an administration that shipped more and more bodies home from Vietnam, a time of an unpopular war that ineluctably shifted the perception of the agency where Ames worked, both in the eyes of the public, and eventually in the eyes of those employed there. Ames had taken the measure of his own culpability, and had found that he did not like the world of political intrigue. His transition to tenured professor had been made almost effortlessly; he had returned, after all, to a friendly alma mater.

"I came here for two reasons," I told the back of Annie's head. "No, actually three. One, I had to drive down anyway.

Two, I did want to find out more about your dad. And three, I wanted to see you.''

She turned to face me. "Why?"

"Why which?"

"Why all three?"

"One, getting rid of the guests is my job. Two, he did leave a puzzle, like his friend said. And three, I don't know. Because you are definitely not my type."

"Maybe all women are your type, Harry."

Annie's mother, Alicia, walked briskly by, carrying two dirty glasses toward the kitchen. She looked harried and shot Annie a look that meant "talk to these people."

Instead, Annie rolled her eyes and wandered over to the stereo to change the music. I followed and found myself at the edge of the hallway that led to the back rooms. A lot of art hung almost randomly on the walls, including a watercolor landscape of the desert, done entirely in different shades of brown. I liked a gritty black-and-white photograph of a tattooed kid—the tattoo depicted the chest skin being pulled back to reveal some microcircuitry underneath. I stopped in front of an oil portrait of Annie when she was a little girl, about eight, I'd guess.

"Like it?" She was behind me.

"It looks like it was painted in Central Park. By one of the many freelance Van Goghs who starve to death in this city."

"My mother did it."

"She paints and plays the cello?"

"She's a Renaissance woman," Annie said. "I'll give you a full tour of her life. All five rooms."

She pulled me down the hall to the den.

The room smelled faintly of perfume, a nice clean no-man smell, and was as carefully arranged as a department store window. There was a red-corduroy sofa bed and a barrel cactus that practically touched the ceiling. Alicia was one of those Southwest-ophiles. A modern, curved table made of shiny yellow wood dominated the den, accented by a way-cool desk chair that could have been yanked from the cockpit of the space shuttle. Fat, ergonomically correct leather pads climbed up the chrome spine.

On the table was a laptop.

"Yours or your mom's?" I asked.

"No, my dad's, in fact. Mine was the one that blew up."

"How come?"

"My dad's has a faster modem, so I was using it for the Web," she said. "The explosion popped the screen on this one. I had to have it replaced."

I didn't say anything, so she reminded me: "After he put the bomb into the other computer, in the bedroom."

I remembered that part.

The screen was filled with languid angel fish, and without thinking much about it, I reached out to touch the mouse. The screensaver disappeared and the computer cycled to life. Now the screen was filled, haphazardly, with little icons.

"Ah, a Macintosh. An anachronism, but supposedly so easy to use," I said, sinking into the chair. "But why is there no button that says 'click here for cool games'? Now, that would be intuitive. I don't think I have any use for these programs. PPP. Fetch alias. Eudora2.1."

I double-clicked on one anyway, and Annie perched on the edge of the table. I felt obliged to entertain at the keyboard.

"Ha, PPP controls your modem, my dear. I have discovered its secret." I closed it down.

I clicked on the Fetch alias icon, which showed a puppy with a lolling tongue. "Here, Spot, bring me my virtual slippers."

"You use that when you want to get a copy of a document that's archived out on the Internet," she said.

I closed it down. "That reminds me."

"What?"

"I want to meet Bootsie."

"My cat? She's traveling."

"Bootsie's on vacation?"

"In England. She lives with my old roommate."

I double-clicked on Eudora2.1, an icon that looked like a little envelope. Sure enough, Annie's E-mail appeared on the screen. Actually, it was more like a stack of unopened mail, just a list of messages, with return addresses.

A couple of messages were from me, ones she hadn't deleted after she read them. Most of the others came from columbia.edu. Classmates. There were several from nelson@spasm.com. "Who's he?" I asked, jealous.

She looked exasperated. "I'm not sure. He's been sending me a lot of mail since the explosion. A former student of my dad's. Says he met me once in his office. He's actually a bit of a pest. I stopped responding."

I clicked to move the cursor downward, continuing my investigation. "Same with davidr@euclid.uk?"

She laughed. "Harry, you're chaperoning me?"

"I'm interested. That's all."

"In that case: David is my old roommate. He's at the London School of Economics now." She reached over and clicked the mouse herself. The program closed down before I had a chance to click on one of David R.'s messages. I guess she suspected that I wasn't above reading other people's mail.

She moved the cursor over to a drawing of a can of dog food. The label read "The Zoo—For Your Health."

"Try this one," she said. "It looks like a game."

"You haven't tried it?" I asked.

"I haven't really done much of anything lately, except E-mail. I couldn't concentrate," she said.

As soon as I clicked on the dog food, we heard the tinny melody of the modem dialing a ten-digit number. Long distance, I noted, just before the whole computer screen went black.

"Did I break it?"

"No, it's just trying to hook up with a computer at the other end," Annie said. She sounded curious, hopped off the table, and came to stand behind me for a better view.

The monitor lit up, and a three-dimensional image of the

Joshua Quitttner

can of dog food filled the screen, spinning slowly like the Earth in orbit. We could see different bits of information on the label as it turned: INGREDIENTS: WIT, CURIOSITY, AND NO ANIMAL BY-PRODUCTS. After it completed a rotation, the can of dog food broke apart into a dozen lopsided pieces, fragments that flew across the screen and rearranged themselves haphazardly in the corners.

"It is a game," I said.

"Let's put it back together," Annie said, moving the cursor over to click on one of the pieces.

But it wasn't so easy. The individual fragments no longer fit together neatly. Some were a solid color, others still bore bits of pattern. Their shapes were almost identical. Annie manipulated them, moving them around, turning them upside down, systematically attempting to fit one piece into each of the others.

"Ha!" she said as two finally clicked together, audibly. "I think the problem is that we're looking at some of the pieces from the inside, so the solid color is the metallic hue that would be inside a can of dog food. So if you just view it as a mirror image . . ."

Her voice trailed off as, intently, she moved the pieces around on the screen. She had cracked the code, and within thirty seconds was fitting in the final missing piece.

As she clicked on the newly restored image of the dog food, the sound of a twenty-five-cent kazoo piped through the computer's speaker, followed by the noise of the computer's modem dialing a ten-digit phone number. Within seconds, the screen changed again and was now covered with text:

WELCOME TO THE ZOO . . . LOADING KNOT VERSION 2.1 scrolled across in tall yellow letters. Underneath, in big type, disclaimer size, was a warning. "YOU OWN YOUR WORDS. BY LOGGING IN, YOU AGREE NOT TO HOLD THE MANAGEMENT OF THE ZOO RESPONSIBLE FOR CONTENT, WHICH WE DO NOT CONTROL. BY LOGGING IN, YOU VERIFY THAT YOU ARE 21 OR OLDER AND UNDERSTAND THAT YOU MAY READ EXPLICIT ADULT MATERIAL."

Then the Macintosh automatically executed a series of commands and new words appeared:

LOG-IN: WOLFER
PASSWORD: ******
LOG-IN SUCCESSFUL
WELCOME, WOLFER! YOU ARE BEHIND THE WOODSHED. IT IS
GETTING DARK, AND MOST OF THE OTHER ANIMALS ARE BACK
IN THEIR DENS.

"It's a MOO," Annie said. "I didn't know my dad was into them."

Most of the guys I knew who liked to log in to these virtual communities were graduates of the Dungeons & Dragons school of games. I used to have a roommate who spent thirty-six-hour marathon sessions logged in to one of these "multi-user dimensions" where people hung out and typed conversations to each other. He got kicked out of school at about the same time his phone service was shut off. I wondered if anyone ever paid that last astronomical phone bill he had racked up.

My roommate's MOO of choice, Maze World, had different labyrinthine paths that players could follow. There was no video, so everything—scenery, people, action—was described as text, no pictures. But he still got so caught up in it that he almost believed he was peering around dark corners, meeting creatures named Gandolf and Thor. His MOO had a very medieval flavor. This place seemed altogether different.

WHERE AM I? I typed.

A description filled the screen: YOU ARE IN THE FOREST BE-
HIND THE UNICORN INN, NEAR THE WOODSHED, AN UNASSUMING
BROWN SHINGLED BUILDING WITH NO WINDOWS. THE DOOR IS
LOCKED BEHIND YOU WITH A PADLOCK, WOLFER. YOU DON'T
HAVE A KEY TO GET IN. YOU DON'T REMEMBER HOW YOU GOT
HERE.

Joshua Quittner

"It keeps calling us Wolfer. I wonder why my dad chose that nickname," Annie said.

On most MOOs, the commands were intuitive. I remembered a few from my inadvertent exposure to Maze World.

LOOK AT ME, I typed.

Text scrolled up my screen:

YOU SEE A MASSIVE, FOUR-LEGGED CREATURE, PART MAN AND PART WOLF. HIS HINDQUARTERS ARE POWERFULLY BUILT, AND HIS FUR-COVERED LEGS CAN RUN FOR MILES WITHOUT TIRING. HIS HEAD IS HUMAN, AND ALTHOUGH THE REST OF HIS BODY IS COVERED WITH SILKY GRAY FUR, HIS FACE IS HAIRLESS. HE HAS HUMAN-SHAPED EARS, BUT THEY ARE UNUSUALLY SENSITIVE AND CAN HEAR THE SOUND OF A FRIEND—OR FOE—QUIETLY APPROACHING FROM AS FAR AWAY AS A MILE. HE HAS KEEN, INTELLIGENT EYES THAT JUDGE YOU QUICKLY. WOLFER'S APPETITES ARE LEGENDARY, AND CAN RARELY BE SATISFIED.

"The Zoo. Looks like everybody who logs in assumes the identity of an animal," I said. But what I was thinking was: "Wolfer's appetites?" Um, check please . . .

I could feel Annie's embarrassment. The computer beeped at us:

YOU HAVE MAIL, WOLFER. READ IT? (Y OR N?)

"Should we snoop?" I asked.

"Well, my father is certainly not going to read it, ever," she said.

WOLFER: I MUST SEE YOU AGAIN IN PERSON. I KNOW YOU DON'T WANT TO AGREE TO MY TERMS. BUT I TRUST YOU WILL REMAIN DISCREET UNTIL WE REACH AGREEMENT.—MINOTAUR

The message gave no clue about who the Minotaur was. But the note was date-stamped; it had been mailed to Fred Ames three days before he died. I read it over again. "They were negotiating over something. But what?" I asked.

"He says he wants to meet my father in person. Does that mean in the physical world? Can you meet 'in person' on a MUD?"

"I doubt it. He would have simply said, where are you. In

F

L

A

M

E

W

A

R

person means face-to-face. I bet your dad never saw this message. It was listed as 'new mail,' unopened mail. He never had a chance to respond before—''

The computer beeped urgently, and text began to scroll across the screen. I knew that in a MOO, many users can occupy the same space simultaneously and chat. That's how users can converse with one another, visit one another in different locations, and convene in public areas. Whenever another user logs in, his arrival is announced on-screen.

MINOTAUR CANTERS TOWARD YOU FROM THE EDGE OF THE FOREST.

MINOTAUR SAYS: WHO ARE YOU?

''That's him? That's actually him, logged on to The Zoo from a computer somewhere?'' I was blown away.

Annie nodded.

''What should we say?'' I asked.

''Tell him we're Wolfer.''

WOLFER SAYS: YOU KNOW ME.

Immediately, and angrily, the computer beeped again.

MINOTAUR SAYS: IMPOSTOR.

MINOTAUR CANTERS AWAY. YOU CANNOT FOLLOW HIM.

I felt as if I had been mugged. The unsettling brush with the Minotaur felt just like some guy had run up, shoved his hand into my pocket, and run off with my wallet. I was left on the sidewalk, paralyzed, unable to get my money back. ''Why can't we follow him?'' I asked.

''Maybe he has a higher level of access to the system than Wolfer,'' Annie said. ''He can block us from following him. But you could look at his description of his character. Try that.''

LOOK AT MINOTAUR.

YOU SEE A TOWERING CREATURE SEVEN FEET TALL WITH THE TORSO OF A MAN AND THE HOOVED FEET, MASSIVE LEGS & GENITALIA OF A BULL. HIS FACE IS TURNED AWAY FROM YOU, AS IF HE IS LISTENING TO SOMEONE IN THE DISTANCE. YOU SEE HIS PROFILE, A DISTINCTIVE, AQUILINE NOSE AND A CHIN THAT JUTS OUT

BELLIGERENTLY. YOU WANT TO KNOW HIM, BUT HE IS ELUSIVE. HIS LEGS CARRY HIM AWAY SURPRISINGLY QUICKLY AND AS HE DISAPPEARS INTO THE DARKNESS, YOU THINK YOU HEAR A WHISPER: I WILL RETURN.

"The Minotaur looks a lot like Wolfer," I said.

Annie stared at the screen.

To break her trance, I said, "Maybe he'll come back?"

"He has to, or else we have to follow him," she said.

I knew why she looked so pinched, suddenly. She had been sucker-punched. Just when she was starting to get used to the idea that her father was dead, gone, over and done with, that now he belonged to the ages—up popped evidence to the contrary. Annie, get this! There was a part of your father's life you didn't share, didn't know Thing One about. But now you get to see glimpses of that, to hear from strangers who knew him, to savor sudden, unexplained revelations of who he was and perhaps how he thought. Lucky you!

This would not be the last revelation to force Frederick Ames right back into the present, into her face, as alive as he had ever been, still evolving (as Annie would say). I could give her an itinerary of things to avoid if she wasn't ready to set the time back to zero on the Grieving Clock every day: don't sort through his clothes, don't open any more mail addressed to him, don't sit in his favorite chair, don't let yourself conjure an image of him walking in the front door at the end of a day.

"Are you okay?" I asked.

"No, I'm not okay. Don't be banal, Harry. My father just got murdered."

She took a breath and started over. "What I meant to say was I'm rather surprised to learn that he was having an argument with some person just a few days before his death."

Frankly, the same thought had crossed my mind. "We should tell the FBI," I said.

"No."

"Okay, we shouldn't tell the FBI—why not, again?"

"Maybe it was some dumb personal thing," Annie said.

"The fact that it happened online doesn't necessarily make it an intrigue."

Her face said the subject was closed, and I followed her cue. "You're right. The Minotaur could be the on-screen persona of anyone. Even someone who's here at your apartment right now. Maybe that guy who worked with your dad at the Department of Defense."

"Uncle Edmund? No way. No, it's—"

We heard a light knock, and then the door, which had been ajar, swung into the room. Alicia stood in the doorway. "Annie?" That clairvoyant whisper, as if calling to someone from the Great Beyond. "Are you—oh, hello, Harry. Annie, the Davises are leaving. Would you like to say good-bye?"

That was my cue to leave too, her tone indicated. I logged off, and we followed Alicia silently down the hall. Annie volunteered to go look for a pocketbook that one of the Davises had misplaced.

I stood at the door with Alicia. "We'd love to see more of you while you're in town, Harry, but unfortunately Annie and I will be going away for a few days," she said, barely audibly. "Did she mention it?"

"No."

"Oh, yes, we're leaving in the morning. It was kind of you to come."

Then somehow I was out in the hall, with the door shut firmly behind me. This woman was not happy to see me. And how unhappy had she been when she learned her ex-husband had died? Clearly our Dr. Ames had a number of volatile relationships in the real and virtual worlds.

Out on the street, I bent to unlock my bike.

Above me, I heard a voice call my name. It was Annie, leaning out a window on the eleventh floor. "Harry, do you always sneak off without saying good-bye?"

I stood on the sidewalk and called back up to her. "Goodbye and have fun on—"

But she was already gone.

chapter four

B laney had warned me not to show up at his cousin's early. I know now that he had a good reason for keeping me "outside the perimeter," as he might phrase it. He did not want to drag me into his secrets. He knew the risks of his actions, and could make an informed decision about whether to participate. I was not to have the same luxury. In his own awkward way, he did try to protect me.

"If you come before eleven, I might not be there," he had said.

I rang the bell at six.

"What?" a voice squawked from the intercom.

"I'm Blaney's friend. Harry."

"Be right down." He said it as if he were expecting me.

Like so many of its neighbors, this sooty brick town house had been designed for a single family to live in. That was about a century ago, of course, when wealthy merchants and ship builders inhabited this part of Greenwich Village with their wives and children, and their live-in servants slept on the top floor. Lifestyles change. The streets were still cobblestone, but the houses had been divvied up into at least six different apartments. In this case, a thick glass door separated the entryway from the hall inside. There was nothing to do but wait at the door with my bike.

Finally, Cousin Eddie pushed open the door, adjusting a backpack across his shoulders. He shook my hand.

"Nice to meet you, but you almost missed me," he said cordially. "Blaney went on ahead to the meeting."

He seemed to think I was headed there too, and for want of something better to do to pass the next few hours, I fell into step beside him, wheeling my bike alongside. Too bad that Blaney would be shocked that I had infiltrated his secret coven.

"Blaney said you were in the hospital for almost a week. Hope you're better," Eddie said. It was an awkward way to circle around what he really wanted to say, which was, So how the hell does it feel to be blown up? Like everyone I had spoken to in the past few days, Eddie was dying to know. Unlike most of the others, he attempted tact.

"Still a little sore," I said. "But thanks."

Eddie was a short man deep in the throes of a serious hair conflict, with a walrus mustache droopily retreating from an aggressive crew cut. He wore green army fatigues, a black T-shirt, and white high-top sneakers—a look I identified as Midwestern Liberal Arts school, circa 1975. He was only about ten years older than me, though, so the uniform was hard to explain. We walked along Sixth Avenue, past ripe and precarious pyramids of fruit in the greengrocers' doorways, and then he surprised me by saying, "I'm not a busybody. It's just that I knew Fred Ames. We all did."

"Blaney too?" The little weasel had never mentioned it to me.

"Ames used to come to our meetings occasionally."

"Small world."

Eddie didn't pick up on the sarcasm. "For now, maybe. But crypto should be everyone's concern, you know. That's part of our agenda."

"I didn't see you at the memorial service today, did I?" I was fishing.

"I didn't know Ames that well. He stopped coming to meetings a while back." Eddie paused. "It's a pretty informal thing, membership. At least it used to be. Most of us knew Ames, but mainly from the Net. We posted to the same Usenet cryptography newsgroups. Every month, Blaney would post the notice of the upcoming meeting on the alt.crypto.policy group, time and place. Ames started to come for a while. Hobby. But he dropped out, months ago."

"It wasn't his thing?"

"Oh, no, I wouldn't say that. Codes were what he breathed—didn't you ever read his papers on algorithm theory?" Eddie asked. "*We* weren't his thing. He wasn't political."

"I got the impression that he was very political."

"Maybe in theory," Eddie said. "He wasn't ready for action."

"He must have been ready for action at some point in his life," I said. "After all, he did a stint at NSA."

Eddie looked at me curiously. "So?"

"So he was a domestic spy."

"You watch a lot of TV?" Eddie said. "Ames was probably a paper pusher. Or a theoretician. Forget the cloak and dagger crap. It's a bureaucrat's dream, working for the government; he probably did it for the health benefits. Not that the government even admitted that the NSA existed back then. We're talking about an agency that came into existence after Truman wrote a secret order to establish it. We're talking Cold War, and the U.S. of A. had learned that code breaking was a powerful way to undermine an enemy. Don't forget the Nazis and their Enigma Machine. The Brits broke the code. Instant heroes. Uncle Sam wanted a piece of that action the next time around.

"You got this agency that existed to *intercept* crap, right? Radio signals. Satellite transmissions. Radar. Crap's encoded, so then the NSA fellows sit around, trying to deconstruct it. They crack anything good, they slip it to their pals at the CIA. That's the way business was conducted for a couple of decades," Eddie said. I had the feeling he'd given this speech before, but his bright eyes and nervous hand motions clued me in to the fact that he really needed to get it off his chest at least one more time. Right here. Right now.

Eddie was so engrossed that he almost fell off the curb at the next corner. "What changed the world, Harry, was computers. Digital communications. The rise of the PC. By the time the 1980s rolled around, we all needed codes. Someday soon we're all going to be sending private correspondence via computer, doing business online, making electronic transfers to our checking accounts. But the government doesn't want us to have the tools to keep our secrets safe."

"Shouldn't be a problem," I said. "The government must have a roomful of strong codes, hoarded over the decades. NSA could just license that stuff to the computer makers and it could come built into the box, right?"

"You think like a capitalist, Harry, not like a spy. That would be the end of eavesdropping, wiretaps, all kinds of standard surveillance techniques. If we had strong encryption programs built into our PCs, the government couldn't crack the code when they wanted to. Ask the NSA about what would happen then, and the answer they give is 'Anarchy.' Bunch of assholes."

"You do codes for a living?"

"No, but I need codes to *make* a living," Eddie said. "I'm a financial consultant. Freelance stuff."

"Oh, one of those guys who tells you how you can live on five hundred dollars a week," I said.

"I don't really tell people how to manage their money. No, strike that—I do tell them how to manage their money. I teach them to manage it so they don't have to pay any taxes."

"Tax shelters, you mean?"

"No, that's not what I mean at all." Eddie's mustache drooped in counterpoint to his eyebrows, which were raised in quiet outrage. The traffic light turned red and Eddie glowered at me to make his point while we waited for it to go green. "I mean not paying any taxes, not a dime, to a government engaged in a tyranny of the people."

A tyranny of the people? Let's take the next caller, please . . .

"I teach people how to hold on to the income they honestly make and hide it from a government that dishonestly tries to seize it. I teach people how to thrive in the new digital economy, where cash flows freely between states and even countries without regard to local laws, government-controlled banks, and all the rest of that state-imposed hogwash. Yesterday, I did a consulting job—anonymously—for an anonymous client who paid me with cybercash. It's a grand world, ain't it?" He snickered self-consciously, unaware that I didn't know what he was talking about, and stuck his hand out, pretending to click a mouse. "Rant, off," he said. "I'm no different from the others."

The light changed and we walked into the intersection. Oncoming traffic had slowed to a stop, but a taxicab, aggressive as always, edged into the crosswalk. In fact, it nearly butted into my bicycle. I turned to scowl at the driver, which is how I typically handled such transgressions. But not Eddie. Without warning, he shifted into Insane Gear.

"You stupid FUCKING idiot," he bellowed at the driver, who was now more startled than me. "Fucking ASShole . . ." Eddie kicked the front end of the cab once, twice . . . "Watch where the fuck you're driving, scumbag!" He kicked it again.

"Hey, hey, hey! Get away from my car, motherfuck!" yelled the cabdriver.

"Get away from your car, dickhead? What the fuck is it doing in MY crosswalk?!" Eddie leaped onto the hood of the car,

I swear to God, and for a second I felt closer to death than I had when I heard the explosion in Cottage 5. Eddie, head high, eyes blazing like gun barrels, stomped across the hood, leaving a couple of small, half-moon dents. The cursing driver groped under the passenger seat. Which was as much as I needed to see. With one hand on my bike, I reached up and grabbed Eddie behind the knees. He crumpled, like an overgrown child, and his sudden weight knocked the breath out of me. I carried him, slung over my back, to the corner—just as the driver whipped open the taxi door. He charged out with a small aluminum baseball bat. He took a few steps and stopped.

"Come here, you goddamn crazy!" yelled the cabbie, whose car was now blocking the intersection. Cars behind him honked unreasonably. I dropped Eddie, upright, at the same time that I dropped my bike, which was a good thing, because Eddie the crazy cocksucker only wanted more. I had to wrap my arms around him to keep him rooted to the corner, where he stood snarling and barking like a mad dog.

The howling clearly impressed the cabbie: You could see him gauge the red-line level of Eddie's rug-biting anger. Car horns blared, and the driver at last succumbed. He jumped back into his cab and roared off.

Eddie was foaming. "Motherfucker," he muttered. "Man, I hate that shit."

"You okay?" I asked, pointlessly. "Want something to wipe your mouth?"

He said nothing but continued to stare down the street at the fleeing cab. "Fucking A," he said, and a weird smile crossed his face. He reached behind him, under his belt, and pulled out a stunted black pistol. I'd guess a Walther PPK, only because that's what James Bond used and this gun definitely looked like that kind of automatic. "Fucking A," Eddie repeated, quickly shoving the weapon back into its hiding place. "The bastard was lucky I didn't get mad."

We walked on for a while, in silence, and I let the heat, welling up from the sidewalk into the early summer night, enervate Cousin Eddie. Fortunately, no other cars, taxis, buses, or stray dogs penetrated his personal space. We trekked on in peace, past empty shish kebab joints that were stoking up for the dinner crowd and outdoor bistros where people nursed five-dollar cappuccinos, stretching them out as if they constituted a form of seat rent.

Soon, Eddie started to whistle, a sign I interpreted as meaning he'd returned from the Land of the Livid.

"So, who's going to be there today?" I asked.

"The usual bunch of Urban Crypto Militia whack jobs." Then he asked me cautiously, "Blaney told you, right?"

"A little."

He nodded grimly. Eddie and I had the sidewalk to ourselves because everyone who can afford it flees the city in July. As I wheeled my bike along, we turned down a side street that smelled of baked garbage, and stopped in front of a battered metal door that looked as if it had been stuck randomly into the side of a decaying brick building. There was no sign, no doorbell, no indication that we would find anything inside other than some overworked boiler room. Scrawled on the wall beside a mailbox was a phrase of hieroglyphic graffiti.

Eddie pulled on the rusty door handle, and amazingly, it opened. "Watch the stairs," he said, and disappeared into dimness.

I used my kryptonite lock to clamp my bike to a NO PARKING sign and followed. As I stepped down, the door banged shut behind me. I jumped involuntarily. Loud noises were having that effect on me lately.

As my eyes adjusted to the dim light, I thought: No wonder the streets were empty. All the people in the world were in here. We were in a deep, narrow room jammed with blinking, buzzing, clicking pinball machines and video games. But not ordinary video games. About ten people were waiting in line

F

L

A

M

E

W

A

R

for a machine whose green neon sign announced it was the Virtual Reality Rocket. The lucky guy at the controls, a lanky pasta rasta with waist-length dreadlocks, wore heavy goggles, rammed a joystick up and down, and screamed instructions to the digital crew members who were visible on the monitor.

Scattered throughout the room, among the islands of sound and light, were tiny bistro tables, each of which displayed its own desktop computer. Phone wires snaked down from each table and disappeared into the floor. The temperature was about fifty degrees, which was probably necessary to keep the equipment from overheating. Judging from the crowds, the machines never got a rest. A clump of muttering computer hackers—I knew they must be hackers because they looked like Russian dissidents and drank Jolt cola straight from the can—hunched over a table piled high with cables and laptops. They poked the equipment with tweezers and wire cutters. Waitresses in T-shirts that read CAFÉ INFO navigated the crowds to deliver drinks.

Places like these, hundreds of which were springing up in hip urban neighborhoods all over the country, were like a version of Disney World configured just for nerds. Everything in America gets its own theme park; every trend gets identified, every niche marketed and then commodified. Now the geeks got theirs. I heard a sound over my head that reminded me of the launch of a bottle rocket and looked up to see a transparent plastic tube running across the ceiling. Relax, Harry.

Sections of the tube veered off toward some booths way in the back. The sound came from a small, pink torpedo that shot through the tube, propelled pneumatically from across the room. I watched it race down the wall behind the bar, where the bartender opened a metal door reminiscent of a dumbwaiter, pulled a slip of paper from inside the torpedo, read it, and poured ice cubes into a blender. Someone had just ordered a margarita, geek style.

Keeping an eye on Eddie's backpack, I maneuvered toward

the booths in the back. I moved past a dozen murky screens, which cast a blue glow onto the tables.

The initials carved into the tabletops made me wonder if the previous tenant had been an Irish pub. Theme bars. It's a tough business, and I'm not saying I have any answers. Just about the time you get the walls sponge-painted apricot, and square away the paper parasols and daily conch deliveries from the Keys, the whole Caribbean craze goes bust. Instead, everyone wants microchips and motherboards hanging from the rafters.

In the farthest corner of the dark room was an oversize horseshoe booth. We found Blaney there. He sat alone, nursing a beer, surprisingly oblivious to the lure of the electronic.

He tensed when he saw me. "What are you doing here, Garnet?"

"I got done early."

"You shouldn't have brought him," he mumbled to his cousin.

"I thought he was with you," Eddie said, on edge. He looked at me, angry, as if I had betrayed him.

"Never mind, he's okay." Blaney suspiciously eyed every person who walked past him toward the rest rooms. Although no one came within ten feet, Blaney kept reaching up with his right hand to pat the bulging pocket of his short-sleeved button-down shirt. Whatever he had stored inside must have had great value, because it had imbued him with an air of expectancy and importance. He was ready to take charge. I had never seen him behave in this way.

"Did you get my message?" he asked Eddie.

"No one followed us."

"How do you know?"

"How do I know? Well, I guess I don't, Richard," Eddie said, glowering, "any more than you know I won't pop you in the fucking head." He stomped off toward the front.

Blaney turned his attention to me, and I could see he had lied to Eddie when he said I was okay. He was looking at me

FLAME WAR

as if I were a rotting, maggot-covered piece of meat. "This is not a place you want to be, Garnet. Get out."

"I'm having a beer in a public bar."

"You don't take me seriously, Garnet."

"That's not true," I lied.

"Sure, when some key on your keyboard is sticking, you call me to take off the dust with a Q-Tip. But that's about all you think I'm good for."

"Knock it off, Blaney."

"Do you know anything about cryptography, Garnet? Anything at all? I'll settle for a simple definition even. Can you spell it?"

I flipped him off. "Code breaking, my man. Cryptography is the science of making and breaking codes."

"Very good, Harry. Say, I am impressed. Anything else you can tell me? Or have we hit the wall on the topic."

"Knock it off, Blaney. I know a bunch of unrelated crypto factoids. The Enigma Machine and Navajo Code Talkers and Morse code and let's see what else? The Urban *Crypto* Militia . . ."

"Spare me, Garnet," Blaney sniffed. "Okay, yes, the Crypto Militia. You do know what militias are, correct?"

"Bunch of doughnut-addicted right wingers in the sticks who like to cross dress in military fatigues and parade around with rifles. Yeah, I read all the newsweeklies and papers on the subject."

Blaney glowered at me and for a second I almost regretted the fatso allusion. "You're wrong on a number of counts," he said. "Who the hell do you think is meeting here? Let me correct you on the more crucial facts."

He ticked them off on his cruller-sticky fingers. "One: Militias, my dimwitted friend, come in all different political stripes—not just right wing. The Urban Crypto Militia, for instance, is composed of many old lefties—and many people who don't even vote. Oh, yeah, while we're on the point, note that this militia is distinctly urban. Not a hayseed among us.

Er, visitors excluded. Two: Militias advocate personal freedom. Freedom of religion and freedom to associate with whomever you want and freedom to live where you choose and freedom of speech. Consult your Bill of Rights for details, Garnet. Some of it might look familiar. Three: As freedom-loving souls, militias intensely distrust centralized governments, which have become dominated by special interests that are opposed to those freedoms. Four: Militias believe that the best way to safeguard freedom is through munitions.

"Now, while you tend to think of guns as munitions," he continued, "your government also includes other things."

"Like cryptography," I said, remembering Eddie's impassioned speech.

"Precisely. To preserve the peace, we need to spy on hostile governments. That's why the Department of State classifies strong crypto as a munition and has long prohibited U.S. citizens from disseminating unbreakable codes abroad."

Blaney swigged his beer and his beady eyes tracked someone moving across the room. "Oh, but that's a sideshow," he said hurriedly. "Crypto is cool because it will bring down the government someday. It's inevitable. With crypto comes real digital cash—cyberbucks—and financial transactions that can't possibly be taxed because they can't be observed. And what's a government without taxes?"

"And that's what the Urban Crypto Militia is about? Bringing down the government with software?" I asked.

"Among other things," said Blaney.

"You're plotting an overthrow?"

"Just remember that I warned you. You just passed the bar exam. You don't want to jeopardize anything. Get out while you can."

I changed the subject. "Weird that you never mentioned to me that you knew Frederick Ames."

"Weird that you never mentioned that you were screwing his daughter, either," he snapped.

"I'm not," I said.

"Oh, she just happened to pick The Vines for a vacation. And just coincidentally asked Daddy to take her there?"

"You're paranoid," I said. What I thought was: Daddy picked the vacation spot, not Annie. He was paying.

"I could use a beer," I said. "Want one?" I fiddled with the pneumatic tube system until I figured out that all I had to do was to put the torpedo inside the tube and latch the door. Intrigue or no, one thing I could count on: I was buying.

We didn't say anything else until a waitress arrived with two mugs just as a scruffy woman pushed up to our table and dropped her entourage of luggage—a briefcase, a backpack, and a shoulder bag—onto the floor in a heap by the booth.

"Irene." Blaney grunted her name.

"I saw Eddie outside, and he said he was sent to do reconnaissance." She was a small and intense person, with dark hair and eyes. A black and white button was pinned to her blouse. It said, "Hiding in plain sight."

"I'll have a Bud," she said to the waitress.

She slid in next to Blaney, and turned to examine me. "You're Harry Garnet?" She sounded surprised, but not unhappy, about that fact.

"Eddie told you?"

"I read the newspapers." She thrust out a hand. "Pleased to meet a fellow warrior. You had it tough. Fred Ames was a friend of mine."

"I didn't know him," I said.

"Right." Her pupils were black deep holes to nowhere. She trained them on me. I looked away.

Blaney said quickly, "Irene, Garnet and I know each other from college. Old friends."

"Right."

"Irene, I mean it. He's not active."

She ignored that, said instead, "Well, it was a good idea to bring him, Richard. You think of everything." Then she asked me, "Have you healed?"

"The burns, you mean?"

"No psychically."

I played along. "Some things never heal."

She nodded. "Blaney," she said, without turning to him, "you should have brought Harry along sooner. He's a lawyer—that's what the *Post* said, anyway, Harry—"

I nodded.

"And you've been hoarding his expertise for yourself. Richard, you are supposed to share with the group." She was teasing him now.

Blaney had a benign, favorite uncle's smile on his face. "Irene, I have a lot of resources at my command."

I offered my hand. Her grip was strong. Her arms were muscular, her face unlined. I couldn't tell how old Irene was, but I would guess that she lifted weights a couple of times a week. The handshake, the shock of warm flesh, disarmed her enough to remind her that strands of her long dark hair had escaped a makeshift chignon at her neck.

As she settled herself into the vinyl booth, she simultaneously urged the hair back with pins, unclasped a heavy black satchel, eased off her sneakers, and inspected me. She captured the essence of multitasking.

"Richard should have told us you were coming," she said.

"Does he have to clear everyone?" I asked.

"Some of the others who aren't coming tonight would have liked to meet you."

Blaney looked uncomfortable. But since I seemed to be some kind of a bizarre semicelebrity in his world, my presence enhanced his status. He had already decided I was staying, so he couldn't back down.

"How did you know Fred Ames?" I asked her.

"Mainly online."

I took another stab. "He told me about The Zoo."

"What about it?"

"People there."

"Don't know any," she said. "What are you getting at?"

"I thought maybe there were meetings online too. Virtual meetings?"

"Not in a place like The Zoo," she said. "Believe me."

Blaney cut in. "Irene helps small businesses configure their networks to get the cheapest deal for Net service, phones, data and voice lines. She wrote the best program for creating virtual conference rooms to connect all their satellite offices."

"I tell them what kind of Net connectivity they need, and who charges the least for it. Then I build the system," she said.

"You could have made a bundle off of Café Info," I said.

"In fact, I did."

"So what do you do for fun?"

"This. The Crypto Militia. I wouldn't call it fun, though, exactly. It's what I do for my soul. It's what *we* do for our souls." She gestured to the room at large and it occurred to me then that all of the people in the bar were there together, waiting for something to happen. Or maybe it was already happening. As I looked closer I realized that each of the clusters of people was linked, like cells. They passed information back and forth, from the long chrome bar to the VR Rocket; hushed intelligence hopped from table to table in a sprawling game of Whisper Down the Lane. It was the Internet made flesh.

Irene's beer arrived, which prompted a new flurry of simultaneous activity. She sipped, pulled a thick stack of business-sized envelopes from her briefcase with her free hand, and called over my head, "Eddie! Just in time."

"Why the envelopes?" he asked, sliding in next to me, placid as a deacon on holiday.

"Pass them out to people at work, wherever." She looked at me, a challenge. "You lick stamps?"

"Not recently," I said. She handed a dozen envelopes to me. I took a few and handed the rest to a slight young man hovering nearby who grabbed them wordlessly and passed them on. The envelopes were addressed to the same mailbox: Senator Francis Dunne, c/o his Senate office in Washington.

"And what are we asking the senator to do?" I asked.

Irene looked up from her envelopes. "Take another look at the Patriot bill. Nobody in either house has the guts to say it stinks. Which isn't surprising. When was the last time you heard of a politician who *wasn't* a traitor?"

From her tone of voice, I realized I should know what a Patriot bill was. I licked a stamp. It didn't taste like arsenic. A stamp-and-lick operation of political activists didn't seem to warrant this level of high alert.

"Will he block it?" I asked cautiously.

"Not with the pressure he's getting from the FBI to ram it through. The Justice Department, on behalf of the FBI, is pushing its own encryption standard: Patriot. If we all have to use it—imagine Patriot chips coming as a standard feature on the hard drives of every new personal computer and telephone—then they'll be able to eavesdrop on all our conversations. You can see why they want it," she said with disgust. "You saw the piece in *The Times* today?"

"No."

"Read it," she said. "It talks about the government's real agenda. A National Eavesdropping Center built in Washington. A place where they store the keys to listen to all the digital conversations people have over phone lines. Sure, they say they need Patriot so they can continue to do wiretaps. They say that unless they can decode digitized data transmissions, they can't protect us against terrorists and child molesters. And they need the Eavesdropping Center to do it. Take a search warrant to the center and get the key. A national center is fast and efficient, right? It also guarantees that some piss-poor sheriff's department in Ringworm, South Carolina, can carry on a wiretap as readily as the FBI. Just get some kangaroo court to sign off on it.

"But why do they have to eavesdrop," Irene added, rhetor-

F
L
A
M
E
W
A
R

ically. "They don't. It's a Big Brother thing, a way to use technology to enslave rather than liberate us."

"They already eavesdrop with a search warrant," I said.

"Not as easily as they'll be able to after Patriot. This thing is an FBI wet dream," said Blaney.

"And that's if it works according to the supposed best intentions of Congress. We can expect a huge increase in eavesdropping if this thing is approved," said Irene. "But that's the least of it. A national center is ripe for abuse—by the police, by politicians, you name it. Every telephone conversation and every computer communication in this country will be funneled through a single building. Find out what stocks huge multinational companies plan to buy or sell on Wall Street tomorrow. Find out whether the mole they removed from the president's ass last week was malignant. It's all right there under the nose of the U.S. government . . . Imagine what a Richard Nixon could have done with that kind of power!"

"Or look further down the food chain, at lowly federal employees," said Blaney, erasing a white beer mustache with a cocktail napkin. "Last year the Internal Revenue Service fired a dozen clerks for being on the payroll of some private investigator. For a hundred bucks a pop, those poor clerks would fork over Social Security numbers and any other interesting personal data to the P.I. That's a lot of money to some guy who makes eighteen thousand dollars a year. Imagine how lucrative moonlighting at the Eavesdropping Center will be."

"Which is what the militia aims to stop," said Eddie. "It's time to take back our government and our freedom."

The three of them looked at me, I guess seeking my approval. Go on, I'm listening, we're all friends here.

"How?" I asked.

"First, defeat Patriot. Then implement our own crypto standard," said Blaney. "It will create truly secure and private communications networks."

"Which brings us to Francis Dunne," I said, waving an unlicked envelope like a flag.

"What about him?" Eddie asked rhetorically.

"He's on the Judiciary Committee, which would approve Patriot," I said.

"Correct," Irene said. "And if a good old-fashioned effort by constituents from his home state doesn't do the trick, we'll move to Plan B."

Plan B. These folks talked like Shining Path rebels, but how sinister could Plan B be, if Plan A was licking stamps?

A man pulled up a chair at the next booth. He wore jeans and a work shirt and peered at us through aviator-frame glasses—I realized, with a start, that he was the same guy who had been scoping out the people at the memorial service. I figured Irene and company knew him, that he was another link in the cell wall, but it became clear from the way conversation stopped that he was a stranger to them as well. After a few minutes of silence, the man moved away, skulking among some wild-haired, printout-waving hackers. Who immediately shut down when Aviator Glasses appeared.

"Fucking feebs," said Eddie. "We're from the government. We're here to spy on you."

Eddie gave up on the stamps and instead reached around me to plug in a computer keyboard he'd picked up off the bar. He touched a key, and a monitor embedded in the wall lit up.

"Welcome to Café Info," words on the screen said.

"Are you sending E-mail to Senator Dunne?" I asked.

"Wish we could," Eddie said. He typed: telnet nyonline.com

A new banner scrolled across the wall screen. "Welcome to NY Online, gateway to the Net! If you're a member, please log in," it said. Eddie did and typed:

YO NELSON ARE YOU THERE? CONFIRM.

Within seconds, a reply scrolled across the screen:

YO BLANEY!!!!!! READY. GIVE ME THE ROLL CALL.

Eddie noticed me staring, fascinated, at the screen, and said, "One of our members can't make it physically to the meetings. He attends virtually. We can chat with each other by

F

L

A

M

E

W

A

R

using the word 'yo' before any message. Cute and cloying, yes, but effective.''

Eddie yo'ed:

RICHARD IS HERE. EDDIE IS TYPING. IRENE IS HERE. ALSO: A FRIEND OF RICHARD'S.

Instantaneously, Nelson responded: DO I KNOW THE FRIEND?

HARRY GARNET, typed Eddie.

AMES'S FRIEND. WHY IS HE THERE?

RICHARD SAYS HE'S OK.

I DIDN'T ASK IF HE'S OK. HAS ANYONE DONE A SECURITY CHECK ON HIM?

Eddie looked at me, then colored. ''Sorry,'' he said.

''What does he mean, a security check? I'm just sitting here in a bar, sipping a goddamn beer,'' I said. ''Who is Nelson, your boss?''

''Who knows? I've never met him,'' Eddie said. ''Nelson insists that these meetings actually occur somewhere out there in cyberspace, in the place where all the little bits of information meet and pass each other. The juncture of energy and intent, he calls it.''

''He floats up there, just a bunch of disembodied, digitized bits?'' I asked.

Eddie relented. ''Actually, he supposedly lives about eight blocks from here. But he's never shown his face at a meeting. He might be home now, or he could be anywhere where there's a wire to connect him. Of course, none of us has ever met him in person. So he could be sitting at another table toward the front of this room, for all we know. He could be that fed. Or he could be at a pay phone at the foot of the Himalayas.''

''I don't think there *are* any pay phones there,'' Blaney said. He should know. Since long before I'd known him, Blaney had been fascinated with pay phones. In what had passed for his personal version of teenage rebellion, he had built red boxes to simulate the sound of coins dropping into the slot, which tricked pay phones into giving him a dial tone to make free calls. He used to brag that in those days he had obtained, and memorized, a full set of New York Telephone proprietary technical manuals for the computers that controlled phone service along the Eastern Seaboard. In his dorm room, he liked to display his collection of photographs of foreign pay phones, odd-shaped kiosks on street corners in Amsterdam or Tokyo.

"If you never met him, how did he pass your security check?" I asked.

"He created the security procedure," Eddie said. "He's kind of the security chief for the militia. Just like I'm kind of the recording secretary."

"Kind of?" repeated Irene. "You're obsessive. You have everything in your archives, every meeting date, every document, every Usenet reference to the Crypto Militia. If I didn't know you better, I'd suspect you of working for the National Security Agency, Eddie. In fact, I do suspect you. Mole. Traitor."

"A virtual security czar and recording secretary? Welcome to the New World Order," I said.

"Don't be so belligerent, Garnet," Blaney said, a plea in his voice. "It's for everybody's safety. Give Eddie your Social Security number, okay? You carry your card with you, right?"

"Are you nuts?" I asked.

Irene spoke up. "If you won't do it, you'll have to leave."

Feeling as if I were standing on the sidelines, watching myself interact with strange aliens who inhabited a parallel universe, I pulled the card from my wallet. I slowly recited the nine digits, watched Eddie type them into the computer, watched him send my soul out over the Internet.

We waited, all of us watching the computer screen.

A minute later, Nelson responded:

IS LIONEL THERE?

NOT YET, Eddie typed. WHY?

HE'LL HAVE TO MAKE THE FINAL DECISION ON HARRY DAVIDSON GARNET.

"He figured out my middle name," I said.

Eddie frowned, then typed: WHAT'S WRONG?

Nelson responded: HARRY D. GARNET, D.O.B. 03/02/71, HAS NO CREDIT CARDS. DOESN'T OWN A CAR, OR A HOUSE, OR A BOAT. THE PRIMARY EVIDENCE THAT HE EXISTS IS A BUNCH OF STUDENT LOANS. ON WHICH HE HAS NOT YET MADE A SINGLE PAYMENT. OH, HE DOES HAVE A GUN PERMIT.

"Bravo," I said, genuinely impressed at how quickly and efficiently Nelson had breached my privacy and laid my affairs out for a bunch of strangers to peruse. And pass judgment on.

"Databases," Blaney said testily. "It's all out there."

"You have a gun?" Irene said.

"Doesn't everyone?"

"In New York maybe." Eddie said this quietly.

"Well, I live upstate. In the woods."

"You use it on deer?" she asked.

"No."

"People?"

Blaney broke in. "Garnet, relax. Irene, back off. It's legal to own a gun."

Another message from Nelson: WHOA. GET A LOOK AT THIS GUY'S MEDICAL RECORDS.

On the screen appeared a stream of personal information about me that had to be authentic. He couldn't have made up the facts I was reading—height 6 feet, weight 170, dime-sized birthmark on the back of the left knee. I felt like someone had just slugged me in the gut.

I was reading the contents of the medical files that had hung on a clipboard at the foot of my hospital bed after the explosion. It was the first time I had seen the notes the nurses had made in the intensive care unit during the first hours after I had been brought into the hospital.

2 A.M.: PATIENT STILL UNCONSCIOUS. PUPILS CONTRACT AND EXPAND WITH LIGHT.

4 A.M.: THRASHING BUT NOT RESPONSIVE TO VOICES.

6 A.M.: PATIENT NOT RESPONSIVE; EXHIBITS AUDIBLE BUT UN-INTELLIGIBLE SPEECH. CALLS OUT FOR PARENTS. MOTHER ALERTED BY NURSES' STATION (5:48). FATHER DECEASED (?)

6:30 A.M.: 50 CCS SALINE DRIP, IV, AS PER DR. MCC.

The records traced my medical history even further back. A broken arm when I was twelve, a broken leg when I was eight. Appendicitis. And, of course, a notation of "psychiatric counseling," mercifully brief.

"That's enough," I said, too roughly, and reached over to grab the keyboard.

Another message appeared on screen: ISN'T IT A COINCIDENCE THAT OUR LITTLE GROUP NOW INCLUDES SO MANY VICTIMS OF THE INFAMOUS COMPUBOMBER?

"What does that mean?" I asked. "Who else?"

Blaney said, "Listen, we should just wait for—"

"Here I am. You can stop waiting."

Although he had just come in from the heat, the man standing at the end of the booth looked cool and calm. I knew him. How could I forget him? Ever since I had lost sight of him on a sunny midday block up by Riverview Chapel, I had subconsciously been searching for the tall man with the ponytail, peering around parked cars, glancing into doorways, looking over my shoulders. Now he had taken me by surprise again. His presence restored order.

"Hail to the chief," gushed Eddie, who typed:

LIONEL IS HERE, NELSON.

His arrival changed the mood, subtly. The waiting was over. He was the one who directed the group's actions, and they all were ready to follow his lead. The room seemed to organize around his presence.

Lionel pulled a chair from one of the nearby round tables. He straddled it backward and nodded hello to each of the people at the booth. I saw others, in adjacent cliques, look at him respectfully. When his eyes reached me, they stopped.

"I saw you at the memorial service," I said.

"I recognized you from the newspaper photos."

It sounded like a lie, but I let it pass. "Were you a friend of Ames's?" I asked.

For just a moment, that same sadness crossed his fine face. But he struggled against it, and it passed, and then he said to me, "Fred Ames was a blunt and honest man. The world could use more like him."

With that, Lionel extended a smooth browned hand to me. I tried to conceal my shock that he was missing a finger as I shook it, as if we had reached some tacit agreement, which made me feel like an idiot as soon as my hand was back on the table. "Welcome to our group."

Blaney cleared his throat. To change the subject.

"Lionel," Blaney said. "I have my half."

"And I have mine."

They smiled at each other and for a moment Blaney basked in rare approval.

"When did you get it?" Lionel asked.

"Last night."

"Will they find out when they look at the audit logs?"

"Only if they know more about computers than I do," Blaney said.

Lionel studied him for a moment. Then he extended his hand. "In that case, my friend, congratulations. Between us, we have pulled off a coup. We have obtained both halves of the key the government will use to decode digital transmissions. Imagine if you and I wanted to topple governments, rather than just educate the fools who run them. What a strange place the world would be."

Eddie looked up from his screen. "Nelson wants to know how long it takes to run?"

"We don't know yet. We have to put both halves together," Lionel said. "He should know that." He sounded slightly annoyed.

A waitress arrived with a plate of nachos. No one ate,

Joshua Quittner

Michelle Slatalla   **81**

and the cheese sauce, slowly congealing, seemed like a sick joke.

The group was getting down to business now, leaning forward on their elbows, conspirators, and talking in low voices in a language that was as foreign to me as Mayan. Words burbled by: checksum, weak algorithms, 82-bit, and factoring primes.

Only Lionel held back from the group. He listened, but at the same time, reached across the table for the torpedo. He turned it over in his hands, and from time to time looked up at the grid of tubing on the ceiling, calculating.

Blaney said, "Now that we have both halves, we need to agree on the timing."

"The end of the month," Lionel said. A small pocketknife appeared in his hand. He reached for an empty paper cup that sat in front of Irene and cut a shape from it. The shape looked like a fin. He cut an aileron in the fin and folded it up, like the spoiler on a sports car.

"Who should go?" Eddie asked.

"As few of us as possible," Lionel said. He positioned the fin along the back of the metal cylinder. He tore a small piece of chewing gum from his mouth and used it to fasten the fin. The contraption now resembled a tiny, mutant dolphin. "We want to limit exposure."

"In fact," Blaney said, "I plan to go alone. It's better."

"What if you get arrested?" Irene said.

"It would be worse if we all got arrested," he answered.

The computer beeped.

ARE YOU TRYING TO STEAL THE LIMELIGHT, RICHARD?

"Tell him that I'm trying to protect him, that's all," Blaney instructed his cousin.

"Not that Nelson would ever show up anyway," Eddie said. "He's the most paranoid person I've ever *not* met. Even for a security director."

"Tell Nelson that he should be thanking Richard, instead of suspecting him of dark motives," Irene said to Eddie.

"There, that should do it," Lionel said. He adjusted the angle of the spoiler on the fin, slid a sheet of paper into the torpedo, and popped the whole contraption inside the pneumatic tube. "Watch this."

The cylinder traveled up the pipe, but instead of heading for the bar, veered east along the overhead grid. Its path took it across the room and down a length of tube at a booth where a young woman sat alone, hunched over a book and nursing a cup of coffee. Lionel had hacked the network.

She looked up, surprised, took the cylinder from the tube, and read the note inside. Then she looked over at our table and smiled. I could see her blush from here. Lionel waved.

"Sorry. I'm married," she called across the room, over the beeps and clicks of the machines. She really looked like she was sorry too.

Lionel shrugged, pantomiming failure. Everyone else at our table looked surprised. But perhaps the stunt had served a purpose, because I felt the tension level recede.

Eddie said, "Who's going to run the program to see if it really works?"

"I will," Lionel said.

Eddie nodded, happily. "And if it does, we're all agreed that Patriot must be stopped, no matter what?" Eddie asked.

"Relax," Lionel said. He held up his hand to restore order. "We should be celebrating our success so far."

Blaney took a floppy out of his shirt pocket and waved it like a fan. "The key to the government's eavesdropping program has fallen into the wrong hands," he said triumphantly.

Lionel reached for it. Now he was in a hurry.

"I'll phone in a day or two. We still have time to work out the details," he said. He picked up the bill from the table and headed toward the bar. He got in line to pay, caught Blaney's eye, and motioned him over.

Blaney gathered his papers and sauntered over to his master nonchalantly. Lionel put an arm around his shoulders and curtly led him into a corner. Then, the tenor of their relationship changed. Lionel was upset about something. Suddenly, Mr. Mellow was gone, replaced by Dr. Type-A, who drove points home into Blaney's chest with finger jabs, and who seemed to pinion young Blaney under his glare as if he were an entomologist mounting a caterpillar. Then Lionel wheeled away, back to the cashier's line.

Blaney slinked over to our table, where he sat quietly for a few moments.

At last he sighed and said, "Garnet, you know almost everything now."

"I understood maybe ten percent of it."

Something about my tone failed to reassure him.

"You're in this as deep as I am," he said.

I had figured out that he and his buddy, Lionel, had broken into government computers and stolen top-secret files. I, on the other hand, had done nothing more than meet a group of acquaintances for nachos and potato skins. Of course, that's what a U.S. attorney defines as conspiracy these days. "Don't worry. Your secret's safe. I won't tell. But don't act like I'm involved, because I'm not. I don't understand what you guys are talking about and I don't do politics. You know that, Blaney."

"I know, Garnet. You're the big-time corporate lawyer."

Irene stuffed her envelopes into her satchel, fished out a subway token, and counted change to leave a tip. She said, "Will we see you next month?"

"Sounds like your business is going to be finished at the end of this month," I said.

"That's just the beginning."

Eddie was the only one still seated. He typed a sign-off to Nelson:

LIONEL WILL BE IN TOUCH.

chapter five

I told Blaney that I'd meet him back at the apartment later because I needed to go for a ride. I split before Blaney could raise any of his usual objections, so I was the first to leave the bar. It was night now. The muggy darkness had weight to it, and I felt it on my shoulders, like an unwelcome backpack.

I unlocked my bike and mounted it and crossed the street. I was looking forward to riding through Central Park at night when everyone else was scared to be there. I'd done it once before. It was the only way to get some privacy in New York City. Loop around the reservoir, look up, see all the color-lit buildings from a distance. I headed north.

But as I rode up a curb, I felt the back tire pulling. I dismounted on the sidewalk, and bent to see what was rubbing. The streetlight was burned out. My hands moved hesitantly over the spokes, over the rim, and I felt like a surgeon hit with a power outage in the middle of a kidney transplant. Was this bumpy part over here a blockage, or just an ordinary brake pad?

As I straightened, ready to wheel the bike back to where the light was better across the street, I saw Lionel walk out of Café Info.

Warm yellow light arced out from the open doorway, and he stood silhouetted in the glow, a tall and thoughtful man who hesitated long enough to make me wonder if he had just realized that he had left his wallet lying on the bar.

I hadn't had a chance to press him on the subject of Annie's dad. Lionel would know more. Lionel seemed to know a lot about a lot of people, in fact. Like Nelson. But before I could call out, he walked up to a Ford Bronco parked a few yards away from the café's door, unlocked the driver's door, and slid in. I waited for the engine to turn over, but Lionel didn't start the car. Instead, he edged over to the passenger's side and huddled low in that seat. He seemed to be peering out of the window at the bar he had just left.

I edged closer to the parked cars on my side of the street, leaning my bike low enough for them to block me from his view. What was he doing? The Bronco looked brand-new, shiny and black, and with a license plate that read TIE IT. How long would he sit there in the dark thirty feet from the café?

Then the door opened again, and out walked Eddie. He stopped for a moment too, feeling around in his pocket as if he sought change for a bus. I expected him to climb into the Bronco, or to wave to Lionel inside. But he didn't notice the car. He turned left, walked down the street past the Bronco, and rounded the corner.

The silhouette in the parked car sat stock-still. It hit me then that he was ticking off his friends, accounting for them one by one, as they left Café Info. Moments later out came Irene and Blaney. He cocked his head anxiously to hear her words even as he protectively kept the door from swinging shut on her. Irene looked up at him as if he were her big brother, clutching her valise like a stack of schoolbooks. Blaney reached to take the bag from her. But she held on. Smooth move. He was trying, but the body language was clear. He didn't have a chance.

They walked in the opposite direction of the one Eddie had taken. They crossed the street, stopped at a pay phone. Irene dialed. Blaney waited until she finished talking, then they turned a corner and were gone.

Lionel watched them. He sat in the parked car for nearly ten minutes more. By then, I had identified the bike's problem as a twig caught in the frame, and had developed a bad cramp in my calf. Then Lionel opened the car door and stepped out. He pushed down the lock button before he shut the door. He left the Bronco sitting there in the dark.

He walked into the street, waited for a car to pass, and then crossed. He was headed for my hiding spot, but at the last second veered and walked between the two cars parked in front of me.

He took off in the direction of Blaney and Irene. So, of course, I decided to tag along. What else could I do? I mounted my bike, stealthy as Cochise.

Lionel was conspiring against his friends. He didn't fit the FBI's profile of a mad bomber on the Net, but there was no way to ignore the facts: Lionel was plotting something illegal. He was breaking into government computers and stealing codes. He had been at Ames's funeral. Ames had spent his life cracking codes.

A garbage truck pulled down the street in front of him, lights blinking, and rumbled to a stop in the crosswalk. Lionel navigated around the guys who jumped off the back and scattered pigeons with their loud boots. By the time I reached the corner, the garbage crew had emptied seven cans. I waited impatiently. They jumped back onto the truck and slapped the side panel to signal their readiness to move. Their conveyance inched forward as majestically as the *QE II*.

But Lionel was gone. The truck had blocked my view for at most thirty seconds. Now I had a clear view for at least two blocks in every direction. The sidewalks looked empty. The light was green.

Green. Same color as the light on the subway entrance a block ahead. I pedaled at sprint speed to the twin lampposts that marked the entrance. A sign on the wall said UPTOWN LOCAL. I peered into the subterranean dark, unable to divine whether Lionel had descended. I didn't want to carry my bike down a flight of fifty steps.

A man wearing a dusty ski parka with a fur-lined hood sat by the railing, drinking from a paper bag. The hood was up. He looked like he was sweating Vaseline.

I pulled out a dollar. "Did you just see someone go down here?"

He looked up, took a long time to focus in the Martian glow cast by the lampposts. "Sure."

"Man or a woman?" I asked.

"Man."

"What was he wearing?"

"Pants."

I gave him the bill anyway.

I hesitated. If Lionel was down there, I didn't want him to see me. I wanted to spy on the spy. I wasn't afraid of him. He had the air of a man who lived by his wits and enjoyed fine manipulations much more than he would a direct confrontation. But no way could I remain invisible if I hoisted my bike up on my shoulders, carried it through a turnstile, and had to wait on the long, exposed concrete platform next to my quarry.

Then I heard it, a far-off roar, like the beginning of thunder, and the ground vibrated.

The train was coming. Below me, a horrible shriek of un-lubricated metal on metal announced its arrival. If Lionel was down there, he would be waiting by the doors, getting on now, grabbing hold of an overhead handhold.

"Hey, buddy."

The man on the sidewalk was trying to get my attention.

"Yeah?"

"He had a ponytail."

I could hear that the train was starting to move out of the station. Uptown local. That meant it would stop about eight or ten blocks up. It was my only chance.

I headed north. I pedaled as fast as I could down the middle of the avenue's many lanes. I knew from experience that there were fewer potholes in the middle. Don't ask me why. Of course, I had to weave in and out anyway, to avoid the random sawhorse construction sites that littered the roadway like squatters' camps, and to stay out of the way of cabdrivers. They were crazier than me, and had no insurance. Head down, knees up, chest heaving, I pumped as fast as I could. I would beat that train.

I thought I could make it through the intersection at Greenwich Avenue on the yellow, and so I pushed the gears up one notch, to give me more resistance to pedal against. I was moving at about thirty miles an hour when I realized that I'd have to run the red, so I just bore down and prayed a little, appropriating a few verses of the Psalm of the Unsung Bike Messenger for myself.

A cab on Greenwich that had been racing its engine, waiting for the green, jumped the light and came barreling at me. As I hit the brake, swerved left, and passed behind the taxi, I felt the fender brush against my pants leg.

I had no way of knowing how fast the train below me was moving, but I imagined it barely keeping pace with me. I could see a green ball glowing up the street, marking the next subway station. It was maybe three blocks ahead, at Fourteenth Street. I had no plan, just to keep moving.

I decided not to stop. A guy as fit as Lionel wouldn't get on a subway if he only had to travel ten blocks. I kept pedaling. I had the greens, and I was in thirteenth gear, a nice hard push that rewarded me with speed. I went through one intersection, two, a third, and I swear I felt as if I were riding on top of that train.

But then the sound of a siren gained on me. I couldn't risk a glance over my shoulder at this speed on this terrain, but within seconds it became a moot point. A shrill ambulance pulled up on the left of me, and the cars before me stopped short. A fiery red wall of brake lights forced me to slow. In any other city, the cars would be in neat rows, and I would slip by, but this was New York, where people drive as if they were playing touch football. There was no space to maneuver. I started banging on my handlebars. "Move it, move it!"

The traffic broke, but I had to start up again from a standstill. My momentum was gone. I couldn't feel the train, only my pounding heart. I got to Twenty-third Street and the green lollipop lights of the subway station as a few stragglers wandered up the steps. I slowly cruised up the street, full of despair, just looking for a juice stand. I gave up.

And then I saw him, getting into a cab.

As the traffic light turned green.

Now, I wouldn't skitch off a car in Manhattan, or even a cab, because the odds were that the driver would think nothing of pulling out a zip gun and ventilating my skull. But a bus? Bus drivers were civil service employees. They were not going to forfeit a cushy pension just because they didn't like some punk on a bike hanging off their bumper on a free ride. I hung off the left, and the driver flipped me the bird, but there was nothing he could do.

As we picked up speed, I considered the situation. I was following a guy who slipped down dark staircases, jumped out of a train and into a cab. I'd be skittish, too, if I possessed both halves of the stolen Patriot key, but that wouldn't cause me to spy on my pals.

The bus stopped every couple of blocks, which was okay, because a couple of blocks was all I needed. I was in twentieth gear when I let go, moving ahead of the bus so fast that my handlebars were vibrating almost out of control. It felt like mowing the lawn.

I still had my eye on Lionel's cab, with its one missing brake light. It turned right onto Forty-second Street and started to pull ahead. I hit a red light at the corner, and without a thought rode up on the sidewalk to make the turn. It was Saturday night on one of the busiest streets in the world. It was like riding through a parade. I yelled and howled like a maniac to get them out of my way. I had to get off the sidewalk, not so much to avoid cops but more because I couldn't see the cab from that angle. After about half a block, I zigged past a sidewalk entrepreneur who had spread out a picnic blanket to display his stolen hardcover books to passersby, then zagged to miss a one-legged woman begging change, launched myself off the curb, and flew over a mound of rags and Styrofoam coffee cups on a sewer grate.

I was back on the open road, heading east on Forty-second Street, riding flat out, while up ahead, Lionel's cab pulled over to drop him off at the corner of Vanderbilt Avenue. He must have had exact change, because he sprinted out before the cab came to a full stop.

Lionel trotted across Forty-second Street, and north up Vanderbilt. My heart sank. He was going into Grand Central Station! By the time I caught up, he had vanished into the train station's double doors. He could go anywhere in the world from there.

I climbed off my bike at the entrance, and pushed my way through the clumps of people trying to hail cabs, and through the glass-paned doors. I emerged on the balcony of the loftiest space in New York and forgot for a second how crowded and miserable this city was. The moody arched ceiling was painted with constellations and the sound that echoed from above was a reminder of all the millions of footsteps, all the travelers who had passed through here.

Directly opposite me, a football field away, were the hundreds of tiny-paned windows, framed in wrought iron, that had been painted black during the war. To confuse the Germans, I guess. I stood at the marble rail, but couldn't see Lionel anywhere. He was lost in the crowd. All I saw were a thousand people scurrying toward the tracks and the ticket sellers and the information desk and the waiting room and the shoeshine booths and the magazine racks. He was in there somewhere, headed for a train. Or maybe not.

There were a hundred ways in and out of this place. The station took up several city blocks and was encircled by street-level entrances. Since Grand Central was the nexus for the East Side subways as well, he could be hiding in the subterranean maze of tunnels and ramps. He could even take the shuttle across town to Times Square from here. A blaring loudspeaker torturously announced the departure of a Metro North liner, bound for some Westchester suburb that sounded like Hudson-on-Crouton.

I remember that cacophonous scene clearly now, but it washed over me as a blur at the time. I was under the influence of a major adrenaline rush and without making a conscious decision, got back on my bike and pointed it down.

I bounced down the first flight of ten steps, on the wide marble staircase, to the landing. I had a choice then of left or right staircases, down more smooth steps where millions of feet had worn gentle, grooved paths. I chose right because, miraculously, no one was on those steps, and rushed around the bend, my teeth rattling and my bike screaming that important components like brakes and the rear derailer were about to snap off. All I could do was hold on for the ride of my life. I once watched a rodeo rider on Saturday afternoon sports as he held on to a snorting steer with one hand while his body kept flying up like a wind sock. That's how I clutched my bike. I couldn't hope to control it, because it had turned mean on me. All I could do was try to stay on, as it bucked me again and again and my teeth slammed up into my brains.

Down the huge long flight I went, weaving back and forth in some dim serpentine effort to slow myself. Somehow I made it upright to the bottom, a changed man who no longer cared about rules or risks. "Where is he, where is he, where is he?" I was yelling it. I had a killer headache by now, and I must

F
L
A
M
E

W
A
R

have looked like a madman, gasping hungrily for oxygen, my hair plastered wet against my head, tears of pain rolling down my cheeks. I rode a crazy figure-eight right through the enormous arena of Grand Central.

I looped past the ticket booths, around the gleaming brass clock on the information booth, up the ramp into the waiting room full of long wooden benches, down the ramp toward the Oyster Bar. I rode through an archway labeled PARCEL ROOM, only to find myself peering right and left down a bleak windowless mall of tobacconists, shoe repair shops, and a Häagen-Dazs franchise. No Lionel. Then I circled the main floor again, and peered back up into the balcony, where I had started, wondering if Lionel sat in the shadows of the bar behind the railing, nursing a beer and laughing at me. But in my heart, I knew. He was gone.

I no longer had the energy or will to summon a thought, but somehow one popped into my head. We had been moving steadily northeast ever since we left Café Info on this wild adventure. He had changed modes of transportation, but never veered off that course.

So I was off, streaking across the tile to the exit at Lexington Avenue and Forty-second Street. Outside, I rode north for a block or so, trolling for him.

Some people see the face of Jesus on a tortilla. I experienced my miracle when I saw Lionel again. He was in the driver's seat of a Mercedes convertible, idling at the exit ramp of a Kinney Fast-Park. There was a break in traffic, and he pulled out. As he crossed Lexington, he turned and looked in my direction, lifted his right hand, waved at me.

Then he crossed Lexington, drove east for a block, turned north on Third Avenue, and accelerated sharply. As his car disappeared from my sight, I thought, The bastard.

He was teasing me. Or else he was testing me. He'd known all along that I was behind him.

But I was hooked. I pedaled again, and farther up on Third Avenue caught up with him. He proceeded uptown past the office towers of midtown and shiny new apartment high-rises. I followed the two-seater at a respectable distance, keeping my eyes on its distinctive license plate: KNOT

In the sixties, he turned right. A couple of blocks east, he pulled into a driveway next to a limestone town house, and stopped. I coasted up beside his car as he climbed out of the driver's seat.

"You have a lot of stamina, Harry."

"You play a lot of games, Lionel."

"Yes, but you won this round," he said.

Did I?

"Come in for a beer," he said. "You can explain why you're so interested in following me."

I would have said more, but with my tongue lolling out of my mouth and every muscle in my body aching, I was either going to have to sit down soon or collapse.

"Come in through the garage," he said, getting back into the car as an electronic door under the house opened.

I surveyed the building. Lights were on inside. On the parlor floor of the town house, a large bay window with dozens of panes of leaded glass revealed a crystal chandelier, a tall potted palm in a corner, and an ornately carved mantel that dominated the high-ceilinged room. But what mesmerized me was the portrait.

Over the fireplace hung a remarkable painting of a young woman in a blue dress, dark-haired and looking off to the right. Although it had been painted in oils, the likeness had a photo's clarity, as though its subject had been caught in midsentence. Her expression was expectant and pleased, as if someone she adored had come into the room calling her name. I wondered who she was and who she loved that much. I could not stop looking at her.

"Are you coming?" Lionel's voice came from inside the dark garage.

I followed.

chapter six

The place smelled rich. Like fresh paint and some kind of exotic spice, maybe turmeric. The floors and the furniture were waxed and the ceilings were high. I sank into one of those overstuffed armchairs that are famous for swallowing the TV's remote control, and put my feet up on an ottoman.

Lionel had led me into the house through the garage, then up a spiral staircase. We emerged into a lofty kitchen, with a stainless-steel prep table and a refrigerator with glass doors, from which he had pulled two bottles of Brooklyn Beer. There was a chrome-edged banquette and wooden tables along the wall. And in the middle of the room, a brass pole shot up through a hole in the ceiling.

"We'll take the elevator," he said.

Now I was upstairs in the parlor, and Lionel was over in the corner, fiddling with the stereo. Before I heard David Grisman's music start to pipe through the speakers recessed in the walls above my head, I had time to study my surroundings. The place told me three things about its owner: he was rich, he had opulent taste, and he lived alone. No, not alone: a red fox, the size of an extremely well-fed house cat, sat alertly on a small cushion near Lionel. The animal's ears twitched like radar dishes and it stared at me, wide-eyed. I stared back. It responded with a nervous, growling noise and bared its teeth, which looked as sharp as Japanese tree-saw blades.

"Stop that, Winnie," Lionel commanded, and the fox did.

Everything in the house, from the position of the stereo speakers to the music stand against which rested a bassoon, indicated that artifacts here were carefully arranged to suit a single owner. A fox would be the perfect pet for such a man: canine companionship with feline delicacy among so many breakables.

On the main floor of the house, all the walls had been knocked down. What had looked like a stuffy Victorian parlor when I was peering in from the sidewalk was in fact modern. Asymmetrical velvet couches with pompous, high backs that curved like violins faced each other in front of the fireplace. One was purple. The other was yellow. Somehow, they matched.

What did it prove? That even a guy with really good taste spies on his friends. As I sat there, I noticed his security system. When I walked into his garage from the street, I had caught a flash, about ankle high, of a laser resetting itself just inside the doorway. After he summoned his private elevator, he punched a long string of numbers into a digitized control panel to convince it to accept us.

"Even if you didn't see which numbers I punched," he said conversationally, "you could figure out the code, eventually, if you watched me try enough different combinations of numbers."

"How?" I asked.

"By clocking me, keeping track right down to the nanosecond of how long it took my fingers to move from a certain key to another."

"I don't keep time in nanoseconds."

"A computer could do it."

"If I had a computer strapped to my chest."

"Say you were sending a digital message over your modem to instruct your encryption software to scramble outgoing messages and decode incoming ones. Then a patient hacker could break your code. By using his computer to time how long the software took to execute each step of the process, he would know how many digits long the key was and he could work from there, to try all possible combinations of numbers."

"Time-consuming."

"Almost anything that's worth doing is time-consuming," he said. "And takes a supercomputer."

The elevator stopped at the parlor floor.

"Too bad you and Blaney didn't have a supercomputer," I said.

"I considered that." He gestured for me to sit before he went over to the stereo that resided inside a black-lacquered cabinet. Winnie, while sitting at attention, began to doze. "Who knows how long it would take to hack the Patriot key? I can't wait indefinitely."

I picked up a Rubik's cube from the table next to my chair. I idly flipped the colored squares. "I've never met anyone who liked games as much as you, Lionel," I said.

"I don't like games," he said. "I like puzzles." He leaned back on his heels to close the cabinet doors, and then came over to throw himself down on a velvet sofa.

"So did Fred Ames. At least that's what his friends said at the memorial service."

"That's a clumsy way to try to lead the conversation, Harry. Why not just ask me straight out what you want to know?"

"What was Ames mixed up in?"

Lionel took a minute to consider the question. "Math, mainly."

He saw my scowl, and held up his hand to cut me off before I could blurt out something rude. "I'm not being disingenuous, Harry. Hear me out. Fred Ames was one of the most brilliant mathematicians of this century. Whatever his personal

Joshua Quitter

problems may have been, his interest in his work was pure. He was a philosopher, and he devised beautiful, theoretical equations to explain the world around him. He was an expert on prime number theory. It was probably inevitable that he became enmeshed in the encryption debate, considering how heavily the science of cryptography relies on the practical application of prime numbers. I met Fred Ames when I was first noodling around with plans to devise my own code.''

"You write code?''

"Sometimes I write code for codes. Other times I just write code.'' He smiled, as if at a private joke. Blaney had told me, during the meeting, that Lionel was the author of ''fucking great software,'' so I assumed he must be enjoying a secret laugh at the fact that I was too dumb to know he was the world-famous author of some *essential* spreadsheet program that was currently all the rage among Fortune 500 bean counters.

"Do you know enough about math to know that factoring primes is one of the most difficult problems in mathematics, and has been confounding theorists for centuries?'' Lionel said he had met Ames after he read an article on Information Theory that Ames had published in an electrical engineering journal called *IEEE Transactions*, and had been captivated by the professor's theories on prime numbers.

What I knew about prime numbers had been learned from Mrs. Binney in junior high, and when I tried to summon up the memory of those interminable math classes, all I saw was the long, dark hair of Katie Millery. She sat in front of me, in the third row from the door, and for forty-five minutes a day, I stared at the back of her head. When I wasn't staring at the Seth Thomas over the blackboard, the clock with the pie face and the minute hand that moved so slowly that I became convinced I would live forever—unfortunate, considering what a high percentage of that time would be spent enduring Mrs. Binney.

From somewhere in my subconscious emerged the image of lock-jawed Mrs. Binney, stern in heavy eyeglasses that made her look older than she was. She liked to stand at the black-board, her back to the class, and call out in a hoarse voice that carried over her shoulder, "Prime numbers are divisible by themselves and by one. Period. You might be interested to know, class"—and here she would turn on her heel to catch us snickering at the suggestion that anything she said could be of interest to the hormonally challenged students she steered—"that there is no shortage of prime numbers. You might think they'd be rare, but in fact, primes occur about every one hundred numbers or so once you get up to very large numbers with, say, one hundred digits."

I had learned from the homework assignments that while it was mathematically easy to determine if a large number is a prime, it seemed impossible to factor a huge number to dis-cover which two primes to multiply to equal the larger num-ber. Katie Millery had been good at math, I remembered that much, and she had been the one to raise a hand, hesitantly, because with Mrs. Binney, it paid to exercise caution, and to ask, "Ma'am, I figured out that the factors of 7,337 are 23, 11, and 29. But why doesn't it work with a bigger number?"

That was the kind of question that Mrs. Binney liked, be-cause it would eat up the clock, but I think I must have lost interest around that time, or maybe Katie wasn't wearing the red shirt and so I started to stare out the window. That's all I could summon from the depths of memory.

"Did Ames's work focus on factoring?" I felt obliged to ask, on behalf of Katie Millery.

Lionel raised his eyebrows, mocking me with feigned sur-prise. "Very impressive, Harry."

While mathematicians have made some advances in that task, much remains mysterious, Lionel explained. "That's why it's possible for most modern encryption schemes to rely on a key that is partially derived from the process of multiplying two large prime numbers. Almost impossible to factor that key, which gets applied to a plaintext message, to garble its con-tents. Maybe you heard about it when a group of researchers recently managed to break the code on RSA, an encryption system that would have taken forty quadrillion years to crack if a single mathematician were using a single computer to try to factor the primes."

Hadn't heard about it, in fact. Also hadn't heard what happened to Katie Millery in the ten years since I'd last talked to her.

"The method of attack on the RSA code was based on a factoring system invented by a mathematician in Georgia."

Known as the quadratic sieve, the factoring system allowed researchers to break up complicated problems like factoring into small chunks, and then pass out the pieces to individual people to solve. At the end, all the small pieces of the puzzle are put together, and a solution emerges. Much of the data is useless, but the important bits are caught, like gold in a sieve, and reveal the answer.

"Ames was involved in a similar project, with a large number of people who were working together on factoring problems. He also had published a number of papers which—if you took his body of work as a whole—indicated that he was formulating his own theories on factoring," Lionel said.

"You knew Ames well."

"I knew his work well. I only met him a few times—once after I had petitioned him for a meeting at his office at Columbia, back when I was working on my own algorithm, and then, years later I was, frankly, surprised to see him at militia meetings. I thought of him as someone who inhabited a theoretical world. Not someone concerned with changing the physical universe."

"You must think that one of the militia members killed Ames, otherwise why take a risk, breaking into a car parked on the street just so you can snoop?"

"I own the car. I parked it there earlier."

I remembered the license plate on the Bronco, TIE IT. And on the convertible, KNOT.

"Tie the Knot?" I stood and paced the perimeter of the

room, entranced by the round, recessed metal plates in the walls, up under the lip of the crown moldings. I saw the indentations blink from time to time, like watchful eyes. Surveillance cameras.

"Knot is software that I wrote," he said. "It's what I do for a living, at least what I did when I needed to earn money. Now I do it to occupy my mind."

"Is Knot a spreadsheet program?"

"It's my encryption program. It encodes messages."

"Like Patriot?"

"There's a difference. Patriot archives messages so that other people can read them later. Knot doesn't do that—it protects the user's privacy.

"It's actually rather simple," Lionel said. "Imagine you had a mailbox that was built exclusively for you to exchange messages with me. A lockbox, built of impenetrable titanium. The box, of course, would need two keys—one for you, and one for me. Assuming I could ensure that your key could not be copied, and never fell into someone else's hands, I would have an extremely reliable, extremely secure system for communicating with you. I would know that every message I found in our box came from you. And you would know that every message you found came from me."

I nodded. Yes, this was the simple part. I figured he was about to add a layer of complexity so I braced myself, by flopping back into the armchair.

"But," said Lionel, "say you wanted to carry on secure communications with a hundred people, or a thousand people. You wouldn't want to carry around a key ring with a thousand keys. A more efficient solution would be to have a master key, a skeleton key, that opened all your mailboxes. You'd keep the master key, and give each of your correspondents a unique key that allowed him to open only the mailbox you had set up for him. Just so."

He twirled a throw pillow on the sofa as if waiting for me to catch up. "Software, it turns out, can do all this, and more.

In fact, it completely stands that hardware notion of 'keys' on its head. Public-key encryption, it's called—which is what Knot is. Perhaps the strongest implementation of public key ever. When I communicate on computer networks, I can choose to publish my 'public' key. Perhaps you've seen public keys on E-mail, or in Usenet?''

"Strings of gibberish down by the signature on an E-mail message?"

"You can use my public key to encipher messages for my eyes only. You merely copy my key, load Knot, and encrypt your message to me, using my key. It's as if you were putting a message in a mailbox shared by just the two of us."

"But if you publish your key, can't I use it to decode your other messages?"

"Not at all!" said Lionel, beaming. "That's the brilliance of it. In fact, that's where my little analogy breaks down. Once you encrypt a message with my public key, even you can't decrypt it. Only I can. The public key only goes one way—toward me. You can use my key to encrypt, or lock up, as much material as you want. Only I can unlock it. This is what Knot does, and does quite well.

"With one major difference. Every message sent using Patriot has a third key, if you will. A key held 'in escrow' for use by the government and law enforcement," Lionel said. "It's a vile idea. With personal computers, for the first time in the history of mankind, we have an opportunity to enjoy complete privacy. And our government wants to thwart us. It's tragic. Obviously, businesses will never agree to such a thing. Some of Knot's biggest users are large corporations, who have a fierce desire to keep trade secrets secret."

"So you have a financial interest in defeating Patriot."

"No. I give Knot away for free," he said. "Not everything is about money, Harry."

"You're very altruistic," I said. "For a man who has a de Kooning hanging in the living room."

He laughed, but not in a mean-spirited way—more at himself than at me. "Let's not play Spy versus Spy. I see that's a waste with you. You're in my house, and so of course you gather bits of information about me. Well, I'll put my cards on the table. I've culled some data of my own. Here's what I know about you, Harry. I read between the lines in the newspaper accounts. Father killed in freak incident when you were at an impressionable age—" His recitation had the singsong quality of being from memory. "You coasted through college, then law school. Frittering away your last summer of freedom working for an old family friend. In a way, Harry, the fact that you were standing in that cottage at The Vines may turn out to be the best thing that could have happened. The bomber didn't know it, but he gave you a second chance."

"To do what?"

"To choose. You don't always have to take the easy route."

"Why do you care?"

"Because you are a clue."

"To what?"

"The bomber. I don't believe in random victims. I've been studying this case rather closely for months now—you might say it's become an obsession. God knows that's what other people say about me. Everything about you—who you are, what you think, why you of all people delivered that package to Ames—could be helpful to me. You're a cog, Harry, a cog in the wheel of this case. I want to understand the mechanics."

Out in the street, a car horn honked. Winnie's eyes opened like window shades, and she slinked off, too feral for a house pet in my opinion, to growl at the window.

Abruptly: "Want to see your file, Harry?"

I wanted to refuse.

But when he gestured to the elevator, I followed. The clank and wheeze of the cables as the machine responded reminded me of an old dog that still lives to please. Wordlessly, we rode up.

As we reached the fourth floor, he pulled his right hand from his pocket and held it up in front of his face, in front of my face. "Count," he said.

Four fingers. Actually, he had three fingers and a thumb, as I had noticed back at the café during his origami demonstration. "Doesn't seem to affect you."

"For a long time, *I* was the only one who had survived," Lionel said. Nelson's mocking tone came back to me: *Our little group now includes so many victims of the infamous Compubomber.*

"But I thought all the previous victims died." I tried to remember what the FBI agents had told me in the hospital.

"I was supposed to die," he said flatly, as if placing an order for coffee, black. "But I didn't. Someone else did, for me."

"When?" I asked.

"Nearly two years ago," he said. He answered my unspoken questions: "After a few months, I stopped reliving the sound of the explosion every single moment. I run in the mornings. Around the eighth mile, I'm free."

"Of what?"

"Rage."

"I don't want to be free of that." I was surprised to hear myself say it.

"Rage can be constructive," he agreed. "If you can harness it."

"Have you?"

We stepped out into another cavernous space. A wall of French doors in the back of the building led to an outdoor patio, lit by floodlights and crammed with plants and wild vines that cast noose-shaped shadows on the walls. Inside, the only freestanding furniture in the room was an immense, S-curved desk that sat off-center on the glossy oak floor. When Lionel sat in the leather desk chair behind the mahogany desk, he had views of all the windows. His back was against a brick wall.

Along the opposite side of the room was a bank of built-in file cabinets, twenty-five feet wide and stretching from floor to ceiling. The cabinets were bright metal, and powerful halogen lights along the ceiling pinned everything below.

Lionel answered my question: "Rage is a curious motivator. I'll do whatever it takes to get him."

He sat at the desk and typed on a digitized keypad to gain access to the desk drawers. He opened a compartment and pulled out a box of Band-Aids. The metal box with its red-white-and-blue flip-top lid looked so *normal* sitting there on his desk, so out of context in this place of weird gadgetry. I stared at the Band-Aids, as if I were seeing an artifact from a world that no longer existed. "Put one on your hand," he said.

I looked down, and saw that a blister shaped like West Virginia had formed in the crook between thumb and index finger, where I did most of my shifting. I didn't remember getting it, and I didn't remember it tearing open, leaving raw red skin exposed to the air. Now I felt it for the first time.

"No, thanks."

"Take care of your hand," he said. "I can't stand to look at it."

He held out the box, and I accepted it. I pulled one out, and ripped on the red thread, and realized that I liked him then. The feeling was as reflexive as reaching for the Band-Aid.

"How are you going to get the bomber?" I asked.

"With your help. I hope." He walked over to the file cabinets. He flicked a button and a drawer slid soundlessly open on oiled casters. He flipped through a row of hanging files, each one tabbed in red, yellow, blue, or green. A perfectly organized system.

"I've studied this case for so long, I no longer understand anything clearly," he said. "He never should have killed Fred Ames. I should have stopped him before then. I'm not too proud to ask for help."

He pulled out a folder labeled BOMB-4 (THE MATHEMATI-CIAN).

"Codes are the link between the victims."

"You think like a G-man, Harry. The FBI asked me about that after Ames died. They were knocking on my door the very next morning, in fact," Lionel said. "But they weren't able to tie it in with any of the other victims except me."

"You don't think they will?"

"I have a different theory," he said. "I think the fact that Ames was a cryptology expert and I'm a political activist is beside the point. Which obscures the real point."

He held out the file to me. "But I don't want to influence your opinion. Not until you know everything."

As I reached for the file, a phone rang. Lionel walked back to the desk, answered. He spoke too low for me to hear. He put the call on hold, said, "I'll be back. Make yourself comfortable."

As the elevator door slid shut behind Lionel, I looked at the folder. Inside was a thick stack of newspaper clippings. I caught a glimpse of a headline: BOMBER INVADES UPSTATE HAMLET. I realized these were the stories of my life. While I'd read the ones in *The New York Times* and the Albany papers, many of these were from publications—*The Washington Post*, the *Chicago Tribune*, the *Times* of London, even—that I hadn't seen yet.

I turned back to the file drawer, still open, its key dangling from the lock. I was alone with all the files. Was it another setup? I didn't care. The whole drawer was devoted to the Compubomber, dozens of files neatly organized. I took out every thick folder. Gentle as a pallbearer, I carried them to the desk, welcoming their weight. I fanned them out.

Emotion told me to start with my own file. But logic dictated a different order. My fingers meandered. The labels were as generic as encyclopedia entries. The files included BOMB (MATERIALS), BOMB (ONLINE RECIPES), BOMB (PHYSICS), SUSPECTS (DESCRIPTIONS), SUSPECTS (PSYCHOLOGY), PATTERNS (GEOGRAPHICAL). I skimmed randomly, admiring the careful cross-referencing system Lionel had imposed. Phrases overlined in pink and yellow linked by folder and document number to

F

L

A

M

E

W

A

R

other related passages. An attempt to control the uncontrollable, to explain the unexplainable. I had the same urge.

I wanted to read them all, at once, plug all that data into my brain. I sank into the chair and sifted through the pile, until I came to a folder as thick as the *New Collegiate Dictionary*. It seemed older than the rest. It was labeled BOMB-1 (THE PROFESSOR).

Inside I found yellowed newspaper clippings, brittle and smelling of rot, held together by a rubber band. Some were marked with paper clips or crabbed notes in black ink. It surprised me to see that Lionel had written messily in margins. I picked up the first story, expecting to be introduced to my enemy. But first, I met my peers.

The U.S. Postal Service delivered death to Edward Barrow on September 10, 1995. It was a time of the academic year when the students hadn't yet settled into their routines, and the weather in southern California distracted the undergraduates from Intro to Morality. Barrow was one of the youngest tenured professors on campus, and usually had a waiting list for his classes. He shaved his head and wore black, Japanese gardener's pants. He looked angry as he strode across the quad. He also, reputedly, liked to date his students. That day, the philosophy department's secretary sorted the mail and put several letters and a larger, padded envelope into Barrow's faculty pigeonhole while he was teaching an honors seminar on Kant, Hegel, and the Dialectic.

The thirty-one-year-old professor had office hours, but after class stopped in the student union to purchase a tofu sandwich on whole wheat toast, which he was carrying when he arrived at the mailboxes. There, he ran into a colleague. They made a date for tennis.

In the margin of the clipping I was reading, Lionel had scrawled: "See PD file." I flipped through the folder, and saw that he had acquired a set of Los Angeles Police Department investigative reports, as well as a thick sheaf of forensic files from the Federal Bureau of Investigation. By now, I was becoming inured to his ability to obtain sensitive information; I greedily dipped into the documents. Barrow would not have had a reason to be suspicious of the manila envelope that he ripped open with a Swiss army knife. He seemed to traffic in floppy disks. Just that week, he already had received at least three others, including two rough drafts of students' dissertations and a screensaver program that infinitely computed pi (from a wry colleague in the physics department).

The articles and reports gave every detail, and I saw Barrow on his last day. He rarely smiled (according to a *Times* profile), so I imagined him bent, serious purpose etched across his face, riffling through his stack of mail. He walked down the hall to his office and closed the door. A few students wandered by. But none knocked on the narrow strip of wavy glass on his door. No one else saw Barrow put the floppy in his machine. He was browsing an American Society of Mathematica newsletter when the A: drive swallowed the disk.

A horrible chain reaction ensued: The disk slid home, closing an electrical connection and charging a microdetonator that issued a tiny blast. That caused a thin pancake of plastique to explode in sympathy. The hard plastic case of the computer and its microcircuits were then transformed into shrapnel. Millions of razor-sharp shards rode on the shock wave and imbedded themselves in the hallway walls and in Professor Barrow.

I felt dizzy when I read the description.

Miraculously, no one else was hurt. But Barrow never stood a chance. The police reports described in painstaking detail the charred rubble of his office, the blackened remains of his goose-necked desk lamp, the hunks of plaster that rained from the ceiling. Of all those facts, the one bit of information that I couldn't shake, the image that would stubbornly incorporate itself into my dreams was this: tiny bits of confetti floating on the autumn wind. The force of the bomb blew out Barrow's third-floor window and spewed fragments of his furniture, his limbs, his books, his unmarked quizzes, and his tofu sandwich out over the commons. And long after the police had arrived, after the yellow tape of the crime scene was in place, after the worried knots of students dispersed, pieces of his papers fluttered in the breeze, settling eventually in the shrubs, on the brick paths, all over the lawn. I wondered if it had been easier to reconstruct the papers than the professor.

I scanned the dozens of follow-ups, the wild goose chases (he had a mistress, he had a gambling debt), looking for a link between Barrow and the little I knew of Fred Ames. I even flipped through the dissertations on the search for meaning in a post-Holocaust world. But where was the killer, and why did he kill? The last bit of paper in the folder was one of Lionel's scrawls: "See BOMB-2."

BOMB-2 (THE SOFTWARE DEVELOPER).

The file was slim compared to the others. And surprisingly impersonal, considering that it had been assembled by the victim himself. Inside was a bare-bones police report. Perhaps Lionel had no need to collect newspaper clippings to get the details of this particular crime because, after all, he had been there. The only two press accounts he included were a long piece detailing the police investigation, and an article speculating on possible connections between Lionel and Barrow.

The facts were these: on August 23, 1996, nearly a year after Professor Barrow's death, a woman named Ilse Sullivan brought the day's mail into the office area of the SoHo loft apartment she shared with her husband, Lionel. He sat at one of the desks as she opened the envelopes and packages. She handed him a floppy disk that had arrived in a small package. Although he was a software developer, and was in fact the author of a well-known computer program called Knot, Lionel did not know who had sent this particular disk. He could not guess the contents. Curious, Ilse walked over to a second desk, next to a window that faced north. She turned on a computer on that desk, inserted the floppy, and was killed instantaneously. Her husband, whose desk twenty feet away was partially shielded by an antique iron folding screen that they used as a room divider, sustained serious injuries. Ilse's wedding ring, a thin gold band set with three small diamonds, was later pried from the office wall, where it had been propelled with such force that it imbedded itself in the building's century-old cinder-block walls.

Nothing else in the file.

So I turned to BOMB-3 (THE HACKER). All I could think about as I read about the murder of Matthew Alan Reese, age fifteen, a high school sophomore in the northern suburbs of Chicago, was how invincible a teenager feels.

At that age, death happens, but only to other people. No way would that kid, waking up too late to make it to his 7:45 A.M. geometry class at Dover Heights High, have believed it if the Grim Reaper had tapped him on the shoulder and said, "Sorry, Matthew, but you wasted all that time doing your homework last night."

I thought about that day, May 1, 1997, and what it must have been like for Matthew. There were some pictures. I could have passed him in the halls of my own high school a hundred times, a wiry dude with fusilli hair and a wary look in his eyes. He wouldn't want people to think they could get away with anything just because he was short.

He was the second son of a successful civil lawyer and a physical therapist, and the previous Christmas he had gotten a new computer. The clips said that he was the kind of kid who had always had a computer, from the time he was old enough to sit on his dad's lap and mouse-click on Mickey.

I imagined him scrambling for a pair of clean sweat socks among the piles of laundry that littered his bedroom. Dashing downstairs, grabbing his backpack, and heading out the front door. On the way, he passed the table in the foyer where the Reese family's junk collected: his sister's hairbands, his mother's car keys. Mail. He must have seen the envelope addressed to him, where it had been placed when it was delivered two days earlier. He jammed it into his backpack. Matthew and his parents were deep in the Adolescent Cold War. It was no mystery that he hadn't seen his mail sooner. He never checked it.

But E-mail, that was a different proposition. Matthew had a secret life online. He hopped fences and trespassed in private computer systems all over the world. He liked to break in, just to see if he could. And usually, he could. Matthew got off on hacking. He got his hands on everything anyone anywhere ever wrote about the fine art of computer intrusion. He taught himself UNIX, the language that computers speak to each other when they connect on the Internet. He knew enough about how computers talked to impersonate them, spoofing other computers and convincing them he was a legitimate user. Hi, remember me, let me back into your system, he would type in UNIX. Sure, come on in. How have you been? they would answer.

The FBI found a cache of spiral-ringed notebooks in an iron lockbox in Matthew's closet, detailing his travels throughout the networked world. Investigators pored over these, suspecting that surely the killer would be mentioned. But they found nothing, aside from a fairly complete diary of the education of a hacker. They also found 968 floppy disks in shoe boxes. That's how they learned that he used to leave programs hidden inside corporate computers so that he would always have a log-in and a password—even if someone saw his digital footprints and attempted to close up the back doors.

Matthew never crashed a computer system, and although he had looked through confidential files in sensitive systems that belonged to everyone from the phone company to TRW to Chiquita Banana, he never stole or harmed anything. At least as far as anyone could tell.

The FBI investigators surmised that Matthew would have believed that the floppy disk had come from one of his friends in the hacker underground. He would have figured it was just

No. 969 in his collection. That would explain why a normally cautious young man would accept an unmarked floppy, sent from an unknown person. And put it into his machine. No questions asked. The forensics team was able to determine that there was no return address on the hand-lettered envelope.

Matthew had lots of friends in the Underground, with names like NetSmasher and Mr. HacK. The feds had done a credible job of interviewing them too. The kids were shaken up and eager to talk. Death never visited their dens; indeed, physical contact was rare.

For a while, the FBI suspected that the bomber was someone Matthew had met in one of the places hackers liked to gather on the Net. Or perhaps the bomber was the kind of person who lurked on an Internet Relay Chat channel, trolling for young boys.

But in the end, the FBI could find no connection between Matthew and the other victims.

Professor Barrow, Matthew Reese, Frederick Ames, Lionel. A philosophy professor, a teenage hacker, a mathematician, and—and a software developer. The only link was computers. All the victims used them daily. But these days, so did almost everyone.

I came to BOMBER (WHO HE IS). Inside was a three-page internal memo written by one Special Agent Peters. It was single-spaced and at the top was a notation that copies were to be sent to a dozen agents in different bureaus around the country. The memo was marked CONFIDENTIAL with that cheesy stamp you can still buy in office supply stores. Whether Lionel had lied, hacked, or bribed to get the report, I did not care. All I cared about was the memo itself, which laid out in detail everything that was known about the killer's personality. It was a curious introduction to my enemy.

The bomber had never contacted the authorities directly to take credit for his handiwork. So the personality sketch was based on the way he committed crimes, the materials he had

had to procure to build his bombs, the long hours of solitary effort that he had put into the construction of his packages. Agent Peters speculated that the bomber was in his late fifties, with an engineering job and a poor self-image. The meticulous nature of his actions suggested that he needed order, that he would function best in a situation with a clear hierarchy. The military? If he had been in the service, that would explain how he learned at least the rudiments of concocting explosives.

The bomber probably lived alone, the report said. He had to have large blocks of uninterrupted time to build his creations. The work required him to be as careful and patient as a watchmaker. He built all the components of the bomb from scratch. Even the tiny screws that secured the detonators inside the floppies were fashioned by hand, from little cylinders of common metals. None of the materials could be traced, except the floppy disks. They were all the same type, a common brand sold in two big computer software chains that between them operated hundreds of stores in forty-one states.

The report was dated May 30, 1997, a month after Matthew Reese died and less than six weeks before Frederick Ames would be killed.

I noticed one other thing: nearly a year had elapsed between the first and second bombing, and again between the second and third. But less than three months had passed between the deaths of Matthew Reese and Frederick Ames. Was the bomber simply perfecting his skills, constructing the bombs faster? Or maybe he had begun to spiral out of control, needing his fix, that power rush of attention, more often.

Of course, maybe he wasn't mad at all. Maybe he had some deadline to meet, some arcane agenda. We live in a world of serial killers and have come to expect them all to murder according to a hidden master plan. We expect neat Freudian solutions (kills women who look like his mom) or Sherlock Holmes-ian denouements (dates of deaths correspond to signs of the Zodiac). Perhaps the bomber merely wanted the authorities to think he chose relatively random victims.

"He had a reason to kill specific people."

I didn't realize that I had spoken aloud until a tinny voice answered me from an intercom system in the wall behind me.

"That's my conclusion as well." The voice was Lionel's. I couldn't tell if he was heartened—or disappointed—by our similar opinions.

"Harry, come upstairs," the spy in the speaker box said, just as the elevator arrived and its door rolled decorously open before me. "Hurry. I hate to wait."

I stepped off the elevator into a room that looked like Mission Control before a space shuttle launch, and joined Lionel at a long table. He sat in front of a big-screen computer monitor, one of many to choose among in this room. Along the walls were metal racks, stacked with more than a dozen computers that trailed numerous gray cords to connect them to phone lines, to monitors, to each other. He had a SPARC workstation, a server with a big disk—"for storing data," he said, noticing that I was admiring it as if it were a vintage Mustang convertible—a Silicon Graphics Onyx workstation that was running UNIX, a router that sprouted phone lines, and endless arrays of cool-glow digital numbers quietly counting. Gentle lighting, no windows.

"Have you figured out the link between the victims, Harry?"

"Unlucky?"

"Ames."

All the victims had worked with Ames on a factoring problem that he had devised. Ames recruited them. It was supposed to be a test of Ames's new theories about prime numbers, and if the method worked, he had planned to publish an article about his technique in an upcoming issue of a mathematical journal. "You can see why Ames recruited me for the project—I had evinced an interest in the same issues. He knew I had a practical interest in the process as well, because whatever I learned from the project, I could turn around and incorporate into practice, in updated versions of Knot."

FLAMEWAR

Ames's project had required massive amounts of human support, and Lionel suspected that as many as a thousand different researchers were working on the same problem with the professor. "I never knew Barrow or Matthew Reese, never had any contact with them or heard their names mentioned in connection with Ames's factoring project until after the professor died. That's when I realized that they and I had a rather startling connection."

I have come to accept the fact that it is my fate to ask the obvious, so I said, "Did you tell the FBI?"

"The FBI already knew," Lionel said quietly. "They knew about the connection well before Ames died, in fact." Lionel had reviewed government documents that he had obtained from law enforcement officials. On the twenty-page list that inventoried the subject matter of the floppy disks confiscated from Matthew Reese's bedroom had been the notation: DISK TITLE: FACTORS. "I phoned Reese's math teacher, who put me in touch with the man who ran the computer lab at his high school, and that's how I learned that Matthew often stayed late in the afternoons to cadge computing time. He told everyone in the lab, in fact, that he was working on a piece of a bigger problem."

"And Barrow?"

"He was a tinkerer. I searched Internet archives for references to him, and learned he had posted several messages to Usenet groups that discussed the project."

"The FBI didn't say anything to me about it," I said, remembering the two agents who had visited me in the hospital.

"And they won't." He let the implications of that sentence hang in the air, heavy and gray, and if I had reached out a hand, I might have felt the cold weight of the accusation: conspiracy.

I asked: "What would happen to Patriot if Ames, or anyone else for that matter, unlocked the secret to factoring huge numbers?"

"Patriot would be obsolete. So would most methods of encryption that we know of."

One thing still didn't make sense. Well, hell, most of what Lionel had said during the past two hours had been over my head, truth be told, but the one nagging question that I could get my brain around, that I could voice, was this: "How did Ames meet the others?"

Lionel turned to the keyboard, stored a file, punched a few keys. "Barrow, myself, Matthew Reese, Ames—we all at one time or another were members of a private online club. It's quite popular among a certain segment of Netizens. It's the equivalent of an underground club, like Studio 54 in cyberspace."

The computer screen went blank momentarily as Lionel's machine attempted to establish contact with another.

"It sounds quite exclusive," I said.

"It is."

I saw an image appear on the screen. A revolving can of dog food.

"It's called The Zoo."

F

L

A

M

E

W

A

R

chapter seven

I had a spy's view of both the sunrise and Annie's lobby. I lurked inside a limestone doorway across the street. I didn't want to blow my cover if her mother happened to look out the window to see if the cab had arrived to take them to La Guardia. The woman didn't want me to see her daughter. That much I had clued in on. The rest was conjecture. In fact, the two of them might not even be headed to the airport; all that Alicia Ames had said was that they were leaving. I still didn't have Annie's phone number, because it hadn't seemed essential after we started exchanging E-mail.

But the truth was that, not possessing the *right* numbers, I was powerless once again. In this case, it was a phone number. Other times, it's a bank ATM code that I forget. Or my Social Security number. Or my mother's date of birth. Digits define our identities. When Nelson the Crypto Terrorist had shown how easy it was to spew those details about me, he also was making a bigger point: he had all the power. Sometimes I wonder if human thoughts, memories, ideas that are number-free deep in the cerebellum even matter anymore. Certainly they provide no real protection. Nelson had exposed me as surely as if he had trooped into a locker room and trained an Instamatic on me while I showered.

But some things remain off limits. Like Annie. I knew nothing about her, except that I kept losing her.

I told myself, as I stood as alone as anyone can be in the early morning, with a relentless stone punishing my back and no breakfast in my gut, that my growing need to find her, to connect to her, was born entirely of frustration. I hate to be thwarted. What was the lure of this woman, other than the fact that she and I had once been blown apart in midsentence, other than that her mother was as determined as a Victorian dowager to shield Annie from riffraff like me?

That must have been it. I mean, what was so special about Annie, anyway? Well, her eyes, for one thing, the startling fact of such clear gray against black pupils. And her high cheekbones, tinged with what always seemed to be a flush of excitement. Or of curiosity. You don't expect so much color, so much *commitment* from the complexion of a redhead.

I might as well mention the ears too. I had noticed, during the fifteen times an hour that she absently tucked her hair back, that she seemed to be asking a lot of such finely sculpted ears. The hair was electrified with energy, with will, with a desire to curl and drape wherever it wanted. How could such small ears, so close against her head, exert authority over that kind of a situation? She had a model's ears, with the kind of delicately pink, idealized lobes that an art major would sketch in an anatomical drawing class.

I checked my wristwatch. I had a backup plan. If no one emerged from the building by eight, I'd go inside and ask for Annie. Eight was a decent enough hour.

My back hurt from leaning against a stone archway. My legs ached from so much riding and standing. I'd been hoping last night to snatch an hour of sleep on a spare mattress at Eddie's apartment. But when I had gotten back there, in what I considered to be the middle of the night, my arrival was clearly an intrusion.

Walking into a cramped, dingy foyer, I had stepped into a bizarre lair of midnight paranoia. I had expected a living room with a dingy couch. So forgive me if I was overwhelmed by the sheer sensory stimulation of entering a secret and vast, fluorescent-lighted digital laboratory. High-powered fixtures that Eddie had custom-fitted into a dropped ceiling had illuminated a scene of intense activity and concentration. Engrossed in the fascinating displays on their computer monitors, people sat at a half-dozen little islands scattered across the floor, at desks jammed up against a piece of wall, at makeshift tables blocking a doorway to another room. Each workstation harbored at least one computer. There were high-powered Indys and stack towers from Sun Microsystems and a sleek server from Digital, barely uncrated, its shipping box discarded at the foot of its owner's desk. Popcorn packaging spilled across the floor.

Two guys, both in their early thirties, were sitting next to a machine, peering at the screen. It looked like they were waiting for a response. Then: "Pepperoni! Definitely pepperoni!" the smaller of them said excitedly. He was a lank, pale fellow in shorts and T-shirt and he was controlling the keyboard. He had a small gold ring through his lower lip.

"Be serious. Ham and pineapple. It's got to be, Dim," groaned his companion, a huge man with a huge head, a jutting brow, and dark red ears that were the color of chicken livers. He sat in an old wooden chair, his arms folded gruffly in front of him. "Pepperoni," he rumbled, and shook his massive crown disgustedly.

Aside from these two, everyone was working alone, but the computers were all connected—by pairs of thick orange cables that ran from the backs of processors, twisted down the legs of the desks and ran across the floor, where they were held flat with pieces of sticky brown shipping tape. One of the cables from each computer seemed to link to all the neighboring machines, creating a nifty ad hoc local area network. The other cables ran to the corner of the room, and up the wall, to attach to one of a dozen red-blinking modems stacked, like stereo components, on wire shelving.

A guy with scalp-short, bright yellow hair sat at an adjacent terminal. He stood and moseyed over to the pizza pals, and leaned in over the huge man's shoulder. "Dim," he said. "What difference does it make? You can get two, can'tcha?"

Dim, it turned out, was not a value judgment but the name of the shorter hacker, who snorted in response: "Two? I could get two hundred."

The massive fellow smiled, tugged at one of his ears. "Delivered. Bwa-ha-ha-ha. Bwa-ha-ha!" He laughed maniacally.

Blondie fell to his knees and genuflected at the computer. "Praised be thee, O Pizza Hut Server! You provideth the dough! The cheese! The sauce and toppings! You delivereth life and art our salvation!"

"Amen," everyone in the room intoned.

"Who's paying the freight this time, Dim?" a dark-haired women in tie-dye asked from across the room.

"Who, indeed?" Dim echoed, arching an eyebrow. He slid his mouse up the keypad and pointed to a field on his screen. "The Mayor's Office. City of Newww Yawk. It appears our pizzas come from a Parks and Recreation budget account."

A polite smattering of applause from the room. Hardly anyone was even looking this way anymore, and the pizza-server hackers went on about their business.

That would explain, I guessed, the dozens of empty Pizza Hut boxes stacked like building blocks under everyone's worktables, by bookshelves, in the foyer, kitchen, hell, everywhere I looked. The grad-student decor was completed by the endless reams of paper that exploded from the wrong ends of laser printers. But here was an odd fashion statement: a glass-fronted gun cabinet against the far wall. I could make out the silhouettes of at least a half-dozen rifles inside. The lethal collection was an apt accompaniment to a nearby target-practice poster, which could have been stolen from a police academy shooting range. The black-and-white poster showed a man's torso, with a bull's-eye centered over the critical internal organs. A bullet hole punctured his heart.

A stack of oversize schematic drawings lay scattered across the floor as if a windstorm had ripped through the space moments earlier. In the background, I could hear a low hum of power, of energy, of the self-satisfied whir of a dozen microprocessors singing in chorus.

Everyone had gone back to their work. I registered: sunken eyes, careless dreadlocks, overgrown beards, all vaguely familiar. Then I experienced the nauseating gut-punch of déjà vu. I had seen each of these people earlier in the evening. They looked out of context to me now, writing code so intently, smoking home-rolled cigarettes, and staring, unblinking, at their screens. Earlier, I had passed them at Café Info as I had walked into the militia meeting. I recognized the waitress who had worn the Café Info T-shirt; the gum-chewing hacker from a nearby table who had held tweezers over a tiny spring mechanism inside a pair of headphones; and at the desk closest to me, the goggled man with a lank dark ponytail who had piloted the Virtual Reality Rocket.

The goggles were gone, but the look of intense concentration he had worn while playing the video game still owned his face. He reached a hand behind his back and groped, without looking, until he discovered a nearby file cabinet, on which sat an opened box of Entenmann's powdered doughnuts. His hand closed on one, but accidentally knocked the box to the floor. As he turned to survey the damage—the doughnuts had disappeared immediately in the general abyss of papers and thick orange cables and discarded cola cans below—his eyes met mine.

"You belong to Blaney."

"Or the other way around," I said. "Have you seen him?"

"He sleeps." He set down his doughnut, wiped powdered

sugar off onto his ripped jeans, and held out a hand. "I am Yuri."

"Harry."

"I assume you have been cleared, Harry. Or else you would not have a key," Yuri said.

"Uh-huh," I said. "Plus, I signed the loyalty oath."

"Loyalty oath," snickered Dim, without ever looking my way.

From a doorway that might have led to a kitchen—I no longer was making any assumptions about the floor plan of this particular apartment—Eddie emerged. He held a laptop aloft in one hand, as if it were a divining rod and he wanted to rule out the possibility of rain. The computer's motherboard dangled, exposed, eviscerated. In the other hand he held an open bottle of Red Dog. When he saw me, he stopped, took a swig, and said, "You disappeared."

"Errand." I gestured at the scene in the room. "I thought the meeting was over."

Eddie followed my eyes, then barked a short laugh. "My roommates."

"Cheap rent?"

"Cost-effective infrastructure. You know how much it takes to run a T-1 connection into an apartment, and then to maintain it every month? Doubt I could afford it on my own. And they sure as hell couldn't."

Eddie's apartment had been turned into an informal kind of a timeshare, where like-minded programmers and hackers and militia sympathizers could pay a low, low monthly fee in exchange for the privilege of connecting to the Net, round the clock, over a superfast hookup that pumped 1.5 million bits of data a second to them. Information-greedy bastards. With that kind of a deal, what did it matter that they probably had to share flea-ridden bunk beds and a single dirty shower stall, bereft of hot water?

Yuri said, "Eddie. You must look. It is algorithm, after all." He pointed to his screen.

"Let me get Harry settled first."

Translation: Let me get Harry out of the way.

I followed Eddie down a narrow hallway lined on both sides with closed doors. As he turned the knob on the last one on the left, he said, "Sleep in my room."

I wondered if he purposely chose the room farthest away from the hackers' beehive because he didn't want me to hear what was going on back there. Or because he didn't want me to catch a glimpse in the hallway of someone who was staying in one of the other rooms.

"Where's Blaney?" I asked.

Eddie shrugged. Then he flipped a light switch, and at first I thought that the place must have been burglarized. I mean, I live like a slob, but my disorganization was nothing compared to this wasteland. Piles and piles of junk covered every surface of the room. Grocery bags stuffed full of papers were stacked on a wooden chair. A makeshift desk of sawhorses and plywood groaned under the weight of more paper, more notebooks, discarded socks, a pyramid of beer cans, a half-dozen candy wrappers, and two more computers. There was a mattress on the floor, and Eddie swept aside a gelatinous mountain of tangled sheets and blankets and work boots and engineering textbooks to reveal a lumpy surface. On it sat a plate of sandwiches, half eaten. Bologna, I'd guess. "What, you don't like pizza, Eddie?"

"I'm fucking sick of pizza," he grunted. Then left me alone.

I closed the reinforced metal door that Eddie had installed on his private lair, and felt the knob click—automatically locking—under my hand. I was as tired as I've ever been, but instead of flopping down, I walked over to the desk. I glanced down and saw a meticulously hand-lettered chart that Eddie must have been working on recently. The coffee stain on the top page was still damp. I wouldn't even have to move other papers aside to snoop.

Fleetingly, I wondered if Eddie was the kind of guy to drape a single hair over his desktop to see if its contents were disturbed while he was away. Screw it; I knew he was that kind of guy. I picked up the paper to examine it more closely—and realized that Eddie had devised his own code. The writing on the paper was grouped as if in words and sentences, but on closer inspection, I saw that instead of letters, the "words" were composed of stiff, inked shapes I had never seen before. The first column had been blacked out, along with one corner of the paper, as if the resident crypto archivist had crossed out some markings underneath. Perhaps in anger? I held up the paper toward the ceiling light, and as the sheet turned translucent, I could make out the telltale alphanumeric evidence beneath: The first column was simply a list of Arabic numerals, while up in the corner he had written "A History of Knot, .01 beta through the present."

I could only guess at the kind of data Eddie had been compiling. But from the groupings in each column of the chart, it appeared that he was recording dates in the first column. And then perhaps synopses of something that had occurred on each date? What changes would he be tracking? Updates in the source code? It looked tedious, and the minute details of the work must have been pure torture to endure for someone as mercurial as Eddie.

The careful black lettering was the work of a man obsessed. But with what? With Knot? Or with Knot's creator?

Now, as I stood on the street outside Annie's building, I could smell coffee drifting down from the coffee shop on the corner. I was starved. Half past seven.

A dark sedan pulled up in front of her building, and double-parked. The doorman came out, leaned his head into the passenger's window to say something, then went back inside. The car idled for nearly five minutes before he returned, pushing a cart stacked high with suitcases and an instrument case. The cello was going. So this was a long trip. Annie hadn't mentioned to me that she was going anywhere. In fact, she had been lamenting that she had nothing to do for the next few weeks.

F
L
A
M
E
W
A
R

The driver popped the trunk so the doorman could load everything. Then Alicia Ames wafted out of the building. She put her hand on the doorman's arm to get his attention while she spoke. He nodded, and she handed him a folded bill, got into the car. It pulled away. Without Annie.

I waited another five minutes, then crossed the street. I went into the lobby, where the doorman sat at an antique writing desk, reading a newspaper. The sports section looked funny spread across the leather and gold-leaf blotter. He looked funny in a military-style doorman's uniform—gold braid and epaulets above a name tag that said Dominic.

His look let me know he thought it was too early to deal with visitors.

"I'm here to see Annie Ames," I said.

"Your name?"

"Harry Garnet."

"She's not home."

He looked back down at his paper.

"Are you sure, Dominic?" I asked. "We were going to jog in the park before breakfast."

He looked up. "You just missed her. She and her mother went out of town. I put them into a cab."

"Both of them?"

"Yeah."

"Could I leave her a message?"

"She'll be back in a couple of weeks."

"Okay," I said. "Thanks."

Back on the sidewalk, I hesitated. Alicia had warned the doorman to keep me away from her daughter. And where was Annie now?

Caffeine would help me think. I walked down to the coffee shop to get a large coffee and a Danish to go. The breakfast rush was on, so while I waited at the register to pay, I popped the lid and sipped. Scalding your tongue is an overrated way to start the day.

Behind the cashier, through the plate-glass window, I could

see Columbus Avenue waking up. A greengrocer swept the concrete to make it worthy of his tomatoes. In front of a bistro, a waiter arranged café chairs and tables beneath a green-striped awning. A constant stream of customers approached the corner newsstand to get a thick Sunday paper.

I reached the cashier.

"Two dollars," she said.

I set my coffee down and fumbled for bills.

As I handed her a twenty, I glanced back out the window—and saw Annie walk past the coffee shop and down the street.

"You got anything smaller?" the cashier asked.

Annie disappeared from my line of vision.

"Got a ten?" The cashier prompted me.

I barely heard her as I rushed to the door, pushed it open, and peered out. Now I could see her again, already half a block away.

"George," the cashier called toward the counterman. "Change a twenty."

George materialized behind me. He was holding eighteen dollar bills and the bag with my breakfast in it. "You in some kind of a hurry?"

"This is New York, isn't it?" I said, and ran as a bus pulled to a halt at the corner, just as Annie reached the bus stop. A woman with a baby stroller was ahead of her, slowly trying to maneuver up the steps. The stroller's wheels lolled crazily, and the front axle got caught in the doorway. But then Annie reached over, grabbed the back wheels, and the two women climbed aboard. I saw all this as I sprinted, blistering hot coffee sloshing onto my wrist. I was barely fifteen feet from the bus doors when they wheezed shut.

The bus pulled away from the curb. I cursed, drained my cup, and tossed it into a garbage can. My bike was still locked up back by Annie's building, so I had no choice but to run.

As the bus continued downtown, I barely kept it in sight, and I prayed it would hit a red light. It didn't, but two blocks later it stopped anyway, to discharge a passenger. Miraculously, it sat still long enough for me to catch up. Panting, I climbed aboard. I was in no mood for another cross-city marathon.

The sign on the fare counter said NO BILLS. I had no coins. The driver glared at me and the spill of dollar bills that I pulled from my pocket, but before he could kick me off, I heard the reassuring ring of quarters dropping into the turnstile. I looked around and saw that Annie had paid my way.

She looked at me worriedly.

"Are you crazy, Harry?"

The bus jerked away from the curb, and we both grabbed for the back of a seat to steady ourselves. There were only about five other people aboard. She pulled me down next to her near the front.

"Hi, Annie," I said. I was still trying to catch my breath. Sweat ran down my forehead. She, on the other hand, looked very clean and cool. I took in the whole picture. Khaki shorts, a bony scraped knee, an errant strand of hair escaping from one of those ponytail bands with the clear plastic balls on the ends, the kind that all the third-grade girls used to wear. A better-looking version of Jane Goodall.

"I looked out the window and saw this nut running after the bus. I thought, no. It can't be," she said. She pulled a tissue from her backpack and handed it to me. I wiped my face.

Between gasps, I managed to get out, "Had to talk to you."

"Why didn't you just come over to my mom's apartment?"

"Tried. The doorman said you left with your mom."

"What?" She looked like she didn't believe that one at all.

"It's true," I said in a plaintive tone that of course made it sound like a lie. Now that I could talk again, I shifted to prosecutor mode. "In fact, your mother lied too. Maybe you could explain why she told me yesterday that you were going out of town with her."

"She did?"

"When she was pushing me out the door of her apartment."

Annie's skepticism faded and was replaced by a small smile. "What's so funny?"

"My mother. She was trying to protect me, I guess. She's suspicious of you."

"Suspicious of me? What, that I might pocket the silver?"

"No, worse. The FBI asked us a lot of questions about you."

"What kind of questions?"

Annie hesitated. I could see her wondering if she should be suspicious of me too.

"FBI," I prompted her. "What did they ask?"

"They kept going over the sequence of events. The events before the bombing, you know. Were you the person who always delivered mail to the cottage? Why wouldn't we just go down and pick up our packages at the front desk instead? Did I notice you hanging around at all before the explosion? Was there anything odd about you?"

The day Annie and her father checked into The Vines, I was thrashing in the bushes behind their cottage, looking for Peterson's volleyball. I emerged with a handful of raspberries, a chigger bite, and the ball just as they pulled around the curve in one of those golf carts the guests loved to use to transport suitcases. Ames's look told me he didn't welcome trespassers. "One of the guests lost this," I had said, holding my treasure aloft. Was that odd? Did Annie consider that hanging around?

"My mother thinks it's weird that you weren't hurt very badly. And that you came down to the memorial service. That's all."

"Annie, can you do me a favor? Don't tell the FBI anything else about me. Do yourself a favor, in fact, don't tell them anything about anybody."

She looked at me oddly.

"Have you ever heard of Patriot?" I asked. I realized, probably too late, that I would sound paranoid if I started to spout off about government conspiracies and secret codes. "Look,

I'm just saying, how do you know who you can trust? Other than me, that is."

"You're a jerk, Harry."

We rode in silence for a couple of blocks, both pretending to look out the window, feigning fascination with the interchangeable merchandise on display at the Gap and Benetton outlets that we seemed to pass at every corner. Certain retail chains have reached critical mass in Manhattan. There's no more room for expansion. I wouldn't be surprised to see the Starbucks sales clerks out in the street wielding sharpened coffee stirrers, fighting the khaki-vested employees of Banana Republic for the right to renovate the last empty storefront on Columbus Avenue.

"Annie."

She turned from the window and looked at me, still mad. Her face was blotchy. "What?"

"We don't know each other well enough to fight this much," I said.

She relented. "I don't think the FBI considers you a serious suspect, Harry. My mother's another story. She's very wary of tall, dark-haired men who act as if they don't respect life's niceties."

She was appraising me as if I were debris she'd just pulled from the ground and she was trying to decide if I was an ancient jug handle or a candy wrapper a tourist dropped yesterday.

"What?" I demanded.

"It's just that another rather odd thing happened. Unrelated to my mother's suspicions, which makes the timing even stranger."

She pulled a folded sheet of printer paper from her pocket.

"Remember that Nelson guy? Who kept sending me the E-mail about my dad?" she asked. She unfolded the paper and handed it to me. I read, MS. AMES. DID YOU KNOW THAT YOUR FRIEND HARRY GARNET IS ASKING A LOT OF QUESTIONS ABOUT

YOUR FATHER? I RAN INTO HIM AT A GATHERING OF SOME OF THE PROFESSOR'S FORMER STUDENTS. IT SEEMED A LITTLE ODD— UNLESS YOU SENT HIM.—NELSON

"A gathering of former students." I snorted.

"What's so funny?"

"The guy is trying to pick you up. What's more, he's a dangerous nut. Gathering of former students. He's a radical, tax-evading crypto flamethrower. And you're thinking of going out with him?"

The bus brakes protested as the driver pulled up to the corner of Columbus and Seventy-ninth. Annie stood. "You wear me out."

She left me sitting there and climbed off the bus. She walked away, not looking back. I yelled out the window: "Do you always leave without saying good-bye?"

The doors cranked shut and the driver put on his blinker. But then Annie turned, as if she wanted to say something, and that was enough for me. "Wait, let me off," I yelled at the driver, adding, for effect, "I'm going to be sick."

I ran to her. "Sorry," I said. It startled me to hear the word come out of my mouth.

"Truce," she said.

We crossed the street and walked a block to Central Park. As we left the concrete and stepped onto a dirt horse path, I felt the temperature drop about ten degrees. It was such a shock to walk under trees again and to see the world through the watery green light of leaves. I forget, whenever I come to New York City, that shade exists. And that dirt has a smell. A good smell. I filled my lungs with it.

"So you never heard of this Nelson guy before he sent you E-mail?" I asked.

"Well, he said he had met me. Once in my dad's office. A while back. It sounded legitimate, because he even described from memory this dress he said I was wearing at the time."

I told her about my online encounter with him at Café Info.

F
L
A
M
E

W
A
R

"I don't think he's dangerous, Harry. But then, I don't think you're dangerous, either. You're both too direct. The bomber doesn't like to confront his victims."

"Thanks for the vote of confidence. Just do me a favor: don't take Nelson up on any of his offers to meet, okay?"

We walked along a winding, hard-packed path, heading deeper into the park. The traffic we'd left behind sounded like a distant ocean. She plopped onto a bench and pulled off one of her washable leather Keds. "I've had a pebble in here for the last fifteen minutes." She rubbed a blister on her heel, and the sun was in her face, so she was squinting. On most women, this would not have been an attractive look. But it worked for her.

"Why don't you seem to care that the FBI thinks you're a suspect?"

"Because I don't trust the FBI."

I stood on a precipice. If I jumped, there would be no return. I could have pulled back at that moment, chosen to protect her rather than to enlist her. But I was a coward. I wasn't afraid for my life. What I feared, at that moment, was being alone. I'd lived with isolation for as long as I could remember. Annie was the first person I had ever met who I wanted to *tell* anything to. So I couldn't resist. I conspired with her. That was my weakness, and I fully expected to pay for it later.

But what a relief to tell someone about meeting Lionel! About the Urban Militia and their mysterious plotting! I admit that the part of the story in which I raced uptown and through Grand Central Station on my bike sounded ridiculous now, in the light of day. A few yards away, on one of the park's shaded avenues, parents wheeled Peg Perego buggies past us and rollerbladers whizzed by carrying boomboxes and wearing kneepads with "Warp Speed" written across them.

Annie listened with such total absorption that I could almost imagine her constructing a complicated mental flow chart with all the facts and variables of the case neatly connected by arrows. She was going to catch this killer. I could either help her or get out of the way.

I said, "About your dad hanging out in The Zoo—" Then fumbled.

"Harry, don't worry, you aren't destroying any illusions."

"Well, I didn't know him. Maybe he had some other reason for being there," I said.

"People don't always have reasons for what they do. Do you think he had a reason for abandoning my mother, leaving her alone with a little kid and a demanding job and moving up from Washington, D.C.? Did he have a reason for not answering the letters I used to send him? About a month before my birthday, every year, I'd write a chatty note . . . 'Hi, Daddy, how are you?' I wouldn't even *mention* my birthday. I'd hope that the mail would jog his memory."

"Sorry."

"That's not my point. I don't think he consciously meant to hurt me. I don't think he had a *reason* for being a rotten father. He just was, you know. I don't think he had a reason, particularly, for coming back into my life later, either. Maybe he was lonely. Maybe he was nervous around kids and was waiting for me to stop being one. Maybe he was afraid I'd find out about his 'Zoo' life and kept me at arm's length until I was old enough to not judge him. He liked equations, logical processes that took one from A to B. Children are essentially random creatures. I don't think he could have explained his actions then. People often try to rationalize things to no avail, Harry."

"I wish we could *reconstruct* some of his actions. Like, what he did online." It was too bad that everything on The Zoo was encrypted, using Knot, or else we could have read the archives. I would have liked to look through her dad's old posts. His E-mail.

"Maybe Lionel Sullivan could do it," Annie said. "You said he helped install the Knot program on The Zoo. Maybe he knows how to get around it. The FBI was asking me about Lionel Sullivan too, you know. Why is *he* still alive?"

"Because the bomber sometimes makes mistakes," I said.

"Maybe. He's some filthy rich software developer or something. The agents actually seemed quite in awe of him," she said.

I told her Lionel wasn't really your classic victim. Sure, he had flailed around after he got out of college, with his parents expecting him to go to medical school. The war had just ended and there wasn't anything left to dodge except the future, so he had declared his intentions with odd jobs. A slummy apartment. A roommate who didn't talk much, just sat in the corner at a computer.

"It was one of the earliest Apples. When his roommate moved to California, Lionel bought it with his savings."

He learned how to write programs, simple applications to make it easy to write business letters. "Pretty soon friends started asking for copies. Then his father's friends wanted copies. Pretty soon, he was also doing technical consulting for big corporations. That's the part of the business he still has."

"Horatio Alger for the end of the century," Annie said. "Then he wrote Knot, right?"

She stopped and looked at a screaming toddler being led firmly away from a cotton candy vendor.

We walked for a while, and then she said, "Other people always thought my father was reasonable and good-natured. Which was true, ninety percent of the time. But once in a while, some little thing would set him off and he'd throw a chair across the room. I saw him do that at the cottage, the day before the explosion. He was reading his E-mail, and something got him upset," she said. "My mother wanted him to take care of her. That made him angry. I think that's really why he left her."

"Why did they get married?" I asked.

"Sex, I guess," she said. "Some people can't help being attracted to poison, if it comes in a beautiful bottle and smells like vanilla custard. At least I can't, and I have an object lesson in my parents."

"Am I poison?" I asked.

"Nope. Nor do you smell like vanilla," she said. "Bicycle grease and Cutter's mosquito repellent is more like it."

"You have a great capacity for forgiveness."

"Because I indentured myself to his ego, typing his correspondence, filing his notes, reminding him the phone bill was due?" She laughed. "I don't think I did him any favor, in the end."

"Why not?"

"He was very competitive with me. I know that seems silly, a grown man with enough graduate degrees to wallpaper the Louvre. For years, every time I'd see him, he'd pepper me with math problems. Long addition. Then later, algebra. Four people on a train, two in yellow slickers, one in a windbreaker, together they travel a total of six hundred miles. The blue shirt gets off at the first stop . . . Where do the rest disembark? I'd have to solve it in my head, immediately."

"Why was that competitive? Wasn't he just trying to teach you?"

"On those holidays when he remembered my existence, he sent me books of puzzles. He wrote to me in code, and I had to crack his encryption scheme before I could see what my father had to say to me."

Ahead of us, I could see the tall iron gates at the entrance to the Central Park Zoo.

Annie had a zoo membership card (of course). We walked through the admission gates, then over to the pool where the seals were doing lazy morning laps.

I should have realized then that someone other than me could have been waiting for Annie to emerge from her building a couple of hours ago. But even now, playing back that scene, and that day, I can't point to anything that would have tipped me off that someone else had followed us across Manhattan. All I remember from the zoo is a little kid up on a man's shoulders by the seals, squealing, delighted. A woman videotaped his reaction. Sometimes I wonder, now, if her camera caught a glimpse of something important that I missed. If I could play that video, who would I see in the background?

"I'm thirsty," Annie said and bought a couple of those frozen cherry push-ups that melt down your hand before you can eat them. "Let's go see the polar bears."

We wound our way up the foot ramp at the back of the zoo, past the native flowers and blueberry bushes that these days required constant Parks Department tending to keep alive. At the polar bear exhibit, we found a small patch of not-so-smeared Plexiglas, a two-by-two space where no other people had their faces mashed up against the wall. Up on the rocks, the bears seemed oblivious to the eyes of a hundred tourists. An enormous white one sunbathed. Another swam. Cubs wrestled. Annie sat on the ground, cross-legged, and pulled her laptop from her backpack. She started to type.

"Notes," she said. "I'm keeping a journal on these bears."

"What does that have to do with anthropology?"

"I like to study how they act. Animals are like dead people. You can get pretty close, pry into what they're doing, their daily habits, in a way you can't with live people."

A cub wanted to go into the water, but hesitated.

"There's a strict hierarchy. The cub knows its limits," she said.

"That's how it used to be in my family too," I said.

She stopped typing. "It changed?"

"When my dad died."

"You didn't tell me your dad died."

I shrugged.

"I won't take notes." She flipped down the lid of her computer. "I have noticed that you seem to know a lot about how to get around New York City for somebody who lives upstate and hates it here."

"We lived here when I was little."

"Was your mother a police officer then?"

"Both my parents were. That's how they met. But she was from Timber Lake, you know, where she lives now. After a while, they had a kid. The usual."

"So they moved back home with you? And they were both on the force in Timber Lake?"

"No, my mom retired for a while."

But my father had become chief of a five-officer force. He liked it because in a small town he could really see the impact of his work—at least that's what my mother told me. I don't have any recollection of him as an idealistic person. I remember how strict he was. Not unfair, you know, and he never hit me. But he didn't give an inch, not when drivers whipped down the town's two-lane highway doing seventy and not when his five-year-old son stole a pack of spearmint gum from the grocery. He wasn't the kind of guy who liked to toss a ball around in the yard. He'd go outside and then realize that the grass needed cutting and the weeds were getting high. He believed in chores.

"When did your mom go back to work?"

"When I was ten. After he died."

One night my father got a call that there was a lot of yelling coming from the Kendricks' house on the edge of town. A domestic, he called out, I'll be back in an hour or so. I remember how he looked in his clean jeans and sweatshirt. He had no time to change into his uniform. He just tucked his badge, encased in a cracked brown leather wallet worn shiny over the years, into his hip pocket. He must have had a sense of humor that I didn't see, because otherwise why would Ellen have married him? But I don't remember how he looked when he smiled, if he smiled. That night he drove off just as it was getting dark, the same way he'd driven off a hundred times before. I can still see the moths, confused in his headlights. That's all we heard until about three hours later, when a squad car drove up the road. My dad wasn't inside.

The sergeant, a bald guy named Peterson who later retired from the force to run an aging summer resort, got out of the car and walked slowly up to the screened porch where my mom was reading to me. When she saw him coming, she sent me inside.

"It was a stupid death," I told Annie. "Husband is waving a gun at his wife. My dad gets in the middle. The gun goes off."

"Your dad was a hero, then."

"I don't believe in heroes."

"But you believe in law enforcement."

"What do you mean?" I asked.

"You're a lawyer."

"Not because I love laws. Not because I want to perpetuate order or anything like that," I said.

"Then why?"

"It's safer than being a cop. You don't have to get your own hands dirty, but you still get to tell people what to do. You solve their problems. Nice and clean."

"You could be a prosecutor. Send the bad guys to jail?"

"Nyah. Corporate law. I'm going to tell big companies how far they can push the envelope and still be legal. I get off on yelling orders at pompous guys in expensive suits."

"You're not a horrible person, Harry. So why do you say such terribly cynical things?"

"So you don't fall in love with me," I said. "I'd hate to break your heart."

"I don't think you want to be that kind of lawyer," she said.

"Just watch me."

We watched a big, cranky bear shoo the cubs into a cavelike indentation in the man-made habitat. Talk about your oxymorons.

"Time for lunch," Annie said. "They do this every day at noon."

Noon.

"I've got to go," I said.

"I thought you were going to protect me from the bomber. You can't disappear just because you have an appointment."

"Had an appointment," I corrected. "I have to drive back upstate. I'm late for my Blaney pickup."

"What's a Blaney?"

Which gave me pause. How to explain the cranky hacker who was no doubt pacing his cousin's apartment, cursing my name? I looked at this woman who liked nothing better than to study unusual life-forms, and I said, "Blaney is an enigma wrapped in a filthy T-shirt. Come and see for yourself."

The sky was clouding up, so maybe the radio had been right after all. There was a green tinge to the air, which Annie said reminded her of Illinois during tornado season. She lived there one year while her mom was on a teaching fellowship at a music school.

We took a cab back to her building to pick up my bike.

"Can I ride on your handlebars?" she said as she hoisted her backpack.

"The subway's just as fast."

The first drops hit us as we reached the entrance to the IRT. We could hear the roar of a train below us, so we ran down the greasy concrete steps. We hit the platform just in time to see the train disappear around a bend, its last car derisively shaking its butt at us. I asked the token clerk if she would open the gate so I could wheel my bike through. She peered through the bulletproof glass surrounding her booth, then leaned way into the sound-distorting microphone that theoretically connected her to my world. I don't know what she tried to say, but what came out on my side of the cage sounded like the enraged protests of a wounded brontosaurus. I gave up, shouldered my bike, and limboed through the turnstile.

Annie plopped onto a wooden bench. "In the movies," she said, "the cute couple always makes it to the train at the last minute."

During rush hour, with the crush of thousands of hot bodies and the fear that you'll never be able to squish onto one of those overloaded trains, you don't have time to really survey your subway surroundings. But on a Sunday afternoon uptown, the abandoned station felt as foreign and unknowable as an ancient tomb. I felt, for a moment, like an explorer who stumbles onto evidence of a long-dead civilization. Some earlier people with customs I would never fully understand had hollowed out this world beneath the world, mortaring public rest-room tiles to the wall to spell out DOWNTOWN LOCAL and TRANSFER HERE.

Annie and I were the only ones down there, in that underground cavern where the temperature was fifteen degrees hotter than the street and the walls were sweating. Correction. About twenty feet away from us, a homeless guy was sleeping in a refrigerator box that said THIS END UP.

I walked to the edge of the platform, peered down into the rail beds. They were so soot-blackened and bedecked with filthy candy wrappers and shredded muck that I marveled at the fact that the trains rarely derailed. I felt a faint rumble under my feet, and miraculously, another train appeared.

"That was fast," Annie said, bounding aboard.

"Like the movies," I said.

A half-dozen other people were in the car, so we had our pick of the molded orange benches. The passengers stared through us, dull-eyed. The train lurched, I sat.

I tried to straighten the front wheel of my bike, which was wedged against a metal column, so that I could stretch out my legs.

The train picked up speed again, hurtling toward the blackness ahead, and as we hit a curve, I was reminded of the bobsled event in the Olympics. But the run down the icy bobsled tunnel would be marked by a lack of sound, or the white noise of the blades below and the wind rushing by. Here on the train, you were mugged by sound. We lurched down the tracks, barreling into the long curve, and I leaned reflexively into Annie. A new move.

The train slowed, hard, and I saw the lights of the next station. Another five or six passengers boarded, including a group of teenagers wearing sneakers with lights winking on their heels. The doors closed and the subway jolted forward again, into the darkness. A couple of older women carrying a hundred shopping bags settled onto the bench behind us.

This time I didn't hear the brakes screech. Instead, the train decreased its speed gradually, like a sailboat when it loses the wind. Eventually it rolled to a gentle stop. Outside the windows, I could see only blackness. We weren't at a station. We were trapped in a long tunnel.

"Another fucking breakdown," the teenager with a pierced nose said to his friend.

"I sat for an hour last week. I can't stand it," said his friend. He stood, peered through the glass, saw nothing. "We should just get out and walk."

The other passengers did not react. To be a New Yorker is to grow inured to the indignities of the subways. Like Pavlov's dog, they had been conditioned. When the train stops, you wait. They made no eye contact. A man wearing a rumpled blue shirt with his name sewn over the vest pocket slumped for a nap. He had probably been headed home to bed anyway. One of the women behind us rustled through her bags, and I heard her say, "Edith, have I shown you the photos of my grandchildren on vacation? They went to a real dude ranch."

Then the lights went out.

We might as well have been at the core of the earth. Dim light came, every few yards, from naked lightbulbs high on the walls of the tunnel. Still we seemed to be in a deep, dense place, where the weight of the darkness got heavier by the second. The world was suddenly a very quiet place.

The only light inside came from the winking bulbs on the L.A. Gear shoes.

"Harry," Annie whispered.

"It's okay," I said. My voice sounded too loud. "There's probably just a traffic jam at the next station."

Five minutes passed. The air-conditioning had gone off with the lights, so it was getting hot in the car. I felt perspiration on my forehead. But no one said anything, or moved. I could feel the tension level ratchet up a couple of notches. The passengers were starting to wonder if they'd spend the rest of their lives down here in the dark.

"Harry."

"What?" Now I was whispering too.

"I'm afraid."

"Of what?" But I realized, then, that I was afraid too.

"This isn't normal."

"In New York, it's normal," I said, trying to convince myself.

"It's been too long. They should have made an announcement."

"They couldn't make an announcement. The loudspeakers don't work."

"Where's the conductor, then?" she asked. "Why isn't he walking through the cars to calm us down?"

"Everybody else is calm," I said, just as one set of winking shoes walked over to the middle of the car and kicked a door. Hard.

"Fuck," the kid said. "I want out."

I heard a soft noise, sort of a whoosh, as if the wind were being sucked into a vacuum. I thought it was a terrible sound, and I remembered why: The last time I had heard it was during a drought five summers ago, when some dry acreage of scrub pines went up in flames near North Creek.

Then I saw the fire. The car in front of us lit up, orange, as the flames rushed through it. The fire took the passengers in there by surprise, the way a brushfire startles rabbits, and I could seem them scramble, pushing against the windows, the doors, rushing down the aisle toward our car. They seemed like a vision of hell, my hell at least, dim and distant silhouettes you could reach for but never touch. I heard someone scream, "Get out! Get out!" The harsh voice was my own.

chapter eight

T he door at the front of our car burst open, and passengers fleeing the fire spilled through. The litter on the tracks was burning, and the paper advertisements that lined the walls of the car ahead were almost melting in the heat. The fire was fueled by the motor; I smelled hot metal and overcharged wires, the PVCs of melting plastic. Blistering heat chased the passengers, and the teenagers tried to push the jammed door shut behind them. But the metal was too hot to touch and all of us were beginning to be affected by the smoke.

I pulled Annie with me to the double doors in the middle of the car. They were locked. I tried to jam my fingers into the black rubber strip where they met, but I could not force them open. Then I threw my shoulder up against the stainless-steel panel, putting all my weight into it. It hurt.

All around us, passengers were scurrying crazily. Some were trying to unlock the door between our car and the one behind. The man in the blue uniform shirt was trying vainly to open a transom window. The New Yorkers had panicked.

"We have to break a window," Annie said into my ear.

"With what?"

"Your bike pump."

I ran back and pulled it off the frame. It was metal. It weighed about two pounds.

"Use it like a battering ram," she yelled.

I climbed up on one of the seats. The fire had invited itself into our car by now, and the seats where the teenagers had sat were melting like ice cream. The boys had run to the other end of the car, where they cursed and slammed themselves against the door that separated us from the next dark car. But it was jammed.

I struck the safety glass with the bike pump. I rammed it again, and again and again, but it did not give way.

Next to me, Annie had opened one of the transoms. The opening was about eight inches deep, and the metal frame felt hot enough to brand. "Can you get through, Harry?"

If I could, so could the others.

I slid my shoulders through, body surfing in the subway. I could see the electrified rails ten feet below. Would the tracks fry us? Attached to the outside of the car was a handle. I grabbed it, somersaulted like Greg Louganis, and landed in the dirty rail bed.

"Come through feetfirst!" I yelled up.

"Over here," I heard her call to the other passengers. "Come this way. Hurry!"

Above me was a bare bulb, crusted in black grime but emitting a glow bright enough to reveal the graffiti on the concrete walls. Someone had sprayed a fat white WOE on the wall. If kids walked in here with paint, there must be some way for the rest of us to walk out. Then I spied the narrow strip of concrete that ran along the edge of the wall about three feet off the ground, a path to inch along. I tried not to think about all the rats that lived down here, tried not to wonder if they were lining up against the walls as curious as a parade crowd on the Fourth of July. See the survivors. If they survive. I turned back and yelled, "Come on, Annie."

But she didn't climb out. Instead, she and the teenagers were hoisting Edith through the window. I reached up to guide her down.

"There's a walkway!" I yelled in the woman's ear. "Head away from the fire!"

The rest emerged one by one. Down the dark tunnel, I could see other passengers scurrying out of other cars and away from the fire, which had by now spread halfway through our car.

How much time did we have before the train blew up?

"Annie! Where are you?"

There was no answer. "Annie, come out!"

Then I heard her voice. "Here, take this first."

Out the window came the backpack, dangling there in the red glow. She had gone back for the computer.

Then Annie was out the window, and I guided her feet to the ground. "Now what?" she said. "That way?" She turned to follow the others.

"Wait."

We were alone by the side of the train. The others had disappeared around the bend. We could hear their voices in the distance.

"Harry, we don't have time."

"Annie, that fire spread too fast. Someone started it."

"What are you saying? Come on, we have to go."

"Annie, listen." I clutched her arm. "I think he's out there."

She stared at me, her eyes wide and terrified. We looked down the dark tunnel. We couldn't even hear voices anymore.

"He's waiting for us down there?"

"Trying to flush us out of the underbrush, like rabbits in a forest fire."

"Oh, God." She hugged herself.

"This way." I pointed to the burning car ahead of us.

"Through the fire? How?"

"Not through it. Past the fire. Climb up."

I boosted her to the ledge. Then I handed her the computer bag and climbed up myself, grasping a metal pipe that stuck out from the sheer cinder-block wall, feeling for toeholds in the crumbling mortar. We inched forward, backs plastered against the sooty wall. In that way, we passed the burning car, flames less than two feet from our faces. I felt Annie reach for my hand, but could not bear to look away from the inferno. We had almost reached the cooler darkness ahead when the cars' windows started to blow out from the pressure. We heard a series of explosions, immediately followed by the glass shattering against the stretch of graffiti we had just passed.

"Harry, look!"

Inside the car, in the motorman's booth, a man slumped over the controls. Blood dripped down his temple onto his lap, from what looked like a bullet hole.

Five more steps, and we were clear. We stayed on the ledge. The farther we walked from the fire, the less we could see ahead. A distant siren echoed, and I could not tell if it came from ahead or behind.

"Faster," I urged, vaguely thinking that we had to put more distance between ourselves and the burning wreckage.

Then I heard the footsteps ahead. We both must have heard the sound at the same time, because just as terror washed over me, Annie froze. "He's here."

The footsteps got louder. I wondered if he meant to shoot us in the head, like the motorman. I wondered about it in a clinical way. But there was nothing I could do. Oddly, the closer he got, the less I feared. In truth, I wanted to face him, to jump for the throat of this madman who had bled terror all over my life. I wanted the chance to try to stop him. I crept forward, as silently as I could, headed straight for the sound of the heavy, steady footsteps.

Then a flashlight went on, about twenty feet ahead of us, and the arc of yellow light swung over the walls and came to rest on my face.

"Who is it?" I yelled. "Who the hell are you?"

"It's me. Lionel," came the answer. He had the police with him.

Even though we only had a few minor injuries, the rescue crew strapped us onto stretchers and carried us through the dark subway tunnel, back to the world.

A bunch of FBI agents, including the two from Syracuse, arrived at the hospital before the emergency-room doctor finished bandaging a cut above my right eye. They had changed their ties. They didn't look happy to see us. Or Lionel, who stayed at the hospital that night, pacing the waiting room like a first-time father expecting twins.

"This is my fault," he repeated to the nurses, the doctors, the FBI agents, and my mother, who must have set a new land-speed record because she arrived at the hospital before dark. I heard my mother approach my room long before I saw her. Her gait is like no one else's, a demand for the confrontation that always lies just ahead. I felt relief when I heard loafer soles slapping linoleum, a sound she didn't try to soften in deference to patients who were asleep.

She pushed open the door, nodded briskly to the uniformed cop who was baby-sitting me in the brief absence of the FBI agent, who had stepped out into the courtyard for a cigarette. She snapped her badge at the officer, pulled a chair up to my bed, flipped it around, and straddled the seat. Her face was about a foot and a half away from mine, her arms were resting aggressively on the chair back, and if I didn't know her better, I would have thought the furrow in her forehead was from worry. But I knew her well enough to recognize her anger. She doesn't like surprises, not anymore.

"New pants?" I asked.

The crease in her chinos could inflict a wound not unlike a paper cut.

"I stopped at Kmart in Albany on my way down," she said dryly.

"You cannot resist a sale."

Other mothers might have fallen, weeping, onto their sons, shrieking, "Oh, my God! Thank the Lord you're all right!" or whatever it is that parents say to offspring who have narrowly cheated death for the second time in a month. Other mothers might have demanded to see the doctor immediately for a progress report. Or grasped their husband's sleeves to steady themselves as they gasped in horror at the sight of their firstborn in a hospital gown.

Maybe my mother would have acted like that too, if she had had the luxury of a spouse—or any other support system. But she, like me, had believed for some time now that there was no one else to depend on, no one except yourself. I knew she would have stopped at the nurses' station already, demanded my chart, flipped through it. She would have answered the medical questions in that way. She was here now to resolve the rest.

We were buying time, taking each other's measure in the same wary way that had defined our relationship since the night, back when I was seventeen, that I had drunk a six-pack of beer and wrapped the family car around the lamppost down near The Vines. Peterson drove me home. She went to get the car. We never spoke of the incident again.

"I think you have been holding out on me, Harry," she said finally.

"I have, Mom, it's true. For years. You know practically nothing about my friends, my sex life, or the job opportunities I've turned down."

"The bomber came after you again. Why?"

"You're asking me? I'm a threat. Or Annie's a threat. I don't know why. I'm not holding out." But I was, of course, because I told her nothing about the urban militia, mainly because I wanted to understand it myself first.

She considered, then said, "I think it's time I introduced myself to Annie Ames."

"Don't scare her off, Mom. You know how hard it is for me to get girls."

The FBI agent came back into the room, notebook already flipped open, an air of preoccupation on his face. Then he stopped, did a double take, and said in amazement, "Ellen?"

I don't think I'd heard my mother's first name spoken aloud in about five years. Back home, she's known as Chief. And I'm sure I've never seen her stand up to shake someone's hand before.

"Bill Dellis," she greeted him. "I wouldn't have recognized you, except for your voice."

"Well, I would have known you anywhere, even after nearly thirty years," Dellis said. "You're working the case?"

"Just tangentially," she said. "I work upstate now. Harry's my son."

Then Bill Dellis said a remarkable thing to my mother. "I like your hair short."

My antennae went up, and I examined the special agent critically for the first time. Buttoned-down shirt, crisp pants, medium-expensive navy jacket. He had a slight tan and a boyish lock of still-brown hair over one eye. Compared to the other law enforcement officials I had recently become acquainted with, he looked like Calvin Klein.

Involuntarily, my mom—er, I mean *Ellen*—shot a look in my direction to see if I was following the nuances of this conversation. To head off an Oedipal crisis, she hastily put her hand on the shoulder of the man who could only have been an old boyfriend, and led him out of the room.

I lay behind, marveling at the world—and confident that, pro that she was, Chief Ellen Garnet would work him for information. Probably over dinner.

The next morning I wandered down the hall right after breakfast to see Annie. I found her untouched meal on a cart outside her room, and discovered her sitting up on the edge of her bed, nibbling a chocolate croissant and wearing a hospital gown tied at the neck and a pair of dust-mop slippers—pink, of course—from the gift shop. On the windowsill sat a bouquet of yellow roses.

She was talking to Lionel, who had dragged an armchair close enough to allow him to stretch out his legs and rest them, familiarly, on the bed frame. He wore a white linen shirt, blue jeans, and woven fisherman's sandals. He looked much better today. He was talking urgently and she was leaning forward, to catch every word. Her face said she desperately wanted to ask him a question, but he raised his hand, like a school crossing guard, to make her wait. When I came through the door, he straightened.

"Harry!" He jumped up and put a hand on my shoulder, indicating that I should take his seat. "You look . . ."

"Like hell. I know." I sat. "I don't remember getting the cut above my eye."

Annie inspected it and announced, "I don't think you'll scar."

Lionel settled lightly on the edge of the bed, comfortable with the idea of invading Annie's space, confident that she wouldn't mind. I said to him, "How long were you following us?"

"I was behind the bus. In the van."

"You weren't in the train?"

"I expected you to go to Eddie's apartment. I was above you, driving south, when I saw people stream out of the subway station at Seventy-ninth Street, yelling 'Fire.' "

"Are you going to follow us around for the rest of our lives now?" I asked. I didn't sound grateful.

"As long as you're my responsibility. I drew you more deeply into this. Have you eaten?" Lionel proffered a paper bag with the familiar Starbucks logo.

"Just crap," I said, rummaging through the pastries. "Don't let me interrupt your conversation."

"We were talking about The Zoo," Annie said, somewhat defensively.

"How Knot works," Lionel added gently.

"It's an ingenious program," Annie said. "The thing is—" She lapsed into the thought she had been exploring before I came into the room. "You wrote it. You know it. You can control it, and I think you have a moral obligation."

"You know better, Annie. You're letting emotion take over, which is what the bomber wants," Lionel said.

"I want you to eavesdrop on the citizens of The Zoo, to intercept their conversations and decrypt them," she said.

"First of all, I can't," Lionel said.

"Why not?" I asked, to remind them that I was present.

"The way Knot works, Harry. It's different from Patriot, where a third party, like the government, would have access to a key. It works on the simple but ingenious principle that says: Why use only a single key to encrypt and decrypt? It's far more secure to split the key in half, keep half to encode and send a message, while the other half of the key goes to the recipient, so he can use it to decode the text after it arrives. Both halves are necessary. That's what ensures security. This has been the dominant form of cryptography for nearly twenty years, ever since three professors at MIT created an encryption technique to take advantage of split keys."

Annie interrupted: "Don't patronize us with a lecture on the history of public-key cryptography. But since you brought up RSA, let me remind you that the fellows at MIT who created it didn't think their algorithm could be breached, either. They offered a reward to anyone who could crack RSA. And let me further remind you, Lionel: They had to pay up. Any encryption technique can be surmounted."

"Annie, you're being disingenuous," he said, but he sounded indulgent, the professor pleased at the efforts of a precocious student. "They paid up nearly twenty years after they issued the challenge. It took sixteen hundred computers, working together, more than six months to crack RSA's 129-digit key. I can't duplicate those efforts. I have fewer than a dozen machines at my disposal, which couldn't possibly identify enough unit vectors to crack Knot."

"Lionel, Knot can be cracked."

"Not by me. I have tried," he clarified. "Unsuccessfully. Of course, you're free to try too. Anyone can. The algorithm isn't exactly secret, Annie. It's been published."

Annie folded her arms defensively.

"Look," Lionel continued. "I want Knot to be uncrackable. I want the citizens of The Zoo to keep their privacy. But I don't for a minute kid myself. Any code will ultimately fall to a brute-force hack, as you said. I'm content to know that mine is secure enough to weather virtually any attack modern technology can muster. I've staked my life's work on the proposition that people have a right to retain what little privacy and attendant individual identity is left to them in this age of technological intrusion. Knot is my humble contribution to that goal.

"Even if there were a way, a trapdoor, say, or some other way to decrypt Knot, I hope to God I wouldn't use it," Lionel said. "I believe in the right to privacy. If I were to abandon that belief, then the bomber would win. I might catch him, I might live to see him behind bars, but I would know he had destroyed me."

Annie slid her legs off the bed, stood stiffly, and said, "Oh, that's absurd. Lionel, don't follow me around anymore. You have the power to protect me, and Harry, and yourself, and all the other innocent people who are fooling around on The Zoo. But you won't. So don't patronize me by trailing me into the subways. That won't stop the bomber."

She hobbled out of the room, still sore from yesterday's acrobatics. Where she was going I had no idea. It didn't look like she would get too far before she needed to sit down again.

In the awkward silence that followed, I said, "So. How do you like Annie?"

Lionel snorted. "I don't think she likes me."

"Well, the yellow roses were a good start," I said, gesturing to the bouquet. "How did you know they're the only flowers she likes to have around?"

"I wish I'd known. I'd have brought some," Lionel said dryly.

"They're not from you?" Curious, I walked over to the vase and plucked the card from the little envelope that dangled from a thorny stem.

I read it aloud. " 'Sorry to hear about your mishap. Feel better and stay safe. Sincerely, Nelson.' "

Lionel looked up, sharply. "He knows Annie? How?"

"He knew her father," I said, surprised that Lionel was surprised. "I thought he was a friend of yours."

"We've never met in person," Lionel said.

He walked over and took the card from my hand, read it again, silently.

"How did he know she liked yellow roses?" I repeated.

"How did you?"

"She told me," I said. "In unencrypted E-mail."

It was getting to be a habit, checking out of hospitals. I inventoried my gear. Belt. Wallet. Oh, shit—key to my bike.

"Don't worry," my mother said, as she hoisted a plastic bag full of my dirty clothes over her shoulder. "Bill Dellis said we can get the bike from evidence in a few weeks. They don't need it."

"What else did Bill Dellis say?" I asked. "Am I still a suspect?"

We walked down the hospital hallway, not commenting on the smell of sterilization that we both were coming to dread.

"Who said you were a suspect?"

"Annie."

"Really must have a private talk with that girl," Ellen mused.

"Well, you'll have your chance."

Annie had agreed, somewhat reluctantly, to come upstate with us for an indefinite amount of time. My mother's invitation to sleep in the spare bedroom didn't exactly qualify as protective custody, at least not officially. But my mother did have a quasi-official status in the case, anyway, with the mandate to help the FBI investigate the bomb that exploded in her jurisdiction. Besides, Annie's only other option appeared to have been to stay alone in her mother's apartment in New York, no doubt lying awake at night wondering if any creaking noise she heard meant that someone was jimmying open the front door. Annie had shown no inclination to stay with out-of-town friends until the case was over, and I could tell she didn't feel safe on her own. At least my mother carried a gun.

She nodded to the nurses as we passed.

"How did he shoot the motorman without the passengers knowing?" I asked.

"Cut the power. Used a silencer made from a Coca-Cola can."

"How did he start the fire?"

"Arson Squad is investigating," she said.

"Did any of the other passengers see anyone in the tunnel?"

"Not so far. A few haven't been interviewed yet," my mother said. "Is that your last question?"

"When are you going to see Dellis again?"

She swatted me with the plastic bag.

When we got to my mother's house that night, I carried Annie's backpack into the second bedroom. She traveled as light as if she were headed for a camping trip. Then I found my mom also making up the sofa bed in the den. I hadn't seen her actually handle bed linens in about ten years. The sheets were mismatched.

"Thanks, but I think I'll recuperate at my own place this time."

"I'll leave the sheets. Maybe you'll move back in after the next hospital stay?"

"Annie's the one in danger."

"You've been in the wrong place twice now," she pointed

out. "You're thinking that maybe it's happenstance? I don't believe in that. I don't think you know what you're doing and I wish to God you'd stay here."

That's the way it was with my family, or what was left of it. We were always making these pronouncements. The things we didn't believe in could have filled a dump truck. Heroes. Happenstance. Happy endings.

I went back to my house to a stack of junk mail, an electric bill for $23.11, and a refrigerator scented by spoiled milk.

As long as he's out there, he'll be plotting to get to us. That thought had set up shop, like an unwelcome mantra, in my mind. The danger was heightened, of course, by the knowledge that I faced an adversary who changed personality, who would abandon the distance of mail bombs to move in close when it suited him. He was a particularly cunning hunter. Unless, as the FBI agents had remarked as they questioned me in the hospital, I had managed to do something *new* to piss off a second killer. I catalogued all the reasons to fight back. There were plenty of things I'd lose forever if the killer got me. I'd miss the way that the hard-packed dirt in my mother's driveway turned to red dust in surprise if we had three days in a row without rain, powdering my shoes with a fine reminder of past mud pies. I would miss the curious sharp quality of the air, which could carry the scent of a distant wood fire right to my nostrils and tweak them with the intensity. I would miss the taste of just-caught trout fried in lemon butter, and the sting of the lemon's juice as it seeped into a torn blister on my palm. Most of all, I would miss the big view, the sweep of the land visible from the top of Burns Mountain, irregular undulations and indentations of the glacier-tamed earth as it fell away toward the sea. It wasn't time to relinquish the big view.

Annie and I had agreed on that point, at least, which was what spurred us to set up a rustic command post in the corner of my mom's living room. As if she were a traveler from an earlier century, she had brought provisions to conquer the Adirondack wilds. But whereas a Victorian woman of a certain age traveling by carriage to a $2.50-a-night hotel on the shores of nearby Raquette Lake might have brought flannel underwear to stave off cold nights, balmoral boots for hiking, and elbow-length kid gloves to deflect the persistent blackflies, Annie's weapons were aimed at defeating the region's technological deficits. She had a surge protector to plug into the wall, to act as a liaison between the lackadaisical electrical current and her computer's delicate innards. She had a mouse pad and glare screen to keep the midday sun from rendering her monitor useless. She had an ergonomically acceptable keyboard, split down the middle and adjustable to fit the angle of her hands. I watched admiringly as she unpacked this gadgetry.

But that was the extent of the frontier camaraderie. Whatever alliance we had struck in Central Park, before the subway fire, was gone, replaced by a wary cordiality that almost made me wonder if she suspected *me* of planting the bombs. I could imagine how her puzzle-solver's mind might twist things: Why did Harry insist that we take the subway? Why did he steer us toward that particular downtown line, that specific train, the one car located directly behind the bomb? The theory would have been outlandish, probably no more than one step away from suspecting me of causing the sudden rainstorm that had splattered us that same afternoon. As Annie had explained to me, you have a better chance of cracking a code if you try every possible combination of solutions. And she had the attention span to do exactly that.

That was what made Annie dangerous. She was the kind of woman who would have the necessary fortitude to hack someone else's ATM card password. In my mind, I could see it: She'd just stand at the machine for 7,351 hours straight, patiently punching in sequential four-digit combinations until she hit the right one. Maybe it would be snowing, yeah, a blizzard, and she wouldn't have gloves. But would she give up?

Not Annie. Her fingers would get sore, then they would bleed, then finally they would develop huge, thick calluses. Still she'd be standing there, brute-force code cracking. Whatever it took.

It was unnerving to sit next to her, hour after hour, watching her focus so single-mindedly on the screen. She was trying to unlock the secrets of Knot. My mind was not equal to the mathematician's daughter's when it came to encryption theory. And so, we were next to each other in the physical world, but she was far away. My leg was less than a foot away from hers, we hunched our elbows on the same edge of the vinyl-covered card table, we breathed the same air. But in truth, she inhabited a different land during those times, and sometimes wouldn't even notice if I got up and walked away.

Once she had settled into a routine, Annie seemed content to stay at my mother's house indefinitely. One night after she had been there for a week I came in to find the computer off and Annie sitting with her legs curled under her on the sofa, facing my mother, who sat in a wicker armchair with her feet up on the edge of the coffee table. Even in midsummer it gets cool at night in my town, and Annie sat under the checked wool blanket that had been on my bed when I was a boy. They looked up quickly—guiltily?—when I came in, and then Annie went back to her post in front of the computer. To this day, I don't know what they were talking about. The case? Me? The persistent E-mail messages she was still getting from Nelson? (My mother had promised to try to track Nelson through the alumni records at Columbia, but so far had no luck. Maybe he'd done so poorly in Ames's class that he had decided to change his name.) Or maybe the dark, bad possibilities that must have welled up in Annie's mind late at night, when she lay in bed, unable to sleep. I know she suffered in that way; she must have, because I did.

Even if my mother wasn't her confidante, her old roommate, David Who Took Bootsie to Europe, was. Close as I hovered when she was on the phone with him, I never could hear a word of what she said. She had mastered the art of whispering without *appearing* to conceal her conversation. One thing I knew about old davidr, though: You don't place daily transatlantic phone calls to a woman just to update her on the condition of her cat.

I, on the other hand, spoke to no one.

Except Annie. When it was business.

And so we sat, day after day, trying to track a killer through the dark alleys of cyberspace. Annie had become obsessed with Knot, because the encryption program had locked up all the secrets of The Zoo. Stored somewhere in a computer were the archives that included her father's E-mail correspondence, the conversations that transpired between him and the others he met at The Zoo, the lines of scrambled code that could explain so much if they could be decoded. But Lionel had refused. Not only that, but he had issued an inadvertent challenge to Annie when he told her that Knot's security was unassailable. I watched her load a copy of Knot's software onto the machine, and then dissect the program. Annie was not the kind of hacker who would sneak around, guiltily trying to hide her footprints. Instead, she had sent Lionel E-mail, warning him of her intent.

"Good luck," he E-mailed back.

His taunts only strengthened her resolve. I couldn't see how we'd find the bomber at all if the two of them were engaged in their own private war over political philosophy. I told her so, but she wasn't paying attention, because Lionel had E-mailed her again: "Don't waste your time. Drive down here and read my files instead."

To which she typed in reply, "Never underestimate the desire of a code breaker."

She told me that she couldn't break Knot unless she got root access to The Zoo. She needed the same universal privileges to mess around the system as the system administrator had. "Then, if I could sit silently and watch all the encrypted packets of information whiz by me as people sent them to each other on the system, I might have a chance."

"Why?"

"Timing, among other things. I could tell something about the program just by watching it work. Even a computer program makes mistakes. I might see a whole chunk of plaintext—that's a portion of the message that didn't get properly encrypted—pass by. That would give me enough information to crack the code."

She scrolled down her E-mail directory as she talked.

When she hit RETURN, the computer displayed a record of all the correspondence she had mailed. Time, date, recipient, all in a neat list.

As I read off the items, I realized that the bomber wasn't after us at all. It was the first true revelation of my life.

"Harry? You look sick."

I pointed, like the Ghost of Christmas Past. "It's the computer he wants."

"What do you mean?"

"Your dad's computer. It was supposed to blow up with him. But it didn't."

"How does the bomber know that?" she asked.

"The broken date stamp. Every time you post something on The Zoo or the Internet, that machine leaves a personal calling card. He must have been following us onto the subway, and so he knew you had it with you when he set the fire."

She stared at the laptop, as suddenly repelled by its innocuous gray case as she would be by a rattlesnake.

"My dad's files."

"Annie, remember the Minotaur's message to your dad. 'I know you don't want to agree to my terms.' Your dad had some information on his computer and the Minotaur wanted it. He still wants it."

Without a word, she typed a command to list every file on the hard drive. The list appeared almost instantaneously: copies of mathematical papers he wrote and submitted to scholarly journals. Copies of correspondence to the dean of his department, from whom Ames was hoping to receive authorization for a new fax machine. A surprising number of games from software that would simulate a pinball machine on his monitor to Omar Sharif's Bridge for Experts to word-guessing puzzles and matching games and five thousand ways to play solitaire.

She studied the list thoughtfully. "You know, Harry, there's not enough here. Not enough files on the hard drive."

She typed another command.

"See?" Annie said. "It says here that most of the room on the hard drive is taken up. But the items listed in the directory don't use nearly that much space. So where is the rest of it?"

"Could files be in another directory, a subdirectory?" I asked.

"No. This should be comprehensive."

"Your father loved puzzles."

"He hid the files somewhere. I know they're in here," she said.

The computer interrupted us. We had logged into The Zoo and the welcome screen scrolled across the monitor. We had been transformed into Wolfer. The neighborhood was starting to seem familiar.

WELCOME, WOLFER! YOU ARE BEHIND THE WOODSHED. IT IS GETTING DARK, AND MOST OF THE OTHER ANIMALS ARE BACK IN THEIR DENS.

"Let's explore," she said. "There's always some starting point, a place where a lot of the players congregate," Annie said. She typed: NORTH.

The screen beeped: YOU COME TO THE ZOOTROPOLIS BUS STATION ON ROUTE 1. YOU SEE A DOOR TO THE MAIN DEPOT— MUCH FURRY FUN AWAITS INSIDE! OR YOU CAN WAIT HERE FOR THE BUS, WHICH WILL TAKE YOU ANYWHERE YOU'D LIKE TO GO. IT SHOULD BE ARRIVING ANY MINUTE NOW . . . WHY, HERE IT IS!

THE NUMBER 7 BUS DRONES INTO THE STATION. YOU MAY ENTER THE BUS. TO THE SOUTH IS THE WOODSHED. TO THE NORTH IS PIG'S PEN.

ENTER BUS, she typed.

YOU ENTER THE BUS. THE DRIVER, A 1,900-KILO ORCA NAMED RALPH CRAMMED-IN IS WEDGED BEHIND THE STEERING WHEEL. RALPH ASKS: WHERE YOU GOING, WOLFER? IF YOU'D LIKE TO CONSULT A MAP, TYPE: SEE MAP. OR, MAY I RECOMMEND A FEW HOT SPOTS?

"I don't get it," I said. "Is Ralph a real person?"

"Software, I think," said Annie. "It looks like he's part of the bus code. Wait. Let's see . . ." She typed:

RALPH, DO YOU KNOW WHO THE PRESIDENT OF THE U.S. IS?

The computer responded:

RALPH SMILES MEANINGFULLY AND WOULD LIKE TO HELP. IF YOU'D CARE TO CONSULT A MAP, TYPE: SEE MAP. OR, MAY I RECOMMEND A FEW HOT SPOTS, WOLFER?

"Software," confirmed Annie. Clearly, Annie had done some research since the first time we had logged in. I raised my eyebrows in question. "I've been checking out MOOs," she said.

"Okay." Her fingers flitted across the keys:

SEE MAP.

The computer beeped and a crude ASCII "map" made out of slash marks and asterisks and dashes rolled up the screen, laying out some of the more popular haunts of The Zoo: Penguin's Polar Cap. Serpent's Rock. Effrodite's Purrfect Playpen and Sushi Bar. Maya's Trunk o' Fun. The Garden of Mirthly Deelites . . . There were easily three dozen places listed.

"So hard to choose," I grumbled. "And they scrolled by too fast."

"Also, there's no way to know if any of these places is currently inhabited," said Annie, who typed:

HOT SPOTS.

RALPH LEERS AND WHISPERS IN YOUR EAR: HENRI'S HOT TUB IS ALWAYS BUBBLING WITH EXXXCITEMENT AND IT HAPPENS TO BE MY NEXT STOP. THEN HE WINKS AND LICKS HIS FINS SUGGESTIVELY. HERE WE ARE . . . HENRI'S HOT TUB! NEXT STOP, SINTHIA'S TERRARIUM . . .

F L A M E   W A R

Annie typed: LEAVE BUS and immediately, more text scrolled by.

WOLFER EXITS THE BUS AND FINDS HIMSELF STANDING IN A COOL GLADE OF GOLDEN ASPEN TREES. HE MARVELS AT THE SHIMMERING, SPADE-SHAPED LEAVES AND LISTENS TO THEM RUSTLE . . . BUT WHAT ELSE DOES HE HEAR? GIGGLES, NEARBY. A PATH LEADS OFF INTO THE WOODS AND IS MARKED BY A SIGN THAT READS: HENRI'S HOT TUB! EAST! HAVE FUN, WOLFER!

"I guess we want to go east," I said. The computer beeped. We had company.

MARISSA SCAMPERS INTO THE ASPEN GLADE.

MARISSA SAYS: HI WOLFER!!!

GREETINGS MARISSA, Annie typed. Then, she typed, LOOK AT MARISSA.

MARISSA IS A PUBESCENT FEMALE RED FOX, read Marissa's description. SHE HAS A SMOOTH & FLUFFY STRAWBERRY-BLOND COAT AND A BUSHY TAIL THAT CURLS COQUETTISHLY ALONG THE LINE OF HER FIRM RUMP. A GOLD RING DANGLES FROM HER NIPPLE AND GLINTS BECKONINGLY. SHE NOTICES YOU LOOKING AT HER AND WONDERS IF YOU LIKE THE SAME KINDS OF DIVERSIONS SHE DOES.

MARISSA ASKS: WHATCHA STANDING HERE FOR, WOLFER? ALL THE FUN'S IN THE HOT TUB. TIGGER'S IN THERE AND SO IS TALLULAH AND BIG TUNA AND XERXES. A NEW GAME OF TRUTH OR DARE IS ABOUT TO BEGIN!!!

"What should we do?" Annie said.

"Up to you. It's been a while since I played chicken with a badger."

We stood there, or rather Wolfer did, as lamely as a missionary at a nudist colony. Then the bus roared up. Ralph Crammed-In to the rescue. Annie typed: ENTER BUS. We scanned the map once more.

"I bet the Unicorn Inn has a lobby where people hang out. And we can pick up the gossip."

GO TO UNICORN INN, Annie typed. A moment later, we debused. Only to find a weird—relatively speaking—banner:

THE INN BURNED DOWN LAST NIGHT, WOLFER.

YELLOW TAPE CORDONS OFF THE CHARRED REMAINS OF THE UNI-
CORN INN. YOU SEE A POSTER SLAPPED ONTO A CHARRED STICK,
STUCK IN THE GROUND. THE SIGN SAYS: "THE OFFICIAL UNICORN
INN INVESTIGATION (#76544) IS UNDER WAY. CITIZENS OF THE
ZOO WILL BE KEPT ABREAST OF DEVELOPMENTS."

"It was virtual arson?"

"Sounds like it," Annie said. "It had to be, didn't it? Everything that exists in The Zoo is just a bunch of lines of code
that people wrote to describe characters, places, and actions.
So then somebody else had to go in and erase the code that
described the Inn. That passes for arson online. There's another of your coincidences. My dad gets blown up in the real
world. And the place he frequented online burns down."

"How did it burn?" I wondered.

Annie typed: SEE #76544.

She got a curt, and official response:

ALL DOCUMENTS RELATING TO THE INVESTIGATION CAN BE
READ IN THE ARCHIVES AT HTTP://WWW.ZOO.COM/INN/INVES-
TIGATION.HTML.

"We should take a look at that Web site," Annie said. "The
people who run The Zoo must have put the documents on
the World Wide Web so everybody could read about what's
going on without tying up bandwidth on the MOO."

"Let's go later," I said. "I need to know more about The
Zoo first."

We were like those European explorers from an earlier century who set sail across the Atlantic, knowing intuitively that a
new world existed but having no specific idea of what it would
be like. The Zoo turned out to be a place that was at once
familiar and unknown. Familiar, because there were other hu-
mans already there, and they spoke the same language. Unknown, because all the plants looked different, and if you
looked up at the sky at night, the stars were in the wrong
place.

I had never before considered the possibility that a place

could be a place if it had no *physical* properties. In the old world, with air and ground and bodies and buildings, everything had mass and texture. You could describe anything based on how it looked or smelled or sounded or felt. In The Zoo there were no atoms of anything. This was a world of bits, of pure imagination, a world where my mind created an image based on minimal descriptive suggestions. Conjuring up the Unicorn Inn was like a dream you have at night, but more vivid. I had envisioned it looking much like the rambling white Victorian lodge at The Vines. What made this experience so different from a dream was that more than one person could inhabit this place at once. Annie and I both saw the same words on the screen. But that didn't mean that we interpreted the information in the same way, that we saw or felt or heard the same thing.

For all I knew, Annie had imagined the Unicorn Inn as a Marriott Hotel just off the expressway in New Jersey, with banks of escalators and a three-story glass atrium just past the registration desk.

A new text block appeared on the screen:

TORTOISE SLOWLY WALKS TOWARD YOU AND THE REMAINS OF THE UNICORN INN. TORTOISE HAS COME TO SEE THE DAMAGE FIRSTHAND.

TORTOISE SAYS: HI WOLFER.

WOLFER SAYS: HI TORTOISE.

TORTOISE SAYS: HAVEN'T SEEN YOU AROUND LATELY, W. HOWS HUNTING?

The surprise that we could communicate with other people on The Zoo reminded me of the early days of the telephone. But this was a lot wilder, because people using telephones have always known who was at the other end—and where the other end was. They could picture Aunt Millie picking up the phone in her kitchen, sinking into a chair at the table, and holding the mouthpiece close to say hello. Cyberspace afforded no such luxuries. Where was the physical spot out there in the universe where our words were meeting with Tortoise's? Was

Michelle Slatalla   **163**

it night or day outside the window of Tortoise's room? Was Tortoise at home or at work, typing surreptitiously in the office while the boss was in a meeting? Was Tortoise old or young?

I asked, "Why doesn't Tortoise know that your dad is dead? Hasn't the news reached The Zoo?"

"Wolfer's real-world identity is probably a secret. All the other players can see of us is our official description."

"And all we can see of Tortoise is his official description, I suppose?"

LOOK AT TORTOISE.

YOU SEE AN ANCIENT TURTLE, WITH GREEN AND GOLD SHELL DULLED BY YEARS OF SUN AND SEA. HE HAS CRACKS AND GOUGES IN HIS CARAPACE AND YOU WONDER WHO HAS TRIED SO OFTEN TO HURT HIM.

WOLFER SAYS: TORTOISE, I DECIDED TO STOP HUNTING ALTOGETHER.

TORTOISE SAYS: DOES THAT MEAN NO MORE PARTIES AT YOUR HOME, WOLFER?

"My home?" I asked Annie.

"All the characters have a home. A place they build and then inhabit. A location where other characters can come to hang out."

WOLFER ASKS: WHEN WAS THE LAST TIME YOU WERE IN MY HOME, TORTOISE?

TORTOISE GUFFAWS: DON'T BE COY.

WOLFER ASKS: WHO DID YOU TALK TO AT MY LAST PARTY?

TORTOISE SAYS COYLY: I WANTED TO TALK TO YOU BUT YOU SEEMED TO BE SO SMITTEN WITH MINOTAUR.

WOLFER ASKS: HAVE YOU SEEN MINOTAUR LATELY, TORTOISE? I NEED TO TALK TO HIM.

TORTOISE SNICKERS! THATS FUNNY. I WAS JUST TALKING TO HIM A MINUTE AGO, AND HE SAID HE WAS LOOKING FOR YOU.

"Ask him where we can find Minotaur," I said.

But another text block appeared on the screen:

WISE TORTOISE HAS DISAPPEARED INTO A CLOUD OF SMOKE. YOU SEE ONLY A FOOTPRINT LEFT BEHIND.

"How'd Tortoise do that?" I asked.

"When you log out, or exit, or go from one location to another, the software signals everybody who's left behind that you're gone. If you want to make a really grand exit, you can substitute your own customized text for the default text."

Annie typed: WHERE IS TORTOISE?

TORTOISE IS ASLEEP IN HIS SHELL.

"Asleep means he logged out. Went back to the real world. His character is idle," Annie said.

WHERE IS MINOTAUR?

MINOTAUR IS ASLEEP IN HIS MAZE.

We had missed him again.

GO MAZE, Annie typed. "Let's see where he lives," she said. But a few seconds passed, and then:

YOU CAN'T GO THAT WAY.

"Why not?" I asked.

"Lots of people 'lock' their homes when they're not online. Now what?"

"I want to know more about your father's parties," I said. "I want to know who he invited, what they did, where his home was. I want to know the geography and the terrain. I want to be able to draw a map of this place."

This time I was the one who typed GO.

WHERE DO YOU WANT TO GO, WOLFER?

GO HOME.

YOU TRAVEL NORTHWEST FOR ABOUT FOUR MEGABYTES, UNTIL YOU LEAVE BEHIND ALL THE HOUSES AND BUILDINGS. YOU ARE IN THE FOOTHILLS NOW AND YOU CLIMB A ROCKY PATH. THE PATH IS WELL CAMOUFLAGED BUT LOOK CAREFULLY AND YOU WILL SEE THAT IT FOLLOWS THE CURVE OF A DRIED-UP STREAM-BED. YOU TURN A BEND, AND BEHIND THE BRANCH OF A TALL FIR TREE, YOU SEE THE OPENING. WELCOME TO WOLFER'S CAVE.

I typed: GO IN.

INSIDE THE MOUTH OF THE CAVE IS A DEEP BLACKNESS. YOU ENTER CAUTIOUSLY, SNIFF THE AIR FOR INTRUDERS. REASSURED, YOU WALK ALL THE WAY IN, BACK ABOUT TWENTY FEET. CONGRATULATIONS! YOU'VE FOUND THE SEX WORKSHOP! ALL AROUND YOU ARE SEXUAL APPLIANCES AND FUN DEVICES. PRIVATE ROOMS ARE IN THE BACK, BEHIND THE STEEL DOOR, WHERE YOU CAN SPEND QUALITY TIME, ALONE OR WITH FURRY FRIENDS.

LOOK AT CAVE, Annie requested.

WHAT AT FIRST APPEARS TO BE AN ANIMAL'S DEN IS ACTUALLY A WELL-APPOINTED LIVING SPACE. A STEEL DOOR IS ON THE FAR WALL. AS YOUR EYES GET ACCUSTOMED TO THE GLOOM INSIDE, YOU SEE A WALL OF BUILT-IN SHELVES, FILLED WITH HUNDREDS OF TOYS. FEEL FREE TO PLAY WITH ANYTHING YOU SEE HERE. YOU ALSO NOTICE AN INDENTATION THAT ON CLOSER INSPECTION TURNS OUT TO BE A FIREPLACE. IT'S STACKED WITH KINDLING AND WOOD, READY TO LIGHT. A PACKAGE OF MATCHES, WITH A VELVET COVER THE COLOR OF MIDNIGHT, LIES ON THE STONE HEARTH. YOU HAVE ONLY TO STRIKE ONE TO GIVE YOURSELF LIGHT AND WARMTH. ABOVE THE FIREPLACE IS A LEDGE, ON WHICH SITS AN UNUSUAL CARVED PIECE OF EBONY. A PHRASE IS BURNED INTO ITS SURFACE. HINT: LIGHT A MATCH TO READ.

READ PHRASE, Annie typed.

IT'S TOO DARK TO READ THE PHRASE.

"Come on," Annie groused, then typed: LIGHT MATCH.

YOU MAKE OUT A PHRASE ETCHED INTO THE EBONY. IT SAYS: THERE IS NO PRIVACY.

Did this description evoke the same image to Annie as it did to me? In my mind, I was seeing Bachelor Pad. I was thinking about how Wolfer was probably a swinging guy, er, wolf, out here in the hills. I was wondering what visitors he had brought to his cave. Neither of us typed anything, so we both jumped when the computer beeped and spit out a phrase without a prompt.

ARE YOU TIRED, WOLFER?

"What a bizarre thing to ask," Annie said. "I've never been in a MOO like this before, where the software suggests emotions or states of being to the players. Why does it want us to go to sleep?"

"What happens if we do?" I asked.

SLEEP, she typed.

THANK YOU FOR VISITING THE ZOO FOR 31 MINUTES, WOLFER. YOU HAVE LOGGED OUT AND LEFT YOUR CHARACTER ASLEEP IN THE DEN. YOU HAVE FROLICKED A TOTAL OF 17 HOURS AND 32 MINUTES THIS WEEK. YOU HAVE USED MORE THAN YOUR ALLOTTED TIME. NEXT TIME YOU LOG IN, TYPE "ACCOUNT" FOR MORE INFORMATION ON HOW MUCH YOU WILL BE BILLED.

"We have to go back," I said. "We need to meet other players. We have to see where the Minotaur lives. We need to—"

I looked down at my arm, which Annie was clutching tightly. "It says that Wolfer has been logged in for more than seventeen hours during the past week."

I read the text again. "Maybe it's an accounting error?"

"No. Somebody has been using my father's identity to sneak around in The Zoo."

chapter nine

A nnie noticed first that the phone had been ringing for some time.

I ran to the kitchen and answered on the fiftieth ring: "What do you want, Blaney?"

"How did you know it was me?"

I could have told him that I had been waiting for his call, with equal parts dread and anticipation, ever since the night of the meeting at Café Info. I could have told him that I had known this call was inevitable. What I hadn't known was the nature of the demands that the new and more dangerous Blaney would make when the moment arrived, or how I would respond. Winging it had always worked for me in the past. But now the stakes were higher, and I had more than the consequences to my own miserable hide to consider. I had Annie's interests to protect as well. The voice on the other end of the line sounded low and unfamiliar, as distant as if he were calling from inside a lead-insulated bomb shelter fifty feet underground. Or from an untraceable, black-market cellular phone that he had programmed to scramble digital transmissions. Or, perhaps from the pay phone outside the laundromat, one of two such open-air kiosks down on Jasper Street that had developed a reputation over the years for static-laden connections.

"Anyone else would have hung up, Blaney. You are the only person alive who loves the mammoth interconnected systems of computers that comprise the phone system enough to stay on the line long after it becomes obvious that no one is going to answer at the other end. Only you love the sound of a phone ringing, for its own sake."

"You answered, idiot. So it clearly was not obvious that no one was going to answer. That's a fallacy of logic, and further—"

"You were sure I was here, weren't you?" I had suspected that he was watching me during the past few days, not because of any evidence I had obtained, but more because the lack of his overt presence, coupled with his sudden absence of interest in my condition, was notable. I wouldn't say that I was looking uneasily over my shoulder every time I turned a corner, seeking the unmistakable shadow of his Pillsbury Dough Boy silhouette. Although the terms of the social contract between Blaney and myself had been altered somewhat precipitously in the past few days, I wasn't afraid of him, at least not physically. I had more immediate worries, what with wondering whether the G.I. G-men who had been assigned to follow Annie and me everywhere were there for our protection—or as a threat. Or maybe they were using us as bait to lure the bomber.

With Blaney, I feared his mind, and wondered at the savage twists his thoughts might take, pulling him away from the comparative safety of Computer Nation and toward anarchy. Or did I fear the ramifications of the shift in our own relationship? In the world I had lived in comfortably for so long, Blaney was the subordinate. In this new, hazardous environment, however, Blaney was something else. The enemy, maybe.

"Why are you spying on me now, Blaney? Can't Nelson tell you anything you might conceivably need to know?"

Silence.

"Hey, I thought you didn't trust phones," I said. I hooked a foot around a chair, pulled it out from the kitchen table, and sat. I propped my elbows on the table. By habit I performed the same lazy motions that had accompanied practically every phone conversation I had had in this room since I was fifteen years old. But for the first time, I was acutely aware of the effects of even such simple actions: the feel of the wooden slats against my back, the harsh scrape of unpadded chair legs across linoleum, the stickiness of my elbow at rest in an errant blob of grape jelly that hadn't been sponged up after breakfast. I was aware of the absurdity of it—of the juxtaposition of the normal and the horrific, of the damp dish towels draped over the stove door while outside in the darkness a killer stalked me.

"Speak to me, Richard."

"The time for jokes is over, Garnet."

"You called me."

But from where had he placed the call? It was unlikely, under even the most mundane of circumstances, that a lifelong paranoid like Blaney would phone from home. And the mundane had long since disappeared from the horizon around here. My mother had informed me, in fact, that Blaney had dropped out of sight rather abruptly after I had last seen him at Café Info. The FBI had wanted to question him after the subway fire, she said. They wanted to talk to everyone I had been in contact with in the days preceding the incident. But when agents had gone to knock on Eddie's door, they got no answer. And when they had breached Blaney's warren upstate, they found a filthy crib, but no Blaney.

My mother had told me that Blaney was presumed to be on the run. "On the run? From what? Did Bill Dellis tell you that?" I had scoffed in what I hoped was a convincingly disbelieving voice. "You know he drops out of sight every once in a while."

"Yes, Harry, Dellis whispered it to me over a candlelight tryst. I was so tipsy from red wine that I fell for his crazy talk," she said dryly. She peered at me calculatingly. "You seem a little defensive. I just mentioned it because I was worried about the twitchy fellow. I'm surprised you aren't."

I had shut up at that point. It's not that I didn't trust my own mother. Or that I was becoming paranoid myself. But you might excuse me for thinking that things had gotten a little confusing around here, what with all the attempts on my life, and stuff. And what good would it do to explain to her that Our Richard was mixed up in some shadowy scheme to subvert the government's attempts to imbed little listening devices into all of our phones and computers? What would it help to tell her that a strange man in aviator glasses—perhaps wearing government-issue lenses?—had been surveilling Blaney and his friends? She would have asked me, in a syrupy voice, if I had taken to wearing an aluminum-foil shield under my base-ball cap to deflect the CIA's laser death rays. She would have demanded that I make an appointment to have my skull X-rayed for fractures. She would have thought I was crazy. Hell, I half thought I was crazy.

"Garnet, can you listen for once? This is an emergency, and the only thing I need to know is if you will meet me."

His voice was desperate and pleading. I found that comforting.

"You're not still stuck down in Manhattan, are you?" I said, my tone light, reeling him in.

The question was not entirely facetious because Blaney did not navigate life gracefully. I could picture him stranded in perpetuity at Eddie's, staring like a loyal dog at the door, waiting for it to swing open. Waiting for me. When I didn't show up as promised, I expect that Blaney panicked. He did not live in the kingdom of common sense. He would not have known who to call, where to look, what to rule out. He would have suspected the worst: government plot! assassination! a ploy to use me to get to him! Even after it became clear that I had been hospitalized after a subway explosion, his worries would not have been assuaged. I saw how my problems would have become mixed up with his own, in his mind, how he could easily have confused the events as a clumsy plot aimed in his general direction.

He had gone underground for sure, but how? While he was a man who considered train timetables a thing of architectural beauty—in the abstract—Blaney never stopped to consider the practical ramifications. He was not the kind of person to know the location of a *train station*. To buy a ticket would have required the foresight to stand on line (not to mention cash).

The memory of being abandoned was still fresh. "You could have called me. Eddie and I were freaked out when you didn't show up."

I let that pass. "So what's your emergency?"

"Not over the phone."

"You want to meet?" I asked. "Where are you?"

"In town," he said, and then I heard muffled sounds from his end of the phone. Whatever he was up to, he wasn't alone. His voice came back on, louder than before. "Meet me at the place where people go to eat."

It wouldn't be hard for anyone wiretapping this conversation to figure out that he meant Raymond's. This town only had one restaurant.

"Maybe." I thought about the missing files on Ames's laptop. "You might be able to help us figure out something."

"Us?" More whispering, then, "You come alone, Garnet."

"Are you coming alone, Blaney?"

But he had hung up already.

I looked up to see Annie in the kitchen doorway. "I'm coming with you," she said. "It's not safe."

"Good reason to accompany me," I said sarcastically. "That way we can both be killed."

"Everything you've said suggests Blaney can't be trusted," Annie said.

I remembered the gun cabinet in Eddie's apartment.

"You don't think he'd hurt us, do you?" I asked as I turned over the idea in my own mind. I didn't think he'd confront me directly.

"He's a coward," Annie said. "But he might very well be using my father's account on The Zoo."

We sat on a red vinyl banquette in the back booth at Raymond's Pizzeria and Eatery. Everybody I knew ate there once or twice a week. The peppers were fresh. The mushrooms were canned. When you got sick of pizza, you could order a sub. "My legs are sticking to the seat," Annie whispered.

"You don't need to whisper," I whispered. Then, louder, "You do look a little sweaty."

Raymond's was always hot. A big air conditioner was mounted in the transom over the front door, and you couldn't miss seeing it if you were a tourist looking for lunch. But the motor in that dinosaur hadn't turned over once in all the years I'd been eating there. And even in the Adirondacks, where the air was usually so cool you wanted to drink it, a brick oven could raise the temperature of a room by about twenty degrees.

"I wonder if this heat will crash the CPU," Annie said.

I was surprised that she had brought the laptop here, and that she would risk logging onto it in front of Blaney. I would have left it at home. The way I looked at it, we had enough problems trying to focus on one problem at a time, and the question of what Blaney wanted seemed to be the most pressing item of new business. But Annie was not easily diverted from her goals, and she had set herself the task of unraveling the mysteries of The Zoo. She would not rest, by God, until she had solved the puzzle. If Blaney's tardiness presented an opportunity to explore the strange terrain we needed to understand, then she would take advantage of it.

By now, the sound of the modem dialing into the Internet was as familiar to me as loons out on the lake.

I wanted to log back into The Zoo immediately, but Annie vetoed me. "First let's check out the Web site they set up to inform people about the fire at the Unicorn Inn."

I agreed, but now it was taking about ten years to get the document to come up on the screen.

"Don't fidget," Annie said. "Your legs make sucking noises when you move them on the plastic."

"Vinyl."

"Whatever."

Another six years passed.

"Why—"

"Don't ask me why it takes so long," Annie said. "Why do you always manipulate the conversation so that I end up playing the role of Apologist for Technology?"

"I was going to say, 'Why don't I get you a refill on that cherry Coke.' "

"Liar."

"So why does it take so long?"

"It's because there are millions of documents archived on the Web and our modem is sorting through them slowly. Not enough bandwidth. If you went into the biggest library in the world, and you wanted to find one little pamphlet in a corner of a reading room on the fifth floor, don't you think it would take a while to put your fingers on it? We're searching through a huge, disorganized card catalog, trying to figure out which computer houses the document we want to read. Okay?" She sounded a little annoyed.

I went to the counter to get more ice.

When I came back, the screen had finally changed. A banner across the top read: MAMMAL NEWS . . . BROUGHT TO YOU BY THE FURRY FOLKS WHO RUN THE ZOO . . . NO NEWS TOO LEWD TO PRINT.

The letters were in big red type, sprawled across a technicolor scene of tranquil mountains ringing a lake. It looked a little like one of those old Budweiser clocks, where the video image of a campsite was on a screen behind the minute and hour hands. The scene moved, as if you were making a full 360-degree swoop of the area, until the image came full circle and you were back at the tent.

The main difference was that The Zoo scene on the computer screen never repeated itself. It was like a home video that somebody made by holding the camera out of a car window. Strange terrain flashed by behind the words, changing from wilderness to some high-tech, chrome-theme City of the Future, and then turning into a desert on the outskirts of town.

Under the banner was a menu of the different topics that you could read, just by clicking on an item.

- ZOO COMMUNITY STANDARDS
- MEMBER DIRECTORY
- HISTORY OF THE ZOO
- CALENDAR OF LOCAL EVENTS
- NEWS: THE DEATH OF THE UNICORN INN

Here's the thing about the Internet. You think you're looking for information about a fire, but on the way to looking it up, it's easy to get sidetracked by all the other data out there. Each menu item was accompanied by a full-color illustration. Next to the calendar item was a small picture of an old-fashioned calendar with oversize numerals, like one that would flip by in old movies to illustrate all the months that passed while the hero was away at war. But on this calendar, some dates were written in blue, and those numerals pulsed. I was dying to click on them, to see what incredible happenings were planned for those dates. Then there was the History item, accompanied by a thumbnail-sized video clip, which showed a bright red and orange volcano erupting over and over. The eruption must represent the dawn of The Zoo's universe. I didn't know where to start.

Michelle Slatalla   **175**

I chose what I thought would be the most logical course.

"Maybe we could find out more about Minotaur by checking the member directory?"

"We said we were going to read about the fire first," Annie said. She was very organized. It bothered her that I wanted to throw out the Old Plan. I once lived with a woman like that. She would be in line at the grocery checkout, *planning* to bag the frozen food in plastic and the dry goods in paper. If you were there too, and tried to be helpful by, say, putting ice cream into a paper bag, she might not have said anything, but you'd know. You'd ruined the plan.

I usually avoided planners. But this one had sneaked past my sensors because (A) she laughed at my jokes fairly often; and (B) when she did, her eyes opened wider instead of scrunching up. I hate it when people look like rodents when they laugh.

"Annie, do you keep a to-do list?"

"What?"

"You know, a list of stuff you have to do every day. When you finish some task, like reading the anthropology newsgroups or phoning davidr or cleaning the bathroom, you get to cross that item off."

"You must really hate me."

"I'm just scared of you."

"Good."

I noticed that when she moved the mouse pointer down the menu on the Web page, she clicked right on MEMBER DIREC-TORY to please me. So this was romance.

A form filled the screen, like one of those insurance-company forms that you have to fill out after you see the doctor. There was a long explanation about different ways you could search the directory to find information about members: by name, by most recent log-ins, by "home." She found the line where it said TYPE NAME HERE and wrote MINOTAUR.

MINOTAUR WAS LAST LOGGED IN TO THE ZOO AT 20:18.06 TODAY. SEND E-MAIL TO minotaur@zoo.com.

"Should we?" Annie asked.

"Why not?"

We composed a message: MINOTAUR: WOLFER NEEDS YOU.

We sent it whooshing through the myriad phone lines that connected our laptop on a scarred wooden table to whatever computer the Minotaur used, somewhere else in the world. I wanted to hitch a ride on the message, to travel along like a rodeo rider on a comet, to see where the Minotaur lived. I said, "Okay, let's read about what happened to the Unicorn Inn now."

"You know what, Harry? You're a control freak."

The Web page about the tragedy at the Unicorn Inn appeared to have been assembled in haste. It had no pretty graphics, just a page of black text with a funereal border. It's funny now to think about how real it all seemed to me. I could almost see the charred and blackened wood, the scorched trees, the shards of broken glass on the ground. I read:

THE DEATH OF THE UNICORN INN

SOMETIME BETWEEN THE HOURS OF MIDNIGHT AND FOUR A.M. ON WEDNESDAY NIGHT, AN INTRUDER USED A STOLEN LOG-IN AND PASS-WORD TO GAIN UNIVERSAL ACCESS TO THE ZOO PROGRAM.

THE INTRUDER ERASED ALL CODE ASSOCIATED WITH THE INN.

AMONG THE ITEMS DESTROYED WERE:

*THE LOBBY AREA AND REGISTRATION DESK. THE GUEST LOG, WITH A COMPREHENSIVE LIST OF ALL MEMBERS WHO HAD ENTERED THE INN SINCE ITS CREATION IN 1991, WAS ERASED.

*ALL GUEST ROOMS THAT MEMBERS HAD CREATED ON THE SECOND AND THIRD FLOORS OF THE INN. ALL PERSONAL POSSESSIONS THAT MEMBERS HAD LEFT IN THE ROOMS, INCLUDING CLOTHING, PHOTOS, FURNITURE, AND TOILETRIES. FOR A PARTIAL LIST, SEE HTTP:// WWW.ZOO.COM/INN/ARSON/ITEMS.HTML.

*ALL VALUABLES THAT MEMBERS HAD STORED IN THE INN'S SAFE. THE SYSOP WAS ABLE TO RETRIEVE A PARTIAL LIST OF ITEMS LOST: MARLIN'S WAND (#48771), BIG TUNA'S SILVER INGOT COLLECTION

(#89221), WOLFER'S JOURNAL (#41104), ANTY MANE'S FEATHER BOA (#52117). IF YOU HAD SOMETHING STORED IN THE SAFE, CONTACT THE SYSOP. A MASTER LIST IS BEING COMPILED.

BEFORE LOGGING OUT, THE INTRUDER LEFT A NEW DESCRIPTION OF THE UNICORN INN. IT READS AS FOLLOWS:

A MYSTERIOUS FIRE BURNED DOWN THE INN LAST NIGHT. AS THE ROOF OF THE INN COLLAPSED, A SHADOWY FIGURE WAS SEEN RUNNING OFF INTO THE WOODS, SILHOUETTED AGAINST THE TREES BY THE HUNGRY FLAMES. THE HEAVY SMELL OF SMOKE THAT HANGS OVER THE CLEARING WHERE THE INN ONCE STOOD MAKES YOU WANT TO GAG.

"Wolfer's Journal? We needed to read that," I said. "What does that number, 41104, stand for?"

"Every time a Zoo member creates a place, like Wolfer's cave, or an object, like a journal or a feather boa or a wand, the member does it by writing code. You add another little piece of code onto the big Zoo program," Annie said. "In your code, you define the object and then you also define the scope of actions that can occur using the object."

I looked clueless.

"You know, you would create the journal, describe the journal as maybe a blue leather book with 150 pages. When somebody typed SEE JOURNAL, it would say BLUE LEATHER BOOK WITH 150 PAGES, right? So then you would write code that would allow other people to examine the journal, to open it, to read words written on the pages. Actions. It can get pretty detailed."

"And every new piece of code has a number?"

"So the sysop can keep track of it."

Annie typed: SEE #41104.

THERE IS NO #41104.

"Well, there's your answer," Annie said. "The code for the journal must have been appended to the code for the inn. The arsonist destroyed all of it."

If everything in the real world were really just software code too, we all would be living in a MOO called The Solar System.

God would have a giant laptop up in heaven, which he would use to create the world. SEE EDEN (#1). A character could EAT APPLE (#2). Of course, that would prompt expulsion from THE GARDEN and necessitate more code, to create other venues. God the Sysop could give certain characters special programming privileges. Einstein for instance. Louis Brandeis. Isaac Newton. Lance Ito.

"What do you think my dad wrote in his missing journal?"

"Something that got him killed."

"Do you think that's why the inn was burned? To destroy his notes?"

"It's the only motive I've heard," I said.

"My dad was careful, Harry. He kept copies of everything he ever wrote."

We both stared at the laptop.

"If only we could break in and get it," she said.

I heard the bell jingle over the front door. Blaney entered Raymond's, wearing the cautious look of an animal trainer assigned to sedate an enraged elephant who had just trampled a child. His eyes darted suspiciously around the room, coming to rest on our booth. He scowled as he looked at Annie.

I went to rescue him. Gently: "Oh, Richard." I put my hand on his arm. He recoiled as if I'd branded him. "We're in the back."

"Has anyone else been here?" he asked.

"Since we got here? No."

"All right."

He turned and practically jumped back out of the restaurant. I stood by the plate-glass window and watched him disappear into the dark night, wondering if he had totally flipped out. And then a crazy thing happened. I almost lost it myself. Standing there on my own turf—in the aisle at Raymond's where I had wooed Katie Millery (she peaked in ninth grade) over a meatball sub, where I had come faithfully every Thursday night for nearly ten years to pick up a Large (half pepperoni, half anchovy) for my mother to devour, where I had bused tables and washed water glasses to pay for next semester's textbooks—I felt the purest rush of terror that had ever hit me. Why? It was no mystery. If my life had been encased in the comfort of the familiar for two and a half decades, then Raymond's had been the epicenter of that safety. Blaney's actions, his abrupt exit, suddenly robbed me of that.

There was a bomb in here. There must be a bomb. Blaney had planted it before we arrived. It was under Annie's seat. I had heard the ticking. I had ignored the ticking. Why had I ignored the ticking? Shit, he just came into the restaurant for an instant to make sure we were in place, and now he had retreated to the cover of the woods to detonate it. Annie!

Just as I was about to scream, to leap, to hurl my shaking pathetic self back down the aisle to grab her, to flee, to cower, to curl in a fetal position—who knows?—I saw a lumpy shape emerge again from the shadows outside the restaurant. I willed myself to calm down. This was my restaurant, late at night, the same as it had always been. Smell the dough charring in the oven. Slow it down, Harry. Make him come to you.

Blaney walked in the door, furtive. Behind him was Eddie.

The two of them were twins, unshaven and red-eyed and jittery, maybe from too much coffee, maybe from too much fear. They wore rumpled jeans and sweat-stained T-shirts. Eddie had a pack of Camels, unfiltered, in his shirt pocket. They said nothing to me as they walked past. They sat down in the booth with Annie.

I joined them.

"Long time no see," I greeted Eddie.

Annie snapped shut the lid on her laptop, which Eddie was eyeing as if it were a feral animal, and said quietly, "You two look wasted. You want some pizza?"

That was how we had decided to play it, to have her take the lead. They wouldn't expect that. Blaney, certainly, would be thrown off balance by the consternation he would feel at having to address a woman directly. Eddie looked at her for the first time, but there was no hostility in his gaze. Only confusion and total exhaustion.

I held up a hand to get the waitress's attention, signaled that we needed two slices.

"My father told me about your work. He admired your ambitions," Annie said.

"It would have been more help if he had taken a more public role," Eddie said.

"Perhaps he didn't want to blow your cover," Annie said.

"He wasn't so worried about security," Blaney said. "Or else he wouldn't have gone so public, supporting Knot."

This was news to me, and to Annie too, I could tell, because I felt her foot nudge mine under the table.

"He wasn't always cautious when it came to the things he felt were right, and the things he felt were wrong," Annie said.

"I'll say." Eddie snorted. "I admired the guy for laying it all out on the line, but no way would I personally have posted to sci.crypto to announce to the whole goddamn fucking world that I was a code freak. I mean, whose business is that? Can't we assume that everyone we *wouldn't* want to know about our politics would be monitoring sci.crypto?"

"Truth may yet prevail. But your old man took it in the gut," Eddie said. "I'm trying to prevent that happening to anyone else on our side."

"Is that why you guys are here? To protect us?" Annie asked, sympathetic but not pitying. Let's get it back on track, boys. The front door jangled, and Eddie startled as if slapped.

Jed and Peterson walked in together, nodded as they went up to the counter to pick up their order.

"You know them?" Eddie's voice was strangled.

"Of course," I said. "I know everyone here."

"They followed us."

"Get hold of yourself, Eddie," Blaney snapped. It made him uneasy for us to see his cousin so tenuously grasping at reality. To me: "We have to go soon. It's not safe here."

"It's not safe anywhere anymore, Blaney," I said, not meaning to sound so accusatory.

"Question. And then we leave," Eddie said.

"What?"

"Will you meet us in D.C. at the end of the week?"

I was transported back to Café Info, to the sound of the pneumatic tube carrying ideas above my head, to the first time I had shaken hands with Lionel, to the strange conversation I had observed during what now seemed to be a distant and ancient time. *We need to agree on the timing. Who should go? We want to limit our exposure.*

"Does this have something to do with Patriot?" I asked, knowing the answer.

"Never mind," Eddie said. "Are you in or are you out? Richard said you could be trusted."

What if you get arrested? It would be worse if we all got arrested. Are you trying to steal the limelight, Richard?

"Are you trying to share the limelight, Richard?" I asked.

Blaney had the grace to color. "Plan B."

"What happened to Plan A? The petitions didn't work?"

"Drop the sarcasm, Garnet. There's a congressional hearing on the Patriot bill, and I plan to testify."

Now that we have both halves, we need to agree on the timing.

I leaned forward across the table, locked eyes with him, and said, "Testify? You stole the Patriot key. Are you going to testify about that? Stand up and embarrass the government by showing how easy it was to subvert Patriot's security?"

"I need a lawyer."

I couldn't help it. I laughed.

"No way. I don't know anything about encryption issues, federal export restrictions, any of it. And if I did, I still couldn't represent you. I'm not licensed in D.C. And I can't aid you in the commission of a crime."

He had steeled himself against my reluctance, of course. He wheedled. No one knows anything about encryption issues, it's a new area of law, just emerging, those with the foresight to get there first will be shaping public policy for years to come. He didn't really need an official lawyer, just a legal adviser, someone who would know what he should say and where to find help if the need arose. And he didn't expect me to commit any crimes. Nowhere was it written that possession of a Patriot key was illegal. Not yet, anyway. Not until the appropriate laws had been enacted.

Peterson and Jed walked out into the night, Jed cradling the cardboard box. I heard the familiar complaint of Peterson's Suburban as the engine turned over, one more time, for him.

Eddie stood up suddenly. "Someone's out there, by my truck." He couldn't see that far, not in the dark, not through a window, no way.

"Eddie, please," Blaney begged. "Sit down."

"Sit *down*, Richard?" Eddie hissed. "Sit the fuck *down*? What the fuck do you think we've been doing for the last four hours, hell, the last six months? It's time to stand the FUCK UP!" He was almost roaring now, and of course, people turned to look. Which, of course, only exacerbated poor Eddie's discomfort. "You moron," he said. "Fucking moron." And lurched out of the diner.

Blaney dropped his head into his hands, slowly rolled his eyes, and sat there for a few moments. I decided to ignore Eddie's outburst. Let the two of them enjoy a time out in their own respective comfort zones.

"Isn't Lionel going with you?" I asked. "To that hearing?"

"No. We decided that if we both went, it might look like we were involved in a conspiracy to overthrow the government."

"Which you are."

He looked uncomfortable. "It'll just be me."

"Won't Lionel hire some fancy, high-powered inside-the-Beltway suit to represent you?"

"We don't want it to look like we think we need one of those lawyers," Blaney said. "Technically, I haven't done anything illegal."

"Stupid strategy," I said. "And I can't believe that's Lionel's reason."

Annie cut in: "Where should we meet you? And when? Harry will need to review a copy of your planned testimony before you actually give it, of course. So there won't be any surprises. And I don't know where you're staying tonight, but you will need to clean up before you show up in front of a congressional subcommittee. I hope you own a suit?"

Blaney looked so grateful that she was emboldened to press further.

"Now, I wonder if I could ask you for a small favor. You see"—and she pulled the laptop over from the edge of the table—"my father appears to have more information on this computer than we can see. I bet you could explain this anomaly."

His pudgy fingers flew over the keys, Paderewski in concert, and then he announced, "He partitioned the hard drive. Not uncommon."

Blaney explained that Ames had used Knot to create a secure moat around an island of confidential files. "There's no way you'll get the information unless you learn the password."

"That brings me back to the same problem: cracking Knot."

"Well, good luck with that one. Your old man tried for months to crack it," Blaney said. "Finally, he posted to sci.crypto just one sentence: 'The algorithm is stronger than I thought.' It's one of the most famous postings up there, ever."

"Then how do we figure out the password?" I asked Blaney.

"He left a clue somewhere. People always do."

"He wrote it on a slip of paper?"

"No, idiot. His password is probably associated with him. Something he could remember easily."

"Like his birthday."

F

L

A

M

E

W

A

R

"If he were incredibly stupid, maybe." Blaney was impatient. "Think like him."

He frowned, as if he had just remembered something painful. "I better go find Eddie. If he leaves without me, I'm fucked."

He exited through the kitchen.

chapter ten

I fumbled with the key in the lock, conscious for the first time of how my place must look. Picture Auntie Em's house after the twister shook the flimsy building around in the air for about ten minutes, then slammed it back onto the ground. Everything flew out of her closets; my situation was slightly worse because I don't use closets.

"You are a cliché, Harry," Annie said, using her thumb and forefinger like finicky pincers to remove a sweat sock draped over the couch. "Did you hire a decorator to capture the Oscar Madison look?"

It was true that the only nonsocked place to sit in the room was on the tool chest in the middle of the floor. Except that it was open, with wrenches spilling out. I'd been working on my old bike, trying to get it into some kind of shape, since I never really expected the New York City Police Department to release my other one from custody. Spokes and derailleurs and brake lines and pedals were scattered around the floor. There was a faint smell of grease. At least, I thought it was faint. The frame looked skeletal in the glare of an unshaded lightbulb that dangled from an extension cord. It was the only light in the room.

"You don't like it?"

"I love it. The whole place is you. Everything apparently on display," she said, and she set the lightbulb swinging gently like a pendulum. "But all the good stuff is hidden."

"What good stuff?"

"The wiring." She shrugged. "The treasures."

What did she expect? The place was a temporary hangout, a summer rental with a futon on the floor and most of my stuff still in boxes by the front door. Why unpack? In another month, I'd be gone, beginning a life sentence in Syracuse.

I examined her as keenly as I could in the bad light, looking for an indication of how she was assimilating all the unsettling bits of information we had been collecting. I saw nothing on her beautiful face except an expression of mild amusement. She was picking up my collection of cigars, one by one, sniffing each.

"Hey, put those back. I got that long one at my roommate's wedding," I said. "It's unlucky."

"Were you the best man?"

"No, an usher. I ushed."

"Is he your best friend?"

"Just a friend."

"Do you have a best friend?"

"I don't know anybody I could stand to go camping with in the rain."

"Not even me?" she asked. She walked over to the make-shift bookshelves, two-by-fours on stacked cinder block.

As she ran a finger over the spines, I spoke to her back. "Maybe you."

"What if I forgot to pack the checkers?"

"We'd do something else," I said.

She turned to face me. "Teach me to gut a fish."

I wanted to walk over to her then. And grab her by those cute, small shoulders. And kiss her.

Instead, I went into the kitchen.

"Good news. You have a bottle opener," she called. "I just sat on it."

"Cold ones," I announced, heading back into the living room with two frosted mugs. There was nothing in the freezer *except* mugs.

"Thanks."

She sat at the desk, where she had opened the laptop, plugged it into the wall, and logged in to The Zoo.

YOU HAVE MAIL, WOLFER. READ IT?

Y.

MESSAGE FROM MINOTAUR: YOU ARE NOT WOLFER. SO WHAT DO YOU WANT?

We had smoked him out. Together, we hunched over the computer, our faces almost pressed to the screen in the dim light.

"I can't believe it," Annie said. "He's actually out there somewhere. Talking to us."

I typed: WOLFER SAYS: WE ARE HERE WITH WOLFER'S BLESSING. WE NEED TO TALK TO YOU.

Interminable seconds passed. Maybe longer. Maybe minutes. Maybe hours. Who knows. It felt like it was the twenty-third century by the time the computer beeped again with its polite announcement of mail.

MINOTAUR ASKS: TALK? WHAT ABOUT?

WOLFER SAYS: ABOUT WHAT HAPPENED TO WOLFER. IF HE WAS YOUR FRIEND, YOU WILL TALK TO US.

MINOTAUR ASKS: US? WE? WHO ARE YOU?

WOLFER SAYS: ANNIE AMES AND A FRIEND.

MINOTAUR ASKS: WOLFER'S DAUGHTER? ANNIE AMES, THIS IS NO PLACE FOR YOU. THIS IS A PLACE WHERE MEN STONE PIGEONS. GO HOME.

We waited again. But this time Minotaur sent no response. "Damn. We lost him," Annie said.

I typed: WHERE IS MINOTAUR?

MINOTAUR IS IN HIS MAZE.

188

"He's playing games with us, Harry."

"How can you tell?"

"His last message. He left us instructions." I read it again. And then I typed:

GO HOME.

We were back at the entrance to the cave. We pushed aside the branch that grew over the door and stepped into the dimness, going through the same steps as before. Once inside, I tried something new.

TURN ON LIGHT.

YOU SEE A BOX OF MATCHES ON THE MANTEL. YOU STRIKE ONE AND LIGHT THE OIL LAMPS THAT LINE THE WALLS OF THE CAVE. A FRIENDLY WARMTH REPLACES THE OMINOUS DUSK.

Time to explore Wolfer's cave. Fred Ames had called this place a "well-appointed living space," which made me think that he might have packed it with little bits of surprise code. He had created a wall of built-in bookshelves, for instance. So what could we do with them?

LOOK AT SHELVES.

YOU SEE ROW AFTER ROW OF BOOKS, MOSTLY HEAVY HARD-COVERS THAT LOOK LIKE REFERENCE TEXTBOOKS. THEY DON'T INTEREST YOU FROM A DISTANCE. BUT IF YOU STEP CLOSE ENOUGH TO READ THEIR SPINES, YOU LEARN THAT THE SUBJECT MATTER IS RATHER UNUSUAL. YOUR INTEREST IS PIQUED BY TITLES LIKE: "HISTORICAL EXAMINATION OF THE ORIGINS OF AUTOEROTICISM" AND "THE RELATIONSHIP BETWEEN PAIN AND PLEASURE" AND "THE BEAST WITHIN."

LOOK AT BOOKS.

THE BOOKS ARE WELL WORN, WITH TATTERED DUST JACKETS, AND YOU CAN TELL THAT WOLFER SPENT A LONG TIME SEARCHING THEM OUT, AT SECONDHAND STORES, ESTATE SALES, EVEN BUYING VOLUMES ON THE STREET FROM THE MEN WHO SPREAD THEIR WARES ON THE SIDEWALK NEAR COOPER UNION.

LOOK BEHIND BOOKS, I typed, hoping for treasure.

YOU LOOK BUT SEE NOTHING THERE.

READ BOOKS, I typed.

READ WHICH BOOK?

PAIN AND PLEASURE.

Not that I really wanted to read a big hunk of text from something that would probably turn out to have been Ames's private diary of sexual encounters. I'm not squeamish about much. But I do hate bad writing. And I had no reason to believe that a mathematician leading a double life as a virtual wolf had any literary aptitude whatsoever. Frankly, I was afraid that his daughter would get upset if she saw something really pathetic on the screen. "My canine malehood," etc. etc. Happily, before the depths of Fred Ames's sexual identity could be laid bare on the computer screen, another line of text scrolled by:

MINOTAUR IS AT THE DOOR. LET HIM IN?

Y, I typed, hit by an adrenaline rush strong enough to knock me over. I had been right. He was hooked. And finally I was about to get a glimpse of the one Fred Ames had feared. Maybe I was about to meet whoever had tried to kill me, as well. Tried twice to kill me, I corrected myself.

MINOTAUR CANTERS INTO THE CAVE AND YOU SEE JUST HOW LOW THE CEILING IS. HIS POWERFUL BARE CHEST SEEMS TOO LARGE FOR THE CAVE, AND WHEN HE SPEAKS, HIS VOICE RUMBLES DEEPER THAN AN EARTHQUAKE AND ECHOES OFF THE WALLS.

MINOTAUR SAYS: HELLO, ANNIE. OR WHOEVER YOU ARE.

I can't tell you how eerie it was, to see these disembodied letters float onto the computer screen. We'd spent hours fantasizing about who the Minotaur was, whether he was the bomber, whether he posed a danger to us, whether we'd ever track him down. And now, without a warning, he was in my apartment. He had invaded our privacy as surely as if he had arrived physically, tromping up the rotting porch steps and banging on the peeling front door. Now he was in the room with us. I felt him breathe. I smelled him.

Annie reached for the keyboard and typed:

WOLFER SAYS: ANNIE AND HER FRIEND HARRY GARNET.

F
L
A
M
E

W
A
R

MINOTAUR SAYS: FROM THE EXPLOSION?

WOLFER SAYS: THAT'S ME, I typed.

MINOTAUR SAYS: YOU'RE BOTH TYPING?

WOLFER SAYS: WE ALTERNATE.

MINOTAUR ASKS: WHAT DO YOU WANT FROM ME?

WOLFER ASKS: HOW DO YOU KNOW ABOUT THE EXPLOSION?

MINOTAUR SAYS: EVERYONE KNOWS ABOUT THE EXPLOSION. WHY? DO YOU SUSPECT ME OF WISHING YOU HARM? IS THAT WHY YOU'VE BEEN GALLOPING ALL OVER THE ZOO CALLING MY NAME?

WOLFER SAYS: WHY DID YOU RUN AWAY FROM US THE FIRST TIME WE SAW YOU?

MINOTAUR SAYS: AMES IS DEAD. I KNEW YOU WERE AN IMPOSTOR.

WOLFER ASKS: YOU WEREN'T CURIOUS?

MINOTAUR SAYS: I WAS AFRAID.

WOLFER ASKS: OF WHAT?

No answer. Minutes passed. "Let's try something else," Annie said. She typed:

WOLFER SAYS: YOU SENT E-MAIL TO AMES BECAUSE HE WAS AFRAID TOO. YOU SAID HE NEED NOT FEAR YOU.

MINOTAUR SAYS: THAT WAS DIFFERENT. THAT WAS PERSONAL.

WOLFER SAYS: DID FRED AMES FLAME YOU?

The Minotaur did not answer. Not directly. Instead, I saw this text block:

THE MINOTAUR SHAKES HIS HEAD SADLY. HE WALKS OVER TO THE FIREPLACE, PICKS UP THE BRASS POKER, IDLY PUSHES IT AROUND IN THE EMBERS. HE IS TRYING TO DECIDE HOW MUCH TO TELL, BECAUSE HE KNOWS THE TRUTH WOULD HURT HIS OLD FRIEND'S DAUGHTER. IS IT NECESSARY TO HURT ANYONE? AT THIS POINT? THE MINOTAUR WONDERS.

WOLFER SAYS: ANSWER THE QUESTION, Annie typed. THIS IS ANNIE . . . I NEED TO KNOW.

THE MINOTAUR PUTS DOWN THE POKER, REMEMBERS ALL THE FIRES HE AND WOLFER BUILT TOGETHER IN THIS STONE HEARTH, REMEMBERS THE DAY HIS OLD FRIEND CARVED HIS PERSONAL

Joshua

Quitter

MOTTO INTO THE WALL: "THERE IS NO PRIVACY." IT ALL SEEMS
SO LONG AGO NOW. THE MINOTAUR RESTS HIS HEAD ON THE
HEARTH, SEEKING STRENGTH FROM THE COOL STONE.

WOLFER SAYS: TELL US, I typed.

MINOTAUR SAYS: I WOULD NEVER HURT WOLFER. AND THE REA-
SON IS SIMPLE: I LOVED HIM.

WOLFER SAYS: WHO ARE YOU? Annie typed.

MINOTAUR SAYS: ALL YOU NEED TO KNOW IS THAT I AM NOT
THE ENEMY.

WOLFER ASKS: WHO ARE YOU OFFLINE? PLEASE. WE WANT TO
MEET YOU.

MINOTAUR SAYS: THAT WOULD BE DANGEROUS FOR YOU TO
KNOW. AND YOU ARE IN ENOUGH DANGER RIGHT NOW.

WOLFER SAYS: DID MY FATHER KNOW YOU OFFLINE?

MINOTAUR SAYS: NOT AT FIRST. WE MET IN THE UNICORN INN.
THERE WERE ROOMS THERE, UNDERGROUND, WHERE YOU COULD
GO TO RELAX.

WOLFER SAYS: WHAT KIND OF ROOMS? I asked.

MINOTAUR SAYS: ROOMS TO BE ALONE.

WOLFER ASKS: WORKOUT ROOMS? SAUNA? I typed.

MINOTAUR SAYS: SORT OF.

WOLFER SAYS: YOU MET AMES IN ONE OF THOSE ROOMS?

> WE MET IN THE WHIRLPOOL.

> AND THEN?

> WE BECAME FRIENDS AT FIRST.

> AT FIRST?

> WE WERE IN LOVE.

> THEN WHY DID HE FEAR YOU?

> HE DIDN'T REALLY. IT WAS A GAME. A PRIVATE GAME.

"Harry, do we have to get into all this?" Annie looked pale.
"It sounds like some kind of sexual game. They met in a whirlpool. The titles of the books. It all sounds like a virtual swing-
ers' club."

I typed:

> WHAT IS THE POINT OF THE ZOO? WHAT ARE ALL OF THE
CHARACTERS HERE TO DO, ANYWAY?

> I THOUGHT YOU KNEW. IT'S A PLACE WHERE WE CAN RELAX AND PLAY GAMES. A PLACE TO LIVE OUT THE MOST EXTREME KIND OF FANTASIES.

> WHAT WERE WOLFER'S FANTASIES?

"Sorry, but we have to ask," I said to Annie.

MINOTAUR GESTURES AT THE INSCRIPTION OVER THE MANTEL. HE IS LOSING PATIENCE WITH THESE QUESTIONS. WHAT DO THEY HAVE TO DO WITH FRED AMES'S DEATH?

WOLFER SAYS: YOU KNEW HIS REAL NAME. DID HE KNOW YOURS? I typed.

> ENOUGH.

WOLFER ASKS: ARE YOU A MAN OR A WOMAN?

MINOTAUR SAYS: I AM THE MINOTAUR. I AM NEITHER MAN NOR BEAST.

MINOTAUR TURNS FROM YOU. HE IS ANGRY AND GALLOPS FROM THE CAVE. HE DISAPPEARS.

"He disappears. He. He. He."

Annie said quietly, "I knew he was a man. I just didn't know *who* the man was. I never met him. My father never spoke of him by name, just, 'I'm spending the evening with a friend,' or, 'I'm expecting a call from a friend.' "

"Did you ever speak to the friend? On the phone? Anywhere?" I asked.

"Not until that day in my mother's apartment, when we read the E-mail the Minotaur had sent to my dad. I knew that had to be him."

"Why didn't you say anything, Annie?" I was angry. "Jesus, what else are you hiding? Didn't it ever occur to you that it could be impor—"

She cut me off. "Didn't it ever occur to you, Harry, that some things are private? That my father's personal relationships weren't something the world needed to discuss? It wasn't listed on his credit report, or mentioned in the newspaper accounts of his death or his personnel file at the NSA. It was one of the few small parts of his life that belonged *only* to him. He deserved that. We all deserve that."

"You knew about it, Annie. So it wasn't private."

"I was his daughter."

"You're jealous, aren't you? You're jealous of the fucking Minotaur. What mattered to your dad was his work, first, and his special friend, second. Where did you fit in?"

"No, I made *my* peace with my father a long time ago." She pointed to the computer screen. "This was his real life. All these artifacts scattered around the cave, these are the objects he used to define himself when he was liberated from his physical life. I didn't know he loved the outdoors, yet here he has a rugged home in the forest with a cozy fireplace. He was so controlled, he planned out every step of his life, but here chose to be a wild animal—a creature driven to howl at full moons. I thought he was a man who didn't read anything that wasn't science or mathematics, but he built bookshelves and filled them with erotic literature. But I can respect that, Harry. So don't project your own problems on me."

"Sorry."

"What if you had an alter ego, Harry?" she asked. "What phrase would you inscribe over the mantel in your cave?"

"I'd steal a line from Kurt Cobain. 'Come as you are,' once you figure out who you—"

But she wasn't listening anymore. She was staring into the distance. A look of sweet realization came over her face, and then triumph. It was the expression of a woman bent over a rare bit of sharp clay that poked up from the dirt bed it had slept in for a thousand years. Hers was the look she would have had as she knelt so gently next to it, brushed dirt from it with a toothbrush, and saw the sharply unfamiliar patterns of a forgotten language etched into its surface.

"There is no privacy."

She clutched my arm, shook me as if she were trying to get the attention of a puppy who was on the verge of darting in front of a truck. "There is no privacy." This time she took my hands and counted off the letters on my fingers.

"What are you doing?" I asked.

"Harry, how long can a Knot password be?"

Fred Ames's daughter had cracked his code. Perhaps he knew she would. The Minotaur had led us to the key, and we were able to decrypt Fred Ames's hard drive. Whether the Minotaur had meant to do it or not, I'll never know, but I like to think that he wanted us to learn the truth. I like to think that his conscience forced him to help us, forced him to repay a debt to his old friend Wolfer. I like to think, of course, that the Minotaur sought absolution. But then I always have preferred the convenience of tidy endings, where the world is put to order and the righteous sleep in peace. Give me Trollope over Hardy any day.

The gibberish on the screen turned, magically, into text. Fred Ames had no more privacy. I had never been so in love with the words of the English language as that instant when I saw Ames's files materialize before my eyes. I loved the solid way that the vowels and the consonants sidled up to each other, the authoritative ring to the syllables, the utter lack of unfamiliar characters marring the meaning that Ames had meant to convey. AmesDiary-1.0 was the first file that popped up on the menu. AmesDiary-1.2 the next. -1.3, -1.4. In all, there appeared twelve long files for us to read.

"He kept his journal on his computer, as well as at the Unicorn Inn," Annie said. "My father had a backup system for everything. Except for saving his life."

I moved the cursor down the list. "Maybe he thought this information would be an insurance policy," I said.

"Then he was wrong." The sadness in her voice made me look up. I saw her wear her grief at that moment more visibly than at any previous time since his death. I remembered that she had looked tired at the memorial service, and I realized that the strain of hiding her pain had wearied her that day. Now, in this jock's locker room of an apartment, sometime well past a dingy midnight, she had no more reserves.

"But, Annie," I said in a low and reasonable voice that was completely out of character for me, "maybe his system will save his daughter's life."

I was foolish enough to believe the mysteries were solved.

So when the screen came up blank, I cursed. I slammed my hands down on the keyboard. I couldn't help myself.

"Nothing in the file? He deleted the contents?" she asked unbelievingly.

She pulled the keyboard to herself, and fiddled. No luck. She called up -1.2. It, too, was blank. Had he erased it? Had someone else? Was there a deeper, impenetrable layer of encryption, a program that worked like invisible ink to hide the very existence of the text? She called up -1.3. Blank. -1.4. -1.5.

Neither of us spoke. The seconds it took for her to complete the exercise were among the longest of my life, and so, by the time she double-clicked on -1.12., I had no more than the sensibility of an old man. I stared, as dull and thick as if the dog had wakened me from a snore in the Barca-Lounger, not sure at first what exactly it was I was seeing on the screen.

It was the final installment of the diary.

F

L

A   HOW ATOMS COLLIDE IN SEEMINGLY RANDOM BUT PRO-
PHETIC WAYS. IN UNIVERSITY FOOD MARKET. BUYING SOAP. MY

A   OLD STUDENT, N, ON LINE AT THE NEXT CASHIER. HE TELLS
ME OF HIS NEW OBSESSION. HE CALLS IT THE ZOO. WRITES THE

M   PHONE NUMBER ON THE BACK OF HIS REGISTER TAPE.

E   "His old student, N?"

"Nelson," she said. How could she always be so sure?

"Was it a trap?" I wondered.

W   "Lying in wait for my father at the supermarket? To entice him online?"

A

R   WEEK LATER. SPRING TERM UNDER WAY. SYLLABUS OUTDATED.
INSTEAD OF FIXING IT, I TRAVEL. I SPEND THE DAY IN THE ZOO.

196

TROMP THROUGH THE WOODS. STAY THE NIGHT THERE. I MET
SOMEONE. WE HAD MUCH IN COMMON.

There were many lines of white space between that entry
and the next, and I wondered if Fred Ames had deliberately
deleted the details of his romance. Had modesty prevailed?
Or had he been trying to protect his lover?

MAY 28. UP ALL NIGHT. PREPARING FOR PATRIOT HEARING,
WHICH MINOTAUR PROMISES WILL OCCUR BEFORE END OF
SUMMER. USUAL WORK WAS INTERRUPTED BECAUSE OF EU-
REKA MOMENT—

MAY 30. IN SUMMARY, THERE APPEARS TO BE A SECRET BACK
DOOR IN THE CODE. I INTEND TO FIND OUT IF THIS WAS AC-
CIDENTAL, OR INTENTIONAL. THE CONSEQUENCES ARE STUN-
NING TO CONTEMPLATE.

The file ended abruptly. Of course, we didn't really need to
read any more. The world had changed, turned upside down
in a moment. We had found what we were looking for, and
the knowledge turned out to be far more terrifying than we
could have expected.

"Your father was working on the Patriot software too?" I
sounded harsher than I meant to.

"He was one of dozens of experts around the country who
had been asked to review the code."

"Why didn't you tell me before?"

"It was pro forma. It was an attempt to coopt the academic
community and gain support for the initiative. At least that's
what he thought." Defensive.

"Did you know he found a flaw in the Patriot code?"

"Of course not." Angry now. "That, I would have told you."

"A back door in Patriot would enable unscrupulous people
within the government to keep tabs on its citizens without a
court order. It would destroy any notion of privacy. It would
create a nation-state where Big Brother might as well implant

electrodes in our brains so that bad thoughts about income tax evasion and anarchy and driving seventy-five miles per hour on the highway could be zapped out even as they occurred. Long before we ever acted on our dangerous, unruly impulses.''

I knew then that I would definitely show up for the hearing in Washington. Annie picked up a stubby pencil that had been lying on the floor, brushed the dust off it, and pulled a small notepad from her pocket. She began to write out a list of questions: Who is Minotaur? What is his connection to Patriot? Senate Committee aide? Who did Minotaur tell about the flaw?

Did Minotaur kill Ames or just arrange for others to carry out the job?

"Did Minotaur kill *Ames*?" I was incredulous. "You call him Ames? Annie, he was your father."

She looked up. "I would not be his daughter if I got emotional now, would I?"

She went back to her work. I watched her gravely. She was so intent that she barely flinched when I reached over and pushed an errant strand of curl behind her ear. Whatever emotions this final contest of wits between her and her father had evoked were not on display.

I knew from experience her hair would escape again in under a minute. Hair so red had the powers of Houdini.

Of course, it must have taken longer than that for her hair thing to occur. I don't know, exactly, since I lost track of time, just sitting there, watching her bent in concentration to her task. All I know, all I remember with wondrous certainty, is that at some point, perhaps hours later, when the silly streaks of dawn had just begun to paint the sky, she sighed, clasped the laptop shut, and nudged me. Her hand on my leg. I felt her fingers trace laterally along my neck, tickling me on the collarbone, and I toyed, briefly, with the idea of keeping my eyes closed, feeling, rather than watching, what would happen next. But I didn't have the willpower to do that.

We embraced then, exhausted but full of the possibilities left to us. And we kissed, of course, and I couldn't believe that at last I got to taste those pouty lips, feel her pulled tight against me. Maybe we had plenty of time, an infinite amount of time after all.

And then the phone rang. The "terror phone" as we used to call it when it jangled at an inappropriate hour. For what else could be communicated at the hours between midnight and dawn but the Terror?

"Garnet." Blaney's voice was taut and I could hear him breathing, hyperventilating.

"Eddie. Oh, Jesus. Eddie's dead, man. I'm here now, in his apartment. I found him. I guess I did, I mean . . . You gotta help, man. He's all bled out and it's a mess and I can't take any more of this, Harry." He was sobbing now. "I can't. I don't want to anymore. I don't want to do this anymore."

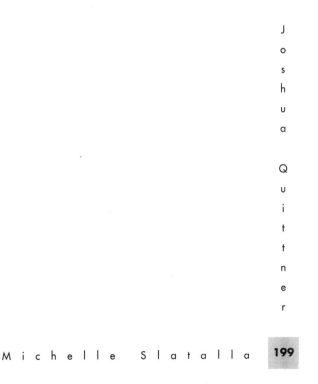

Joshua

Quittner

chapter eleven

H is roommates had found Eddie in the bathtub.

I remembered that tub. Not so long ago I had endured its curious, old-fashioned faucets and the tease of its scald-and-freeze showerhead. It was a deep tub, and more than six feet long, with ancient claw feet that raised the whole contraption a couple of awkward inches off the ground. The porcelain was yellowed around the drain, and chipped along the outer lip. A moldy shower curtain, transparent with a colorful map of the world printed on its side, was pushed aside.

It was probably fortunate that the old tub was so big, because Eddie's compact body fit neatly into it. The blood dripped down the drain, not out onto the floor.

I tried to think of which of his roommates would have had the stomach to mop up the bathroom after the police had finished their gruesome catalog of the corpse, the fingerprints on the door handle, the pubic hair caked to the bottom of the bar of yellow Dial soap. Their footprints mingled with the sooty gray powder they dusted on every surface, and left a gritty film behind. I don't think Yuri would have been able to bear the ordeal of cleaning up after the rubber body bag exited the apartment. Nor Dim the pizza lover. Nor Blaney, if Blaney had still been there.

I think it must have been Irene who walked down the street to the nearest Duane Reade drugstore to buy Lysol cleanser, a scrub brush, and a black plastic pail. I saw those items in the apartment later, when I visited, and I know they were not the kinds of supplies that ever would have passed over the threshold for any less compelling reason than to erase the strong smell of death. I see in my mind the form of Irene, as she scrubbed, on her hands and knees, the grout crumbling between the black-and-white floor tiles.

I see her lean back onto her heels to wipe a strand of dangling dark hair out of her eyes and to stare, bleakly, for a moment out the unwashed transom window. Even if she came to the conclusion that she and the other militia members were in danger as well, I don't imagine that she would have allowed herself the luxury of a good hot cry.

Irene would have had the fortitude to clean up any mess. And Irene would have the courage to face, head-on, the coarse reality of what had happened to her colleague. I was going to say "her friend," but the truth is, I didn't know if any of the odd assortment of skittish militia members who had banded together to pay the rent really called each other friend. I do know that Irene would have been the first to go get a tape measure to try to determine if the murderer could have escaped through the transom.

Her conclusion, which she related to me the next time we spoke, was that only a child would have fit through the opening. For some reason, instead of comforting me (Blaney is bigger than a child, right?), that information terrified me.

The police had called it an execution-style murder.

I called it surgical. Annie, when I repeated the details to her, had turned pale and looked away from me—as if in relating the facts, I somehow became personally responsible for the horror of the act itself.

The body, when the police photographed it, was still fully clothed. A purplish contusion swelled up over his forehead. The picture I saw made me think of something incongruous: an eggplant-colored potato. That injury was probably the first.

He was dressed as he had been less than twelve hours earlier when I saw him at Raymond's Pizzeria. The belt was missing from Eddie's blue jeans, but it turned out that it was still on his corpse. Whoever had killed him had used it to cinch Eddie's hands behind his back, looping the makeshift leather handcuffs tight enough to cut off his circulation and leave greenish bruises on his skin. That was how they knew he had been cuffed before he was killed, before his blood stopped trying to pump to his fingers. So: blunt trauma to the head to subdue him. His belt wrapped around his hands to restrain him. And finally, when he had been dragged to the bathroom—quietly, none of his roommates heard a thing—Eddie's throat had been slit. The cut was so deep that his head was almost entirely severed from his spinal cord.

The weapon was gone, of course, but the sharp clean cut to his flesh could have come from a fishmonger's shiny long blade.

The dirty white T-shirt that he had worn when I saw him had been saturated with enough of his blood to be described simply, on a police report, as a "red? shirt." The pack of Camel cigarettes was missing from the shirt pocket.

Maybe he had smoked them all. He'd certainly seemed nervous enough to try to calm himself with the soothing self-medication of nicotine and repetitive inhales. Had he driven alone through the night to reach his downstate lair, propelled by some inner demon I could not recognize to return to his apartment? Had his killer been waiting there? Had Eddie been trying to keep an appointment?

Or, had he met his murderer in the shadows outside Raymond's? Perhaps Eddie had been right when he said he saw someone hanging around in the darkness, near his truck. But if that were the case, why wouldn't the watchers—the faceless,

F

L

A

M

E

W

A

R

nameless men who followed Annie and me—have noticed someone outside? All they remembered seeing was Eddie getting into the cab of his truck. They noted the bright flare of orange when he lit up a cigarette. They noted that when the truck started, its right blinker was on. Eddie had shut it off and pulled away.

Maybe Eddie had accidentally brushed against the turn signal lever when he slid into the driver's seat. Or maybe someone else had done it, climbing surreptitiously into the cab while Eddie was still inside the restaurant.

In any case, that was the last time that anyone had seen him alive, and the surveillance report noted that it seemed unusual that Eddie left the scene without Blaney. "Did they have some sort of a fight?" my mother asked me when she read the report to me. We were sitting in the uncomfortable gray office she inhabited down at the local police station. It was a room that had always reminded me of metal, with its hard clean surfaces and lack of invitation.

"They were jittery and paranoid," I said. "But under the circumstances, that didn't seem unusual."

I could see where this was headed, of course, but for some reason I refused to buy into the concept of Blaney as Eddie's murderer. I wouldn't say it was because I felt protective of Blaney, in particular—despite my panic attack only hours earlier about Blaney, I no longer harbored any illusions that Blaney was dangerous, that Blaney was a threat, personally, to me. So as I sat on the wrong side of my mother's desk, in the uncomfortable schoolteacher's chair into which she maneuvered her infrequent guests, I found myself unwilling to add any bits of circumstantial evidence against the missing cousin. Why should I help out the FBI? Or more important, betray Blaney?

I didn't mention the phone call from Blaney, for instance. There was no really logical reason for the omission, no, for the outright lie, let's face my actions for what they were. My gut told me, for the second time that morning, to shut up about it. I had felt the same way when Lionel had phoned earlier. He had heard the news, of course. He asked me directly if I knew where Blaney was—the question of the hour—but I was able to say honestly that I didn't know. I had wondered then, fleetingly, if Blaney also had contacted Lionel and if Lionel was in fact concealing that information from *me*. But why? To see what I would say? A loyalty test? The possibility made me feel as if I had been transported physically into an Escher drawing, where repetitive images played out for a wearying eternity.

Annie, who had been listening to me obfuscate to Lionel, picked obsessively at a loose thread on her shorts and wondered aloud what good it would serve to obscure evidence.

Of course that's when I had suggested that I visit my mother's office—just to see what else I might learn. Annie had wondered, reasonably, how I would be able to talk to my mother about Eddie's death without revealing how I found out about it. "I'm not going there to report the murder," I said. "I'm going there to see if she reports it to me. Do you have any laundry to take into town?"

It was a measure of how inured to death and violence we had become that neither of us remarked much on the fact that Eddie had ceased to exist. Was this how soldiers trapped in a foxhole started to behave, when yet another guy in the company took a direct hit from a machine gun? Eddie's dead. Oh, that's interesting. Now pack up your delicates and let's go to the laundry. Got enough quarters?

I dropped Annie at the coin wash with a bag of dirty shirts to create our cover. As she hauled the army-issue duffel bag out of the backseat, she said, "You don't even trust your own mother, Harry?"

"I'll pick you up in an hour." I leaned over to pull shut the door. I drove over to the police station, just to say good morning.

But my mother wasn't buying. "The waitress at Raymond's said that Eddie seemed angry."

"Eddie was always angry. The first time I met him, he tried to kill a cabdriver for sport."

"Blaney has been acting like he was on the run for a while now, Harry. I would imagine that their cat-and-mouse game with the federal government would have provided a nice background flavor of suspense in their lives," she said. "Why didn't you tell me that Blaney was mixed up in the Crypto Urban Militia?"

"I figured Dellis told you."

She shrugged. That's not the same as hearing it from your own son, her judgmental shoulders said.

What kept tripping me up was the timing. It was well after midnight when Eddie left Raymond's. The body had been officially discovered at 9:30 A.M. in Manhattan, by Yuri, who was the only roommate to hold a day job, and therefore usually the first to shower. He had walked into the bathroom with his dingy towel (embroidered accusingly with the label HOLIDAY INN) flung over his shoulder. He didn't remember screaming when he saw Eddie. But the others heard his hoarse cries. They must have been pretty loud to wake up that crew.

"It's a six-hour drive down to Manhattan," my mother noted.

"Five when you drive."

"I wasn't driving."

She said that the police believed that Eddie had traveled alone to Manhattan, parked his truck on the street outside his building sometime before sunrise, and walked up the steps to his apartment. They conjectured that the killer had been inside, waiting. Maybe the killer had waited until everyone in the apartment went to bed, then slipped in through the front door. That theory required the killer to have a key, as no signs of forced entry were noted.

Or maybe the killer didn't have to break in. The police seemed to believe that any of Eddie's roommates would make a good suspect. They were mixed up in enough dirty business to be obvious candidates, after all. In that case, the list of possible suspects was big enough to create the rudiments of a board game. Let's see, was it Yuri with the pizza box in the living room? Or was it Dim, wielding a laptop in the kitchen?

"The official theory is that a single killer knocks the victim over the head, knocks him unconscious, or at least stuns him," my mother went on in a dispassionate voice, flipping efficiently through the stack of notes she had taken. She sipped a bitter taste of cold coffee from a Styrofoam cup. She usually nursed a single cup for the whole morning.

"Then, the killer removes Eddie's belt, restrains his hands, drags or carries him into the bathroom," she continued, "where the actual event occurred."

"The event was a murder, Mom, and the killer must have been a man, if he carried Eddie anywhere."

"Maybe there were two assailants." A long silence.

"Annie and I have alibis."

"I remember."

Then she said, "I hope Blaney does too."

There was little more she could tell me. When I got back to the Laundromat, Annie was waiting at the curb. I turned left to head out of town. I was getting so used to the appearance of the unmarked cars that usually followed us on the road that I didn't always notice when one fell in behind whatever vehicle I was piloting. But today I noticed the gray Chevy sedan, although its only unusual feature was a second roof antenna. In the days after he discovered the flaw in Patriot, did the same kind of car start to follow Ames's movements around the city, maybe even tag along when he drove upstate with his daughter, maintaining a discreet distance of a quarter mile or more on the Thruway's straightaways? Funny how I didn't feel *protected* by my watchers.

So we zipped along a two-lane back road, following a winding route along the banks of Hazard Creek. I nursed the gas pedal, testing my car's limits. I was surprised that the government-issue car behind me could keep pace. I was confident going forty-five mph only because this tricky terrain—twists through scrub pines and rocky overhangs—was as familiar to me as the individual parts of my bike's brake mechanism. I'd driven this way at least a thousand times before. But I would have felt reckless going that speed around unknown bends.

"What did your mother say?"

"She thinks it's Blaney. Warned me not to have any contact with him."

"The thing that bothers me is why he didn't come back inside to cadge a ride from us after he realized his cousin had taken off without him."

Maybe he wasn't given the choice. I took a hairpin turn too fast and skidded. I corrected the car's trajectory a full three seconds before we would have smashed into a guardrail. Annie didn't seem to notice. Or maybe in the weird new world of death and danger that we inhabited, this kind of behavior had come to seem normal. As I say, we were under a lot of pressure by then.

"You're trying to avoid the subject because you don't want to admit the possibility that something horrible happened to him," Annie said.

I didn't like to think of him as dead.

I didn't like to think of him as a killer.

But those were the two possibilities that seemed most likely. I kept going back to the description of how Eddie's body had been found. Not once had anyone mentioned seeing Blaney, speaking to Blaney, phoning Blaney.

And yet he had known, before anyone, that Eddie was dead.

"Could he have gotten back to Manhattan in time to see Eddie alive again?" Annie asked.

Of course he could. As soon as the news spread through town about Blaney's troubles, I expected that someone would drop in casually to my mother's office and just happen to mention picking up Blaney at the side of the road last night.

"You're frowning," Annie said, obviously annoyed that I hadn't answered her.

"It's that car behind us," I said.

Ahead, I saw a semitrailer groaning up a steep hill. I knew that the straightaway would give way to a series of snake coils about 150 yards beyond. Could I pass the truck before then? I floored it.

"Harry, are you crazy?"

The engine whined, but responded, for once, in an obliging way. It must have been feeling some gratitude toward me for religiously changing the oil every fifteen hundred miles. The car probably could sense that if it had been left to my mother's devices, the engine would have burned up years ago. It rewarded me now by overtaking the truck, and sliding easily back into our lane a good eighty feet before the first curve. I braked serenely. I knew all the variables of this particular journey.

I figured I must have lost the feebs behind us, but the next time the road straightened out for a few hundred feet, I caught a telltale glimpse of sunlight glinting off a windshield far behind. They'd passed the truck too. But when? Whoever was driving was more of a risk taker than your average FBI agent entrusted with a government car.

Annie glanced over her shoulder at the sedan, which had caught up and was now, in fact, tailgating. It was unusual that the driver was alone in the car; our watchers usually came in pairs.

"The driver is not one of the agents who usually has the day shift," she said. "I don't recognize him."

Unfortunately, I did.

Maybe he wore contact lenses. Or else the aviator glasses had just been part of his cover, a clumsy disguise that the man had worn the last time I had noticed him watching me. I hadn't seen him since the night of the meeting at Café Info, but I remembered Eddie's disgust: *Fucking feeb.* Today he didn't look myopic at all. Today he just looked crazy.

He was riding our bumper, so I easily recognized his chunky, bucket-shaped head, which seemed to affix itself to the top of his broad shoulders without benefit of a neck. A neck would have seemed too delicate, too slender a piece of piping to support his heavy brow.

"Annie, hold on, we need to get away from this guy."

"Who is he, Harry? Where is he from?"

Ames found something that he thought could change the course of history.

"Your dad was afraid of him."

Ames called the office of a well-respected and powerful man. He told him he had some information that he needed.

"You think the Minotaur is following us?"

"Maybe he just sent someone to do his dirty work for him," I said. Maybe the Minotaur preferred to stay clean in the off-line world.

I was forced to speed up, because if I hadn't, the grille on the front of his hood would have slammed into my trunk. Traveling at better than fifty miles per hour, any impact would have been too risky.

"Harry—" Our tires squealed as I involuntarily crossed the solid yellow line coming around Antler Bend.

"I saw him at the memorial service, and later that same night. Both times, though, he was just watching."

"Then he just disappeared?"

"Nothing weird about that these days."

"Is he FBI or local police? That's what you think?"

"Eddie thought he was some kind of agent, sent to spy on the militia."

"Eddie knew him?"

"He knew Eddie."

We had almost reached the suspension bridge over the gorge. I floored it. So did he.

I had a plan, though, and I hoped that it was the thing that separated me from the enemy.

About fifteen feet before the ramp to the bridge was a last-chance, curving stretch of asphalt, and then, at the lip of the bridge, a sudden turnoff that led down toward the state park. The road to the park was bumpy, and unpaved, and little used.

But the county kept the brush cut back enough to clear a right-of-way.

I slowed to take the curve, and I heard the screech of the Chevy's brakes behind me. I steered into the road, and around the bend, and made the turnoff perfectly.

But the sedan made it too.

"How the hell did he know about the turnoff?" I said.

I cut the gas then, and just coasted down toward the park, trying to avoid trees and rocks in the roadway and any stray deer that might take it into their heads to wander into my path.

Annie was holding on to the door handle, white-lipped and silent, as we made our descent. Halfway down the side of the gorge, I hit something. It sounded like rock against the undercarriage of the car, and it spun us out of control.

"Hold on," I yelled, and wrestled the wheel. But now we were in a bumper car, and we bounced off a fir tree on the left, then came to rest, engine smoking, in a narrow ditch along the edge of the track.

I looked at Annie, and saw that the force of the impact hadn't knocked her unconscious. She looked rattled, and scared, but then so did I, I'm sure.

He screeched to a halt about twenty feet behind us, and came bounding out of his car, gun drawn, yelling, "Exit the vehicle! Exit your vehicle and put your hands up, up, where I can see them!"

My door didn't seem to open anymore, and so I slid across and out Annie's side behind her. We emerged as cautiously as a pair of tortoises who expected, upon sticking our heads out of our shells, to be greeted by a drunken teenager wielding a baseball bat.

"Put your hands on your heads! Get down on the ground!"

He was only three feet away from us now, and he looked like he was about to lose it and shoot us in the face. But somehow, both Annie and I reacted instinctively, and in the same manner. We just continued to stand there, befuddled, staring at him.

He pushed me, roughly, face first into the side of the car, and I felt him search for concealed weapons. Then he did the same to Annie.

"You fucking idiots!" he screamed. "You almost got all of us killed!"

A tiny part of the old smart-ass me still lived, somewhere deep in my battered psyche, and it was that rogue cell that now prompted me to say, "Do you have any identification, Officer?"

Which was a mistake. The goon elbowed me, hard, in the back of the head, crushing my face into the car. I didn't need a mirror to know that my nose was bleeding. Hell, it was probably broken.

He backed up a couple of steps and said, "Turn around. Slowly."

We did, and that's when I realized that something was wrong with this picture. The guy was wearing the same kind of dark, almost-cheap suit that I had seen on most of the FBI agents in recent days, but there the similarity ended. What remained of his hair was ragged and unkempt around his ears. A dark stubble covered his jawline. He was agitated, and his BB eyes darted everywhere and nowhere, all at once.

He waved his gun at us, then pointed: "Get in my car."

Annie and I exchanged a look. Hers said: "What if we don't?" Mine said, "Nice knowing you."

"Let me drive," Annie said, and before he could stop her, pulled open the passenger's door and slid across. Would she have driven off and left me behind? I don't think so, but who knows? She had that almost vicious streak of determination, of course, and here was someone who was trying to thwart her. I wonder if, at that precise moment, she even remembered that I was there.

The man jumped into the passenger's side before she could

floor it, and so I slid into the backseat. It rattled him that we were in two different locations, and he kept moving the barrel of the gun back and forth, sighting it on both our foreheads.

It occurred to me that this would have been the perfect time and place for him to kill us, on this silent and isolated stretch of land that wasn't visible from the main road. He could just drag our bodies into the trees and leave them. It might be weeks before anyone came this way again. Instead, he fished around in the glove compartment for a paper towel. To me he said, "Mop your fucking nose." I took the paper towel.

To Annie: "Reverse it up the hill."

She glanced over her shoulder, ascertained that his face and his gun wore the same expression, and obeyed.

"Where do you want me to go?" she asked.

"Over the bridge. Slow."

On the other side, he said suddenly, "Pull over here."

We parked on the deserted shoulder, and I turned slowly to face my captor.

"Who are you?" I said.

"Fuck do you care?" he answered. "You writing a book?"

Neither of us said a word.

"Where's Blaney?" the man asked.

"We don't know."

"He call you? After he popped his cousin?"

"He phoned this morning."

The man's busy eyes searched my face, then Annie's, rav-enously seeking clues about our truthfulness. He must have been satisfied with what he saw, because he lowered the barrel of the gun a notch and said, "Repeat the phone conversation. Word for word. Don't leave anything out."

"He said, 'Harry, it's me. Eddie's dead. He's dead, man.' "

"Go on."

"That's it. That's all he said."

"The fucking phone went dead on you, Harry? Like in the goddamn movies?"

"He repeated it. That's all."

I tried not to think about all the other things Blaney had said to me, his words tripping over each other in the rushed hysteria that had overtaken him, because I did not want them to show on my face now. I had never heard anyone sound as scared as Blaney did, his voice cracking, when he whispered: "Garnet, Eddie's the second."

The first conspirator to die had been Fred Ames, Blaney had said. Ames had not disassociated himself as completely from the crypto militants as Eddie had led me to believe. Maybe he had stopped attending meetings. Certainly, he disapproved of their plan to create a circus at a congressional hearing—Ames was, after all, a man used to working *within* a system. But if he had been uncomfortable with the more anarchic notions the militia harbored, he had remained philosophically bound to them. He opposed Patriot; he opposed any key-escrow encryption standard that would give the government a license to rummage in its citizens' affairs. His distrust was the result of personal experience. He knew very well, after a stint at NSA, just how seriously the spooks took certain laws. He knew which laws were considered gospel and which were mere *technicalities*, like requirements to get *warrants*, those permission slips signed by judges. So Fred Ames had retained ties to the militia, and was plugged in enough to know they were trying to get both halves of the Patriot key. And no one would know better than Ames that the militia could succeed. "I was surprised that he cared, either way," Blaney had said. "At the meetings, he seemed so apart from it all, nasty little smile on his face, like a teacher in the playground watching a bunch of kids kick around a ball but not bothering to tell them the rules of the game."

With his new, lower profile, Ames had pretty much disappeared from Blaney's personal radar screen weeks before their last, unscheduled meeting. But was it really a surprise that Fred Ames hadn't been in search of restorative tennis or soul-searching talks with his daughter when he booked a week at The Vines? The old warhorse had merely been creating cover, and a measure of its plausibility was the fact that not once had any FBI agent suggested that the presence of a finicky, book-bound man like Ames was unusual in the rugged rock-bound region where he died. No, a summer vacation in a cool, mountainous climate was an obvious choice.

It had been ingenious to use his daughter—a lot of fathers might not have stooped to that—but Ames had been more careful than most veterans of his agency. The government was keeping a close watch on the urban militia members; that was a given. He couldn't meet Blaney in the city, couldn't attend any more meetings during this time of heightened strategy and danger. It would have been foolish to risk a phone call on a tapped line, or a public encounter at Café Info that might be photographed clandestinely. No, for what Ames had to say to Blaney, a casual, spur-of-the-moment visit was far more appropriate.

"He came walking into the store, middle of the day. I'm with a customer, you know, and I wonder at first if it's a hallucination. The sun was shining through the plate glass, and I saw the outline of his frizzy hair, kind of silhouetted there. I had to blink."

By the time Blaney had disengaged himself from his customer, Ames was at the end of an aisle, studiously concentrating on the fine print on a software box that held a game of Myst. "I could have just gone into the stockroom, avoided him completely, thought about doing it, I mean it couldn't have been good news that he was there, Garnet. But it was too weird," Blaney had said. So instead he had sidled up to Ames and asked, "May I help you?"

Ames had looked up pleasantly, vacantly almost, so that if anyone were watching the encounter, the only logical interpretation of the meeting would be that a salesclerk had approached a customer. And that the two were strangers. In a low voice, in the tone he might use to ask "Is this IBM-compatible?" Ames said carefully, "Don't react.

"I heard about your recent efforts and that you're close to obtaining the key," Ames said, his eyes on the software box again, his finger running down the ad copy on its face as if he were asking a question about RAM requirements.

"Who told you? Nelson?"

"That doesn't matter, Richard."

Blaney, more worried about the possibility that the floor manager's observant eyes were trained his way—a recent memo to the employees had warned against fraternizing with acquaintances on company time—than about his more generalized fear of government surveillance, had reached over to take the box out of Ames's hands. He turned it in his own, as if searching among the software specs for the answer to the customer's odd question about the product.

"Have you come all the way up here to offer to help us, Ames?"

"You're not stupid, Richard. You know better. I came to ask you to wait."

"Why?"

"I need more time."

"For what, Ames? You're not part of this."

"I found a flaw. A vulnerability. There's something strange about it. As if the code were deliberately written that way. I need more time to understand it."

Blaney stared at Ames, amazed, unable to conceal his admiration. "How?"

Perhaps Blaney didn't react as quickly as he should have to process the unusual information that Ames was conveying, but truth be told, the demeanor of a supplicant was so unusual in Ames that Blaney was thrown off guard. He was more used to the blunt, aggressive utterances of a man completely in control of both his subject matter and his students, a man who rarely found cause to question his own impulses or conclusions. The idea of someone like Ames asking a favor of anyone—much less of a mere mortal such as Blaney—was nearly inconceivable. Here was someone who had *cracked the code*, who by dint of intellect and instinct had rendered moot the militia's whole scheme to steal the two halves of the key. Why bother to steal the key to Patriot when a mathematician could use simple brainpower to deconstruct the algorithm?

"Think of it like a skeleton key. I wrote a number of programs that work together to unlock it. I'm still refining it."

"Why should that change our timetable?"

Ames paused, considering how to phrase the request. "It would be a personal favor to me, Richard. Well, actually a favor to a friend of mine, a close friend who has a strong professional interest in the outcome of the debate over Patriot. I don't want to embarrass him if it isn't necessary. I don't want to jeopardize your movement, either. What would it hurt to wait three months?"

"And you'll share your discovery with us, of course? You know this information is worth more than gold."

Surprisingly, Ames laughed. "Yes. But to whom? I don't know that yet."

Ames had hesitated then, trying to decide whether to tell Blaney about the rest of the problem he was wrestling with.

"Trust me, Professor." Surely the slightly sweaty sheen to Blaney's forehead, reflected in the fluorescence of the store's lighting, would have undercut the remark. For there was an oily aspect to both Blaney's appearance and to his manner—the way his eyes darted to the ends of the aisles and back, always on the lookout for the boss, always on the lookout for trouble—that would have made it seem laughable to an onlooker that a man as composed and controlled as Ames would put faith in Blaney. But Ames was confused. And scared. If only he had known enough about himself to know that, then maybe he would have known enough to save his life.

Ames said he had recently met his friend—who appeared to work for the government in some capacity, from what Blaney could glean—in a public plaza, where they sat stiffly along the ledge of a tepid fountain, pigeons at their feet, heat in the air, no doubt an odor of old urine rising from the concrete path below their feet. They would have been more comfortable in an air-conditioned restaurant, ordering wine with lunch, as they had on so many earlier meetings. What concerned Ames most was that when he confided his secret—that he had found a flaw—to his friend, "He became enraged," Ames told Blaney. "I hadn't expected that. I was looking for advice, a sounding board, and instead he was in a rage. I felt as if I were in the presence of an unpredictable stranger."

The two kept in touch online, even when they couldn't meet in person. Ames said, "We frequented the same online communities, we sent E-mail to each other nearly every day, but now days passed without any response to the E-mail I sent. I realized something was very wrong."

Ames sent an urgent E-mail to his friend, asking for a meeting. This time, he got a reply. "My friend asked me to meet him at a hotel outside Washington where, he said, no one would recognize him. He wrote that he wanted me to explain to him exactly how I had found the flaw and how it worked: 'Please bring all computer programs and documentation that you possess relating to this procedure.' "

Blaney was not sure how to react to this revelation, or whether to react at all. Ames saved him the decision: "So, Richard, there is my problem. I seem to have stumbled into a situation that has broader ramifications than the code itself. I seem to have hit a sore spot with my friend."

"What did he say to you when you went to meet him at the hotel?"

"I didn't go. I came here instead."

Blaney promised Ames that he would talk to Eddie and the other militia members. "You should come to the next meeting yourself, Professor. If you told us that we wouldn't have to go to all the trouble of, uh, obtaining the key on our own, I think we could work something out on timing."

"Think about it, Richard."

After the professor left, Blaney had been filled with two wild but contradictory impulses: to share his news with his militia colleagues, or to keep his incredible secret to himself. He wrestled with the two delicious possibilities all the rest of that day, throughout his shift at Computer Nation, later in the cramped apartment where he opened a can of Dinty Moore stew for supper, and through the long hours that the screech of a Metallica album kept him company. Before Blaney could decide, Ames made the decision for him. He died.

And so Blaney had realized that no one needed to know that he had been one of the last people on the face of the earth to see Ames alive.

Why Blaney chose to come clean with me, at that moment on the phone, was obvious. Eddie was dead. The situation had escalated, had become far more of a crisis than Blaney could handle; he wanted to absolve himself of the responsibility of cleaning up the mess he had made. He wanted me to own the problem. The possibility that Blaney would confess his secrets was evidently as novel to our captor as it had been to me, because he did not press me for such indiscreet details. Instead, he emitted a dry whistle of short airy pulses, and considered something. Then, he said to me: "So he didn't say whether he still had it?"

"Had what?"

"The key. His half." He looked at Annie. "No more games, okay?"

She held up her hands. "No more rough stuff, okay?"

"The key?" he asked again.

"I have no idea," I said.

Suddenly he reached back over the seat and grabbed me by the hair. My head jerked back and when my eyes stopped tearing up, I was looking at the roof of the car. There was a little tear in the fabric up there.

"You have the other half, Harry?"

"No."

"But you're making plans to drive down to Washington in the very near future?"

My neck burned painfully, and he jabbed the cold muzzle of his gun up against my Adam's apple.

"I'm a lawyer. Blaney wanted legal advice."

F

L

A

M

E

W

A

R

He barked. I realized, mainly because he released his hold on me, that the harsh sound was what passed for laughter from him. "Well, he fucking needs it, that's for sure."

I tried not to make an obvious show of how grateful I was that I could swallow again, and turn my head, and smell something other than metal and cordite.

Now his voice was low and almost gentle. "So who does have the other half?" he said conversationally.

Was it possible that he didn't know? It was possible, I guess, that even Blaney, the hacker extraordinaire, had made some blunder when he broke into a computer network to steal his half, possible that he had left his electronic fingerprints behind. What surprised me was that Lionel had been so much smarter.

"Not us," Annie said shrilly. "We don't know."

"Well, you take a message to your friends for me," he said. "You tell them that I will be very, very unhappy—let's say personally disappointed—if I find out that some other hacker has been fucking with my agency's computers."

"What agency are you from?"

"The talent agency." His watery blue eyes blazed from behind the aviator glasses, but gave away nothing.

"You killed Eddie," Annie said.

He laughed again. "Wish I'd thought of it. Truly do."

He lowered his gun, pushed the nose of it into his belt. "I have some advice for you, kiddies. Best advice you'll ever hear."

He opened the door, got out of the car, and laced his hands together behind his back. He faced us like a professor addressing a class of halfwits. "Stay the fuck away from Washington. *Capisce?*"

We nodded our heads.

"Now get the fuck out of my car."

chapter twelve

W hat else could we do? We went to the hearing, of
course. We had come way too far to be scared off by
... what? A rogue federal agent? A mad bomber? A minotaur?
The many knives that lay in wait for us, the bear traps with
gnashing stainless-steel teeth, the two-ton safes dropped from
the skies—together we had reached a shell-shocked kind of
acceptance of our new and dangerous world. I'm not saying
we'd become hardened or even emboldened by our experi-
ences. We simply plodded on, intuiting that we would end this
thing. Or it would end us.

Annie and I had driven from Timber Lake to Washington
alone, racing through the gelid summer night. At around 3:00
A.M., we pulled over at a rest stop outside of Delaware and
slept for a few hours, upright and snuggled close, like canaries.
We had taken my mother's car, after telling the chief we
wanted to attend the hearing in honor of Annie's father, who,
we said, had been scheduled to testify. Doubt my mother
bought that one. Her only response was a gravelly warning:

Expect to see FBI types lurking in the background, keeping an eye on us.

We grabbed breakfast in the nation's Capitol at a dining room in the Rayburn Building where the too-polite African-American staff wore white linen uniforms and worked a steam table and where the cashier called us "sir" and "ma'am." Eggs and grits. It was weird, driving ten hours from one eco-system to another. From one political landscape to another, from the North to the South.

I was content, of course, to wear one set of clothes for the rest of the week. Annie, being Annie, brought a single back-pack that somehow managed to include a toothbrush and all the other mysterious stuff she required. Was this how she roughed it on digs? I wondered as I watched her glide away to a rest room. I lingered in front of the hearing room, killed time by hitting the water fountain, buying a *Washington Post*, reading the various bulletin boards and their announcements of upcoming events. People began queuing up for the hearing; some looked familiar.

"Hey, hey!" said a short fellow as he streamed by me to the front of the line. It was Dim. He was so jazzed by wherever he'd spent the night and by the anticipation of the impending hearing that he barely slowed down. "You dressed up. Good," he said. Aside from leaving his gold lip ring home, he hadn't. I didn't think an acid-green sweatshirt, calf-length surfer shorts, and Doc Maarten clogs were going to go over big with the U.S. Senate, but I kept my mouth shut. Why add to his stress?

"Hey." I nodded. "Any word from Blaney?"

"Nada," said Dim, who was practically jumping up and down in place. "Nada fucking thing. Whew. Weird doin's, no?" He shook his head.

"Were you there? When Yuri found Eddie's body?"

"Yuppers. Sleeping. I mean, until all the noise, all the commotion. It would have been hard to sleep through that shit.

Sick scene. Very ugly work. I liked Eddie," he said quickly. "He had a temper on him but he never gave me a hard time."

Two security guards were busily readying the metal detector at the doorway to the hearing room. I felt as if we were waiting to get into a rock concert.

"I went into Eddie's room. After," Dim said. "Stupid cops couldn't figure anything out from the mess in there." He snickered. "One of 'em asks me, is it always like this? Of course, they took samples of everything they could find, vacuumed up every last hair and all. Forensics work—it might be kind of cool. But the dumbasses missed the forest for the trees."

"How's that?" I asked gruffly, suddenly feeling like Joe Friday.

"Eddie's computer. They missed it."

"You mean they left it behind?"

"No, they took it. They just didn't understand what they were taking."

I looked at him blankly.

"There was nothing on it," said Dim. "The whole machine had been wiped, reformatted. You understand, dude? Whoever killed Eddie did it because of something he had on his box."

"Did you tell the cops this?"

"Fuck, no. They're probably the ones who killed him. Hey— save me a seat inside." Dim preceded me through the metal detector, but by the time I joined him he had spied a pal and run off.

I found three seats in a spectator's aisle, first row actually, sat down, and tried to read the *Post*. But the surroundings were too grand and I couldn't concentrate. At one end of the hearing room, the senators were to sit behind a mahogany table long enough to skate on. Its high-gloss finish was as smooth as the ice after the Zamboni man's midgame pass. I imagined the men behind it would wear the stern expressions of referees whose calls are not to be overruled. Paneled in a rich walnut that bespoke an earlier generation's Anglophilia, the cavernous room smelled of cigars smoked a hundred years ago.

"Look at the nameplates. Why are they all men?" Annie whispered as she slid in next to me. I barely recognized her in her belted navy-blue jacket and pants, neat French braid, and leather loafers. She looked like Katharine Hepburn. I was still wearing my lucky suit. My only suit. The same suit I wore from Timber Lake on down. I looked like I itched, because I did.

Reflexively, I scanned the crowd for Blaney. But Blaney was still missing.

By the time the senators arrived half an hour late to claim their overstuffed leather chairs and to shuffle important papers, the hearing room was standing room only. A line had formed behind a velvet rope in the hallway and people were giving me dirty looks for saving a seat for Dim. Two hundred chairs were filled. Their occupants had the earnest look of civil libertarians, the savvy expressions of lobbyists representing the computer industry, the dull-eyed stare of midlevel managers in federal agencies. All were poised to take notes. An air of expectancy accompanied a harried young woman with a clipboard who trotted up and down the plush carpet with her Senate name tag askew on her collar, checking off the names of each person scheduled to testify.

The senators filed in. The long table, the identical dark blue suits from Brooks Brothers, the identical aides positioned two feet behind their master's chairs—all of it had been designed to limit individual liability. I was willing to bet that more than half of the dozen senators had first heard the words "Patriot software" this morning, in a hasty briefing in the back of the Lincoln Town cars that had transported them to the hearing. The administrative assistants who sat behind them were the ones who knew, the ones who had researched case law and the U.S. regulatory code, picked the brains of experts ahead of time, anticipated all possible questions—and the ramifications of any answers their bosses could give. The backup boys were the safety net, eager on the edges of their seats, ready to lean forward and whisper just the right advice into an ear that smelled of expensive cologne and late nights at the club.

As the chairman of the Judiciary Committee ceremoniously perched a pair of reading glasses on the end of a righteous nose and began to read his opening statement, I saw Dim in the doorway. He hovered there, anxious, suddenly afraid to come in but more afraid to stay in the hall. Barely had he settled into his seat when he whispered, "Lionel."

"What about him?"

"He's here. He came." I turned and searched the room, but I couldn't see Lionel anywhere. I was surprised Lionel hadn't mentioned his plans when we had conferred yesterday, by phone, about my strategy for saving the militia's hide.

"He took the first shuttle down this morning," Dim said. "Couldn't sleep all night, he said."

"Are you relieved?" I sure as hell wasn't. I had been dreading the moment when somebody got hauled off in handcuffs, me playing the role of the impotent legal adviser, wringing my useless hands as the coppers clapped my pseudo client upside the head with a billy club. I had never defended anyone, not in court, not on the streets, not in the hearing room of a Senate subcommittee. I might never be ready.

"He wants me to sit at the table with him."

The first witness was Maynard G. Bentley, director of the Federal Bureau of Investigation. Here was a civil servant who proclaimed his independence from the senators who voted on his annual budget by donning a gray suit instead of blue. He pushed up the aisle with the full knowledge of his authority, with a few boys of his own in tow (blue suits), and they all settled portentously at the witness table facing the senators. The locks on fine-tooled leather briefcases clicked open. Microphones were rearranged. Notepads, silver pens, and a perspiring pitcher of ice water materialized, miraculously, in front of Bentley's folded hands. He was calm.

Along the side wall, a long video screen silently lowered

from the ceiling. It was twenty feet square, bigger than the screen in a lot of multiplexes that charge you $8.50. A tasteful spotlight above drew attention to its creamy, parchmentlike surface.

"They have their own demonstration planned," Annie whispered. Worried.

"And theirs is probably legal."

Bentley took his time arranging his notes. He knew his audience, and he would play to them. "About a month ago, I received a phone call from one of you gentlemen, seeking background information on the issue of adopting a federal encryption standard," he began. "At the time, I was sitting at my desk in my inner office, the safest and most unassailable location I can name. To come into my office and hear my private phone calls, one would first have to get past the uniformed guard and the metal detector in the lobby of our building, then use a specially coded, computerized identification card to convince the elevator to stop at my floor, then persuade another uniformed guard in the hall to open a reinforced, bulletproof door that leads down a corridor to my secretary's office, where she would be ready to push a panic button if an unannounced visitor appeared.

"One would believe, with all those precautions, that my conversation with the senator—regarding matters of public safety and national security—was safe from prying ears. But the next morning, I logged into my E-mail account and found this transcript of the conversation sent to me."

The transcript appeared on the video screen. We all could read it. SEN: THIS SHOULD REMAIN CONFIDENTIAL BETWEEN US? BEN: AGREE IT WOULD BE DANGEROUS TO DISSEMINATE AT THIS POINT, EVEN TO SENIOR STAFF . . .

What a cheap trick, I thought, but you had to admire the drama of it.

"Now, let me assuage your fears, gentlemen—our national security has not been hopelessly compromised. My phone conversation had been intercepted at my own behest. The task

Joshua Quittner

was accomplished by one of the bright young hackers who actually works *for* the Federal Bureau of Investigation. I had called the agent into my office a week earlier and issued a challenge: How hard would it be for you to intercept an unencrypted voice transmission from a phone line in our building? As you can see, the bright young hacker answered my question fully. Within the course of a few days, he was able to pinpoint and intercept a specific communication on my own private line. My point, quite simply, is that unencrypted transmissions are inherently vulnerable.''

Bentley paused for that statement to sink in, and then he continued smoothly: "How did this interception occur? Simple. The senator was calling me from a cellular phone on an airplane. We might as well have broadcast our talk over network TV during halftime of the Super Bowl. A scanner captured the conversation.''

The senators pretended to be deeply disturbed by this recitation, each probably replaying the audio from a sensitive phone conversation he had conducted sometime in the past twenty-four hours. Seated at the far left of the table, Senator Owen Larch blushed so deeply that the color of his face perfectly matched his rep tie. Maybe he really didn't know how easy it was to eavesdrop on cellular calls, though it was hard to believe. This was a story as old as sin. Still, Larch, the old reprobate, probably wouldn't be making any more calls to his mistress from Air Force I anytime soon.

Bentley continued: "In this instance, we were lucky. No law enforcement operations compromised. But who knows about the next time? We live in an increasingly digitized society, where our means of communication have changed radically in the past ten years, where our ability to promise privacy has been steadily eroded, and where law enforcement's best efforts are threatened by the Internet.

"We need a weapon to fight back, gentlemen, not only to encrypt our own legal conversations, but also to ensure we have the means to decrypt the data transmissions of those who would use technology to break the law. Our society is headed, inexorably, for a day when all data communications will be encrypted to protect privacy. We need to actively manage that evolution, to provide the government with the ability to assail felons who would wrongfully employ encryption for nefarious purposes.

"I have spent the past six months conducting a detailed examination of the Patriot software," he said. "I have come to believe that, carefully deployed in the National Eavesdropping Center, it is the only viable alternative. Our plan has the clear advantage of maintaining a government role in interception of illegal transmissions. If we don't move forward today, events may overtake us. The federal government's attempts to mediate and regulate this new area of communications will be swept aside by the public's rush to embrace untested and uncrackable code making."

Bentley paused for a sip of water, and to read the slip of paper one of his aides slid across the table to him. He cleared his throat and gave the senators a quick history lesson. He told them that until the late 1970s, the federal government was one of the few entities to use encryption. In those days, code making and code breaking were synonymous with national security, with spy talk. I wondered briefly where Fred Ames, toiling at the Department of Defense, had fit into that scenario.

But after the Data Encryption Standard was adopted as a federal standard to scramble data, everything changed. Banks discovered the usefulness of DES to protect cash transactions. The private sector discovered the value of encrypting sensitive data that might otherwise fall into the hands of ambitious competitors.

"The DES standard, and other methods of encryption—up to and including the Patriot program—were made possible by the fact that phone and computer communications are digitized. The machines that convey information back and forth first translate the data into a string of ones and zeros, to be pumped over digital phone lines to their destinations, where the original message is reconstructed,'' Bentley said.

He picked up a remote control clicker from the table. We were about to see a video show. Click, and on the screen appeared a line of text that read, "This sentence is in English and now I will digitize it." Before our eyes, the text turned into a stream of *0*s and *1*s.

"Now I will scramble it with the Patriot algorithm, a set of mathematical steps that you can think of as a recipe. The recipe transforms the bits so that they seem random. Now, when the message reaches the recipient, its ones and zeros have been rearranged to look like this:''

ker3ie 944rxk p4e90sd 34ou483 f94402m 94vc9c 4u8f28d 668c84j demdd93 2717xki offfp0s 8cfuid8 d8weyds qw89xzu r9349ss 2398s87 389sfq2 09312by i49921j

Senator Larch asked, "Are you guaranteeing that this is essentially uncrackable?''

"By the capabilities of today's technologies, yes.''

I felt Dim fidget. Annie sat as still as toast.

Bentley went on to describe how the Patriot software would achieve, in his words, the "dual felicitous goals'' of protecting the privacy of the populace and giving the government access to individuals' personal conversations where warranted. It was a nimble performance.

He described how a computer running the Patriot software would invoke the escrow feature anytime that, say, a user wanted to send E-mail. The Patriot program would, without drawing attention to its activities, create a Law Enforcement Access Field that would act like a folder.

Up on the video screen appeared a folder, labeled LEAF. He clicked again, and the folder opened to reveal a long string of characters labeled "key,'' and another string of numbers labeled "serial number.''

Bentley explained that every session, or every separate message encoded by Patriot, generated its own unique key. Every copy of the Patriot program would have a twelve-digit serial number, as well, that would correspond to a master list maintained by the government, to enable verification of an origination site for each transmission. Up on the screen appeared an image of a hand, dropping the LEAF folder into a mailbox.

"The program will automatically send the folder to two destinations—the government agencies authorized to hold the keys in escrow," Bentley said.

"Two separate agencies, the National Institute of Standards and Technology and the U.S. Treasury, would each possess half the key. If a law enforcement agent suspected that the encrypted conversation was a high-level strategy session between a Mafia kingpin and his second-ranking lieutenant, for example, then the agent would obtain a court-sanctioned order to obtain, from the escrow agents, the two halves of the key to decrypt the conversation," Bentley continued. "On receipt of the court's order, they would turn over the information in the Law Enforcement Access Field. Then, and only then, could the law enforcement agencies actually decrypt the data."

The encoded message reappeared on the screen. An orange arrow labeled "key" shot onto the screen, struck the message, and turned it back into its original text:

"This sentence is in English and now I will digitize it."

Bentley said a number of safeguards would protect against random snooping. Today, FBI agents might run a recreational check on a vehicle identification number. But thanks to this new separation of powers, tomorrow's agents would have to jump through a number of new hoops to breach our privacy. It was a compelling argument. Too bad it was wrong.

"Gentlemen," he said, and I sensed a big finish. "I would like to close my testimony with a real-life demonstration."

Up on the video screen, in gibberish five feet high, appeared another long string of random numbers and alphabetic characters. Bentley explained that we were looking at the encrypted text of an actual data transmission, E-mail he himself had sent to one of the subcommittee members, Senator Francis Dunne, a few weeks earlier to test the capabilities of Patriot.

"If the Patriot standard were to be adopted, we would have to obtain a court order to get the key to decrypt this message," he said, as an image of a judge's signature superimposed itself on the screen, and then disappeared. "After we obtained both halves of the key to our session, we decoded it for you to read."

The gibberish melted into words we all could understand: SEN. DUNNE: WE CANNOT STRESS OUR POINT ENOUGH: PATRIOT WILL ENSURE PRIVACY AND PROTECTION, ITS ADOPTION IS ESSENTIAL.

A murmur swept through the room. It was the same hushed response the crowd offers up to Andre Agassi after he aces an opponent in the finals at Wimbledon. Bentley sat.

The words lingered on the wall.

A senator near the middle of the table pulled one of the microphones closer to his face and prepared to speak. I didn't need the prompt of his name tag, which announced him as Senator Francis X. Dunne of New York, to know who he was. I was used to seeing his bumper stickers on pickup trucks, and used to seeing his face on the current events roundtables that dominated the Sunday morning television lineup. He had made a career of excoriating government's regulatory intrusions into everyday life. That he had managed to maintain that platform and still coolly collect his salary from the U.S. Senate without seeming hypocritical was a testament to his powers to charm.

Dunne had been the senior senator from my state for as long as I could remember. Although he was best known in my county as the politician who had managed to secure a sixty-million-dollar construction grant for shoring up a series of bridges that crisscrossed the Big Moose River, he would doubtless prefer history to remember him as the author of *Educable Poverty: The Betrayal of the Welfare System*. I had actually tried to read it once in a political theory class.

With his aristocratic slimness and ruling-class posture, he easily could have been a member of George Bush's wedding party. Early one morning this summer, I had opened my cabin door as the sun rose. I was headed to Peterson's on my bike. In the yard, I saw a fox, paralyzed in fear by my intrusion into his world. Dunne reminded me now of that red fox, because he had the same sly nose, the same barely noticeable quiver at the nostrils, the same vulpine wariness. His voice betrayed a lifelong association with prep schools, old money, Harvard, and the best tailors. His polished tone was seldom disrupted by the less logical arguments proffered by colleagues. "Mr. Bentley."

"Senator?"

"What, in your opinion, would be the consequences if this body failed to press for the approval of the Patriot software?" the senator asked. Polite. Making cocktail party chitchat, nothing more.

The quick tilt of Bentley's head, his brusque reply, and the whispering between two of his aides at the end of the table were the clues that convinced me this exchange had not been rehearsed.

"Without Patriot, we will lose our ability to use wiretaps to gather evidence. We will no longer be able to seize documents, because encrypted documents would be as unintelligible as the Tower of Babel. Those investigative tools will belong to an earlier age. And if that happens, I fear for the lawlessness that will grip this nation."

The senator signaled his desire to follow up.

"Mr. Bentley."

"Senator?" I had the distinct impression these two were long-time antagonists, that they had battled before and that those clashes had wearied them for each other forever.

"Can you cite a single case, a single instance, where wiretaps or document seizures were the only source of evidence required to convict a criminal?'' The senator's voice was still conversational. "You must be well aware of the growing feeling, among forensics experts, that law enforcement officials rely far too heavily on wiretaps to gather evidence that would be stronger, and more useful in court, if it were obtained through good old-fashioned gumshoe detecting.''

Bentley blushed. He was saved from a response by the subcommittee chairman, the silver-haired Benjamin Wells of Massachusetts, who judiciously suggested a brief recess.

Forty minutes later—I suspected that a *long* recess would have carried us through the evening and into the next day—the senators reconvened and we learned that Mr. Bentley had been unexpectedly called back to his office. Despite the industrial-strength central air-conditioning in the Capitol, the room was becoming uncomfortably warm.

The second witness was Lionel.

He walked up the center aisle, wearing the only cream-colored linen suit that I had ever seen stay pressed in the middle of the summer. He carried a beautiful, buff-colored leather case, just big enough to house a laptop computer, and as he passed our aisle, he looked down the row and locked eyes with me. Briefly. Dim got up and followed him to the witness table.

Where the senators harbored a dull and overfed look, Lionel met them with a straight and steady stare. He was focused on only one thing—his mission—and he hurtled toward completion. Every muscle of his body, every glance, every small movement he made to set up his laptop, plug in cords, arrange the monitor to cut glare, was directed at the senators. And at a higher goal: His very presence emanated his belief that his was the side of right. That he would prevail. That there was no other possible outcome. His concentration was hypnotic.

He pulled the microphone to him. "Honorable senators, I

would like to introduce myself to those of you I have not met. I am Lionel Sullivan, a computer consultant and the author of one of the publicly distributed encryption programs that Mr. Bentley scorns. My software is called Knot, and its use guarantees to any citizen of this nation the right to privacy that the authors of the U.S. Constitution meant for us to enjoy.''

The senators didn't exactly look bored. They wouldn't risk such an expression with newspaper photographers in the room. So they maintained mild concern on their faces. But they slumped a little in their chairs, and surreptitiously took up pens to write notes to their aides about what they wanted for lunch. They had to hear Lionel's testimony in the same way that they had to work out three times a week. In this room, they had to make a show of considering all sides of the issue, all the facts, before making a reasoned decision. But I had spent the last two summers accompanying Peter Weinmiller, Esq., to the courtroom where he would address juries on behalf of his clients. He was the partner who handled malpractice cases, and he assigned me one job during the case in which he argued for a malpractice judgment, because look how that butcher of a surgeon had disfigured Mrs. Manning. I was supposed to watch the jurors' faces during testimony, and then tell him at break which were for us, which against, and what questions might sway the undecided.

Weinmiller said I got pretty good at it. Mrs. Manning was awarded $465,000 for a scar on her thigh that only showed in a bathing suit.

If the senators were jurors, they were reluctant ones. And Lionel would have to win them over.

The only one who showed any real interest in what he had to say was Francis X. Dunne, who leaned forward in his chair and fixed his gaze on Lionel's computer, which I had never seen before. Unlike the souped-up computers he had strewn about his house, Lionel's laptop was a compact, outdated model that had a small hard drive and a cracked DELETE key. He didn't want to risk damaging any of his expensive hardware on the trip to Washington.

Lionel remained confident. "I won't dwell on the civil rights issues, however, because there are more qualified experts scheduled to testify. What I wanted to show you today is my specialty: computer security."

He picked up a small plastic box that sat on the table next to his computer. It was connected to the laptop by a cord. "This is a dongle. It is a piece of hardware that enables me to log in to my computer system at home in Manhattan. To make sure that no one else can break into my system, I have to use a specially coded card"—and here he pulled a credit card from his pocket and ran it through a reader on the dongle— "to announce my authorized identity to my system at home."

He hit a key on his computer, and the screen on the wall lit up. In harsh black type, letters five feet tall, was the message: PATRIOT HAS A FATAL FLAW: ANYONE CAN EAVESDROP ON ANYONE ELSE.

He clicked again, and the screen went blank. "The point, gentlemen, is this. By giving both halves of the key to everyone's encrypted sessions to two government agencies, you will in effect be killing privacy in this country."

He typed again, and on the screen appeared a brief block of text, gibberish.

"This, senators, is an E-mail message that was encoded using the Patriot software. The message was mailed from a Justice Department computer to another government computer earlier this month. It was intercepted on the Internet—which, as you know, is an easy task to accomplish in these days of vulnerable phone lines and sophisticated hackers. Because the message was encrypted, however, its contents remained secure. For the moment."

He clicked again. Up on the screen appeared two strings of numerals, strange punctuation marks and alphabetic characters.

"I am sorry to say, gentlemen, that here we are looking at both halves of the key needed to decrypt that message. I was told the key was obtained from two servers connected to the Internet: one at NIST, one at Treasury."

Another click, and by now the room was as entranced as if Harry Houdini himself were straitjacketed and hanging from the chandelier. The E-mail message reappeared, and as more than two hundred of us watched, the gibberish transformed itself into readable English.

SEN. DUNNE: WE CANNOT STRESS OUR POINT ENOUGH: PA-TRIOT WILL ENSURE PRIVACY AND PROTECTION. ITS ADOPTION IS ESSENTIAL.

Even the senators were paying attention now. If they were sitting in a jury box, I would have leaned over to Lionel and said, "Wrap it. You've got them."

Dunne was the first to recover the composure necessary to frame a question. "Mr. Sullivan, are we to believe that you have shown us an actual copy of the classified message, independently obtained days before it was revealed here today?"

"As you can see from the time stamp, it is authentic."

Lionel was at peace with himself now. He had delivered his news. He had achieved the goal of warning the senators, and the nations, of the insecurities of key-escrow encryption.

Dunne asked, "But how? How did you get it?"

Larch spluttered in: "You have committed a felony!"

Pandemonium broke out. A half dozen of the senators' aides hastily excused themselves and exited through a back door. They had phone calls to make. I wondered how many of them knew Bentley's private line.

Two or three of the senators were talking at once into their microphones, competing for Lionel's attention, prompting an earsplitting screech of electrical feedback to echo in the room. Against one wall of the room, two dozen members of the

Joshua

Quittner

press—newspaper reporters, photographers, TV cameramen—had been herded into a small area secured by a red velvet rope. They strained against the rope, ready to bolt across the room for comment. In the spectators' seats, the lobbyists had run for the phones too. The civil libertarians were conferring in urgent whispers: Was it indeed a felony?

And at the witness table, amid the turmoil, sat Lionel and Dim, calm as two sailboats anchored in the sunshine off Bimini.

The chairman pounded his gavel. "Come to order!"

A semblance was restored. Larch spoke again.

"Senators, I suggest that Mr. Sullivan has committed a felony, by tampering with private computer systems and phone lines to illegally obtain the content of the message."

Dunne grabbed a microphone and spoke tersely. "Now, Owen, let's not jump the gun here. I think that Mr. Sullivan's demonstration was meant to educate us on a very important point. The point being, colleagues, that as long as the Patriot keys are lodged with key-escrow agents, the keys themselves are vulnerable. If Mr. Sullivan has found a way to obtain an actual key, you can be assured that any number of fifteen-year-old teenage hackers have done the same."

Annie clutched my arm. "Teenage hacker!"

I was thinking the same thing. Matthew Reese—who had lost his life to the Compubomber. Had he somehow stumbled on the same flaw in the software that Ames had found? If so, how had he unwittingly communicated his discovery to the wrong person?

But before I could respond, my attention was drawn to Dim, who had turned in his seat and was waving plaintively at me. Come here, he gestured. Help us.

Annie saw it too. "Your moment," she said. "Go up there and be their lawyer."

"Legal adviser," I corrected her automatically.

"Just get up there and save their butts. You can do it." The vocabulary was such an extreme departure from her usual choice of words that it made her point for her. This was one of those once-in-a-lifetime moments, Harry, old boy. This was one of those tests you were always preparing for. Now pass it.

So I stood. In the long, long seconds that it took me to squeeze past seven sets of knees in the seats between my chair and the aisle, I considered the implications of my actions.

I was about to become involved, politically. I was about to stand up in the middle of a Senate subcommittee and reel off a lot of half-baked nonsense about civil rights and deliver a wholly unsubstantiated opinion of why Lionel and Dim shouldn't be led off to jail. The whole damn thing was sure to be on C-SPAN. I would probably get a call by nightfall from the prestigious offices of Hart, Monroe & Weinmiller. Harry, old boy, there's a bit of a problem after all. We've reconsidered the job offer. Would the call find me in jail too?

It surprised me that Lionel hadn't brought his own lawyer. A real lawyer. Then a dissenting voice from inside my head: You are a real lawyer, Garnet.

I strode past the hectored woman with the name tag as if my name were at the top of her list, and pushed through the wooden gate that separated the important men from the masses. I was in the subcommittee's territory now, but no one tried to stop me.

It helped to walk fast, I learned. And to move as if you meant it.

At the table, I took a seat at the end. I pulled the microphone to me. I said, without stopping to think of where this monologue was headed, "Honorable members of this subcommittee. My name is Harry Garnet, and I have been retained to act as a legal adviser to Messrs. Sullivan and, uh, his associate." I doubt his name was Mr. Dim. "If you will allow me to explain their position, I think we can regain our composure and move on with the day's business."

I stole a look at my clients. Legal adviser—a nice way of

saying I had yet to take the bar exam. Dim looked thrilled. Lionel, of course, looked cool. He looked placid. He smiled at me, and winked. I had his blessing. For whatever reason.

I decided to act as if I deserved it.

"The first point to dispose of, Senator Larch, is your question as to the commission of a felony. I'm sure you, as an attorney, are well aware of the seriousness of making such a charge, and so it might temper your view to hear the facts. Simply put, they are these: These men are heroes. Shower them with medals! By coming here today, they have saved you a lot of trouble and protected their country from disaster. Mr. Sullivan and his associate are in possession of both halves of the Patriot key. They also possess the text of an encrypted data transmission. But nowhere under the U.S. Code or federal regulatory structure is it stated that possession of information encoded by the Patriot software is a felony. In fact, as it stands, they are not in violation of any U.S. laws, regulations, rules, suggested guidelines, or internal office memos. While they possess the key, you can't prove that they either stole it or broke into any private computers to obtain it."

The senators' attention was riveted. Emboldened, I moved on.

"These men have put their own reputations on the line to convey an important truth: There is a fatal flaw in Patriot. By doing so, they have saved you the embarrassment that would have tainted this subcommittee if Congress were to adopt Patriot. Better to learn about the problem now, before every personal computer and telephone in the country has Patriot corrupting it. Better to know now, before some wily and manipulative hacker cracks the system and uses the keys for illegal purposes."

I wanted to tell them about the back door, of course, because another flaw, and one of such great magnitude, probably would have been enough to cause Congress to lynch Bentley. But something inside me said: Wait. I still didn't un-

F

L

A

M

E

W

A

R

derstand the back door itself, or know exactly how it worked. Back in law school, one of the first lessons I learned, from a professor who liked to think he was starring in *The Paper Chase*, was never to introduce a subject in the courtroom unless you knew exactly where it was headed. I sat down.

Larch was seething. "Mr. Garnet, I don't see your name on my list of approved witnesses. As such—"

The chairman cut him off. "Mr. Larch, we'll investigate the hearing's procedural improprieties at length, but at another time. Be assured that the breaches in conduct are disturbing to us all. But for now, let's look at the larger issues."

He trained his attention on me. "Do you mean to argue, young man, that in this case the ends justify the means?"

"Sir, I mean exactly that. And I think we all should heave a collective sigh of national relief because this security hole was discovered before something disastrous—such as the premature adoption of the Patriot standard—sparked widespread illegal eavesdropping."

Dunne cut in. "For the record, I would like my esteemed colleagues to know that I am grateful that this flaw has been brought to our attention. Of course Mr. Sullivan has a vested interest in discrediting Patriot, because he has stated publicly he would like to see us adopt his Knot software as a federal standard instead. However, in this case, I think we share the same vested interest with him. Knot *would* provide security. Period. I think it might be time for us to consider different ways for law enforcement agencies to investigate crimes. Perhaps their arsenal of weapons will no longer include wiretaps. In any case, I don't think Mr. Sullivan has done anything to merit incarceration. I think to pursue that aspect of the matter would be to condone stoning pigeons."

He went on to say a lot more on the subject, but those were the last words I heard. "Stoning pigeons." An unusual turn of phrase, to be sure. I turned and looked back over the wooden railing, into the front row of the spectators' seats, into the eyes of my partner, Annie Ames. And over the roar of the proceedings, she mouthed the word of confirmation that reached my ears immediately: "Minotaur."

The chairman called for another break then. The senators would not be returning to this room. Not today, at least. They fled with the haste of field mice who were only a few steps ahead of a hawk.

A reporter from *The Washington Post* reached Lionel first. Just a word, Mr. Sullivan. Please. Can we talk in the hall for five minutes? As they left the room, I saw the cameramen scramble after them, hustling out the door protected by their extension cords and klieg lights and big-bellied aggression. I feared as much for Lionel at their hands as I would have if he had been locked up for the night in a District jail cell. Dim skipped jubilantly from the room. He had triumphant phone calls to place.

Unnoticed, Annie slipped up the aisle, through the gate, and to my side.

She was beaming. She shook my hand. "You were wonderful, Harry."

I wanted to kiss her. I wanted to slug her. I wanted to collapse in a heap of nervous exhaustion. Instead, I said, "Sit."

I pointed to the seat in front of Lionel's laptop, the computer that was still actively connected to his system at home.

"Forget the key they stole," I said. "I want to see how your father would decrypt the same message."

I watched the screen on the wall. The room around us was almost empty now. The crowd had cleared out, for the most part, except for a few stragglers arguing ethics in the aisle and one or two Senate aides who were clearing away piles of documents from in front of their bosses' chairs. Read these in the car, sir.

I looked away from the screen and saw, standing in the senators' private doorway, the Honorable Francis Dunne. How long had he been there? He stared straight at us, or rather straight at Annie, for a long moment. Then he turned without speaking, and he was gone. The room had an altogether different feeling now. Gone was the circus atmosphere. Now, there was a faint echo. The air was chilled again.

Annie inserted into Lionel's terminal a floppy disk that contained copies of all the salient files from Fred Ames's computer, called up a copy of the original garbled message, then double-clicked to the command field. It must have taken no more than three seconds for her to retrieve her father's skeleton key. But up on the screen, nothing happened. The gibberish did not rearrange.

"Try again," I said. She executed her father's program once more.

Nothing. We both stared at the screen on the wall, as horrified as if we were reading a racial epithet courtesy of a deranged graffiti artist.

"Harry," Annie said, "the back door doesn't work."

Joshua
Quittner

chapter thirteen

T here is no better sound than the *thwock* of a champagne cork as it hits the ceiling. And if throwing a huge victory party to celebrate the demise of Patriot was in poor taste, considering the unfortunate coincidence of the recent demise of one of the Urban Crypto Militia's own leaders, the attendees of this particular gathering didn't seem to give a damn. The party was riotous. It had been going on for hours, with speech-making, with newly arrived guests rushing up to Lionel to slap high-fives, and with the most peculiar sight of Yuri, for once beaming and holding court at the center of small clumps of people. Lionel was paying for it all.

He had rented two suites at the Marriott downtown, one to dance in and one to sleep in later, and as soon as word of the hearing's outcome had filtered north to New York, the militia crowd had set out for D.C. and the hotel. After all, they needed something to celebrate, needed it in the worst way.

For the past six hours, Lionel had fed that need. He had made the requisite victory speeches, phoned room service twenty minutes before we would have run out of beer, and smoothly introduced to each other people who were likely to hit it off. His linen suit was by now wrinkled, but that only made him look as if he had been on safari for a week. And returned with the head of a lion.

There was a defiant edge to the celebration, and an undercurrent that said, hey, we won one for Eddie. He did not die in vain. Irene and the rest of the roommates flew down on the shuttle, but now I had lost them in a room full of dozens of giddy, shouting, toast-making revelers. I hadn't realized how widespread a movement the militia was, how many of its members were located in regional cells up and down the Eastern Seaboard. And all, apparently, within driving distance of Washington. Annie was here somewhere, of course, but the din and my sudden celebrity had conspired to separate us. Who had brought the balloons, dozens of bright balloons filled with helium, bumping against the ceiling, with the phrase TIE THE KNOT emblazoned on each one?

Although I now knew who my enemy was, I kept watching my back in this overheated room. A TV set was on in every room of the suite, tuned to CNN and the major networks, and whenever I glanced at a screen, I saw interchangeable commentators with shellacked hair discussing the implications of the Patriot hearing. A producer at *Nightline* had phoned, seeking an interview, but Lionel had put her off. I wondered what was more pressing.

At a little after 8:00 P.M., Lionel clambered onto a desk to rally the troops.

"Tonight we celebrate," he said, "and then, tomorrow, we will begin to fight again. We cannot rest until the president signs legislation enacting Knot as *the* national standard for encrypting messages. Long live privacy, long live Knot, and long live the man who first said: Sometimes the ends justify the means!"

The applause was so loud that if it had been an hour or two later, I would have expected the hotel manager to evict us. As Lionel bent to jump off the desk, a dozen arms reached for him, picked him and passed him, disheveled and horizontal and laughing uproariously, over their heads toward the doorway. It created an unofficial mosh pit, appropriate to the mood of the evening, which felt like the first stop of a long-awaited tour of a favorite rock 'n' roll band.

I was scrunched up in the corner, between a dresser and the door to the bathroom, a good place to observe the action. Whenever anyone looked my way, I waved a beer can in acknowledgment. A hale fellow, a little drunk. At least that's how I hoped I looked.

The collective temperatures of the throng of bodies had steamed up the plate-glass windows in front of the air conditioner. The noise level was so loud I expected the walls to crack open, like an egg that gives way to the flailings and elbowings of an emerging baby bird. I would have bet fifty bucks that not one more person could squeeze into this groaning, straining space of barely restrained hysteria and hilarity.

I would have lost my money. The door inched open, pushing against the force of the nearest bodies who were engaged in avid conversation, and into the party came the man who had expected, only a few days ago, to be the guest of honor.

Not everyone noticed Blaney right away. If they had, they would have given him a hero's welcome and bodyguard protection, of course. The consensus, in this room at least, was that Eddie had been the victim of a conspiracy that did *not* include one Richard Blaney. It was no secret that federal agents had been shadowing the militia for weeks, no secret that the man in the aviator glasses had been trying to infiltrate the group. Eddie's death was ascribed to an act of desperation by a corrupt and morally reprehensible government, the overreaction of a rogue federal agent who had gone too far in trying to protect his employers.

Most of the people in this room expected Blaney to die next—that is, if he hadn't already been offed, his body dumped surreptitiously into marshy wetlands miles from home. In fact, tonight he looked as if he might recently have dug himself out of a watery grave somewhere in New Jersey. His clothes were filthy, his grayish shirt caked with dirt and what looked like dried blood. His jeans were smeared with stripes of grease and some resilient white substance, as if he had brushed against a just-painted pillar in the subway. His hair was so dirty that it was no longer possible to say what color it was. His eyes darted and scanned the room constantly, seeking danger, seeking confirmation that his journey hadn't been in vain. His whole body was taut, and poised like a runner on the starting line. He was here, his demeanor said, because he had news to impart.

Lionel saw him first. As I made my way across the room to join their tête-à-tête, they embraced. Blaney pulled back just far enough from Lionel's face to breathe heavily on him as he delivered a fierce recitation. He ticked points off on his fingers. He looked extremely agitated. But then, so would I, probably, if I had spent the last few nights sleeping under bridges, expecting to hear the hounds close in on me at any minute. Lionel listened intently. His expression changed, imperceptibly, from relief to worry.

I parted the bodies as quickly as I could, but I felt like I was walking through a sea of fast-hardening Jell-O. I couldn't get there fast enough.

Suddenly Blaney pulled back. He held his hands out in front of him, as if to push Lionel back, and by now I could hear him yell, "You can't stop it! No one can! It's a juggernaut, it's out of control, and it's going to take us all down."

Lionel grabbed his wrists to get his attention. He glanced grimly in my direction and said, "Richard brought bad news."

Blaney didn't acknowledge my presence, just stared at me with the hopeless, pitiable fright of a puppy getting hosed down after a shampoo. He sagged suddenly and said, low, "They fucked us."

"Who fucked us?" I directed the question to Lionel, because I didn't want to set off another tirade.

"The Judiciary Committee."

I couldn't believe it. "They're going to try to ram Patriot through after what happened today? No way. They'll be laughingstocks."

"Worse," Lionel said, and now his eyes were as sad as I've ever seen them, as sad as they had been the first time I saw him at Fred Ames's funeral. "Dunne was on TV saying he's going to urge Congress to adopt Knot."

"But that's what you wanted."

"It's not what we wanted, you idiot, Garnet! Not like this, don't you see?" Blaney whirled in my direction, shook his finger up and down perilously close to my eyeballs. He was enraged again. "The whole thing was for shit! They beat us, outsmarted us."

Blaney had begun to attract quite a bit of attention, and I saw Irene and Dim making their way toward us from separate corners of the room. I saw Annie too, for the first time in hours, standing by the doorway that connected to the next suite. She had changed from the office-armor suit into a pair of her signature naturalists' shorts and a sand-colored thermal-knit T-shirt. She wore thick white socks and a pair of white leather Keds. She looked like her old self.

Lionel cut in. "Richard, calm down. You aren't helping anyone." Then, in a lordlier voice, "Somebody get a chair! Richard's turned up at last, and he's exhausted."

Now Blaney was surrounded. He had no chance of speaking again for nearly ten minutes, as he was clapped on the shoulders, ensconced in a wing chair, offered a beer, offered a sandwich. I stood by, studying him as if he were new to me, and indeed he was. I was as surprised as anyone to see him here.

Through it all he struggled, trying to surface, trying to deliver his awful prophecy of doom.

Lionel climbed back up in the center of the room then. He put his index fingers into his mouth and emitted a shrill whistle.

The room went silent.

"Some news you should hear, not necessarily good news. As you can see"—he gestured toward Blaney, who had stonily refused sustenance and was now cradling his head in his hands, as if he held a fragile, pulsing melon that was about to receive a fatal blow from a ballpeen hammer—"Richard is here. He has come tonight at some personal risk to himself, he believes, because the authorities are searching for him. He brings us bad news."

Here Lionel paused theatrically, long enough to search the faces of everyone in the room. Satisfied that his audience was mesmerized, he continued: "Richard has been to see a certain source of his, someone closely connected to the doings of the Judiciary Committee, and from that person has learned that the senators do indeed plan to urge adoption of Knot as a national encryption standard. Senator Dunne confirmed that himself on network news about an hour ago."

A smattering of applause broke out, in spite of itself, but a frown from Lionel quieted it almost immediately.

"The problem is that Knot will be corrupted first. Even as Knot is being spoonfed to the American public as an unbreakable device for 'privacy protection,' its code will have been modified. The problem is that before Knot gets loaded onto the computers and cell phones that the rest of the world will be buying in the next couple of years, the government plans to graft a key-escrow provision onto the program. In essence, they are going to turn Knot into Patriot, and hope the general public doesn't notice."

"You mean add an eavesdropping provision to Knot?" Irene called from over near Blaney. "Oh, God, they can't, can they, Lionel?"

"I'm afraid they can."

From the other side of the room, near the dresser: "They can't alter your code, Lionel! It's a copyright violation! It's intellectual property theft. Sue them—"

"I can't," Lionel said simply. "Knot is in the public domain.

Its source code is freely available to anyone who wants to examine—or change—it. They can do whatever they want. Anyone can."

I thought there would be a riot in the room. Almost everyone started yelling at once, at Lionel, or at Blaney, or at Irene, who now stood protectively in front of Blaney's chair, arms crossed, to block the assault of questions. Dim smashed an empty beer bottle against the wall, and as I heard the glass shatter, I thought, So this is it. They're going to tear themselves apart. It's a mass suicide. Another Jonestown, and Annie and I are going to go down with the rest of them, in the middle of this Dionysian frenzy of unthinking violence and vented frustration.

I fully expected to see someone ignite the contents of the overflowing wastebasket and then toss the whole burning mess at the long, flammable drapes over the window near where Annie stood. But in the next terrible seconds, Lionel took control and somehow restored order. He clasped his hands around his mouth, creating a bullhorn effect, and ordered, "Quiet! Everyone, quiet!"

Slowly, grudgingly, the crowd calmed, at least enough to assure him that they weren't about to cannibalize their neighbors. "Now listen to me. We are not defeated. We have alternatives. The first, and most important, is to stand firm in our resolve to fight this battle on our own terms, not theirs. If we destroy ourselves, then we destroy everything we have worked for. Don't make it easy for them. Not when we've come this far."

"What are the alternatives, Lionel?" Irene, again.

"I'm going to explore them," he said mysteriously. "I'll be in touch."

This time, the crowd didn't reach for him. He jumped down lightly, like Robin Hood, and turned to search the room. He found me.

"Harry, I may need a lawyer again."

"You know where to find me. You always have."

He left then, and with him took the spirit of the party. He sucked the emotion from the room, and after the door closed behind, the crowd became listless. Blaney slumped farther in his chair, and Irene dropped to her knees and buried her head on the armrest.

I placed the sweating beer bottle I had held for the past hour onto a nearby night table. It was half full. The missing ounces had been poured, in surreptitious dribbles, over the balcony into the evergreens or down the bathroom sink. This was the sixth beer that I had emptied in the same manner. I had made sure, in selecting each successive bottle, to choose a different, distinctive label. If anyone had been watching my drinking habits, it would appear that I had consumed nearly a six-pack in the last few hours.

I stood up, and looked for a quiet way out of the room.

But before I could put my plan into action, I heard someone pounding on the suite's door. Irene walked over and opened it, an action that had an effect similar to pulling a finger out of a dike. At least a half-dozen uniformed police officers rushed into the room at once, arms spread wide, pushing the crowd back into corners. They fanned out, calling harshly, "Police! Back up. Back up. That's it, easy."

Another three or four officers surrounded Blaney. "Mr. Blaney?" barked the tall, hollow-faced sergeant who was in charge. His voice was harsh enough to get Blaney's attention. "We've been looking for you, sir. We need you to come with us to the station. Some questions." Blaney looked up at him, almost blankly, as if trying to translate the words into a language he understood. He looked wholly unable to take care of himself.

Dim, who had been forced up against the wall near the door, called out, "Is he under arrest? Are you going to read him his right? Richard, you need to get a lawy—"

Dim doubled over, choking and sputtering, and that's when I saw that Agent Aviator had entered the room as well. He must have delivered a sharp elbow to Dim's gut—that would have been his style and he was certainly in range. But the agent stood there in his dark blue suit, unruffled, looking as if the tortured choking noises that Dim emitted bemused him. Kooky hackers—who could explain them?

Aviator looked over to where the sergeant stood, watching two officers propel Blaney from the room. "Take this one too," Aviator said, jerking his head toward Dim. "He looks like he might have something to tell us." Luckily, for once, I managed to stay out of the line of fire. He never saw me.

Then it was over. One minute, the room was full of uniforms. The next, they were gone, leaving behind an empty chair, Blaney's abandoned throne. The last glimpse I caught of Blaney as the cops nearly carried him through the door was of his shirttail, crumpled and defeated, hanging out of the back of his jeans. There was no explanation for the benefit of the rest of us, no warnings even, no herding of the whole crowd into a paddy wagon for a ride downtown. There was only a vacuum, and the lingering questions.

Annie and I slipped out of the room through the side door that connected to the next suite, and from there to the hallway. It was empty. The light above the elevator door at the end of the hall indicated that the cops and their quarry already had reached the lobby.

We took the stairs, two at a time, the slap of our steps echoing off the cinder-block walls as we flew past the FIRE EXIT ONLY signs. Two floors, three, five, and then the lobby, where we emerged into the comparative luxury of carpet and brass sconces to find no evidence whatsoever of the entourage.

Annie rushed, reddened and puffing, to the doorman. "The cops," she panted. "Which way?"

He looked surprised. "Excuse me, miss?"

"A group of uniformed police officers came through here two minutes ago? Escorting a guest of this hotel out to police cars? Which way did they go?"

The doorman looked troubled, as if he couldn't decide whether to mollify Annie because she was a registered guest or whether to get tough with her because her breath smelled of beer. "No one has come through here," he said finally. A concierge wandered by to see what the ruckus was about.

"Not in or out?" I asked.

"No."

"Is there another level with an entrance to the hotel?" I asked. "A parking garage?"

"Get into the elevator and press G" he said, then turned to hold open the swinging glass door for a bellboy who was wheeling a dolly piled high with luggage.

Back to the elevators, where Annie fairly hopped with anxiety as we waited for a car. She looked as if she had to go to the bathroom. "Where do you think they took him?"

"It's possible they really were police," I said. "In which case, he's being interrogated about Eddie's murder down at the precinct."

"But the agent who was sent to scare us. He wasn't a police officer," she said. "He wouldn't be accompanying them, not if they were legitimate."

That was my fear too, of course, but I hadn't wanted to voice it. Now, as we stepped finally out of the elevator and into the cavernous parking garage, I saw only cars. There was a strong smell of gasoline, and greasy spots of motor oil stained the concrete. All the spaces in all the aisles of this eerily fluorescent cave were full. The silence nearly echoed. There was no empty spot to indicate that a patrol car had recently pulled out.

We had lost them. We had run out of choices. All but one, that is.

We stood outside the ornate front door of a brick town house, one of a dozen on this self-satisfied block of row houses. It was past midnight, and while a gaslight burned by the base of the stoop where we stood, there was otherwise no sign of life on the street. Georgetown was asleep. "Let us in!" I banged the heavy brass knocker. Just then, water began to pour down, drenching the two of us with such suddenness that at first I thought someone had poured a pailful from the second-floor window onto our heads. But it was rain, a summer storm.

"Open the door" I called again. Annie and I were totally exposed here in front of Senator Francis Dunne's house. The gas lamp cast our long shadows on the wall. There was no shrubbery to hide behind, no protection of a vestibule. The ivy on the trellis behind our heads would offer no camouflage if anyone was out there with a rifle.

"Maybe he isn't home," Annie said. "We've been standing here almost ten minutes." Our hair was plastered to our heads, and water dripped off it, down our necks, down our backs, under our shirts.

"He has to be."

"Why?"

"Because we need him to be."

"Harry, that's not logical. Things don't just—"

The door swung open, and I saw only blackness inside. I sensed depth in the dark, as if we were about to enter a yawning maw of a hallway. It reminded me of the socket in my mouth where a wisdom tooth had been pulled a few years earlier. It was a deep hole, and no one had thought to fill it with anything.

The senator stepped around the edge of the door, and faced us. He wore a dark silk dressing gown, the sash hastily knotted around his waist, and leather slippers. We had gotten him out of bed. But he hadn't been asleep. He was too alert, too unsurprised to see us. His hair was combed.

"Who are you?" he asked. "What's going on out here?"

His face wore a perfect image of befuddled aristocracy. Late as it was, odd as this was, it wasn't in his nature to be rude himself, his expression said. Perhaps there had been some mistake, and we could all straighten it out in the morning? At a more decent hour?

Annie stepped into the light. "I'm Fred Ames's daughter. I saw you at the hearing today."

He stared at her, his face betraying nothing. But his knuckles, clenched around the door frame, were white with tension that even generations of good breeding could not hide.

"What are you talking about?" He still appeared genuinely confused. "I don't know who you are; you can't barge in on people in the middle of the night like this."

"Annie Ames. Frederick Ames's daughter," she repeated.

His face said he didn't know who she was.

His face was lying.

"I'm Harry Garnet. I testified at the hearing this morning on behalf of Lionel Sullivan, who demonstrated Patriot's insecurities," I said.

Now the senator looked angry. "You can't come here to my home in the middle of the night to question me about political policy. If you have official business, call my office in the morning. But now, go away, or I'll phone the police." He stepped back, tried to close the door. But I stuck my foot in the threshold.

"We came to find out what you did with Blaney."

"I don't know what you're talking about. Or who."

"I'm talking about your goon. Your head goon, the boy with no neck, the one you sent to kidnap my friend."

"Get out of here or I'll call the police," he said, trying to kick aside my foot with his own.

"We know you're the Minotaur," I said.

For a fleeting moment, something resembling panic passed across his face, but then disappeared. "I don't know what you're talking about."

He took a step backward into the hall.

Annie took a step forward, over the threshold, and said to him, "I know you and my father had a relationship. He told me all about it. And I'll be happy to call a friend of mine at the *Post* and tell her about it too."

"I don't know who your father is, young woman, or what you're talking about." He found a light switch on the wall, to the right of the door. A crystal lamp on the ceiling came on, throwing sharp prisms of light onto the pale blue walls and the full-length, gilt-edged mirror on the wall behind him. The main staircase curved over our heads, and the second floor was visible through the balusters. I could see three doors leading off a central hallway to bedrooms.

It occurred to me to wonder if all the rooms were empty. I hoped so.

"You assume an alias, you call yourself the Minotaur, and you inhabit an online world called The Zoo," I said. Then I bluffed, "We've seen the registration records."

"And we've spoken to you there," Annie said. "Your choice of vocabulary is quite unique. It's obvious that you and the Minotaur are the same person."

Dunne had backed up to a magnificent lacquered commode that sat against the wall. On it was a telephone. He put his hand on the receiver.

"I don't know what you're talking about. I want you to leave this house now, and if you don't, I will call the police." He picked up the receiver.

I tried one last gambit to crack through years of hard-won composure, to penetrate the shell of official life that protected him from our accusations. I wanted to shock him into compliance, and so I took a wild guess, "We know you know about the secret back door in the Knot program, the one that allows you to eavesdrop secretly on people. And yet, you engineered things so that Patriot will be abandoned in favor of Knot. How will that look to your constituents?"

He reached with his other hand toward the phone's vintage rotary face. But instead of dialing, he pulled open the dresser's top drawer and drew out a pistol. He pointed it at us. Without taking his eyes off us, he hung up the receiver: "Close the door."

chapter fourteen

T he gun was generic, an ugly .9 millimeter and dull gray in this light. It had a snubbed nose that reminded me of a pit bull and was the kind of weapon that almost any law enforcement agent carried around. The FBI agents, the twins with the neckties, had worn theirs in holsters under their jackets. My mother, who also had a gun, kept it in the night table beside her bed. It wasn't quite as stylish as Cousin Eddie's concealed weapon had been, but it looked functional.

I had never handled one, but I could guess at its heaviness. I knew that big, ugly bullets came out of it, efficient slugs of metal that tear through flesh and bone with the same ease as a sharp knife slices through filet mignon.

Dunne closed the front door, shutting out the driving rain that had been spattering the wallpaper and the dark blue Oriental runner. "Into the drawing room," he said. "Quickly." He gestured with the gun to one of the four doors that led off the center hallway. It was dark inside.

He walked behind us. In the darkness, I felt the gun aimed

between my shoulder blades. My back felt hot. It itched in that spot.

When the lights came on, we found ourselves in an elegant green room, with silk on the chairs, heavy damask drapes, and a high ceiling adorned with elaborate molding and an ornate chandelier. Its crystal teardrops tinkled softly as the four of us walked beneath. Portraits of the senator's father and mother flanked the fireplace. His grandparents' faces were on the opposite wall. They wouldn't have condoned his behavior tonight.

"Sit," Dunne said. "Don't worry about the upholstery. I certainly don't."

He threw himself down on a leather club chair. "You were so helpful earlier today," he murmured. "Hard to believe how much trouble you're causing me tonight."

I willed myself to take my eyes off the barrel of the gun before it hypnotized me.

"You have forced this situation on yourselves," he said quietly. He addressed us both, but his eyes were on Annie.

When I glanced at her, I saw that she was pale, and sat very straight and still, staring back at Dunne, facing her father's lover for the first time. Her gaze was dispassionate, almost clinical, as if she were trying to categorize the species before her, the strange and dangerous creature who had entered her father's life, gotten under his guard, and betrayed him. She was trying to learn, I think, what charms Dunne possessed, trying to understand the particular nature of the temptation he posed to Ames, the things he offered that the professor wanted. By training and nature, she was an anthropologist, and the study of the behavior of this particular human must have been of special interest to her. What conclusions did she draw about the cultural and social development of Dunne? Did she see the same things I saw, the haughty tilt of his head that could only have been bred into him by generations of casual wealth? Or was she looking for subtler manifestations of his behavior, searching for the small gestures and throat clearings, the nearly invisible signals of intelligence and curiosity and availability that he must have emitted in order to pique the interest of Fred Ames?

Dunne looked away first, down at the gun in his hand, then back at Annie, as if to convince himself he really would have the courage to shoot someone who reminded him so much of Fred Ames. I had never noticed before how many of her father's traits she carried, how her peerless posture and quiet sense of absolute *rightness* echoed Ames. Even when he was wrong—as he had been on the tennis court at The Vines the day before his death, insisting that a second serve was good even in the face of two contradicting witnesses—he had exuded an aura of total assurance that Annie now possessed. Her hair and her skin tone may have been her mother's, but her rigidity and inherent demand that others live up to her standards she had learned from her father.

Dunne, finally, had failed Fred Ames, and he must have realized that Annie found him wanting as well. Did he care? I suspect he did, if only because he was not used to defeat of any kind. After winning three successful Senate campaigns, ramming hundreds of pork barrel projects through Congress, and receiving eleven honorary doctorates from universities, he had grown accustomed to success. To his credit, he flinched when she asked him coldly, "Are you going to shoot us?"

His answer was an obfuscation—"What's another scandal in this town?"—and I wondered then if he would have been as unwilling to own up to the consequences of his actions if his lover had asked him point-blank: Are you going to have me killed, Fran? Will you betray me to save your job? Will you stand by while someone builds a deadly bomb and packages it cunningly and mails it to me and I open it and lose my hands and the rest of my body becomes riddled with wounds and blood runs into my shoes, pooling there before the ambulance workers can get the heavy beams off my body? Will you, Francis? Or will you save me?

Of course, I did not understand enough about their relationship to frame the questions. But Annie knew enough about her father to guess, and so I knew that this would be her moment, her meeting, her confrontation. She was a surrogate for her dead father, and it was her place to ask the questions of his betrayer. However it ended, I would accept the results. But for now, I had no right to interrupt her terrible reckoning—not unless she asked for help.

Dunne was working out the details for himself, talking himself through the moves he would make. "You were at the hearing this morning. Everyone saw you there. And then, later, two political zealots broke into my house in the middle of the night. They tore apart the drawing room"—he stood, walked over to a delicate high-backed settee covered in alternating stripes of burgundy and gray silk, and suddenly kicked one of its curved legs with a savage anger. The love seat toppled backward, crashed into a curio table behind it that displayed historical papers under glass. The table shattered, and shards of glass flew across the room. The settee's broken leg dangled in the air, its raw inner wood exposed beneath the expensive veneer—"and destroyed my priceless collection of personal letters signed by Thomas Jefferson."

He began to pace, gesturing theatrically. "I woke to the sound of shattering glass and feared burglars. Perhaps I should have called the police then and there. But I was disoriented from a late-night drink"—he walked to a buffet table, uncorked a crystal decanter, poured whiskey into a highball glass, and tossed it down his throat—"so perhaps I was too foolhardy."

He walked back to the leather chair. Sank into it as if he were about to relax with the newspaper at his men's club. He had so much control. He might as easily have been describing his latest congressional fact-finding trip to Latin America as planning the cold-blooded murders of two people.

"I came down the staircase—no, make that crept down the staircase—in the dark, with the pistol I keep in my bedroom cocked and at the ready," he said. "I saw shadows moving in here, and I just started shooting wildly. After I emptied my gun, I stood shaking in the dark for a long time. Finally, I turned on the lights and found the two of you, dead and bleeding on my great-aunt's Aubusson carpets. You had been trying to run from me, or maybe at me, to attack me, but you didn't know which way to turn in the darkness. Tragic. But then, perhaps, there was a history of mental illness in one of your families. Perhaps you had been under a great deal of stress lately? Perhaps you had fantasized that I was some sort of powerful, mythical villain?''

When he stopped speaking, we were all quiet for a moment, trying to understand how it would play out. And then Annie spoke, in a low tone that I had to lean forward to hear, "I do not know what my father saw in you, Mr. Dunne."

She sounded more curious than angry, puzzled, as if she were trying to work out the equation for herself. "I see that he must have been lonely, but my father was a good man. You are not. How did you hide that from him?"

"How well did you know your father, Miss Ames?" This was not a path she would want to follow too far, I knew, because she had already proven to me that she needed to create a mythology around her relationship with her dead parent. The previous day, driving down to Washington in the chief's car, Annie had been looking out the passenger window, counting telephone poles, counting road signs, counting her losses, I guess, because she suddenly had faced me and said, "He didn't use me as his cover, Harry." I had turned down the radio. No big loss, since we were cutting through the back roads of Maryland, avoiding the interstate, and the local oldies station was treating us to Carole King, anyway. "You know, the reason my father took me to The Vines with him was because he needed to use me as a sounding board. After he talked to Blaney. He was going to need someone to bounce ideas off. Help him sort things out. That was the whole reason he had me working for him in the first place."

"I know, Annie." That was the end of the first and last time she ever offered me a justification for anybody's behavior, including her own. She had reached over then, turned up the radio. I don't remember what was playing.

Now Annie looked at the evidence of the formality of Dunne's life, and said, "I probably didn't know my father as well as you did. You certainly knew his weaknesses."

She looked around the room, stood restlessly, apparently unaware that he trained the gun on her as she walked toward the fireplace. "He must have been in this room, wasn't he?" The question was rhetorical. "How many times, and for what reasons? Did he sit on the same couch? Did he notice the wallpaper, no—he felt more of a general impatience with the fussy surroundings, if they registered at all."

"He admired the architecture," Dunne said dryly.

She asked, "Did you ever cook for him?"

The question surprised him, must have surprised him, because he answered almost automatically, "Dinners."

"He told me. I mean, not that *you* specifically cooked for him, of course. He protected you. I never knew your name or where you lived, just that he had these wonderful evenings, of good food and wine, and talk. Omelettes. He loved the way you flipped your omelettes—" She mimicked the delicate wrist gesture.

"He told me once that you were the first real friend he had made since he graduated from high school. Four decades ago."

Dunne just looked at her, whether because he was speechless or because he was jealous of his memories, I don't know.

"Can I see the kitchen, Senator?"

"Maybe later." Something shifted in the senator's face. "He wasn't here that often." He looked down at the gun in his hand and said, "What do you want? You came here seeking something. Surely you weren't banging on the door in the middle of the night because you wanted to hear anecdotes about Fred Ames's dinner conversations."

"I need to know why he died," Annie said. "You say you

never supported Patriot, yet you trained a private stable of undercover hitmen on the militia to stop their efforts.''

He walked over to the buffet table and fixed himself another drink. This time, he spritzed in soda and used silver tongs to pick up a piece of lemon peel from a bowl. He didn't ask us to join him.

"You know nothing, do you?" he asked. "You may think you have evidence. You may even have made copies of your conversations with some creature you believe was named Minotaur. But that proves nothing.''

"Tell me,'' she said, the confessor.

"There's nothing for me, personally, to tell,'' he said. "But your story has an interesting premise. Let me tell one of my own.

"Now, what if one day, a U.S. senator were to be riding in a back elevator at the Capitol, hurrying to the floor for a vote on increasing funds for a U.S. peacekeeping presence in the Middle East, say, and a colleague got onto the elevator next to him. No one else was aboard. What if the colleague, in this rare moment of privacy, were to mention that he had discovered a glorious new world, where physical identity and status no longer mattered. A place where one could reinvent oneself. Do you think such a concept might be tempting?''

"The Zoo,'' Annie said.

"Well, for the sake of the story, we can call it The Zoo, or we can call it Pandora's Box, or whatever name you want. It would be wildly intoxicating to log on to such a place, to create a whole new personality, to call oneself—what name would be apt—yes, the Minotaur. Charming. A powerful creature. Huge appetites. Lives to satisfy them.''

He put his drink down carefully on a coaster on which a hunt scene had been needlepointed. "You can see how such a place could lure a man like myself—any man in a public sort of position, whose whole life is on display—with the promise of ironclad privacy.

"Living like this''—he gestured around the room—"could

be construed as living in a cage, where one is constantly on guard as to what to say or do, careful of whom to invite to the house, living constantly and precariously on display."

But you locked yourself into the cage, I wanted to say. You chose to live a public life among the ghosts of your ancestors, to carry their torches, to accept the legacy of their lives for safekeeping. You chose that path because it seemed easy. If it came with a high price tag, you should have been prepared to pay.

He laughed self-consciously. "Here, in this world, someone perceived as powerful is courted only for what he can accomplish. People with agendas want to use a senator. But in a place like The Zoo, all that would matter, all that a person would be judged by, would be his mind."

"His intellect?" Annie asked.

"Certainly. And creativity. And affinity for certain traits in others. It would be liberating to be judged by who one was, not what one could do."

"How did you meet my father?"

"I told you. In one of the underground rooms. It was all such a marvelous masquerade party. Was my esteemed colleague from the Senate online as well, disguised from me and calling himself Tortoise? Or was he Anty Mane? Or someone else? He wouldn't recognize me, because online we could reveal ourselves. The masks we wore somehow allowed us to be more ourselves there than anywhere else."

He really wanted us to understand his position now. It had become important to him that we empathize. He had lowered the gun's muzzle so slightly that it now pointed more directly at Annie's shoes than at her heart. I wondered if he knew. I wondered if he cared.

"The joke with The Zoo was, of course, creating new species. Pretending to be some new kind of animal, some amalgam of human and nonhuman creature. Because what did that matter? Nothing but the mind mattered. Great intellects floating in space, in cyberspace. Age didn't matter. Gender meant nothing."

Dunne had felt immediate affinity with Fred Ames. They shared the same jokes, the same quirky way of looking at the world, the same love of puzzles. They had become inseparable partners, online and off, even traveling to Sicily for a two-week vacation when, one day, a disturbing E-mail message was sent to the Minotaur's mailbox.

"I should have known better, of course, but here I was, at my age, the target of a crude blackmail demand." The body of the message contained the following items: a copy of the character registration form that Dunne had filled out, requesting use of the name Minotaur; a partial transcript of a recent intimate conversation the Minotaur and Wolfer had conducted online; and a request. The E-mail noted that the senator was a member of the Judiciary Committee, which soon would have to decide whether to support Patriot. "The E-mail said, 'Knot is a better choice, Senator.' The sender noted that he didn't want to put me in the uncomfortable position of explaining to the voters in upstate Canojoharie that I liked to pretend I was half man, half animal, and have sex with other animals."

"And that was all?"

"There were little follow-up reminders that I was being watched. From time to time, snatches of my conversations would be sent back to me, copies of private E-mail messages that no one should have had access to."

"There is no privacy," Annie said.

"There is a lure to eavesdropping, certainly," Dunne said. "God knows, I've thought about it for a long time. If I had that kind of power, would I resist? I doubt it. Imagine being able to look inside the medicine chest of the most powerful person in the world. Imagine knowing the contents of the intimate love notes that a certain Cabinet member's wife exchanges with an ambassador from a not-altogether-friendly

Michelle Slatalla

Third World nation. Imagine being able to predict, from the tenor of locker-room conversations among Wall Street analysts, the exact date that a hot new technology company is going to go public. What could you do with all that knowledge? The question is, rather, what couldn't you do?"

"Who was the blackmailer?" Annie asked.

Dunne looked confused. "The same one who sent the bombs. That's all I know."

"You never met him?"

"I spoke to him once. He phoned at a prearranged time and said he had a new task for me: Keep him informed of any bits of political gossip that crossed my desk regarding the encryption issue. He wanted to know anything I heard about Patriot or about Knot. I was to convey information in the form of E-mail messages, to be addressed to sysop@zoo.com."

There was a long pause. Then Dunne sighed. "You know, it was so unnecessary. I would have supported Knot anyway. Frederick was very convincing."

On the day when Ames came to Dunne and told him he had found some troubling problems, a back door, Ames had counseled Dunne to withhold his support for either Patriot or Knot. Dunne had panicked. He sent E-mail to sysop@zoo.com with a warning that Ames had found the flaw in Knot.

"I had no idea that Frederick would be killed. I had no idea that the bombings were connected to Patriot. You believe me." It was an order, not a question.

"Were the others killed for the same reason? They were all on The Zoo; they all were involved with the encryption programs, you know," Annie said.

"I didn't know any of the others."

"Why didn't you go to the police?"

"I liked being a senator."

The statement was simple and absolute. And in the past tense.

The senator looked down at his hands, seemed surprised to

F

L

A

M

E

W

A

R

see himself holding a gun. He smiled shyly. "Of course, we never had this conversation, did we?"

He put the gun into his bathrobe pocket, stood. "Good. Well, it was pleasant seeing you. Do stop by again," and then he led us through the doorway back to the hall.

Outside, the rain had stopped. Annie stopped in the doorway and said to the senator, "Something I don't understand."

"There are many things I don't understand, my dear."

"If the blackmailer wanted to see the Patriot initiative fail, he should have been thrilled that my father found a flaw in Patriot. It would have been a perfect way to kill the issue."

"Oh, no, you really don't see it, do you?" Dunne looked sad for us. "Your father didn't find the flaw in Patriot. He found it in Knot." He closed the door then, firmly, behind us.

I flashed on what Ames had said to Blaney:

There's something strange about it. As if the code were deliberately written that way. I need more time to understand it.

I glanced in through the senator's parlor window and saw Dunne sitting in the same leather chair, staring up at the ceiling, contemplating his last moments on earth. He looked as if he were studying a minute crack in the plaster rosette that surrounded the chandelier. I doubt he was praying.

By the time we got back to the hotel—the only place we could think of with a reliable phone line for the modem—it was nearly dawn. Annie pulled the key card from her pocket and slipped it into the slot on the door. The red lights turned green, and I felt like we were scientists with a vial of deadly virus, passing through an air lock to the safety of the lab on the other side.

The room was utterly black. Annie had drawn both layers of curtain hours earlier when we had checked in and dropped our overnight bags on a luggage rack in one of the bedrooms. We hadn't had time to set up the laptop then, not with Lionel accompanying us and the phone ringing and an air of expectancy above our heads that required jubilant participation.

Now, I groped for the light switch. I stumbled against a bureau, steadied myself with a hand, and felt the cord of a lamp. "Hurry, Harry," she whispered, more urgently than I had expected. "We're running out of time."

I followed the route of the cord to the cold metal base of the lamp, and felt a knob. I twisted. Light flooded the room.

A scene of such chaos and storm met our eyes that I said, reflexively, "Are we in the wrong room?"

But we were in the right place. And we were staring at the evidence that someone else knew our plan. The bedspreads were on the floor, the dresser drawers were open and cockeyed, my windbreaker dangled precariously from one sleeve in the closet. Through the doorway into the other room, I could see similar disarray. Chair cushions flung against the wall, a card table toppled, its humble plywood underside exposed to the ceiling. I saw Annie's backpack, opened and upside down on the plush, mauve-colored carpet in the next room.

"We've been robbed?" she asked disbelievingly, even as she ran into the other room to find her hairbrush under a chair, her blue jacket wadded into a ball on the closet floor, and the contents of her makeup case scattered on the floor. Someone had been in a hurry, and had trampled over the vials of lipsticks, the case of blusher, the eyebrow pencil. They were crushed, and the powders and dyes had spilled out, staining the carpet in deep, accusing colors.

"We've been searched," I corrected her. Cautious, I walked toward the bathroom door. It was ajar. The lights were off. I stood in front of it, studying the smooth painted surface for what seemed like hours, trying to divine whether a living presence crouched on the other side. I kicked the bathroom door, as hard and as fast as I could. It slammed open and struck the tile wall inside with a satisfying clap of noise. I rushed into the room, threw on the light. And stood appalled.

On the mirror, written in Annie's lipstick, a demure, almost nude pink: I DON'T PLAY GAMES.

She was behind me, carrying her computer. I saw the shock register on her face.

"He knows," she whispered.

We righted a couple of toppled chairs and pulled them up to the reproduction Sheraton writing desk. We pushed aside the folder of classy Marriott stationery to make room for the computer. Annie dropped down to her knees with the power cord, searching for an electrical outlet. As she booted the machine, I reached into my pocket and pulled out my treasure. Lionel's dongle.

We needed it to get into his computer system. I knew that was where we would find the truth. I had pocketed the small, unobstrusive piece of hardware at the hearing, while the melee had distracted everyone around me. By the time Lionel had broken free from the reporters who all wanted the same quote repeated specially for them, Dim had packed up his computer equipment, locked the bag with a key, and handed it to him. Dim hadn't asked about the dongle. And Lionel hadn't opened the bag. He checked it with the clerk at the hotel's front desk when we arrived.

Annie logged on to the Internet, and only at that moment, as we sat poised to break into Lionel's most private sanctum, did we realize that we had no clue how to actually operate his security device.

Annie had Lionel's security card too—"How'd you get it?" I'd asked, and she'd smiled enigmatically, then mimed an expert pickpocket's thrust. There was no end to the mystery of Annie—and we ran it through the groove down the center of the card reader. It worked.

She moved now by instinct more than by design, I believed, calling up a program on the hard drive, typing a new string

of commands in the instructions to the modem, then reboot-
ing the machine. For her, this part of the job was as rote as
tying her shoelaces. We were connected.

> UNIX(r) System V Release 4.0 (knot.com)
>
> log-in: Sullivan
> password: *******
>
> $

"There you are," she said. She noted that Lionel was running UNIX, probably on a workstation that was connected to
other terminals in his house. I could confirm that.

"Find the code for the Knot program," I said.

She scrolled through the directory of files relating to the
Knot program. "You know, Harry, even if there's some corrupted source code in the program, that doesn't prove that
Lionel wrote it. Knot is freeware. We both heard him say that
earlier tonight. It's in the public domain. Anyone could tam-
per with it."

"Or update it?"

*I glanced down, and saw a meticulously hand-lettered chart. The
coffee stain on the top page was still damp.*

I was transported back to that uncomfortable night when I
had tossed on Eddie's lumpy mattress, sleeping fitfully, dream-
ing of fevered dates and times and algorithms, waking early in
a panicked sweat, waking before the sun came up to take a
shower in the same bathroom where Eddie later died.

"Annie, I told you that night I stayed at Eddie's, I saw those
papers on his desk. He was compiling statistics about Knot,
about changes that had occurred in the code. And—"

I was trying to remember. Don't force it, Harry, I told myself, because then you'll lose it. Think of something else, the
weather, the task at hand, the number of beers you poured
into the plants when no one was looking. Don't think about
the chart, the writing, grouped in meticulous blocks of black

ink, each little hieroglyph perfectly formed with such a sure hand.

Don't think of how you held it up to the light, squinting at the paper, trying to discern its secrets.

"A History of Knot, .01 beta through the present."

The left-hand column on the chart had appeared to be dates. Had Eddie discovered a correlation between the dates when the source code changed and . . . Oh, shit, I had seen the plain text numerals that he had tried to scratch out. Why hadn't I realized it at the time? Why hadn't I made the connection that could have saved Eddie's life?

The very first date on the chart had been the day after Professor Edward Barrow had become the first victim of the Compubomber.

"Annie, Lionel did change the code himself. After every bomb exploded. He must have gone back into the program to erase or fix the flaws that had caught someone's attention. His victims served the same function for him as canaries in cages do for miners."

"They went into the code first?" she asked.

"And if they found anything suspicious, he killed them."

"Eddie figured it out?"

"No. Not exactly. He saw the pattern that emerged when he compared the dates of their deaths to the dates when Knot was revised. All those archives of the Knot program online all over the world. And on a few very specific dates, bingo, they all change. Slightly. Version 2.1 becomes 2.2."

"So why didn't Lionel blow him up?"

With Eddie it would have had to have been personal. He was so devoted to Lionel. He wouldn't have believed what his own research was telling him. He would have called Lionel, hinted at a problem, scheduled a meeting, all the time hoping that his suspicions were wrong. Hoping that there was some easy explanation.

Had Lionel set up the meeting for Eddie's apartment? It made sense, no, it was more, it was brilliant. He was hiding in plain sight. If he was discovered sitting on the sofa by one of the roommates on the way to the kitchen to grab a glass of water, Lionel would have the perfect excuse: He was always hanging around. He was one of the gang, as much a part of their surroundings as the pizza boxes.

But no one did see him when Eddie was killed. Lionel could have waited quietly for as long as it took. He could have hidden all the equipment of death that he needed—a knife, perhaps a bandanna to gag Eddie—under his shirt. Untraceable.

"I think he wanted to touch Eddie," I said finally. "I think he wanted to feel the life drain out of him."

Annie scrolled down. "Lionel's very anal. I'm sure he would archive all versions of the program he's ever created. Isn't there any file in here that was created before he released Knot into the world?"

The cursor came to rest on Alpha.0.0.1.

She hit RETURN, and a long document came up on the screen: the first draft of the Knot program, a document that predated by nearly twelve the first beta versions distributed over the Net.

"There," Annie said. "Thousands and thousands of lines of code."

I looked at my watch. I was guessing that Lionel had tried to catch the last shuttle back to New York City last night. His private fortress on the top floor of his house would be his only real choice at this moment. He had to regroup. He had to exercise control over the Minotaur somehow. After all, the creature was *his* creature. Lionel would have needed at his disposal the full computing power of his headquarters at this critical juncture. He could have been home by now.

"Let's test the back door," I said. "Does he have any Knot-encrypted documents on the hard drive?"

Annie scanned the directory: "Just about everything's encrypted. I can search his E-mail," Annie said.

She typed: $grep ames.

FLAMEWAR

270

The computer found three matches.

The first was a message that had arrived a month ago, in late June. The sender was anonymous; the mail had passed through an anonymous re-mailer. The contents were terse:

> I SPOKE TO HIM TODAY AND I WILL TRY TO REASON WITH HIM. AMES IS KNOWN FOR HIS REASONABLE NATURE.

The second file had come from Ames himself. E-mail to Lionel Sullivan:

> LIONEL S: I SPOKE TOO HASTILY LAST WEEK WHEN I SAID I WOULD TESTIFY TO THE UNBREAKABLE NATURE OF KNOT. HAVE FOUND DISTURBING ATTRIBUTE. WE MUST CONFER.—FA

There were more E-mail messages, of course, sent to Lionel from the bomber's other victims. Even as we greedily decrypted them and devoured their contents, I paused to wonder at the remarkable gall that Lionel had. Storing such incriminating evidence on his own computers. Knowing that the encryption program had a back door. So sure—and so very wrong to be sure—that his secrets were safe, that no one could bridge his security. Professor Barrow, after discovering the back door, had believed it was an unintended error. He had mailed Lionel a note to alert him to the problem. Two weeks later, he was dead.

Matthew Reese, teenage hacker, had also believed his discovery of the flaw would help Lionel. He even included, in an attempt to be helpful, a suggested fix, to close the hole in the code. His last words to Lionel: "I don't know if you need any freelance coderz. But I am available. Would also be happy to beta test for new versionz. You are one of my heroes. Signed, fantomphriend (Matthew Reese)"

In less than a month, he was dead. I wondered if he had any inkling that the package with the bomb was from Lionel.

Had there been a return address? Had Reese hoped that his idol was sending a thank you note?

"He killed everyone who found the back door," Annie said.

"And his wife," I said, remembering the haunting portrait of the beautiful woman. $grep ilse.

"No reference to her," Annie said. "Maybe he can't stand to be reminded of her."

"I think he likes to be reminded," I said, flashing again on the painting.

He killed everyone who discovered the back door.

"Annie?" I asked. "Can you cover our tracks in here?"

"First I'll make copies of these files," Annie said, her fingers already starting to fly. But suddenly, his cursor stalled. It froze on the screen.

He killed everyone who found the back door.

Annie hit ESCAPE. She tried to cancel her latest command and start over. But still we were locked in place.

NO CARRIER.

Those were the two words in the English language that I hated most.

"Why did we disconnect?"

"I don't know yet." Annie was typing fiendishly, trying to log back in.

UNABLE TO CONNECT TO KNOT.COM.

"Did Lionel's server go offline?" I asked. "Or was there a problem with the phone lines?"

"I'll check. To get to KNOT.COM, we had to travel over a number of different, privately held networks. Maybe the problem is in one of them," Annie said.

"Find out. Fast."

Annie typed: $traceroute knot.com.

"It's an Internet command that shows up all the phone lines we hoped to get to his computers in Manhattan," she explained. "It should show us where the wires are down."

Within seconds, she had the answer.

```
traceroute to knot.com (174.325.2.70), 30 hops max, 40 byte
packets
1 interramp.com (38.8.17.2), 4 ms 2 ms 2 ms
2 tlg-cust-link.tlg.net (140.174.202.2) 5 ms 5ms 5 ms
3 rgnet-bl-serial3-1.SanFrancisco.mci.net (204.70.32.50) 5 ms 5
ms 5 ms
4 border1-fddi-0.SanFrancisco.mci.net (204.70.2.162) 5 ms 6 ms
5 ms
5 core-fddi-1.SanFrancisco.mci.net (204.70.3.161) 72 ms 71ms
71 ms
6 mae-west.SanFrancisco.mci.net (198.32.136.12) 72 ms 75 ms
74 ms
7 San-Jose6.CA.ALTER.NET (137.39.100.1) 81 ms 79 ms 78 ms
8 New-York3.NY.ALTER.NET (137.39.126.8) 104 ms 84 ms 85 ms
9 ilse3.KNOT.COM (184.39.71.29) 91 ms 92ms 89 ms
```

"That's bad," she said. "There's no disruption on the route.
You see there weren't any unusual delays at any of the com-
puters we moved through, from Washington, through San
Francisco and San Jose, to New York. We had an open route."

"But that doesn't prove that KNOT.COM was still opera-
tional. That just shows us our request got to Lionel's front
door, right?"

Annie typed: $ping knot.com.

Almost instantly, the computer answered: knot.com is alive.

"No, it's there," she said. "But our access to it has been
blocked."

He killed everyone who found the back door.

I should have known he would outsmart us. He'd disappeared in broad daylight at the memorial service. He'd known
I was tailing him from Café Info. He'd arrived on the scene
in the subway tunnel, barely ahead of the police. What if he'd
reached us, down there among the flames and the chaos, five
minutes before the police? Would we still be alive?

I realized, too late, that he must have been there all along, waiting for us to break in, watching us look through his system. He'd known that we'd taken the dongle. He'd searched the hotel suite on his way out of the building. He was a master spy, and I was his quarry.

And like a cornered animal, I fought back. I did the only thing I could. I phoned my mother.

F

L

A

M

E

W

A

R

chapter fifteen

T he FBI arrived at Lionel's door less than an hour after Chief Ellen Garnet called the commander of the bureau's bomber task force. Two dozen agents, including Bill Dellis, surrounded the town house. Another dozen fanned out to block traffic on the quiet East Side block where he lived.

Lionel didn't answer the knock at the door.

But when an agent turned the doorknob, it opened.

Inside, they found a note: "I'm on the third floor. Take the elevator."

There wasn't time for a big law enforcement huddle about whether to drop in the SWAT team from a helicopter to the balcony. Instead, a couple of agents put on bulletproof vests and rode up to Lionel's computer room.

When they got off the elevator, shrieking "Freeze" and waving their guns, they were greeted by Lionel, in a wing-backed chair, sitting in the center of an entirely empty room. The echoing, cavernous space had the feel of a wholesale rug warehouse on an industrial block in Long Island City, Dellis later told my mother. Except even the rugs were gone.

The agents most likely did not comprehend all the nuances of the case: that Lionel was the systems operator at The Zoo, that he had created the online sex club for the sole purpose of amusing himself, of eavesdropping, that he was a blackmailer who believed he could one day know all the secrets in the world if he wanted. They did not realize the full extent of his Machiavellian intent, to replace the National Eavesdropping Center with the Lionel Sullivan Eavesdropping Center, to pull the strings like a master puppeteer whenever he cared to see someone squirm. They did not know that he had controlled a U.S. senator, who had been forced to recruit a rogue federal agent to do Lionel's dirty work for him. They did not know the whole spectrum of his lies, did not know the elaborate duplicitous story about widespread government conspiracy that he had told me in this very room—the convoluted tale of how Barrow and Reese had worked on a factoring project with Ames—and had not seen his performance, so convincing, when he had lectured Annie on the morals of code breaking. Had they been aware of those elements of the case, perhaps they would have proceeded more carefully, perhaps they would have had a better understanding of his wiliness and would have taken care to make sure he did not outwit them yet again. They could not have known that he had originally created the eavesdropping back door in Knot just to see if the swaggering academics and cipher experts in his world could find it. It was the ultimate puzzle. The agents didn't know that Lionel had been corrupted—as the months went by and his colleagues failed the test of wits—by the nagging question he asked himself: Were the great cryptographers frauds? The agents from the FBI only knew that they had been summoned from sleep to hone in on the criminal known as the Compubomber, and that he must be a madman. Maybe they were intent on searching his house for a manifesto. Maybe they thought they had cornered another lonely introvert. And so they lost their advantage.

"Can I help you, gentlemen?" Lionel asked. Winnie, the

fox, growled a high, nervous sound, but sat patiently at his side.

He acted as if he didn't know what they were talking about when they demanded to see all his computers, his phones, his boxes of floppy disks. "My lawyer will be here within ten minutes," he said. "Perhaps he will be in a better position to explain."

It was a spooky setup, according to Dellis, because when they grabbed him roughly and hissed in his ear and forced him facedown on the floor, Lionel acted totally unperturbed. They'd handcuffed him and left him there, one agent's foot planted firmly in the center of Lionel's spine, while the other called on the walkie-talkie for the rest to come up.

But the elevator wouldn't budge.

"You have to take the key and ride down to the first floor. Unlock it manually down there," Lionel said courteously. "The key's in my jacket pocket."

"You didn't ride down in the elevator to let us in," the agent with the heavy foot said, digging his heel into Lionel's shirt for effect.

"I set the mechanism to allow one ride," Lionel said. "You can do the same. You'll see when you examine the control panel down there. And if you insist on continuing your physical abuse of me, I assure you I'll have my attorney bring charges against you and your agency."

When the elevator returned to the third floor, full of agents, the door slid open noiselessly to reveal a new tableau.

The only person left in the room was Lionel's guard. The FBI agent was dead, seated in the wing chair facing the elevator, with his tie knotted around his waist to hold him in the chair and his legs crossed. There wasn't a mark on him. But his black steel-toed shoe had been removed from his right foot. And stuffed in his mouth.

Lionel (and Winnie, I presume) had escaped through a back door, of course. Or maybe trapdoor is a better description. A closet on the third floor hid a shaft and another fire-

o
s
h
u
a

Q
u
i
t
t
n
e
r

man's pole, which led down to the cellar, the trapdoor, and a maintenance tunnel. The tunnel, which must have been dug years ago to hook up to an old firehouse supply depot, had been more recently extended. It now connected to a subway tunnel a few hundred yards down the block. Where Lionel disappeared. No attorney ever appeared. Ditto Winnie.

The physical evidence was gone with Lionel. Why he had even waited for the FBI agents to confront him was a mystery. But Blaney once told me, a long time afterward, that he thought he understood. "To him, the whole thing was a hack," Blaney said. "You figure out how to get from A to B in your code. You try to do it as simply and efficiently as possible, with as few lines of extraneous commands as possible, Garnet. But sometimes, you put in a little twist. Bury an application or a command in there that doesn't disrupt the program, but embellishes it. So everybody can see how smart you are."

We all could see, by then, how smart Lionel had been.

They found his computers in the basement, but all the hard drives were erased and reformatted, of course. Even the FBI's forensics people were unable to resurrect a bit from those remagnetized drives. The Zoo, which once thrived in one of Lionel's computers like a beehive, was erased. It was as nonexistent as a deleted paragraph. With one click of the DELETE key, he had killed off its population. There was no evidence anywhere that it had ever been a place—and no evidence of the time he had masqueraded as Ames, using the dead man's log-in to cover his tracks when he "burned down" the Unicorn Inn.

No one even tied the senator's death to the case, at least publicly. The same day the authorities announced that Lionel was the prime suspect in the Compubomber case—and that he was wanted for the murder of the FBI agent, was presumed to be Eddie's killer—*The New York Times* ran an apparently unrelated, and tasteful, obituary of Francis Dunne. The article

F

L

A

M

E

W

A

R

didn't mention that the cause of death was an overdose. The raciest paragraph revealed that friends said Dunne had confided that he had been despondent for some time, since the death of his long-time companion. They assumed he meant the widow of a prominent industrialist, a woman who had raised five million dollars for the Democratic party's coffers in the year before her recent death from breast cancer. The senator had been her frequent escort at political fund-raisers.

Washington Metro Police released a hugely relieved Blaney from custody. With Lionel on the run and the odds-on favorite suspect in everything from serial murder to a string of unsolved 7-Eleven stickups, the authorities quickly came to realize that Blaney was an unwitting accomplice in a web of deceptions that stretched into . . . where? No one yet knew the extent of Lionel's damage, let alone his whereabouts.

Someday they'd find Lionel, probably sooner rather than later, and it probably wouldn't be a result of spectacular investigative techniques, either. Maybe they'd get him during a routine customs check in a European airport, maybe for a routine stop if he was driving with a broken taillight, maybe because one of his new neighbors in a suburb outside of a city like Boise recognized his face on an episode of *America's Most Wanted.*

Or maybe, just maybe, we'd find him first. Using the Net.

Naturally, Blaney & Co. were feeling deeply burned and betrayed by their erstwhile guru. Sadness, despair, and fear quickly gave way to anger and a growing resolve to Do Something. The folks who gravitated to the Urban Crypto Militia, after all, were doers, not just talkers. But what could they do?

Well, a lot, if you considered the pervasiveness of the Net and the ability of Blaney, Dim, Yuri, Irene, and the rest to pull on its millions of threads as if it were a harp. Over the course of a few days, Eddie's apartment came to resemble a war room as the militia methodically and relentlessly undertook the task of rooting out Prophet, Thing of Evil, as Yuri nicknamed Lionel one night after he had discovered the collected poems of Edgar Allan Poe online.

The militia was harnessing the power of the worldwide network to spread news of Lionel's escape to tiny hilltop towns in Venezuela, to university laboratories in Switzerland, to grade schools in Dubuque, to every one of the forty-five million people around the world who hooked up to the Net. Blaney and his friends nailed their notices up on Usenet's electronic bulletin boards, blared their warnings in the conference rooms where Internet users gather online, and posted all known information about the fugitive Compubomber on a site they created on the World Wide Web.

It began with a simple home page: "Where's Lionel? The Net's Most Wanted!"

Among Eddie's boxes and archives of papers were a number of excellent pictures of Lionel—originals that Eddie had tracked down over the years after feature articles about Lionel and Knot had appeared in newspapers and magazines. These images were dutifully scanned into a Web-based rogues' gallery, as were sound clips of Lionel's speeches and even a Photoshop-tweaked "artist's projection" of how Lionel might look in a wig, bald, as a woman, in a bowler hat . . . This last project was so much fun that Dim figured a way to make it interactive: visitors to the page could choose attributes from a drop-down menu for Lionel, including hair color and length, beards, mustaches, goatees, sideburns, and submit their à la carte selections to a Silicon Graphics workstation, which would render an on-the-fly permutation of Lionel, suitable for printing.

Yuri put together a "VRML walk-through" of Lionel's house and put it up on the Web, where people could visit. This was a 3-D map that you could click navigate, using something called virtual reality mark-up language. For instance, a visitor could click onto the elevator, go up to Lionel's bedroom floor, click over to the night table and open up a drawer, even pull out the contents of said drawer. Irene helped Yuri seed the place with bits of personal data about Lionel, including "Lionel's Paper Trail," a hypertext document that assembled every bit of personal credit, medical, and academic data ever compiled on The Evil One.

It was a monumental accomplishment, a testament to the irony that such a private creature as Lionel had been so fully revealed to the world, and initially, at least, became a cult favorite online. Within a few weeks, it had been anointed a worldwide Cool Site of the Day, which drove more than a hundred thousand people to stop by during a three-hour interval. Apparently, the true-crime, amateur detective stuff appealed to Netizens and the site teemed with vistors around the clock. Irene cobbled together a bulletin board area for people to post messages and kibitz about the case. A kind of community started to grow around the search for Lionel. The Where's Lionel site garnered so many hits each day that Dim advocated selling on-site ads "to defray expenses."

The popularity of the site was further fueled when the off-line world cottoned to it. A slow-burn of media coverage carried the story to the places and people that the Internet had not reached: a story on the militia's Find-Lionel efforts in *Newsday* gave way to one in *The New York Times*, which in turn begat the *Los Angeles Times*, *The Washington Post*, zillions of locals, and the newsweeklies. Not to mention the international press, which first covered the story as an American phenomenon, then got sucked in as well. Network TV news picked it up too, as further evidence of how the Net was coming of age. "The world must feel like a small place indeed for Mr. Sullivan," Ted Koppel intoned at FBI boss Bentley. The G-man nodded his head and sagely concurred that the "greatest manhunt in the history of the world is currently under way. And the Bureau is playing but the smallest part."

E-mail tips flooded in, and Dim duly forwarded the promising ones to the FBI, proving that the politics of revenge makes for strange bedfellows.

*   *   *

Michelle Slatalla   **281**

Meanwhile, all I could think about were the things the authorities didn't find at Lionel's house. No floppy disks. No tapes. No evidence of the thousands of conversations he had monitored on The Zoo. Who knew what he had taken with him? The Zoo census, for sure, and no one knew whose names were on the list. For all I knew, the list could include the president of the United States. The chairman of the New York Stock Exchange. The pope. Lionel still could be blackmailing them all with information already gathered. He could be controlling them. He could be controlling the world.

The FBI felt like a wet bedsheet on my shoulders, a constant, itchy presence, although I didn't think Lionel posed a physical danger to me. I had been his protégé, and had fulfilled my role ably. He had put me into the position of junior investigator, had given me all the background, had tutored me in the fine arts of suspicion and deceit solely to see if I could be educated. That the student had learned so well only testified to the greatness of his teacher. That the lessons forced the student to betray his teacher was another of Lionel's sourly ironic twists.

I tried to picture Lionel in some far-off place with his computer, living equally anonymously in an igloo at the North Pole or blending into the middle-class blandness of a small town in America. But the only image I had was of a comfortable chair. Lionel would never suffer physically. He tanned easily, so I like to think that he fled to a tropical place where no one speaks our language or cares about our laws, where he lives in a hut with an electrical generator he rigged up to run his ceiling fan and laptop.

FLAME

WAR

chapter sixteen

W eeks later. Image of calendar pages flipping in the wind, August is moody and the heat of July seems like a memory as we reluctantly put on sweaters. A late-summer chill rings down on the Adirondacks like the curtain in Act V.

I stand behind the desk in the main lodge at The Vines, flipping through the latest stack of new registration cards, conscious of how for the first time in months, cold molecules are squeezing out the hot ones. I am in a hurry because I promised to meet Annie down at the docks. She decided not to go away, not to London to see David, not to Belize on a dig, not back to her mother's apartment in the city. She spent some time in Manhattan packing up her father's effects, sorting through the obligatory stacks of tweedy jackets and cardigans that still smelled like him, coming to terms with the fact that while the clothes could go to the St. Vincent De Paul Society's thrift shop, the more personal objects had been transformed by death into detritus. Prescription eyeglasses that no one else could see through. An address book that contained the phone numbers of strangers. A stack of unread journals. A holey afghan that someone had knitted long ago, and which had rested there, stretched across the back of his desk chair, for years. She also found stacks and stacks of record books, one for each semester he had taught and listing the names of the students in each section. There she found Nelson's name, and the incomplete that her father had given him after he failed to show up for either the midterm or the final exams. Maybe Nelson had suffered, like Blaney, from the inability to follow through, or maybe he was just crying out for attention from a professor he admired. In either case, he had been rebuffed. Nelson had failed with Ames's daughter as well; he stopped sending her E-mail eventually.

I wondered if Annie had made any sort of peace with Frederick Ames as she sifted through the artifacts he left for her to explore. She kept more of that stuff than I would. Then she drove up here, in Fred Ames's ancient Mercedes two-seater, inherited by his daughter and liberated from a two-hundred-dollar-a-month parking garage. The red leather seats surprised me. So did she, when she knocked on the door of my cabin one morning before dawn. I never asked Frank, the FBI agent, if he had been surprised as well by the sight of her on the threshold, clutching a cardboard box full of her notebooks and looking slightly defiant. She never said how long she planned to stay. I never asked. She told me she didn't feel like being alone anymore, not even for an hour. Maybe she was still afraid.

I go fishing with her in the mornings, when the mist rises thick from the black obelisk of the water's surface. Annie isn't squeamish about worms, after all. I blew off the corporate job in Syracuse, like she knew I would. I was the only one surprised by that announcement. The chief took it in stride that her son was morphing into a slacker, made no cracks about Gen X, did not ask if I planned to get my navel pierced, for which I was thankful. Peterson could use me for a few months, even off-season, to fix the leaky roofs on the cottages and rebuild the sagging porch on the lodge, and generally keep an eye on the premises when he fled to Ft. Lauderdale in January and February.

The mail truck came by a couple of hours ago. It's late in the afternoon and now the heap of letters and FedEx envelopes spills across the polished wooden counter. I write the correct cottage number on each envelope, thinking about how I haven't personally delivered mail to the cottages since the day Fred Ames died. Peterson is out behind the dining hall, pointing out some spray-painted graffiti to Chief Garnet, who dutifully came by to take a report. I left the two of them scuffing among the pine needles, bickering over how many teenagers were to blame and whether the culprits broke a hole through the fence or just exploited an existing vulnerability in the pickets. The argument had the wholly comfortable manner that accompanies an old friendship.

Now the screen door creaks open, and Peterson walks in, squinting from the sun. Which happens to be low in the late August afternoon sky. His bald head is pink and I wonder for the zillionth time if he'd ever consider sunscreen.

"Jed can take the mail," he says to me.

"I'll take it. I'm going now."

"There's a tree, blew down in the storm last night. Too near the tennis court."

"You want me to cut it up?"

"Take your assistant."

He means the kid from Brooklyn, the boy in the sailor hat who still owed me a replacement pair of sneakers. It turned out that the kid who almost drowned had a name, and it was Nate, and he had taken to trailing me around the place, carrying the extra paint can that I couldn't handle in one trip, taking an end of a canoe and helping me to hoist it from the water, holding the ladder so I could scrape the underside of the eaves of the main lodge. Nate had lost his taste for boating, at least on his own, although I saw him out in a two-man kayak with his older brother one evening after supper. They both wore life vests that time.

Joshua Quitter

I see him round the corner by the toolshed as I load the chain saw into the back of the pickup. He's given up the sailor hat, in favor of an old Red Sox cap I left on a peg in the game room once, and he no longer looks pale enough to audition for the part of Casper the Friendly Ghost. Covered in mosquito bites, smeared with calamine, skin on his burnt noise peeling, the kid is a walking, talking advertisement for the benefits of the Cure, The Vines style. "Harry, you need some help, you want me to hold that? Can I use the saw? What are we gonna cut?" He hops aboard.

We barrel around a bend and come to the scene of the accident. The beech tree that came down in last night's winds had a noble, straight trunk that climbed sixty feet or more toward the sky. Peterson had been lucky that it fell unevenly, its crash broken by the low scrub brush to the west of the tennis court. Its roots have ripped free of the ground, thick and fat and covered with dirt and dangling in the air. I can smell the dirt. Its trunk hasn't had a chance to fall all the way to the earth yet; it is partially supported by a smaller stand of new pines and juneberry bushes, and the tree's branches create a green and leaf canopy for anybody who might care to picnic underneath. The immediate problem is a stout branch, barely three feet in diameter but a good twenty feet long, which threatens the net. Already laden with smooth-shelled nuts, the branch will likely come down onto the tennis court tonight if the winds pick up. The branch is at least ten feet up, well beyond my reach. I study it from the ground.

"You gonna climb the trunk, Harry? You gonna shinny up? Can I hold the saw? Want me to do it?"

I see now that I should have brought the ladder, and calculate whether I can reach the base of the branch if I pull the truck in closer and stand on the cab.

"Nate, would you mind running back to the shed, getting me that length of rope in the corner by the door?"

He is thrilled, and crashes off into the woods. Shortcut. I slide into the driver's seat and slowly inch the truck forward through the low weeds at the edge of the clearing, trampling branches, crushing moss, wreaking havoc among the raspberry bushes and staghorn sumacs and sheep laurel that have been vying for position in the sunniest spot by the tennis court. I pray that the nasty scraping sound I hear against the side of the truck doesn't mean a scratch in the paint, although of course it must, and I lean my head out the open door on the driver's side, look up in the vast leafy greenness above my head, and feel all of a sudden as if I am drowning. I am dizzy, I am filled for the first time in years with a healthy respect for the forest, I am almost drunk with the possibilities borne on the scent of cedar and blue elderberry. I think I have the truck where I want it. I turn off the engine.

I can hear Nate coming back already, he's fast, so I vault onto the hood of the truck, then up onto the roof of the cab. With the winch I will fashion from the rope the kid is bringing me, I should be able to pull the branch low enough to reach it with the saw. Nate will be thrilled to hold the rope, and I call behind me for him to hurry. I turn, lightly, to greet him, and from my perch, high above the world but below the tree, vulnerable on the slippery roof of the pickup, wearing a pair of ripped jeans and worn sneakers, I must make a pretty picture.

Otherwise why would Lionel smile like that, so thrilled.

Of course the kid can't make it to the toolshed and back this quickly, and it is not my eyes playing tricks on me. I have never understood the concept of that old cliché anyway, because how could you mistake the image of Lionel emerging from the underbrush, picking a burr from his flannel shirt and wearing a shoulder holster, for anything other than what it is: doom. My death. The end of the Last Summer, and, I realize calmly, the fitting, final end to my miserable, misguided life. How fucking naive I was to think that I could live here in peace with Annie, live in the present for once, for the first time in years not experiencing the sinking dread in my stomach when I wake up in the morning. In that instant when

Michelle Slatalla

287

I register that the shoulder holster is really a sheath, and holds a long sharp blade, probably the one that took off Eddie's head, in those split seconds before he grins crookedly and says in a gentle, determined voice, "Hello, Harry," in the digital microseconds left to me, I remember that Annie is waiting at the dock. And I feel such a sorrow that I will never see her again, such a longing for the rough feel of her gray T-shirt against my face, that I think my heart will break. I am not afraid to die, I realize now, but I am fucking angry at being cheated out of the long, leisurely progression of ordinary years that other, luckier souls will take for granted.

"You've been spying on me again."

"I never stopped."

I have so many questions for him, but the only one I can think of is, "Aren't you afraid you'll be caught?"

"No, Harry." He mocks me, of course, for no one has come close to catching him in the weeks since he disappeared. Even an international manhunt conducted on the Internet—enlisting the aid of forty million amateur sleuths—has not interrupted his routine. For his hair is still neatly cinched in a ponytail band, his jeans unwrinkled. He looks well fed and tanned, and it occurs to me now that the first thing Lionel would have done, all those months ago when he began to plot, would be to establish a safe house for himself. A getaway. Maybe two—since by nature such safety must be temporary. It would have been an enjoyable diversion for him to plot his strategy—would he need a disguise? A second, untraceable identity? Keep it simple. Solve the puzzle. Eliminate obstacles. Eliminate Harry.

He doesn't have time for me today, that much is clear, and his eyes dart around the clearing, taking in the possible routes of escape, measuring the distance to cover in every direction. I have never seen him jittery before, never seen him not in a mood to talk, and I wonder how closely his demons are following him.

He sees me bend my knees, start to crouch, and he says, "Don't come down."

I stand there, a buffoon, splayed against the sky: "What if I do? Will you throw an explosive floppy at me?"

The joke doesn't register, maybe none of my wisecracks ever did. "I need the computer."

Now I am confused, and he can see that this is more than I can take in, because he says, in the same slow cajoling tone that he might use to lure a mental patient in off the window ledge, "I wasn't after Ames's diary entries, Harry. I need his papers on factoring primes."

So that part was true, I think, and why should it be a surprise if it turns out that the father of Annie Ames really was brilliant, truly stood on the edge of a discovery that would change the science of mathematics for the next centuries?

"You think you can do it all again, Lionel? Use Ames's work to help you crack all the codes in the world?"

"Not unless you're dead, Harry. Because you would tell everyone, wouldn't you?"

It makes sense to me now that he has come, because what does Lionel need to survive in this world? He needs money, and lots of it, and enough new identities and new places to hide to last a lifetime. He needs to construct an impregnable fortress of safety to cocoon him for decades, with machicolations around the turrets, so he can crouch there unseen, ready to drop boiling water on his enemies if they approach. He needs to replace Knot.

"The laptop's in my cabin," I say.

"Liar." So he came from there.

"I'll show you."

"You'll tell me," he says, and pulls the blade out to show me. "You can come down now."

"If I don't?"

From the pocket of his jeans, he pulls a weasely little gun, and he points it right at me, and cocks the hammer. "I'll blow your kneecaps off." He says it conversationally, and certainly there is no reason to doubt him, given the vast repertoire of his evil deeds. The Versatile Murderer. He bombs, he sets fires, he shoots, he stabs. Fucking Lionel could be marketed as an action doll. But still I might not have moved, might not have had a big enough dose of the righteous foolhardy heat of anger to believe I could fly, if Annie had not at that moment emerged from the woods.

She stands blinking at the truck, her eyes adjusting to sunlight after the dim cool filter of the woods. "Harry, Nate said—" She stops, because she sees Lionel there.

A look very like regret crosses his face, as he turns toward her, and of course he means to shoot her, but he hesitates just an instant. It is then that I know he did not mean to kill his wife. Ilse was a mistake, and if he can make one mistake he can make many. I take two steps to the edge of the truck's roof, and I leap.

I fly like Carl Lewis in the old glory days, and I land on Lionel just as he turns back to meet me. I knock him down with my weight, I must have three inches and ten pounds on him, and the laws of gravity are on my side. I love science at the moment of impact, because Lionel is knocked to the ground, and he breaks my fall with his body. The wind is sucked out of me, and he is struggling to point the gun at my face, and I see the tension of his thumb on the trigger, his white-knuckled determination, but I have a grip on the gun. I want to go for his throat, but instead I am playing a new variation of the old contest of arm wrestling, our hands clasped together around a gun, while he flops like a dangerous fish under me, seeking purchase, an angle, an opening. That's when he stabs me.

I feel the heat of the blade in his other hand as he buries it into my shoulder, and so to keep from screaming, I bite him in the arm, the only part of his body that presents itself conveniently. He tastes like iron. He tastes like hate. He curses, the gun goes off, and I feel more heat spread through my shoulder, and I hear Annie screaming. I don't care, because I feel his flesh under my hands, and I slam my fist once, twice, again, into the soft spots of his face. I want to kill him. I knee him.

"Harry! Harry!" I hear someone's voice.

Rough hands pull me off Lionel, and as I realize they belong to Peterson, I see my mother standing there, Chief Garnet, in the academy-approved position, legs akimbo, gun trained on Lionel's face. He is conscious, but bleeding, and that's the first I realize that the bullet ripped into his own gut and not mine. My mother is screaming obscenities at him as she pulls the cuffs from her belt. I see the kid from Brooklyn hovering, wide-eyed, by the truck, and I realize that he doesn't owe me a pair of sneakers anymore. It occurs to me that maybe it was a good thing that my mother went back to work, after all.

The next thing I see is Annie's face. She looks at me as if she loves me. The last words I hear before the ambulance arrives are the ones she whispers in my ear as she bends over me, wiping blood from my face so gently with the hem of her shirt. I could tell you what she said, but that's private.

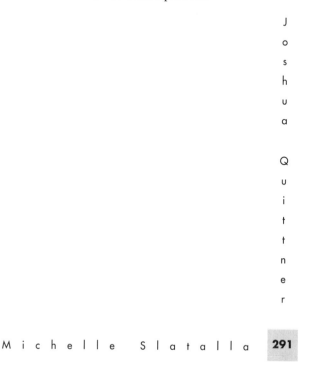

Joshua Quittner